THE
SHEPHERDESS
OF SIENA

THE
SHEPHERDESS
OF SIENA

A NOVEL OF RENAISSANCE TUSCANY

Linda Lafferty

LAKE UNION
PUBLISHING

Text copyright © 2015 Linda Lafferty
All rights reserved.

Published by Lake Union Publishing, Seattle

www.apub.com

Amazon, the Amazon logo, and Lake Union Publishing are trademarks of Amazon.com, Inc., or its affiliates.

ISBN-13: 9781477822074
ISBN-10: 1477822070

Cover design by Mumtaz Mustafa

Library of Congress Control Number: 2014951482

Printed in the United States of America

This novel is dedicated to the good people of Siena
Il Palio e' Vita
(The Palio Is Life)

PART I

A Medici Princess and the Little Shepherdess

ANNO 1569–1574

CHAPTER 1

Siena, Contrada del Drago
AUGUST 1569

One of my treasured memories—one of the few I have of my parents—is riding on my father's shoulders through the streets of Siena, my mother walking by our side. On sunny days, when there was little work or none at all, my father would close up his tiny leather workshop. His eyes would sparkle with a light of conspiracy as he lifted me up and set me behind his head. I could not have been much more than two.

As he locked the door behind us, the fresh air chased away the scent of oiled leather: saddles, bridles, halters, sturdy bags for travelers. If my father could not afford to have horses, at least he could create the tack to put on their glorious backs.

He pointed across the deep ravine that cut into the heart of the city, between two hills. We gazed at the black-and-white marble walls of Il Duomo, the great cathedral. The view from our neighborhood, the Drago *contrada*, across Siena, and up to Il Duomo was the most magnificent vista in our beloved city. A great swath of green farmland edged the yellow and deep red flanks of brick buildings and ocher stucco. Beyond the city, set on three hills, lay a patchwork of green and gold, the rolling lands of Tuscany.

"We will go visit your horses," my father said.

My horses.

"But first we must cross the Contrada dell'Oca, the Goose. Are you ready, my brave little girl?"

I nodded solemnly. I knew one day a Goose *contradiolo* would ambush us. In Drago, we were taught from the cradle to distrust our neighboring contradas. As they distrusted us.

"We must be careful of the goose," whispered my father. "I can smell perfidy in the flap of its feathers. It is a most foul bird."

My mother rolled her eyes.

"Why do you teach her this foolishness? Do not listen to your *babbo*'s silly stories."

My father paid her no mind.

"Keep watch, Virginia. Be vigilant," he warned.

For all the suspicion and anger, the Geese of Oca were our neighbors. If my father threw a rock from his shop, it would land in Oca territory. And we shared more than cobblestones. Although we of Drago had the basilica—which enshrined the preserved head of St. Catherine—Oca was the saint's birthplace. (Her body remained in Rome, but no one spoke of that in Siena.)

My mother did not join in when we spoke of Oca. Her best friend lived in Oca, and she knew not all Geese were treacherous.

"Stop filling her head with these alliances and enemies!"

"I want her to grow up as a proud *dragaiola*. She needs to know her heritage."

At this, my mother's lips tightened. I was too young to know it, but it cost us dearly to live within the city walls. My father's leather-goods shop did not bring in enough money for us to survive there.

But my parents desperately wanted me to be born here, in the city, in the Contrada del Drago, whether they could really afford it or not. It was my heritage, they told me. My Tacci grandfather had been born here.

"Here we go!" said my father, joggling me atop his shoulders. "Into Gooseland!"

My head twisted and I scowled, keeping a sharp lookout as we descended, then climbed up the steep hill of Oca and toward the Contrada della Selva.

"I will spit on them, Babbo!" I said, proud that I had learned to spit quite accurately through the gap in my two front teeth. "No Goose—"

"You will do nothing of the kind!" snapped my mother.

So, no spitting, but I would not let those Ocas pinch my cheek, no matter how friendly they seemed. I kept a wary eye, glaring at my foes.

"Virginia! Stop that behavior, *subito!*" my mother would cry, and I was forced to let an occasional Goose pet me or kiss my cheek.

A plump, wattle-necked Goose Lady laughed, her dimpled chin wiggling. "Oh, Virginia! We are not truly adversaries! Drago and Oca have lived side by side peacefully for centuries."

The Goose Lady gave me a sweetmeat, patting my chubby leg. "Do not listen to your babbo. He makes up wicked stories about the noble Goose simply because he is so proud you were born a Drago, like your grandfather."

"Ah," said the Goose Lady. "I think I have not convinced you, sweet Virginia. All seventeen contradas have their rivalries. Tartuca and Ciocchiola—how those two carry on!"

My mother rolled her eyes in agreement, and we moved on.

"Do not hate the Goose, *ciccia*. We are all Senesi," called the woman.

Still savoring my sweet, I nonetheless heaved a sigh of relief when we crossed the boundary into Selva, for the jungle beasts were our allies.

I kicked my heels against my father's chest.

"Go faster, my pony! Gallop to the Duomo."

My father's ears served as reins. I pulled them on either side, directing him left and right. "Faster, Babbo, faster. We are almost there."

Panting in the heat of the day, my father made a valiant effort to run up the steep hill to the Duomo.

As we emerged from the shade of the little *vicolo*, I shielded my eyes.

"There they are!"

My favorite part of the city sparkled white in the Tuscan sun.

"The horses!" I shouted.

Our magnificent Duomo has a façade as white and thick as cream frosting. Its marble was fashioned into every kind of creature, both fantastic and real. Lions, bulls, winged griffins, saints, and angels emerge from the polished stone.

But my favorites are the horses—*my* horses—supporting the corners of the façade, lashing out of the stone in full stride.

Perhaps I learned to love horses with such passion from those few precious memories of my mother and father.

They left me nothing but memories when they died just a few months later.

CHAPTER 2

Siena, Pugna Hills
NEW YEAR'S DAY, 1573

The young painter stood shivering at his easel, gazing over the sheep-studded hills. A towered castle loomed above him, and beyond that rose the dust-colored walls of Siena.

Dawn cast a rosy wash over the city's walls, and a flash glittered from the distant silver cross atop the Torre del Mangia, which soared above the Piazza del Campo at the heart of the city. A coating of hoarfrost clung to Siena, roof tiles sparkled in the sun.

The artist's hands ached, his freckled skin chapped raw. The scratchy wool wrap around his palms could not compete with the cold of the Tuscan winter.

He had risen in the dark to walk with his paints and easel through the lonely hills to this spot, this clump of oak trees in the shadow of Quattro Torra, a castle abandoned since the siege of Siena nearly two decades before.

He stood, brush in hand. Waiting for the dawn. Waiting for her.

He had painted her from a distance for a year now, the *pastorella*—the shepherdess—and her woolly charges. Virginia Tacci intrigued him, this skinny girl of six years.

His father, Cesare Brunelli, who knew everything there was to know about horses, said he recalled the day his best friend brought newborn Virginia to the stables.

He said all the horses stopped shuffling, eating, snorting. They lifted their heads, listening. "The silence was eerie," Cesare said, "like before a great storm."

That silence held until it was finally broken by the baby's laugh.

"She has a gift. The horses are never wrong," Cesare Brunelli said. "They recognize her spirit—a wild spirit like their own."

It made the young artist feel an emotion akin to jealousy. A burning itch to capture her. He felt the urge to dig in his nails, bright with color, to scratch her form on canvas.

But she's a girl. And a shepherdess. What good will it do her, this wild spirit?

His father's words resonated in the artist's mind. The young man would paint her, over and over, from every angle.

The sound of baying hounds broke into his thoughts. His eyes searched the rolling hills, blinking back tears against the cold wind.

———

Four velvet-cloaked riders paused on the crest of the hill, its grass bleached to straw by the Tuscan sun. Three brothers and a sister, their horses liveried with the red ball of the de' Medici, emblazoned on the cheekpieces and browbands of their bridles.

A cold-throated gust tore at the cloaks of the riders. The woman's billowing skirts filled like sails in the wind.

Her chestnut horse spooked, taking a sidestep leap as swift as a thunderclap. Hooves smashed the frosted grass as the gelding spun around.

"Easy, *cavallo*," the rider cooed as she gathered her skirts, tucking them tight between her leg and the saddle. She sat deep in the saddle, her heels stretching low into the stirrup irons. The horse snorted, his nostrils flared. White puffs lingered in the winter air.

Her lips curved into a smile at the horse's excitement.

"This is why women should not hunt," said her eldest brother, dismounting. He flung back his cloak angrily, his fingers counting the holes in his stirrup leathers. He adjusted his left stirrup slightly shorter.

"Where are the grooms?" he grumbled. The well-oiled leather snapped as he yanked down the stirrup. "The Granduca of Tuscany should never have to dismount except for the kill."

"I commanded them to leave us in peace," said his sister, Isabella. "How often can we speak without witnesses? I do not trust the stable servants. They are paid to carry our secrets to other courts."

Granduca Francesco grunted as he finished with the stirrup. He straightened up and drew a silver flask from his riding jacket.

"That, unfortunately, is the truth." He took a long draught of grappa, his eyes scanning the Senese countryside. "With Ercole Cortile's spying and his wagging tongue, I'd wager the Duca di Ferrara knows the precise lacework of my mistress's chemise."

He offered the flask to his sister, his mouth twisted in a lascivious smirk.

Isabella shook her head, declining the grappa.

"Bianca Cappello's chemise is silk," she retorted, "studded with seed pearls. Everyone knows that, even in the streets of Florence."

Francesco's face darkened. But Isabella straightened her elegant back in the saddle and continued.

"Your Venetian mistress is fanatic about underclothes, Francesco. I wager she will ask to inherit my camisoles and underskirts when I die! And you are wrong about women and hunting, *fratello mio*. The lesson is that a woman should dress herself in breeches when riding, as men do. The horse is terrified of Florence's fashions."

The other two brothers laughed, their horses prancing in place.

The Granduca of Tuscany scowled up at his sister from the ground.

"Oh? Do you not agree, Francesco?" she said, casting an innocent look down at her eldest brother.

His dark eyes, inherited from their Spanish mother, Eleonora di Toledo, smoldered with rage.

"Give me the flask, Francesco. Mine is empty," said Pietro, the youngest brother. As always, he seemed incapable of reading the emotions of others. He did not sense the growing fury of the grand duke.

"You drink too much," snarled Francesco, gesturing at his brother with the flask, his fingers tightening. "Is this the way you comport yourself in Madrid? King Felipe and the Spanish Court must think our family drunkards."

"And worse," he almost added, for Pietro had strange ways about him. His brother's hooded eyes and cruelty chilled Francesco's blood. The witches of Fiesole had pronounced Pietro cursed by the devil himself.

"You may be the granduca," said Isabella, turning her horse toward her brother, "but that does not give you the right to insult your own family!"

Francesco grabbed her horse's bridle in his free hand. The horse jumped back, but he held tight. "If I am insulting my family, you, my dear *sorella*, come to mind first and foremost."

"*Davvero*, dear brother?"

"Your immoral ways make tongues in Rome flicker like snakes', threatening our alliances. A princess who rides like a man. A de' Medici princess espoused to an Orsini and keeping intimate company with his cousin—"

"Paolo himself asked Troilo Orsini to watch over me in his absence—"

"How convenient!" called Pietro, from his horse. "A husband to name his own replacement in the marriage bed."

"Shut up, Pietro!" said Isabella, turning in her saddle. "You are indeed a fool!"

She knew Pietro had suspicions about his own wife, their first cousin Leonora—concerns about his wife's fidelity while he bedded the most common whores in Florence.

Isabella was glad he would be leaving early the next day. She could not bear the sight of him.

"You should live at your husband's side as a good wife and mother," snapped Francesco, still focused on his sister. "Not linger year after year in Florence."

"I married the bastard," snapped Isabella. "Is that not enough? De' Medici blood is mixed with Orsini. Your Highness seizes my husband's land to pay off his debts—my land, my children's!"

"I never said he was not a fool. My concern is with the de' Medici name, the de' Medici fortunes."

His hands loosened their grip on the bridle. Isabella's horse backed away, rearing. She whispered comforting words, steadying the gelding.

Francesco turned, tipping the flask to his mouth. The grappa stung his wind-chapped lips. He winced, rubbing them with his gloved fingers.

"You ride like a *puttana,* sister, straddling the horse."

"Francesco!" said Isabella.

"*Serenissimo,*" interrupted the middle brother, silent until now. "May I remind you that as cardinal of the Holy Church, I cannot condone—"

"Stay out of this, Ferdinando! It was you who came to me, outraged at the salacious gossip and jeers in the streets of Rome! The Florentine cardinal has a whore for a sister. What chance do you have of becoming Pope with a sister like this?"

Ferdinando raised his chin, the muscles in his jaw tight.

Francesco stabbed a finger at his sister. "Why do you not use the saddle I gave you?"

"You jest! How could I jump fences sitting sideways? Or do you wish me to break my neck?"

The ensuing silence stretched out in an answer too clear to be mistaken. Finally he said, "Our cousin Catherine de' Medici rides in a properly modest fashion, and she commands Europe's respect as the queen of France."

"Ha! You choose your model carelessly. Catherine despises you! She despises our alliance with Spain! And do you really want me to fashion myself after a woman whose husband lies in the arms of Diane de Poitiers—who does ride, I am told, very much astride. To King Henri's delight."

"Isabella!" said Francesco.

A hound bayed, catching the scent of prey. Isabella spurred her horse, plunging down the hill toward an enormous fallen tree trunk, her skirts flying back over the horse's flanks.

And a young shepherdess forgot her flock of sheep for a moment as she stared, open-mouthed, at the woman and her horse, who seemed to fly over anything that barred their way.

CHAPTER 3

Siena, Pugna Hills

JANUARY 1573

At age six, I was painfully thin—all angular bones and knobby knees, with shoulder blades sharp as knives under my skin, not unlike a newborn foal. My body did not thrive on the sheep broth, gristle, and rough bread that were all we had to eat, but it was not just my body that was undernourished. My spirit felt hunger more keenly than my belly. I was starved, loved too little by a childless aunt and a kind but weak-willed uncle.

"Zia Claudia!" I shouted, opening the door. A wake of dried leaves chased in after me in a gust of wind. "There was a beautiful woman on a mighty horse who jumped the old olive tree—"

"Close the door! You let out the warmth!" snapped Zia Claudia. "Sweep up these leaves this minute."

"But Zia! I saw a woman astride a horse. A woman who could ride as well as any man!"

"Speak not one more word of horses or I will take a broom handle to you, I swear it," said Zia Claudia.

I fell into silence. I knew Zia's threat was not hollow.

"You are late. The beans need shelling," she said.

My fingers, numb from the cold, fumbled over the yellowed bean pods. I dug my broken nails into the withered shells, stripping the beans from their casing.

I bent over the cast-iron pot, my loose hair obscuring my view of Zia Claudia, though I could smell her sheep scent and mean-woman sweat across the room.

"Virginia!" snapped my aunt, bent over the soup pot. "Keep your hair out of our food!" She strode toward me, her cracked leather shoes kicking against the hem of a soiled apron.

Zia Claudia drew a dirty piece of string from her apron pocket and wrapped it around my hair. Her sooty fingers yanked it tight.

"Ow!" I cried.

"Next time you will remember to tie back that mop yourself. I have no stomach for picking your long hairs out of my soup."

She turned away, leaving the mutton stink in her wake, greasy and rancid. I continued stripping the beans from their hard yellow shells. They rattled into the cast-iron pot.

For comfort, I glanced up at a crude painting of Santa Caterina fastened to the wall. My mother had bought it in the markets of Siena just before I was born. It was my christening present, fitting for a child born in the Contrada del Drago.

Though I was a *villanella*—a country girl—my mother and father had sacrificed everything to make sure I was born in the Drago contrada with Santa Caterina as my patron saint. No one could take away that birthright.

Santa Caterina was my protector. I prayed every night for her intercession, telling her my secrets and fears. And I was quite sure she hated Zia Claudia of the muttony hands.

"And stop daydreaming!" my zia called across the room.

My uncle Giovanni stomped his boots on the threshold, and I smiled.

"A little kindness, Claudia," he murmured.

"Kindness won't get supper on the table," Zia Claudia snapped. Her mouth puckered like a withered raisin. "It's only the beans the soup lacks. And don't encourage her daydreaming. Horses, horses, horses! As if we could even afford a lame donkey."

I felt a twist inside my gut, as if she had punctured something. Giovanni sat down in his chair near the hearth.

"What harm does it do?" he said.

"She is a shepherdess! She fills her head with notions of riding horses, as if she were a *signore*'s daughter! Your brother—"

"Claudia!" he said.

"Well, it is time she accepted her lot and gave thanks to God. And to us!" she snapped.

Giovanni stepped away from her sour breath, looking at me with sad puckers around his brown eyes.

"She is a lonely little girl, Claudia," he whispered.

He looked over at me and said in a louder voice, "Virginia, when you finish shelling the beans, I will tell you more of your grandfather."

Zia Claudia grumbled, clanging the wooden spoon against the soup pot.

"Yes, Zio!" I cried. Now my fingers flew. The rattle of dropping beans filled the smoky room.

The moment I gave Zia Claudia the pot of shelled beans, I begged my uncle to tell me the story of my ancestors and the siege of Siena. He smiled, stroking my hair.

"You want to hear about the horses, ciccia?"

"You spoil her," said Zia Claudia, stirring the beans into the pot.

"She has been out alone with the ewes for five days and nights. She deserves the comfort of a tale, Claudia."

"Not a long story, the soup will be ready soon."

My uncle winked at our victory. I hugged him tight.

His hands patted my shoulder blades.

"So thin, Virginia," he said, shaking his head. "You need to eat more."

"She eats enough," said my aunt. "She is strong enough to hold a ewe for milking. A shepherd's life will give her the brawn she needs."

My zio let a moment of silence pass before he began his story.

"Your grandfather was a skilled iron smith with the Senese cavalry under the command of Piero Strozzi, the most powerful enemy of the de' Medici," he began. "All the world was at war in those years. And the European powers eyed Siena like vultures above a bloody kill. The French were our defenders, but that only drew in their enemies: the Spanish, the Swiss, and the Habsburgs. Siena was a bright penny on the table, surrounded by snatching hands. Strozzi was a great general, and his cavalry needed good blacksmiths, like your grandfather Tacci."

I knew this story by heart—but I still loved to hear my zio tell it over and over again.

"But Grandfather *rode* the horses, didn't he?"

"Yes. Piero Strozzi needed cavalrymen. Strozzi did not care that Grandfather wasn't a noble. Pounding iron had forged his muscles, making him strong. He could sit on a horse and wield a sword. Another mighty warrior to kill the de' Medici."

"He rode well!"

"He killed many a de' Medici soldier; Spanish, too. His sword tasted their blood—"

Claudia called.

"Soup is ready, *subito*!"

"Sì, Zia," I answered.

"But Zio," I whispered. "How did the de' Medici defeat Siena and our fierce warriors?"

"We could not defeat all Europe," said my uncle, sighing, "and Duca Cosimo de' Medici wanted Siena more than any prize on Earth."

"*La più bella!*" I sang the ancient Senese anthem "Per Forza o Per Amore." "*Viva la nostra Siena, la più bella delle città!*"

The most beautiful! Long live our Siena, the most beautiful city of all.

The song made any Senese's eyes shine. Even a country peasant like my uncle. He nodded his head to the words.

"But how he made Siena suffer," said Zio, rubbing his eye with a knuckle.

My uncle Giovanni was a good storyteller. I was as hungry for his tales as I was for hot broth after shepherding.

The siege of Siena was the most painful of his stories—the most painful story for any Senese. Now I needed to hear that story again, even as Zia Claudia tried to command us to come to the table.

"A year of siege," my uncle intoned, recounting the story we both knew too well. "A year with no food from beyond the walls of the city. Many from the countryside risked their lives, running food to the walls at night for the city men to haul up in buckets. Many were slaughtered, their houses and fields burned for aiding the city. Inside the walls, the brave citizens weakened day by day until they were as weak as baby birds, straining their necks for food. They ate sawdust, rats—"

"Dogs?"

I ducked my head, my face hot with shame. I could not meet my uncle's eyes. I knew they would be gleaming with tears. But I needed to see those tears. I lifted my eyes to his, drinking in his sorrow to match my own.

I knew too well that my great-grandmother had died of starvation in the siege of Siena, refusing to eat her pet dog. The mutt curled up and died at the foot of her pallet, a circle of fur and bones, within an hour of her passing.

Her daughter-in-law hurried past the corpse, snatching up the dog's meager body. She stripped the fur and boiled the carcass for soup to save her starving children.

And with that terrible thought in our minds, Zia Claudia's screeching shattered the story and brought us to the table.

Aunt Claudia's cooking was invariable. The broth shone with a bubbling slick of grease, the beans shiny white pebbles beneath the gray scum. Wild garlic and dried parsley defeated some of the old mutton's acrid taste, but the strong essence of our ancient flock still lingered on my tongue.

My belly growled for the repast, despite its grim look. Walking the Tuscan hills tending sheep in the raw cold of winter left me ravenous. For days at a time, I ate nothing but hard, stale bread with ewe's cheese and greasy olives.

I lifted my wooden spoon to my mouth, my lips puckered to blow on the broth to cool it.

That is when I heard the dogs growl in their pens and, a moment later, a pounding on the door.

"Who knocks?"

"Open up, in the name of the Granduca of Tuscany."

Giovanni slid open the iron bolt.

Two men dressed in chestnut woolen jackets and crimson velvet hats stood at the threshold. Their leather riding boots shone copper-bright against their woolen leggings.

"We have come to warn inhabitants of Vignano that the de' Medici family are hunting these hills. Keep your dogs under control and your sheep in a tight flock, close to your sheds. Should you see the hunting party, keep out of their way under penalty of law."

"*Sì, signori.*"

"Do nothing that might spoil their sport. Is that clear?"

"Yes, certainly."

As he turned to leave, the huntsman called over his shoulder, "*Buon appetito.*"

I saw him wrinkle his nose in disgust as the door shut.

"The de' Medici! Here?" I gasped. "That is who I saw, the woman who jumped the fallen tree!"

"What?" said Zia. "Isabella de' Medici? Why did you not tell me—"

"You should have seen her, Zio!" I said, ignoring Zia. "She plunged down the hill from Quattro Torra at breakneck speed. Then her horse lifted off the ground like a bird taking flight. Never have I—"

"Your flock might have frightened the horses!" said Zia Claudia, her hands flying to her face. "We would be held responsible if she had fallen. They would think nothing of confiscating our home, our flocks—"

Zio Giovanni tipped his bowl of soup to his lips. He wiped his mouth on his sleeve as he stood up and took his cloak from the peg by the door.

"Where are you going?" demanded Zia Claudia.

"To the lambing sheds," he said. "I will need to make sure everything is in order for castration this week. And if the de' Medici are in the western hills, we will need to move the flocks closer to the sheds, as the signori ordered."

"I want to go, too!" I said, jumping up from the table. Secretly I hoped that Zio would stop by Smithy Brunelli's stable, and I could pet the horses' muzzles.

"No, it is getting cold and dark out. I will whistle for Franco and the boys to move down from the hills for the night. But after Sunday Mass tomorrow, you can help us herd the old ewes, Virginia. We will need another shepherd by evening after the tupping."

He lit his lantern and closed the door behind him. My chin dropped to my chest in disappointment.

"*Odio le pecore,*" I muttered. I hate the sheep.

I felt the sting of a slap.

"You! You ingrate! How dare you curse our sheep!"

Zia Claudia—her muttony breath hot in my ear—insisted I thank God for each blessed ewe that bleats, each ram that ruts.

"The flocks keep you alive," she said, shaking her finger in my face. "They clothe you, give us their meat and milk."

"I do not curse our sheep. It is just—"

"You think you are above shepherding," said Zia. "Just like your good-for-nothing father, who brought pestilence into the House of Tacci."

"That's a lie!" I shouted.

"He brought killing sickness to this house," she spat at me, her face an ugly mask of hatred.

I knew she was right. My father—then my mother—had died of the fever after his journey trading leather in Piombino, on the swampland coast near Pisa.

"Your dream-sick father, traveling so far from his God-given land. For what? To earn money to buy a horse."

A horse?

"My father was going to . . . buy a *horse*?"

"Bringing home sickness instead. And ruin! He killed your mother with the swamp fever, and he nearly dragged you to the grave with him."

A horse? I felt the ghost of my father draw his arms tight around my shoulders.

For you, ciccia. A horse.

Then I smiled. My father wanted to buy me a horse! Zia Claudia had told me a secret I would never forget.

CHAPTER 4

Florence, Pitti Palace

JANUARY 1573

Leonora di Toledo, first cousin of Isabella de' Medici, and thus first cousin—as well as wife—of Isabella's brother Pietro, sat in front of the polished looking glass as her attendant brushed her red-gold hair.

"Do not put the tortoiseshell comb in my hair, Maria. It makes me look too Spanish," Leonora complained. "I am a de' Medici now." The stiff rustling of brocaded satin made Leonora turn as two women brought in her dress for the afternoon.

"The peacock blue is a beautiful color and contrasts magnificently with your glorious hair, signora," said Maria, addressing her mistress in Italian, though her tongue still yearned for Castilian sounds.

"Yes, it suits me, I think," said Leonora, "though Pietro despises it. He calls the color vulgar. It is good that he will not attend Isabella's salon," she added, smiling, which made Maria's job easier as she outlined her mistress's lips in beet juice and beeswax.

"Our discussions bore my husband," sighed Leonora. "But there are others who find Isabella's concerns quite stimulating."

Leonora's retinue exchanged knowing looks. Their mistress saw their reflection in the mirror. She raised an eyebrow, causing the women to look at the floor.

"If it were not for Isabella, I would die of boredom," Leonora continued, her ladies properly chastened. "Isabella and his grace, Cosimo, the old duca."

Again, two of the ladies exchanged looks. Maria scowled at them.

"Duca Cosimo calls us his huntresses, his Dianas! Ah, if only the de' Medici sons were like their charming father—"

A knock on the door interrupted her. Maria stopped powdering her mistress's face, the plumed puff in midair.

"See who it is, Clara," said Leonora.

The attendant nearest the door opened the door a crack.

"Mistress, it is your husband."

Pietro de' Medici threw open the door, slamming it hard against Clara. She shrieked with pain, her hands thrown up over her face.

Leonora rose from her vanity, pulling her dressing robe tight around her.

"What—you've returned from Siena earlier than—"

"The stablemaster informed me you requested the gray mares tonight to pull your carriage. We have no engagements this evening!"

"I am attending Isabella's salon—"

Pietro took two strides toward her. Maria stepped closer to her mistress, blocking him.

Pietro flung the elderly maid to one side.

"Do not dare to come between me and my wife," he snapped. "You ignorant Spanish cow!"

"Do not address my lady in that way, sir!" said Leonora, squaring her little shoulders.

"I will address her as I see fit."

His eyes shifted to her mouth.

"And what is that red sap on your lips? You look beastly—"

Leonora's hand flew to her mouth, covering it.

"It is only beet juice to enhance my—"

"Since when does a de' Medici have to enhance herself in order to discuss linguistic dilemmas?" said Pietro. "Take it off immediately, you look like a puttana. And you shall not have the grays tonight. I have my own plans in Fiesole."

Leonora's back stiffened. Pietro's favorite mistress lived in the hills of Fiesole, in a villa he had paid to furnish despite the debts he could not pay for his own family.

"But—"

Pietro grasped Leonora's arm, twisting it.

"You are hurting me—"

He whispered, his breath hot in her ear, "If you do anything that brings dishonor to my name—if I hear gossip of another man—I will kill you, as God is my witness. Do you understand?"

"Sì, Pietro, but let go of my arm! Please!"

He flung her arm away. She rubbed her skin, her eyes blurry with tears.

"I mean what I say," he snarled, moving to the door. "Do not trifle with me, Leonora, you Spanish whore."

The ladies-in-waiting scattered like pigeons as Pietro de' Medici strode out the door.

Leonora stood clutching her arm, her face crumpled in pain.

"Write to the Spanish king, your uncle!" said Maria, rushing to her side. "A di Toledo should not endure such a beast as this man!"

"I cannot hide behind the robes of my uncle," Leonora answered, her voice hushed. She blinked away the tears, her reddened mouth hardening. "I am a de' Medici now."

CHAPTER 5

Siena, Village of Vignano

JANUARY 1573

Zia Claudia cursed Cesare Brunelli and made the sign of the cross every time his name was uttered. She called him a gambler and a pagan who never crossed the threshold of any church. And it was true that Cesare Brunelli never set foot in a church if he could help it. That stubborn refusal made him all the more mysterious and feared by the faithful.

"He has the weird Etruscan ways about him," she said, narrowing her eyes.

"But, Zia! He cures horses. People from all over Tuscany travel to see him," I said.

"He consorts with the devil," she spat. "A horse witch. He brews sorcerers' concoctions from devil weeds. Never speak with him, or he will steal your soul."

"But he is my *padrino*," I protested.

Cesare Brunelli had been my father's best friend, and he was my godfather. I was proud of his reputation.

"Padrino!" scoffed Zia Claudia. "A *scherzo* your father played, entrusting him with your soul."

My zia might not have approved of my padrino, but he was often summoned by wealthy *nobili* to shoe their finest horses. His meaty, gifted hands could fit a shoe to the most cracked hoof and make it hold, and they could deliver a breech colt. His shoeing could cure a lame horse; his liniments performed miracles on sore legs and fetlocks. His tinctures made from herbs, roots, or bark could save a horse from colic.

My Zio Giovanni swore he saw him seize a crippled Palio horse by its neck with his great arms, give it a twist, and straighten its spine. The horse dipped his head. His tongue made smacking sounds against his lips.

"Just as if the beast were trying to talk. Trying to thank Cesare. Then he dropped the halter and smacked the horse on the hindquarters. It trotted off, cured and sound."

No wonder the Senese whispered that old Brunelli was a horse sorcerer. But I sensed only his solid strength. His hands were always sticky with the pine tar from spackling cracked hoofs and the white sugar crystals he used to cure festering wounds. I smelt the clean scent of wintergreen oil on his skin as he pounded iron shoes on his anvil.

Smithy Brunelli was so sought after that he had to refuse work, shaking his enormous shaggy head.

"I cannot come," he'd say. "No time to leave my forge."

The rich noble families would send their horses to him, along with a servant who begged or bribed old Brunelli to work his magic on their ailing animals.

"Just a few hours of your time, maestro. *Per favore!*"

And so it was at his stables that I met the Duchessa d'Elci and saw the most beautiful mare in all Tuscany.

After a grueling morning in church—with Zia Claudia pinching me to emphasize each point the priest made about the sins of pride—I finally escaped, walking to the village with my uncle.

"I must negotiate prices for our wool," he told Zia. "Virginia will accompany me." He raised a finger. "And we must tend the sheep close tonight, once Franco brings them down. The rams sense when the castration knife is sharpened. We cannot risk having the flocks scatter."

Before Zia Claudia could open her snapping-turtle mouth to object, we turned down the lane toward the center of the village.

Purple-gray clouds gathered overhead, and soon icy rain pelted our heads. I pulled my cloak around me, its rough wool scratching my neck.

We slipped inside the dark stables of the smithy, where my uncle liked to throw dice a few hours a week. I kept his secret faithfully from Zia Claudia. And I would have traded my soul for the time I could watch Padrino Brunelli work his miracles on horses.

Shivering from the winter rain, we stomped the mud off our shoes. The warm horse smell—spicy and intoxicating, mixing warm hay and grassy dung—welcomed us.

I drew in a deep breath.

"Take your fingers out of your mouth, *cara*," whispered Zio. He said it gently, knowing the spell horses cast on me. I twisted my wet fingers into the folds of my overskirt.

Zio Giovanni was greeted with backslaps from other men, who rose from their crouched positions on the floor. They passed a terra-cotta jug of red wine. He took a deep draught and gave a lopsided grin, his teeth berry red.

Zio took his place in the gambling circle as Smithy Brunelli leaned over a horse's hoof aligning a shoe, five nails clenched tight in his teeth.

"You smell like a dirty sheep, Tacci," said the baker. Flour gathered in the furrows of his moist brow, etching white lines in his ruddy skin.

"It is the livelihood God provides me," said Zio. "I am not ashamed of it."

"Better than the tanner," grumbled the miller. "I swear I cannot draw a breath near him."

Brunelli grunted, removing the nails from his mouth. Tanning leather in urine and feces was a vital but unpopular occupation.

"Stinking but honest," he declared.

The cobbler laughed. "I agree. Let him stink—I need his good leather!"

"Roll the dice, Giovanni," said the baker. "See what luck your sheep-scented hands can throw today."

I sat close to Padrino Brunelli on a section of tree stump, watching my uncle throw the wooden dice on the stone floor. The men hunched over the dice, straining to see in the darkness.

Padrino lit another oil lamp suspended above us on a chain, the storm having snuffed the late afternoon light. He looked up at me, showing his broken teeth in a smile.

"You love the horses, don't you, cara?" he said pinching my cheek with his blackened fingers.

I nodded, staring wide-eyed at the horse he was shoeing. There was a gnawing in my belly like hunger.

"You must be careful how you love these creatures," he said. "One day, you may give your heart away forever."

He watched my face in the lantern light.

"You have the fever, I see it in your eyes," he said with a sigh. "What a pity you are a girl."

Sympathy glowed in his eyes. My smile dissolved. I turned away from my beloved padrino before he could see my tears of frustration—the unfairness!

"*Le due!*" called Zio from the circle of gamblers, rattling the dice in his hand.

The dice rolled from his palm and came to rest next to the lantern.

Two black dots stared up at the small group of men.

"*Ho vinto!*" shouted Zio Giovanni.

As he reached for the coins strewn in the dusty circle, we heard a clatter of hooves, the clanging of iron shoes on the courtyard cobblestones. Brunelli, an enormous pair of tongs in his fists, stopped his work and listened.

There was a sharp rap on the wooden door.

Brunelli gave a quick jerk of his chin to the gamblers.

Zio Giovanni slid the coins into his pocket, and another man grabbed the dice just as a well-dressed rider strode in.

"La Duchessa d'Elci requests assistance from Cesare Brunelli."

"That would be me, signore," said my padrino.

He extracted a glowing red horseshoe from the forge with his tongs. With two deft blows of his hammer, he shaped the open ends. Beads of sweat glistened on his forehead.

The d'Elci messenger stood fidgeting in the doorway.

Brunelli tossed the shoe in a trough of water. The sizzling hiss filled the sudden silence.

"What does the duchessa require that cannot be done by the good men in the Contrada dell'Oca?" asked Brunelli, wiping his brow with the back of his hand.

The men nodded. Oca—represented by the noble house d'Elci—had won the Palio more times than any other. The d'Elci horses were legendary.

"A Palio mare is in foal, but something is wrong. We fear she is dying. She is the duchessa's favorite horse, La Stella."

"La Stella," the men murmured in reverence. They had seen the mare race the narrow streets of Siena. I, too, made the sign of the cross at the mention of her name.

"A mare with a great heart," said Brunelli. Concern knitted his sooty brow.

"Please, won't you come to see her? Per favore—"

Brunelli rubbed his hands on his leather apron.

"Is she within the walls in your contrada?"

"No, no. She is pastured just above, in the hills beyond your village of Vignano—in the shadow of Castello di Quatro Torra. There are some wooden lambing sheds close by. If we could get her to move, she could rest there for the night in shelter. You could tend to her—"

"Zio Giovanni!" I whispered. "Those are our sheds!"

Brunelli shot a glance at me. He considered.

"And what will the Duchessa d'Elci give me if I can save her mare?"

"She will reward you commensurate with your skill, I assure you. You can name your price."

Brunelli snapped his finger against his stout thumb.

"Giorgio!" he called.

A red-haired boy appeared: one of his sons—the one Brunelli had sent away to Florence for years, who was said to have talent for painting pictures.

He was about nineteen, almost a man, with big hands and long fingers stained brilliant blue and crimson. What had stained his skin, I wondered. Scarlet St. John's oil, tincture of violet? So many horse potions I had seen in the illustrations painted in Brunelli's book of horse remedies.

"Fetch me my gray gelding," Brunelli said to his son, "and my doctoring kit."

"Sì, Babbo," said the boy, bobbing his head. His red curls brushed his freckled neck.

I squinted at him, my fingers crossed to protect me from the hex of his flame-colored hair. Aunt Claudia had warned me about those witches' locks. Licked by Satan with his fiery tongue, she said.

A loud whinny erupted. The horses tied to a rope highline down the stable nickered and fidgeted as Giorgio hurried away.

Brunelli looked out the open door, past the rider. The cold gust made me shiver.

A black carriage with a crowned, double-headed eagle insignia stood waiting. An elderly woman pulled the velvet curtains apart, exposing her face to the rain. I watched her silver hair slowly mat against the pink crown of her head.

"That is the duchessa?" asked Brunelli.

"Yes," said the rider. "She is distraught. She begged to accompany us." He tilted his chin up and sniffed. "Though I assured her this stable is no place for a duchessa."

"She is a true horsewoman," said Brunelli. "One of the few noblewomen who still is. Of course she belongs here, though I am not sure you do."

The gamblers chuckled, watching the servant flinch.

"Tell her I will attend the mare," said Brunelli. "But on one condition. You must give the owner of the lambing shed and his niece a ride to their home in the carriage. Those sheds are their own."

Zio Giovanni stood up in amazement. I stuck my fingers in my mouth.

"But—" protested the servant, taking a look at him and then at me, wild-eyed with excitement. "She is the Duchessa d'Elci!"

"You told me that. You also told me she was desperate to save her mare," said Brunelli.

The servant swallowed hard.

"These are your terms?"

"Absolutely. Ah, no. One more thing. I will ask for some paints for my son. He fancies himself another Michelangelo."

Laughter erupted again from the gambling circle.

"Lapis blue is what he craves now," said Padrino Brunelli. "I trust you can procure it in the markets of Siena?"

"*Oltremarino*, Babbo!" Giorgio called from the recesses of the stable. "But I must pick the stones to crush myself for quality. The vendors will cheat us if I do not choose them myself.

"And some madder lake!" he called out. "From the cloth dyers by the Arno in Florence. They hoard the best from the Silk Road."

"You heard him," said my padrino. "That will be my payment. Paints and transportation."

The servant gave a curt nod and ducked back into the rain. I scrambled to the stable door to watch him. I saw the old duchessa's swollen eyes, the flash of a white linen handkerchief.

As the servant spoke, a look of amazement mixed with annoyance crossed her face. She looked up and saw me staring at her from the stable door.

She dipped her chin once, consenting.

"We are going to ride in a carriage, Uncle!" I cried.

"*Grazie*," said Uncle Giovanni, grasping Brunelli's hand. "You know what this means to my niece. And the honor—"

"Nothing, my friend. This is for my goddaughter. But I will ask for shelter for the mare if we can make her stand and walk. You will help me."

The smith retrieved the horseshoe from the trough. He slapped the horse's rump, raising a cloud of dust.

"No shoes for you today," said my padrino. "I will finish the job tomorrow."

A hand clutched my arm, and I jumped. The red-haired Giorgio held me in his grasp. I stared at his color-splotched fingers.

"Make an excuse for a minute, and come with me."

"What?"

"Tell them you need to make water before you ride in the carriage. I will wait for you in the back stalls. It is important, *ragazza*! *Molto importante!*"

I bit my lip. When I turned around again, he was gone.

"Come, Virginia! Did you hear? We are to ride in the Duchessa d'Elci's carriage!"

"Yes, Zio! Oh, Zio, I am so excited. I must first excuse myself to—"

"Ah, but of course, Virginia. Make haste!"

I ran back to the mangers, where a line of horses was tethered to a rope.

Giorgio seized me by the arm.

"What are you doing?" I cried, squirming. "Let go of me!"

"I am preparing you to meet the duchessa. You smell like sheep dung."

He wiped a sweaty rag over my face, neck, and chest. I smelt the tang and tasted the salt of horse sweat from the rubbing cloth. Horsehair stuck to my skin, my clothes, but the rag came away grimy with dirt, mutton grease, and soot.

"The duchessa would not tolerate you for one minute in her presence, smelling like you do."

My eyes stung. I struck out at my assailant with my bony fists.

He only chuckled as he dodged my struggling blows.

"You are hot-blooded, Signorina Tacci," he laughed. "But you do not realize the favor I do for you."

My fist tightened at his mocking use of *signorina* when I was only a commoner, a simple *sora*.

"Leave me alone, you red-headed demon!"

We heard my uncle's voice.

"Virginia! The duchessa awaits us!"

The gamblers hooted and whistled.

"Go, little Tacchina. But do not bore the duchessa with stories of sheep."

I spat at the flame-haired devil, then turned to run toward the stable door. I could hear him laughing behind me.

CHAPTER 6

Siena, Pugna Hills

JANUARY 1573

The duchessa moved as far away from us as she could. She was dressed in satins and velvet, with thick furs drawn up over her lap.

Zio Giovanni wrung his cap in his hands and tried to bow inside the coach. He struck his head against the roof.

The duchessa wrinkled her nose. She drew a lace handkerchief over her mouth and nose in disgust.

"*Puzza di pecore!*" cried the duchessa. He stinks of sheep! "The peasant must ride outside the coach with my footman! *Dio mio!*"

Her attendant grabbed Zio by his elbow.

"Come along, Virginia," he said to me.

"No," said the Duchessa d'Elci. The pale nostrils pinched and flared. "The girl may accompany me. She stays."

My uncle stared, his mouth open wide.

"Come on, *villano*," said the servant. "You will ride the footboard with me."

The footman closed the coach. We heard the two men scrambling up the back of the coach.

The duchessa pulled the velvet curtains closed.

"Sit close to the brazier, my child," she said. "You must be chilled in that thin cloak."

I moved closer to the coals, glowing through perforations in the brass pan. I sighed in comfort.

The duchessa stretched out her finger, touching my shepherd's coat. Her hand drew back quickly as if it had been burnt.

"Such scratchy wool! How can you bear such coarseness next to your young skin?"

I shrugged. "It is all I have ever worn, Duchessa. I do not find it so rough."

"Are you the farrier's daughter?" she asked.

"No, I am the shepherd's niece. My mother and father are dead."

The duchessa nodded. She lifted her chin slightly, sniffing the air.

"Hmmm? But the farrier insisted you ride with me as payment for attending my mare."

"He is my padrino and was my father's closest friend. He knows how much I love horses," I said. I turned around on the bench, upholstered in dark blue velvet. I peered out the small window toward the horses.

"You cannot see them well from here," said the duchessa, smiling slightly. "Pity. Perhaps you would like to see my mare. Ah, but when she is well again!"

I watched as the lady made the sign of the cross.

"Do not worry, Duchessa. My Padrino Brunelli can cure any horse," I said, turning to face her. "He has a way, Zio says."

"Magari," said the duchessa, in the Senese fashion. God willing. Her gray eyes were sad. "There is no finer horse. She has won the Palio twice for the House of d'Elci."

I stared at her. "The Palio," I whispered.

"Yes, and she is with foal," she said. "A very special foal." A gleam shone briefly in her clouded eyes. "She will have the most magnificent colt ever born."

"I love colts," I whispered. "How they gambol and kick in the air at nothing. I watch them as I tend my flock."

"The father of this colt is Tempesta," she said. "He is the swiftest horse in all Tuscany. He was born in the wilds of the Maremma."

"Has he won the Palio?"

"No," she said. She looked out the window at the sluicing rain. "He has never been ridden. Many fine horsemen have tried, but he has thrown them all. He cannot even be approached now, he is so wild."

"A dangerous horse?"

She lifted her eyebrow. "Deadly."

I shivered. The vision of slashing hooves haunted me, for my padrino had told me stories of mad horses that haunted my dreams.

"Sit closer to the brazier, my child," she said, drawing the fur rug over my legs. "You will catch a chill, mia cara. Feel how damp you are."

I looked up at her in awe. Except for old Brunelli, no one had ever called me "mia cara." The hot coals warmed us as we listened to the pelting rain against the wooden coach.

"Why would you want a colt from a dangerous stallion, Duchessa?"

"I want his bloodline. I believe his blood mixed with my mare will make the fastest colt Siena has ever seen. But the real secret is the mare. Mares have heart," she said, pressing my hand.

I watched a smile grow on her face. She looked twenty years younger, like a young mother herself. She patted my knee.

"If your padrino is worthy of his reputation," she said, "we might see the birth of that colt tonight."

CHAPTER 7

Siena, Pugna Hills

JANUARY 1573

The mare lay on her side, her flanks black with sweat. Cesare Brunelli, still wet from riding hard and fast in the rain, rubbed the mare's belly, squeezing her teats.

"How long has she been in labor?" he asked the duchessa's attendant. He looked up from the man's polished boots, now splattered with mud.

"Eight hours," said the stableman. "She can barely lift her head now. It is a miracle we got her to these sheds."

Brunelli shook his head. "She still has a little kick to her—I can see it in her eyes."

"Will you bleed her?" asked the man, shifting his weight in his boots so they creaked. "I have heard that a cut to the fetlock purges the black humors—"

Brunelli snorted. "Certainly not. This mare needs all the blood God gave her."

His fire-scarred hands rummaged through his leather bag and extracted a ceramic jar sealed with beeswax.

He used the blade of his knife to break the seal.

"You got her?" he asked Giorgio.

"Sì, Babbo."

"Easy, girl," said Brunelli. He knelt, bringing the little jar below her neck where she could not see it. Rings of white circled her eyes, where panic shone bright.

His finger slipped between her front teeth and back tusk—knowing too little about horses, I gasped. I was sure the mare would bite off his hand.

The mare opened her mouth, her tongue moving. With his other hand, Brunelli swabbed the contents of the jar into her throat. She jerked up her head, trying to stand. Then she fell back to the straw with a groan.

"What did you give her?" asked the duchessa.

"A potion to relax her. She needs to be tolerant for what must be done next."

He stroked her salt-encrusted neck.

"*Brava ragazza*," he whispered. "Good girl."

The mare's breath stirred the straw, her nostrils flaring.

Brunelli petted her with calm strokes. He listened to her breathing, not moving until she had quieted.

Giorgio wielded a pitchfork, clearing away the soiled straw. His red hair was wet and matted against his skull.

"Bring more straw," he told me.

For a moment, my anger at the way he had mocked me—and my disgust at his devil's red hair—flared. But I knew there was no time for that. We were working together to save the mare and her foal.

When I returned to the stall with fresh straw in my arms, Giorgio was behind the mare, lifting her tail away from her body. I watched as Padrino coated his arm with sheep lard.

His hand disappeared into the mare's body.

"Come, Virginia," said my uncle, turning away. "This is not for the eyes of a young girl."

"No. Let her stay," said the duchessa. "She—"

Bleating from the ewes in the next shed interrupted her words.

Brunelli nodded. "With your permission, my friend. Your niece should stay."

"Never tell my wife," said my uncle, wringing his cap. "She would never forgive me. The blood, the birth—"

"Why?" sniffed the duchessa. "These are things of women. It is a mare who gives birth, may I remind you good gentlemen."

Giorgio and Brunelli smiled. Uncle Giovanni wore a bewildered expression. His fingers continued to fumble with the cap in his hands, as if he were trying to tear it apart.

"Of course, good lady," he said, bobbing his head in respect. "Forgive my ignorance."

"I have helped birth dozens of sheep," I said to my uncle. "Is it so different?"

"Sit with me, Virginia," said the duchessa. "Stay away from the mare. She may stand up and lash out."

My padrino chuckled.

"With respect, Duchessa. I gave her belladonna—it is doubtful she will rise within the half hour."

Padrino's right hand was inserted inside the mare past his elbow. He touched under the mare's belly with his left, as if trying to grasp his hands together through the abdomen wall.

"It has begun," he said.

He pulled his hand from the mare's insides. His arm was slick. A few seconds later, a gush of pinkish water soaked the straw.

The mare groaned. Her sides heaved like the bellows in my padrino's forge. Her snorts blew a thick stream of mucus from her nostrils.

The duchessa rose quietly from where she had been sitting in the straw by the mare. She drew out her linen handkerchief, cleaning the nostrils with a deft hand.

"Good. That will help her breathe," said Padrino, looking up from the mare's hindquarters.

Suddenly Padrino's face turned rigid. The duchessa held her breath beside me.

"May I see, per favore?" I asked her.

She nodded. I moved toward my padrino.

Between her legs, the flesh of the mare was now bright pinkish-red, as if she were turned inside out. She groaned and made a strange sound deep in her throat.

Something glistened in Padrino's hands. A translucent sac was beginning to emerge from the mare.

"Yes," he said. "This is what I felt. The foal is coming tail first."

The duchessa closed her eyes. "She has no strength left."

Padrino glanced at the duchessa.

"But she has the heart of a champion, duchessa mia."

The duchessa nodded, opening her creased eyes wide.

"Come on, mia cara," she said in an urgent whisper. "Just a little more." Her breath made the mare's ear's twitch.

My padrino pulled out his knife, making a slit in the sac. I could see two little hooves inside. He grasped the hooves with his hands and pulled in a twisting motion to release the foal's haunches.

"Oh," I whispered as I saw the waxen form, the tiny hooves.

This miracle horse in miniature chased away words.

The duchessa beckoned to me. "Help me clean her nostrils," she said. She ripped her fine handkerchief in two, giving me half. "She needs air."

I mopped at the long strands of phlegm. The duchessa stroked the mare's neck.

"I wonder if she can win this race," she whispered. The deep wrinkles around her eyes were red like raw meat from being clenched with weeping.

"Of course she can, Duchessa," I said, laying my hand on her arm. "A mare who won the Palio. Twice!"

Padrino's hand disappeared into the mare again. I could see his muscles working as his hands fumbled deep inside the birth canal.

The wind rattled through the timbers of the lambing shed, powdering us with snow. An attendant brought the duchessa her furs from the coach. She patted the straw, inviting me to share the warmth.

"No, grazie," I said, my teeth chattering as I hunched over the mare's nostrils, dabbing away phlegm.

I saw Padrino's lips moving. My young ears heard muttering. Almost a chant, though I could not decipher his words.

Was Zia Claudia was right? Was he a horse witch, speaking their language?

My padrino's jacket pulled up, but he was too engaged in his work to notice. I saw the buckle of white skin, the muscle forged from pounding iron now rimmed with fat.

Was he too old now to perform miracles?

As soon as I thought it, I cursed myself for my doubts.

Padrino can perform any miracle with horses!

I watched the pale flesh bulging over his belt turn bright red in the cold as long moments passed.

The duchessa's fingers twitched, her puckered lips quivered. My eyes darted back and forth between the two souls who fought desperately to save this colt.

My padrino sat back. He withdrew his arms from the mare. The tiny foal lay quiet—so quiet—in his huge hands.

"Stillborn," he said at last, his voice weary. "I am so sorry, Duchessa. I did all I could."

The Duchessa d'Elci made not a sound. Her mouth was a perfect *O* of sorrow. She slowly raised her blue-veined hands to her face.

Giorgio stared at the dead colt. His eyebrows drew up in red peaks, his freckled face pinched. He shifted his rabbit eyes to mine. We stared at each other, terrified.

Then I realized he was not so much terrified as beseeching. I looked away, confused.

The duchessa was silent, her face hidden behind her hands, which were still slick with phlegm.

Her shoulders shook.

I stared at the foal's body, perfectly still in the straw.

Deep inside me, deeper than heart or gut, I felt something move. Move and twist of its own accord, like a small animal had harbored deep within me.

I crawled across the rustling bedding to the wet foal, my eyes unblinking. The red and blue umbilical cord led from the mare to the belly of the foal, bits of straw clinging to it. I followed it, this lifeline between dam and foal.

"Come away, ciccia," said my padrino. "You shall see other foals birthed, happy moments. Forget this one," he whispered, pressing my hand in his.

I pushed his hand away. I barely heard him, my body trembling with a force I did not recognize. My fingers snatched at the knot in my head scarf, and my hair tumbled down loose. I wiped the slime from the stillborn nostrils with the coarse linen cloth.

I pressed my lips over one tiny nostril, closing the other with my cupped hand.

"What is she doing?" I heard the duchessa say, her voice choking.

Padrino watched silently. I could feel his eyes on my back.

I pulled air down into my lungs as deep as I could. My chest expanded until I could feel the beating of my heart, tight within my rib cage. I breathed deeply into the tiny nostril.

I felt Padrino touch me.

"Come away," he whispered.

I shook my head violently, pulling away from his hand.

No!

I do not know how long my lips cupped over the velvet soft muzzle, damp and salty. Time disappeared—I felt only the rush of air out of my body and into the colt's.

Padrino took my free hand gently. He placed it on the horse's tiny ribs, my fingers draped over the quiet heart. I felt the foal's chest expand and lift with the air that gushed from my lungs.

I tasted the saltiness of newborn life on my lips, the moisture of the mare's womb. The foal was so close to life, still struggling for the world as he dipped under the waves of death. The umbilical cord still united mare and foal. I felt myself a part of them both.

The three of us, hovering between life and death.

My eyes were closed tight. I imagined the flicker of life in the darkness, if I could just reach down far enough.

We shared the same breath, the same life, all three of us. My lungs ached—ached as they did running for help on the night a wolf carried away a lamb when I was alone with the flock.

I coughed, sputtering. But I did not stop breathing, breathing for all of us. Until at last I felt the air, my own breath, whispering back to me—mixed with the scent of horse and new life.

"You can stop," whispered my padrino, his hand gentle on my shoulder. "Rest, Virginia."

"Dio mio! He breathes!" I heard the duchessa cry.

Only then did I pull my mouth away from the colt. My cheeks aching, my lips still slick with the colt's snot.

The foal lifted his head. His brown eyes flickered, unfocused, soft with wonderment.

From the corner of my eye, I saw the duchessa rise with the help of her attendants, escorting her out of the lambing shed. I heard their footsteps crunch on the frozen mud outside.

"Just a few minutes, ciccia," said my padrino quietly. "Then we must leave the mare to break the umbilical cord."

I nodded, looking at the colt. His white blaze reminded me of a constellation, one of my favorites in the winter sky. My finger reached out to trace the jagged outline on his wet face.

"Orione," I whispered. "The hunter."

The lanterns threw buttery light across the straw, casting our silhouettes large and black against the timbers of the lambing shed.

The wind ceased. All that could be heard were the gurgles of the mare's insides, and the soft puffs of her breath scattering the straw.

The colt tossed his head, regarding me. His soft brown eyes slowly focused, never moving from my face.

"You shall run the Palio some day, little one," I said.

I whistled the ancient song of Siena.

Nella la Piazza del Campo, ci nasce la verbena
Viva la nostra Siena . . .
La più bella delle città!

The colt watched me, his head wobbling slightly as he listened to my soft hymn, hummed to him only.

Padrino Brunelli said I blew my heart into the foal that day.

CHAPTER 8

Siena

JANUARY 1573

Dawn filtered slowly through the narrow streets of Siena. Giorgio hurried on foot, winding his way from Pispini Gate through Contrada del Niccio, Contrada del Leocorno, and Contrada della Civetta to Contrada della Selva and the heart of the city. He had slept little, arriving home long after midnight. Yet before sunrise, he had ridden his horse to a stable just beyond the city walls, and now he strode along Banchi di Sotto to Via di Città, where the richest merchants and nobili lived. The cobblestones were swept clean each day, with the rubbish carted away by the municipality, the wandering dogs, and private trashmongers.

A washerwoman was stooped over with a yellow-stained cloth, soaking up the street puddles from the night chamber pots in front of Palazzo Lombardi. She twisted her cloth mercilessly, wringing out the urine into a bucket. Her sons threw the rest of the slops into a rickety donkey-drawn cart with splintered wood.

Despite the cold, flies buzzed lazily around the cargo.

"*Buongiorno,* Giorgio," she said.

"*Buongiorno.*"

"I hear your father saved Duchessa d'Elci's mare and foal last night. And a little shepherdess performed a miracle!"

Giorgio whistled in amazement. How quickly the news spread, servant to servant and mouth to mouth within the walls of Siena.

He nodded, dodging a splash of urine from a chamber pot above.

"Ah, a good haul today!" laughed the washerwoman, seeing him jump.

"Arrivederci!" said Giorgio, dodging past the stinking barrel and trying to hurry, for he was late for his art lesson.

"The tanner pays extra if he knows my goods are from Via di Città!" called the washerwoman. "No better piss, not even from the de' Medici chamber pots!"

"Certo," laughed Giorgio. He stopped and winked at the laundress. A Senese is never in too much of a hurry to join in a joke. "De' Medici piss? Their sheer meanness sets stains," he whispered as loud as he dared.

Giorgio brushed his cloak vigorously, then swept his fingers through his hair. He swung his head left to right, looking for any trace of hay, straw, or barley husk that might provoke a jeer from the wealthier students, especially the Florentines. He took a deep breath and cast a glance at the horse-drawn carriages blocking the entrance of Palazzo d'Elci. Young men descended onto the gray pietra serena cobblestones of the Via di Città.

The noble class and merchant sons arrived on horseback or in carriages, servants toting their paints and easels, their soft soles scuffling behind the hard clicks of their masters' heels.

The caped attendant at Palazzo d'Elci took the gleaming swords, daggers, and even the dining knives from around the necks of the art students as they filed into the ancient palazzo. The Duca d'Elci, patron of the Accademia d'Arte Senese, permitted maestro Antonio Lungo to use the great white marble hall overlooking the piazza for his art classes, but only under strict conditions. The duca believed in the cultivation of Siena's new generation of artists, but he also recognized artists' fiery nature. He required everyone to surrender their weapons before crossing the threshold into Palazzo d'Elci.

"*Pace,*" he said. "There shall be peace within the walls of my palazzo—only art shall thrive."

Giorgio stamped his feet against the cold. Despite the woolen rags he had stuffed in his boots, the sepulchral cold of the marble floor permeated the thin leather soles. The brass braziers had not defeated the brutal chill of the great hall so early in the morning.

Giorgio wondered how the nobili could abide the cold in their *palazzi.* At least in his father's stables, the horses' bodies provided warmth during the Tuscan winter and radiated heat to the house above. But as Cesare Brunelli had told his son, "They are different than we are, *figlio.* They are cold-blooded creatures. Watch them walk, move. They are awkward with inbreeding, their foreheads long and narrow, their skin dry as parchment, their rib cages not wide enough for a sparrow to roost, their lips thin and brittle. They are simply not put together properly, these bluebloods. Unless they have some good bastard blood. A new stud or dam to enrich the stock, make them hearty. Inbreeding withers strength and conformation, even in humans."

Giorgio smiled. With a horseman's eye, his father judged everything and everyone by spirit, conformation, and heart.

The farrier's son cupped his stiff brushes between his hands, forming a cave with his fingers and blowing warm breath to soften the bristles.

His easel was close to the windows that looked out over the Piazza del Campo. The thick panes of crystal warped the view of the marketplace. He gazed at the vendors' stalls, their cabbages and carrots, carved chairs, and baskets twisted into strange proportions by the crystal—the Chianina cattle's creamy white buttocks misshapen as a twisted hunchback's, the farmer's head three times bigger than his torso.

Giorgio thought of Michelangelo's *David*, the enormous hands. How would he portray a Chianina's ass, he wondered.

His breath fogged the window glass. He ran his sleeve over the pane, wiping away the vapor. His chest expanded with pride as he surveyed the most glorious public space in all Christendom, the fanned panels of red brick paving the piazza below and the Torre del Mangia rising into the sky, its crenellated white tower majestic above the brickwork.

Siena might have surrendered its gates to Florence. It might have swallowed bitter bile as the conquerors tore down the city's magnificent towers. But the city had never lost its pride. And never its spirit as an independent republic.

But then his eyes fell on the Palazzo Pubblico, Siena's city hall. There, next to the windows crowned with the black-and-white emblem of Siena, was the huge granite shield of the de' Medici: five balls—*le cinque palle*—and a metal crown glinting with the first rays of the morning sunlight.

Giorgio wiped his mouth in disgust.

Branding our Palazzo Pubblico with their coat of arms—the final insult.

Gradually he became aware of the sounds around him in the hall, the rasp and creak as other students set up their easels, unpacking their pens and paints.

A gray-haired man entered the hall, two attendants following him with an easel and a velvet-draped painting.

"Buongiorno," Maestro Lungo greeted the class. "We have a special treat this morning. A painting by the great master Domenico Beccafumi, whose artwork is so admired in the marble floors and ceilings of the Duomo."

The maestro gestured to the draped painting. "I have procured this from an anonymous patron," he said. Then he nodded to Giorgio. "Especially for Brunelli." He winked his creased eyelid like a napping lizard.

Giorgio started. He felt the eyes of his fellow art students. His pale eyelashes blinked, his freckled face reddening.

"No doubt a plow horse," sniffed a bearded young man in an ermine cloak and polished boots.

A few of the Florentines laughed.

Giorgio flexed the bristles of his brush aggressively against the heel of his hand. He hated Giacomo di Torreforte. He and his clutch of Florentine nobili scorned Giorgio as a peasant.

Maestro Lungo whisked off the velvet drape, exposing the painting as he announced, "Beccafumi's *Flight of Clelia and the Roman Virgins.*"

Fifteen pairs of eyes studied the painting. The students fell silent, knowing that their first impressions would be the most powerful when they interpreted the work onto their own canvases.

The story of Clelia was popular with Renaissance painters. The Roman women were led out of their captors' camp by Clelia, who stole horses from the Etruscan corrals while the soldiers lay sleeping. She and the women rode the horses to the Tiber and, still mounted, swam across to the safety of Roman shores.

Giorgio squinted hard at the painting. The vivid colors of Beccafumi, a signature flourish, brought light and life into the cold studio. Clelia, in a red and black tunic, rode an ivory-colored horse, galloping into the waters of the Tiber. The bright greens, reds, and yellows of the togas glowed eerily in the winter light. The voluptuous flesh of a half-naked virgin shone, the contours of her breasts and stomach alive on the oil-painted panel.

"Garish," pronounced di Torreforte, breaking the silence. He raised his chin from his white ruffled collar.

The word echoed in the palazzo hall.

"Positively garish! So typical of the Senese School. Maestro! Why do you choose a dead Senese when we could study Leonardo . . . or even Michelangelo?"

A Senese student, Riccardo De' Luca from Contrada del Drago, leaned over to Giorgio. His blue eyes glittered. "Michelangelo escaped the claws of the de' Medici, fleeing to Rome," he whispered. "Would that Siena had been so blessed as to escape Cosimo!"

"Beccafumi is a great master, true to his art and his theme, Signor di Torreforte," retorted the maestro. "You would be wise to appreciate his skill and learn from it."

Giacomo di Torreforte's bearded face twitched.

"His theme? Ha!" said di Torreforte, gesturing with his palms open. "What would that be, maestro mio? Prostitutes on horseback?"

The maestro swallowed his rage with difficulty. He, too, resented the Florentine's insolence. Yet the di Torreforte family was deeply allied with—and distantly related to—the de' Medici. He would have to endure the young artist's insults.

"Virgins, Signor di Torreforte. Not prostitutes," he said. "The escape of the Roman virgins from King Porsena and the Etruscan camp. Clelia's honor, her bravery—"

"Honor! Everyone knows that only a prostitute rides astride! Look how he portrays her."

Riccardo felt Giorgio stiffen next to him.

"*Tranquillo,*" he said, reaching for his arm. "Do not listen—"

Giorgio shook off his friend's hand.

"That is a lie!" he snapped.

The maestro gave him a wary eye. The other Senese students leaned away from their easels.

"Whether women ride astride or sidesaddle is a question of choice, not honor," said Giorgio. "Only a fool would turn a rider sidewise to her horse."

Di Torreforte smiled slowly, relishing the challenge.

"Oh, really, villano—you country peasant! Have you ever seen a reputable painting of the Virgin Mary astride her donkey? The great masters show her dignity—and virtue—by painting her seated properly. Sideways."

He smirked at Brunelli, and the Florentine artists chuckled.

Giorgio thrust out his lower jaw, debating whether to answer. He looked at his colleagues around him, then to the maestro. At last, he could not resist.

"I have seen a painting of the great Lorenzo de' Medici's sisters astride their horses," he said. "Benozzo Gozzoli, *The Journey of the Magi*." He raised his red eyebrows. "The de' Medici women seem quite at ease astride. Comfortable, even. As if they were . . . born to it."

The Senese students snickered. Di Torreforte whirled around. If he could identify the culprits, he would deal with them.

"Your words smack of treason, Senese!" di Torreforte said, shaking a finger in Giorgio's face. "Peasants like you should not cast aspersions on the de' Medici family!"

"Merely an observation of art," said Giorgio. "Hardly treason."

The maestro took a long step forward between the two students.

"I will remind the signori that this is an art class, not a public forum. I want no more discussion. *Nessuna parola*—not another word, do you hear me? Or I shall dismiss you from the accademia!"

The murmuring stopped. The students stepped back behind their easels. Di Torreforte still scowled at Giorgio.

"You will copy this great masterwork," the maestro emphasized. "Begin your preliminary drawings now."

An intense silence fell over the studio. The students began to sketch their outlines in pen. As they started, their muscles tensed and their tendons stood out from their necks. Then gradually—ever so gradually—their tension eased as art cast its spell, demanding their focus.

"Bravo!" whispered Riccardo to Giorgio.

The maestro's footsteps echoed in the long marble hall as he walked behind each student's drawing.

Giorgio kept his eye pinned on the painting. He dipped his pen in his inkpot, making deft lines, sketching Beccafumi's composition.

"*Bello forzo*, Brunelli," the maestro said, tapping Giorgio on the shoulder.

Good effort.

Giorgio wondered if the maestro was referring to his preliminary sketch or something else.

CHAPTER 9

Siena, Pugna Hills

JANUARY 1573

My flock of mud-flecked ewes, whose muzzles ripped ferociously at the dry grass, paused for a moment and lifted their heads at the sound of baying hounds. I pinched the end of my braid, listening.

Deh! The hounds must have cornered their prey in the depths of the wooded ravine.

I let out a shrill whistle through the gap in my front teeth. Dog, my Maremma shepherd, yelped and sprang at the ewes. He nipped at their heels, herding them away from the blood call of the hounds. The sheep *maaa*-ed and sprinkled the ground with black pellets of manure.

"Virginia!" called my uncle from his work castrating rams in the pens beyond the shepherd's hut. His hands and arms were slick with blood. "Lead the ewes away from the hunt!"

"Sì, Zio Giovanni!"

I shook my staff at the ewes, shouting at them. When they did not react, I charged at them with the ferocity of the dog, shrieking obscenities in Tuscan dialect.

The riders had returned. They stood at the top of the hill. *The woman—it was her!* She made agitated gestures toward a man in a black riding cloak. Her horse reared as she wheeled it around, plunging down the embankment.

I stood transfixed, clutching the crooked staff in midair.

The rider's skirts blew behind her like wings. Her skin was white as a newborn lamb's wool, and her cheeks glowed wine red with the cold wind. Her hands moved in rhythm with the horse, pulsing in time with the thoroughbred blood that coursed through his veins. The gelding's neck and shoulders were lathered in sweat, despite the cold. I could hear his throaty breath as he punctuated each downbeat of his gallop with a snort.

My mouth fell open in awe. I felt something drop deep in my chest, like a heavy stone into a well.

This union, a woman and horse, was powerful like thunder and lightning in the same instant. The fine hairs on the back of my neck bristled with excitement.

Please jump it again!

The rider guided her horse toward the fallen olive tree. The muscles of his hindquarters bunched and exploded as the rider's hands glided up his neck, giving him rein.

For one instant, the two flew together through the air, a surging pulse—a heartbeat—unbound from the earth.

The howls of the hounds echoed beyond. The rider reined her horse toward the sound deep in the hollow.

No!

I dropped my staff and ran. The banks of the ravine were dangerously steep and rocky.

"No, signora!" I cried.

But the rider never hesitated. Even from afar, I could see her flinty determination, her set jaw. Never had I witnessed such fierce spirit in a woman.

Never had I imagined it: the freedom of horse and rider, loosed just moments ago from the bounds of Earth and man as they soared above the fallen tree. Now plunging into the rocky ravine.

I never forgot that steely vision. Never.

Now this *pazza*—mad!—noblewoman careened again across the sheep pastures, jumping over dead trees and plunging into the ravine.

I raced down the steep embankment, stumbling on the rocks and breaking through vines and brambles. I could hear my two dogs behind me, barking at the flock. I heard my uncle call, his voice hoarse with shouting. From the corrals where he stood, he could not see the rider's descent. He could only see me racing away from the sheep, leaving them milling about with the dogs nipping at their heels.

I saw the riderless horse scramble up the opposite bank of the streambed, the stirrup irons clanking wildly. He stopped at the rim, nickering loudly, calling to the rest of the horses from the hunting party.

Below me, I heard a groan and saw a white hand stretched over a birch limb.

"Are you hurt?" I called.

"*Grazie a Dio*," said a voice accented with musical Florentine tones. "Please help me!"

I fought my way through the brush and low-hanging limbs to the rider.

"Are you hurt?" I repeated. As I approached, I saw the fineness of her clothes, the silks and velvets filigreed with rich embroidery. Her boots, polished with oil, shone like a looking glass.

She moaned softly, then opened her dark eyes.

"You are only a child," she said, her voice betraying disappointment. She tried to sit up. Her gloved hand dug into the rotting leaves and soft dirt.

"Help me," she said, extending her hand. "I cannot bear to let my brother see me like this."

I helped her sit up. She was very tall but not heavy. She winced and drew in a quick breath.

"*Madonna!* You are hurt! Let me run and get my uncle. He will carry you to our lambing sheds. We can send for a doctor."

"Yes," said Isabella. "Call your uncle, but do not tell my brother the granduca that I am hurt."

As I turned to go, I heard her mutter, "It would only cheer him."

She lay back in the bed of moldering brown leaves as I scrambled up the bank, running for help.

By the time I climbed out of the ravine, Zio Giovanni and Cousin Franco were running toward me.

"What happened?" shouted Zio. "You left the ewes!"

"It is the de' Medici princess," I said between gasps of breath. "She has fallen off her horse and is hurt."

Zio stared at me, slack-jawed. He whirled around, his eyes squinting in the morning sun.

"The hunting party must be close—"

"Has she no attendants?" asked Franco. "Where are the hounds, the huntsmen?"

"No, she made me promise not to involve the granduca—"

"What? The granduca is here?"

"She does not want him to see her hurt and dirty from her fall."

"*Diavol!* Where is she?"

"Just there." I pointed to where I had emerged from the ravine.

My uncle and Franco raced down the steep slope, grabbing at exposed roots and vines as handholds.

"Your Highness," shouted Zio, "we are coming!"

As they reached Isabella, she was trying to struggle to her feet. She set off a cascade of rock and dirt tumbling toward the stream below.

"Let us help you," said Zio, drawing off his cap as he approached. He lowered his eyes in respect.

Isabella looked in horror at their bloodstained arms and hands. Their woolen shirts were smeared with urine and manure.

Franco followed her stare. He backed away.

"Forgive us, Duchessa. We have been castrating rams. This is no sight for a princess—"

"Let us find the hunting party and the granduca," said Zio.

"No!" she commanded. "I would rather you help me. I can stand the sight of blood. I hunt and watch the kill." Her teeth were clenched in pain. "It makes no difference."

The two men bowed their heads.

Isabella de' Medici straightened her back, lifting her chin with dignity.

Then she winced. Her face puckered as she took in their scent, the sheep's blood on their hands.

"I shall lean on the girl," she said, reaching for my shoulder. "Wash your hands in the stream. Then take the hem of my skirts so they do not drag or catch on the thorns."

I helped the de' Medici princess to her feet, then up the embankment. The two men trailed behind, holding the edge of her silk and velvet skirt above the muddy ground.

The mad bleating of rams greeted us as we approached the pens. Two of the shepherd boys looked up from a ram's arched back; a leather strap tethered his hindquarters. They wiped the sweat from their eyes, blinking at the sight of the noblewoman approaching.

"Madonna!" muttered one. He wiped his hands on his leggings. Then he rubbed his face hard with the hem of his linen tunic.

He remained speckled with sheep manure, blood, and mud, despite his efforts.

"Take her into the shed. Get her a stool," ordered Zio. "And a jug of wine."

Inside the shed, it was warm from the heat of the animals' bodies. The ewes made way for us, a parting sea of white wool.

The weight of the de' Medici princess shifted from my shoulders as she moved onto the stool. She held up her hand to ward away the shepherds.

"Just let me compose myself. Leave me alone with the girl." She looked at me. "Shepherdess, what is your name?"

"Virginia. Virginia Tacci."

"I thank you, Virginia Tacci, for finding me. I fear I might have spent quite some time trying to climb the embankment without your help."

Isabella swiveled her lovely head toward Zio Giovanni. Two lines creased her porcelain brow.

"Look for the hunting party," she commanded. "We were on the far hill there to the north. Beyond the dead olive tree—"

"I saw you jump it!" I said. "You flew!"

"Virginia!" admonished Zio. "Do not interrupt! Forgive her, Duchessa. She is mad for horses."

Isabella managed a weak smile.

"I can understand that. Now go. Look for the hunt party."

"Of course, Duchessa," said Zio.

"Come, little pastorella. Stand near me."

I knew better than to sit in front of a noble. I managed a curtsy.

"How quaint," she observed with the hint of a smile. "I suppose you do not have the habit of curtsying here alone with your sheep?"

"The Duchessa d'Elci taught me. The night her mare foaled."

"Duchessa d'Elci? Davvero?"

"Yes, it is true. Her mare nearly died, but my padrino saved her. And I saved the foal. Orione. The most beautiful colt ever born."

"If it is a d'Elci horse, it may well be. Of course, you have never seen one of our fine de' Medici horses," sniffed the princess.

"But I have seen your horse. You jumped the olive tree! You rode like the strongest man!"

"Ah, yes," said Isabella closing her eyes for a second. "I remember my father the granduca speaking of the remarkable Duchessa d'Elci. I think he was half in love with her."

I frowned, thinking it impossible that a Florentine—especially the granduca—could love a Senese.

But what did I know of love between a man and woman? My passion was horses. Only horses. My imagination could not paint an image that did not include a mane, withers, and tail.

"But, madonna! To see you jump—it was the most magnificent sight, more beautiful than anything. More beautiful than—the Duomo!"

I quickly made the sign of the cross, feeling quite certain I had blasphemed.

She studied me with a puzzled look.

"You love the horses, as your zio says. Have you ever ridden?"

"No," I said, shaking my head. I met her eyes, swearing with my immortal soul. "But I will. One day I will ride the Palio."

The de' Medici princess laughed again, her gloved hand flying to cover her mouth.

I sucked in my breath, indignant. Not even Zia Claudia's rebukes had been as sharp an insult as Isabella's merry dismissal. I squinted at her in the way I do when I'm enraged.

"Oh! I have offended you, little shepherdess. Diavol! What a hot temper you have."

Isabella reached out her hand and stroked my arm. I stood still like a nervous lamb, trying hard not to bolt.

"You do not have a horse, but you will ride the Palio. I see. And what contrada will you ride for?"

"I am Drago by birth."

"I see, a true Senese. But you know, dear Virginia, only men ride the Palio."

"But I saw you! You galloped on the horse like a man."

"Yes, cara," she said, squeezing my hand. "But I must do all my riding, all my jumping, far from prying eyes and wagging tongues. Men will not let a girl ride the race, her legs astride a horse's naked back! They will never, ever let you compete, believe me—"

I snatched my hand away from hers.

"No, you are wrong. I shall ride the Palio one day!"

Isabella de' Medici dropped open her mouth. I doubt she had ever been told she was wrong in her life. I had not addressed her as duchessa or even donna, but as an equal. I had used the informal *tu*, not the formal *Lei*. A grave insult to one of her high position.

She narrowed her eyes, no longer amused by my quaint manners.

"You are very stubborn, Virginia Tacci. A poor shepherdess, a little girl who has never even ridden. Do you understand how ridiculous that is?"

"I don't care. I will ride the Palio. And I shall think of you, jumping the old olive tree without the permission of men."

Isabella stared at my face. She cocked her head as if she recognized something.

"You—"

She stopped suddenly, her hand flying to her belly.

"No," she cried, her face crumpling. She bent over in pain.

"What is wrong, Duchessa? Is it your stomach?"

"No," she said. "No!"

"I will run for help. My padrino Brunelli can—"

We heard the hard beat of galloping hooves approaching, the snorting of a horse.

"Isabella! Are you within?" said a gruff voice.

"Help me," she whispered. "I want to stand. I shall not let him see me in distress."

She leaned her weight on me. As soon as we reached the threshold, she walked on her own, facing three nobili on horseback.

"Yes, I am here."

As we emerged from the flapping canvas door of the lambing shed, I saw a dozen or more men on brilliantly liveried horses. One led Isabella's horse by the reins.

"We shall speak later, Isabella," said a bearded man dressed in velvet. His horse pranced under him. His face was dark with anger, his shoulders as rigid as Brunelli's anvil.

Ah! I thought. *Granduca Francesco de' Medici!*

"Groom!" Isabella said, ignoring her brother. "Was my horse injured in the fall?"

"No, Your Highness," answered one of the entourage. "The horse is unharmed. You may ride him back to Quattro Torra."

As they brought the gelding to her, she ran her open hand down his legs, checking for swelling and wounds. The gilded brocade of her sleeves shone as she moved around to feel all four legs, her fingers gently squeezing the tendons and fetlocks.

"Mount, Isabella!" snapped the bearded man. "Leave that to the stablemaster."

Four attendants dismounted to help the de' Medici princess remount her horse.

As they boosted her up into the saddle, I saw blood seeping into the satin of her beautiful skirt.

Granduca Francesco broke the silence.

"What led you to commit such a foolish act? You could have broken your neck."

Isabella turned in the saddle, as if to respond to her brother's harsh words. Then she groaned, clutching her belly.

"Are you all right, sister?" asked Ferdinando. "Are you hurt?"

Isabella lifted her head only enough to regard him.

"I am afraid the fall may have injured the child, brother."

"What child?" demanded Francesco. "Do you mean to tell me you are hunting while carrying Paolo Orsini's child?"

"*My* child," said Isabella through clenched teeth. "Get me back to the castle. I will hunt no more today."

All three brothers stared in horror at the white pallor of her face.

CHAPTER 10

Florence, Pitti Palace

JANUARY 1573

Whether carried by Isabella's ladies in waiting, her laundress, the stable attendants, or the huntsman, the news spread to every corner of Florence. The butchers spoke tragically of a "lost prince" as they hacked a chop from a pig's carcass. The herbmonger swore she could have prevented the loss had only the de' Medici consulted her for a tonic. The silk traders whispered that a fortune of embroidered cloth was ruined with bloodstains.

Inevitably the news reached her father, the Granduca of Tuscany. Cosimo de' Medici admonished her gently, for he loved his daughter more than anyone in the world.

"Cara, you have wrested a grandchild from my loving breast! You should not hunt, but be in confinement during these days—"

"Confinement!" said Isabella. "You sound like Francesco, fettered with caution. Not the man I know, Papa."

Cosimo took his daughter's hand, caressing it. "And what man is that?"

"The man whose father, astride a prancing horse, ordered a nurse to throw his baby son from the second-story window into his arms. The one who—as that tiny baby—smiled and cooed, without the slightest fear, when his father caught him."

Old Cosimo smiled. The story was legendary, reflecting the courage he would show throughout his life.

"My father was proud of me that day." His smile widened.

"'This baby is indeed my son,'" Isabella reminded him, mimicking the words of her grandfather, the great Giovanni dalle Bande Nere. "'And he shall be like me: afraid of nothing from birth! The grandson of the Tigress of Forli, Caterina Sforza—'"

Cosimo pressed his daughter's hand to his cheek. "Ah, my Isabella." His brown eyes softened. "What shall become of you when I die?"

Isabella blinked in confusion. She recognized the soft gaze of tragedy in his eyes. "What a strange thing to say, Papa!"

A shiver coursed through her spine. He squeezed her hand, sensing her fear.

"I fear I should not have turned the dukedom over to Francesco before my death. After ten years of apprenticeship, I hoped he would learn the feel of the reins in his hand. A good rider learns when to give the horse its head, to ride with the lightest touch."

Isabella stared at a Bronzino portrait on the wall—Francesco as a child. She focused on the firm line of his lips.

"Francesco was not born with light hands, Papa."

The granduca studied his favorite child, her eyes steady on his own.

"Ah, my daughter. You are most like me."

"It is true, my father. I am like you in every way."

"More the pity you are a girl, my Isabella."

She snatched her hand away.

"Is it such a tragedy that I am not born with the de' Medici palle, Papa?"

De' Medici balls. Her father laughed.

"And let us be grateful to God for the two children I already have, Nora and Virgino," Isabella said. "Have I not proved myself an adequate brood mare for the de' Medici stable?"

"My treasures, those grandchildren. And of course you have courage, *figlia mia.*"

"Then why do you appear so sad?"

Cosimo sighed. "I do not want your husband to take you back to Rome."

Isabella scoffed. "Rome? Rome could never be my home. And Paolo will never insist. Did you not pay a dowry of 50,000 *scudi* expressly to keep me here in Florence? I shall remain in Tuscany with you always."

"What will your husband say when he learns of your hunting accident?"

"I will tell him the blood came from a wound, and the scandalous gossip of a miscarriage is fantasy. He will know he could not have possibly fathered a child in the past few months. Besides, he is too busy with his mistresses in Rome."

Cosimo studied his daughter's face.

"You truly hate him."

"Paolo Orsini is a brute," she said, looking away. Her eyes rested on the portrait of her brother.

"Will you ever forgive me for forcing you to marry him?" asked Cosimo.

"Never, Papa," she said, still turned away from him. *"Mai!"*

She felt her face quiver. She took a deep breath, composing herself, then turned back to her father, offering him a smile.

"Perhaps forgiveness might be found if we go hunting again. Quite soon. Just the two of us. And perhaps Leonora. She needs to escape Pietro's ill humor. He really is quite unbearable."

Cosimo's face creased in pleasure. Youth flashed in his eyes.

"Ah! My two favorite companions. I will have the huntsman make arrangements for the coming week. I shall ride with the most beautiful women in all Tuscany. No, in all the world!"

Isabella smiled. "And the three of us will inspire the most delicious gossip!"

Cosimo loved to spend time in the company of his daughter and daughter-in-law. The fact that half of Florence thought Leonora's child was fathered by the granduca made no difference to Cosimo.

Isabella turned her back on Bronzino's portrait of her brother. *The artist depicted his cold eyes too skillfully.*

"Papa," said Isabella, as her father escorted her into the dining hall, "I forgot to tell you about the shepherdess I met in the Siena Hills. A mere child, but quite remarkable. Stubborn as I was as a little girl—"

"As you? Ha! Quite impossible."

"Davvero, Papa. Really. She had the most determined little chin."

"A Senese shepherdess! Of all people to make an impression on a de' Medici princess," marveled Cosimo. "I look forward to hearing more."

CHAPTER 11

Florence, Pitti Palace

FEBRUARY 1573

The de' Medici family waited, their hands on either side of their plates, observing an ancient custom: the showing of hands in peace and respect as they waited for the granduca to proceed.

Cosimo speared the tender venison with his fork and popped the meat into his puckered mouth, chewing carefully with the remaining teeth. Despite his advanced age, the abscesses in his jawbone, and painful gout, the granduca had a good appetite for both food and sex.

After Cosimo had swallowed and taken a sip of Montalcino, the rest of the family began their repast. It was a rare occasion these days to have all the de' Medici siblings at the table. Pietro's wife, Leonora, was not there, nor was Camilla, the granduca's second wife. Isabella was relieved that Camilla, a commoner, had not joined them. Isabella found her flighty and unable to follow any conversation that did not involve fashion and costly fabrics. And of course, Duchessa Giovanna, Francesco's wife, would never accept a commoner in Court. Cosimo respected his daughter-in-law's wishes, as she was the sister of Emperor Maximilian of the Holy Roman Empire.

Isabella glared at Pietro, who still insisted on eating only with his knife, like a soldier on the battlefield.

"It is not as if we are hunting, little brother," said Isabella. "Why do you insist on eating in such a primitive way?"

Pietro sucked at a piece of meat lodged in his teeth.

"I am a military man, sister." He shrugged, spearing another piece of venison with his knife and shoving it whole into his mouth.

Isabella glared, and he returned her look in kind. Finally, their father broke the angry silence.

"Isabella. Please tell us about the Senese shepherdess you encountered."

"Isabella fell from her horse," sneered Francesco, "and the flea-bitten, knobby-kneed *villana* came to her rescue!"

"How dreadful," said Giovanna, who had a terror of commoners, especially Italians. She surrounded herself with German-speaking ladies-in-waiting from the Imperial Court of Vienna.

"It was not dreadful at all, Giovanna," said Isabella. "Quite fortunate, actually."

"A perfect stranger—a peasant—came to your aid?" continued Giovanna. "How truly astounding! Where were your attendants? Your ladies-in-waiting?"

"My ladies could not possibly keep up with me on a horse. And the perfect stranger was a charming little girl. Full of fire and spirit, a true Senese."

"Even more intriguing," said Cosimo, running his tongue over his front teeth.

Isabella turned to her father.

"This little scrap of a child has never been on the back of the horse. But she insists she will ride the Palio one day!"

Her brothers laughed. Giovanna joined in. Only Cosimo remained silent.

"She shall have to compete against our horses," said Cosimo, making a temple with his hands. He rested his lips against his fingertips. "And the Borgias."

"I do not think the Borgias race anymore in Siena, Papa," said Isabella, patting her father's hand. As of late, he remembered occurrences from yesteryear while forgetting the recent past. It had been many years since the Borgias had contested the Palio.

"Not since they annulled Cesare Borgia's win," she said softly.

Isabella squeezed her father's hand. She darted a look at her brother, Cardinal Ferdinando. He met her eyes, saddened at his father's decline.

"Ah, yes," said Cosimo, nodding his head. "I remember. A false start. Borgia's jockey was disqualified."

"I have heard rumor that Siena wants to stage more Palios."

"It would be good for their spirit," said her father, shrugging his shoulders.

"I find the very suggestion ominous, Papa," said Francesco, setting down his glass. "The Senese have too much spirit as it is. It cost us many soldiers' lives in the siege, did it not?"

"They are a defeated people," said Cosimo, dismissing his son's concerns with a wave of his hand. "Let them recover their heart with sport. They are Tuscans, just as we are. Let them race their horses."

He turned away from his son, his attention riveted on his daughter.

"Tell me more about your shepherdess, my dear."

Isabella smiled, content that her father paid her such rapt attention. She saw Francesco glowering at her.

"Her name is Virginia—Rucci? No, Tacci," said Isabella. "She saw me jump a fallen tree and was mad with admiration."

"Jumping!" said Francesco. "With child!"

"She said that she had recently met the Contessa d'Elci," continued Isabella, her voice rising to cut off her brother and any mention of her pregnancy.

"Duchessa Lucrezia? Davvero?" said the old granduca, his eyes sparkling.

Isabella and Francesco glared at one another, while the granduca—perhaps noticing the tension and anger, perhaps not—went on with an eager smile.

"Now, Isabella. Tell me more about the charming Duchessa d'Elci."

CHAPTER 12

Siena, Pugna Hills

FEBRUARY 1573

From the day Orione was born, I wanted to be at his side.

The first night he returned to the pastures, I packed my sheepskin coat and coarse wool blanket to sleep in the lambing shed, where I was so often sent to care for the aging ewes.

"You seem eager to sleep away from our roof," said Zia Claudia. "Perhaps there is a boy you meet in secret."

I stared at her, incredulous.

A boy? What boy could have the charm of Orione?

"The field ewes' pens border the horse pasture, Claudia," said Zio. "Leave the girl alone. She is crazy for the new colt, nothing more."

"A colt?" said Zia Claudia, raising a skeptical eyebrow. "Huh! She may be turning sly in her womanly ways at an early age. I do not want her ruined. She and the tanner's son—"

"I want to be with Orione," I said, glaring at her. "He is more important than any stupid boy."

Zio Giovanni smiled, stroking my matted hair.

"It is an innocent love, Claudia. The love of a girl and a horse. I will have her cousin Lorenzo camp with the sheep on the hill above. She can eat a warm supper with the boys, then sleep in the lambing sheds. I will make it clear to Lorenzo that his duties include caring for her, as a matter of family honor."

Although I am certain that Claudia hated losing this argument, I suspect she was relieved to have me out from underfoot. She had long begrudged me space in the tiny cottage, pushing my straw pallet under the window where the winter draughts chilled my bones.

I thought of what Zio Giovanni said. *It is an innocent love, Claudia. The love of a girl and a horse.*

Innocent, yes. But ardent—the love I had for Orione burned as bright and fierce as any emotion that had ever seized my heart.

I ate greasy mutton stew and shepherd's bread for dinner with my two cousins. Their filthy hands pulled at the bread, stuffing it into their mouths with their muddy knuckles. They chewed with their mouths open, swilling down the food with sour red wine that stank like the vinegar Brunelli used to clean horse wounds.

Shepherds lived a rough life, rarely bathing or sleeping. The cold ground, the coarsest wool blankets, and meager rations were all my cousins knew.

"You helped Cesare Brunelli save the Oca colt," said Lorenzo. I watched the white dough and cheese tumble about in his open mouth, his tongue pushing the food over his uneven teeth.

"I helped the foal to breathe," I said.

"There's they who say you are a witch," said Franco, Lorenzo's younger brother. He narrowed his eyes to slits, staring at me. "That you delivered the devil's horse that night, that by all rights he should have died."

I pulled my scratchy blanket around my shoulders, feeling a chill trace my spine. I had never liked Franco. He was sixteen and stank of sheep dung and meanness. His eyes were set so close together that they looked crossed.

"Shut up, Franco," said Lorenzo. "Do not mind him, Cousin Virginia. He is always seeing the evil instead of the grace of God."

Franco's mouth twisted, the light in his eyes flat. "That colt is sired by Tempesta, the black devil. He has killed two men who tried to break him."

"Orione is also the foal of the gentlest, fairest mare in all Tuscany," I countered.

"That cannot wash clean the blood of Tempesta," said Franco. "That horse is cursed. The colt never should have been born. You interfered with the will of God!"

I shrugged. "If God really wanted that colt, he would have taken him, despite all I could do."

"You breathed life into a corpse. He will grow up to be just like his father. They say Tempesta eats human flesh, ripped right off the bodies of his victims—"

"Shut up, brother! You are a cross-eyed simpleton," said Lorenzo, clearing away his words with a slash of his hand.

"If Tempesta ever jumps the wall to join his mares, he will tear our cousin here—or us!—to bloody shreds," warned Franco, shaking his greasy finger at me.

"The Contrada dell'Oca has built a wall so tall he cannot even see over it. He would break a leg before he could ever clear it," I said. "That is ridiculous."

"I have seen his nostrils flared and red, raised above the wall," said Franco. "Snorting his fury. You cannot confine the devil—or his curse."

"A curse?" scoffed Lorenzo. "Brother, I do not think it is a curse to have the Duchessa d'Elci beholden to you. Is that not right, Cousin Virginia?"

"The duchessa is not beholden to anybody," I said, irritated with both my cousins. I pulled up the muddied hem of my dress enough to stand.

"Are you leaving so soon?" said Lorenzo, the corner of his eyes drooping with disappointment.

"Thank you for the meal, cousins. I must return to the ewes. It will be dark soon."

"We'll be watching out for you down there," called Lorenzo. "Call out if you need us. And keep the fire burning through the night to chase away the wolves."

Franco said nothing. He turned to spit on the ground, and his dirt-caked hand made the sign of the cross.

Orione sniffed the air, his nostrils flaring as they took in my scent. I could make out his eyes, gleaming with curiosity. He nickered a high-pitched call, shaking his head.

As I approached the stone wall, he ran toward me at a full gallop. At first I thought the long legs churning under him would never stop, that he would crash into the stones and break a bone. But he pulled up just before the wall, darting off bucking and kicking at phantom challengers.

I tied my ragged skirts in a knot and climbed the white stones. By this time, Stella had approached at a trot, whinnying.

She seemed to be apologizing for her rude baby, dipping her head for me to stroke her neck.

"Beautiful mare," I murmured. *"Bellissima."*

She closed her eyes, delighting in the caress. I wondered if the duchessa petted her the way I did now. She tilted her head and let my fingers move up to scratch between her ears.

I felt a warm puff of air on my back, then a nip.

"Ow!" I said, whirling around. I slapped the colt's nose and he reared back, snorting. Then he ran off, his tiny hooves churning up the loose earth.

The milk teeth of the foal did not tear my dress, but I could feel a welt blossoming beneath the cloth. It stung and ached deeply, like my finger once did when it got pinched in the chain as I drew water from the well.

Stella nuzzled against me, unconcerned that I had just smacked her foal.

"You will have to teach him some manners," I confided to her. After sulking for a few minutes, the black colt came back around.

"What? Are you going to bite me again, just to show me how alive you are—thanks to me?"

Orione shook his head, snorting.

"Yes, you see how your mother likes to be petted," I said, looking at the chestnut mare.

Orione pushed against me, plucking at my hand with his lips.

"If you bite me again, I will pummel you." Tentatively I moved my hand from the mare's neck to Orione's. His skin prickled and fidgeted under my fingers. "Ticklish? You will get used to it."

He stared up into my eyes, his brown eyes wet. I stroked the curly stock of mane between his ears—all spongy fuzz, not at all like an adult horse's hair. He tried to nip me again, but I pulled my arm away just in time, giving him another smack on the nose.

"Maybe you aren't the devil," I said. "But you are my little demon."

CHAPTER 13

Siena, Pugna Hills

MARCH 1573

A few weeks after the birth of Orione, there was a knock on the door of our *casetta*.

"In the name of Duchessa d'Elci, I come bearing a gift," said a voice.

I licked my fingers clean of grease, threw the bolt, and opened the door.

Outside stood a rider dressed in green and white, Oca colors. Since it was not a Feast Day, I marveled at his dress, and that a contradiolo would visit our little cottage in the hills.

In one hand, he held his horse's reins. In the other, he carried a package wrapped in paper painted deep green with white stars.

"Are you Virginia Tacci?" he inquired. He was a tall, dark-haired youth. His accent was thoroughly Senese—but cultured.

Zia Claudia pushed past me, staring bug-eyed at the package. She stretched out her hands to grab it.

"*Per la piccola,*" said the young man, his green eyes fastened on mine. This is for the little one.

Avoiding Zia's grasping hands, he handed the package to me.

"This is from the Duchessa d'Elci. I am to put this token of her appreciation into your hands. There is a letter attached."

I touched the beautiful paper wrapping the package. A folded parchment sealed with crimson wax lay on top.

My fingers eagerly unwrapped the paper. My zia grabbed it.

"Such a green!" she exclaimed. "This must be worth—"

"*Silenzio, moglie!*" admonished Giovanni.

I held up a leather halter, oiled to a deep walnut color and bearing medallioned rosettes painted with the emblem of the Goose in green and white with red trim.

"It is the *collo di cavallo*—the processional Palio halter—of Stella, our blessed horse of two Palio victories," said the Oca contradiolo. "Stella wore this to the cathedral for the blessing of the horse and jockey." His voice was low in reverence.

The image of the beautiful mare standing before the altar dazzled me. I could imagine the priest raising his hand, making the sign of the cross, sprinkling the *fantino* and his racehorse with holy water.

"We of the Contrada dell'Oca thank you for saving her colt. When the House of d'Elci wins, we *ocaioli* share in the honor. Now you do, too."

He nodded to me, then winked.

I stared down at the parchment, folded in four and sealed with wax. A two-headed eagle was embossed in the red seal, its faces pointing in opposite directions. I did not open it, for I could not read.

———

I raced toward Vignano, my package hidden under my coat.

Breathless, I pushed open the stable door.

"Padrino!" I shouted. "Look what I have!"

Brunelli was straightening nails on his anvil. He turned his head slowly to me, blinking sweat from his eyes.

"Duchessa d'Elci sent a collo di cavallo to me—the one Stella wore to the cathedral for the benediction of the horses!"

Brunelli's face transformed, the creases relaxing, erasing the years.

"Dio mio," he said. I pulled the star-studded package from my coat.

With the reverence of a priest handling the host at the altar, Brunelli pulled the leather halter from the paper. "A two-time Palio winner," he whispered. "There is magic in this, ciccia," he said.

"And she sent a letter!" I said, waving the parchment at his face. "Please, could you read it to me?"

Brunelli gazed at the letter. "Giorgio, *veni*!" he called.

I winced at the name. I remembered the rough toweling before my meeting with the Duchessa d'Elci.

The red-haired young man approached us, a pitchfork in his paint-stained hand. His hair and clothes were littered with bits of hay. He looked as if he hadn't slept in days.

He stared at me, hollow-eyed. I looked away.

"Come, figlio," my godfather said. "I have something for you to read."

Giorgio looked at the letter in Brunelli's hand and the adorned halter on his shoulder. Then his mouth dropped open at the green wrapping paper cast aside on a hay bale.

"My God!" he said. "Where did you get that paper?" I looked at the crumpled wrapping.

"The Duchessa d'Elci wrapped the halter in it—a halter worn by the Palio mare—"

"Do you know how precious that color is?"

He dropped the pitchfork and picked up the wrapping paper gingerly. It rustled in his hand.

"And this yellow," he said. "Look how the colors permeate—"

"Son, would you read this letter for little Virginia?" said Brunelli, calling Giorgio out of his reverie.

The artist had almost forgotten about both of us. To see the glitter in his eyes, focused on the colored paper, gave me a strange sense of forgiveness. He revered paints with the same ardor I felt for horses.

I handed him the folded parchment.

"Go on!" I said, shifting from foot to foot. "Read it, per favore."

He turned the missive over in his hand and read aloud: "To Virginia Tacci."

I felt my cheeks burn, and my lips pulled back in a wide smile. "Let me see it," I said, grabbing at the letter. "Show me that part that is my name!"

Giorgio's fingers hovered over the writing, tracing the two clusters of letters. "That is your name. Virginia Tacci."

I stared at the two words.

"I would give almost anything to read," I murmured.

"You should open it, not I," he said. He handed me a knife from his pocket. "Slide the blade under the wax and break the seal."

"What are these eagles?"

"They are the insignia of the Pannochiesci. The duchessa's ancient family is mentioned in Dante Alighieri's *Divine Comedy*."

Who was this Dante Alighieri? Was he Senese?

I worked open the seal without cracking the eagles. I unfolded the vellum. "Now read it, Giorgio. Read!"

He nodded and started to read with a fluency that belied his lowly birth.

"This halter was worn by the Contrada dell'Oca mare before and after her second Palio victory on August 16, 1571. May it bring you luck, dear Virginia. With tremendous gratitude, La Duchessa d'Elci."

My padrino gave me back the halter. I rubbed the ribbons and felt the enameled medallions under my fingertips. And a brass buckle! My padrino's halters were made of coarse rope that tied on one side. But this—

I glanced up at old Brunelli to share my joy. My smile faded as I recognized the same sad look in his eyes.

Too bad you are a girl.

CHAPTER 14

Florence, Pitti Palace

APRIL 1573

Isabella de' Medici, Duchessa di Bracciano, stared up at the gray walls of the Pitti Palace as her coach rounded the curving drive. The massive stonework resembled an ancient Roman aqueduct, a severe line of repeating arches.

The de' Medici princess never understood why her mother, Eleonora di Toledo, had insisted on buying this monstrosity. True, it was far more spacious than the Palazzo Vecchio, but the Pitti's façade was charmless and brutal, flaunting cold power rather than embracing beauty and Florentine grace. Its series of arches reminded her of a gigantic serpent.

The de' Medici slept in the belly of the serpent, and Isabella had nightmares of being consumed by a snake.

Leonora's valet met Isabella as she descended from the coach. Bowing deeply, he led her to her cousin's apartments in the palace.

The reek of sickness filled the bedchamber, forcing Isabella to cover her nose with a linen handkerchief.

"I am sorry to have missed the hunt, dear cousin," whispered Leonora. Her ladies-in-waiting had propped up their mistress against down pillows so she could receive her visitor. "Did you and my uncle enjoy the riding?"

"Open a window at once!" said Isabella, ignoring the question. "My cousin should have fresh air. The stale air of sickness permeates this room."

The attendants scattered like wild geese at Isabella's command. The sashes flew up, and the sound of birdsong rushed in from the Boboli Gardens. Leonora's delicate nostrils quivered at the soft breeze floating through the room.

Light streamed in the open windows, illuminating Leonora's pale face. She blinked at the sunlight. Isabella took a seat across from the ailing twenty-two-year-old. There was a dark bruise across her cousin's cheek.

Isabella rose from her chair, her fingertips tracing the bruise.

"Is this why you could not join us?"

"No, no," said Leonora, her hand moving languidly to her face. "I have been terribly ill for days now."

"Indeed, you look it. But more than ill, you look frightened—"

"Pietro's physician brought in a bloodletter, but I fear I have not profited from his attention. I abhor the leeches sucking at my veins."

Isabella's eyes grew wide. She started to speak, then stopped and looked around the bedroom apartments, scanning the pallid, worried faces of Leonora's attendants.

The servants followed protocol, lowering their eyes to the floor as the duchessa regarded them.

After a moment's thought, her lips set in a firm line, she spoke in the commanding tones of the princess she was. "Leave us now," she said to the servants. "All of you! I would speak to my cousin. Alone."

When the room was clear, she leaned closer and spoke fervently but quietly.

"Get up, Leonora. Now. You shall ask your ladies to dress you and pack your belongings."

"What? But I am ill, Cousin!"

Isabella lowered her mouth to Leonora's ear.

"If you are ill, it is mostly likely with the pox of prostitutes my brother has brought to your bed. But I think it is poison that you suffer from, not pox. It may be the food and drink you are served that are slowly killing you. My mother and uncles will curse me from their graves if I do not take you away from here. You will stay at my villa until you are well."

"Your villa!"

The faintest trace of a smile crossed Leonora's face. Then it faded.

"Would Francesco allow my husband to murder me?" she whispered, her eyes searching her cousin's face.

Isabella pressed her lips together firmly.

"Bring only your most trusted ladies with you," Isabella said. "You shall recover your health under my watch."

Leonora's face crumpled.

"He found Bernadino's love letters to me hidden in the footstool."

"More discretion would have benefited you both," said Isabella, her chin lifting above her ruffled collar.

"Bernadino has been imprisoned in Elba. Pietro means for him to die."

Isabella swallowed briefly, regaining her de' Medici composure.

"Your news is stale," she said, squeezing her Leonora's hand. "Your affair reached the ears of my elder brother, not just Pietro."

Leonora gasped.

"When Francesco puts his mind to evil, the workings are well-oiled and swift," said Isabella. "Your Bernadino was strangled."

CHAPTER 15

Siena, Pugna Hills
APRIL 1573

Zia Claudia's snores filled the room as I crept from my straw pallet and slipped out of the house. I had hidden my cloak, slippers, and the collo di cavallo in a bundle outside. I grabbed it and ran into the night.

Moonlight spilled over the tufts of spring grass, the olive trees throwing stout shadows on the pasture. Horses stood sleeping, frozen like toy figures. Lying on the trampled grass, the foals slept, safe from wolves. My eyes scanned the field, searching for the duchessa's mare Stella and her colt—my colt—Orione.

With the collo di cavallo over my shoulder, I tied my skirts in a knot above my thighs, the dew wetting my skin.

I thought of the de' Medici princess. I recalled her grace, the brief smile as she cleared the old olive tree, her horse leaping through the air.

Did she ever have to worry about being married off against her will? The tanner's son! Was that my future?

A horse snorted. Another one stirred, moving away. A mare nickered to her foal, nudging him to his feet.

"Tranquillo," I said, approaching. I clambered over the stone fence. "Look, I brought an apple from our cellar. Look!"

I walked slowly toward the silhouetted horses. They shied away, unsure of this phantom who approached them in the darkness.

Suddenly, a black horse charged toward me. He exploded from the blackness like the devil himself. His neck curled in fury, exposing the thick band of muscle running under his long tangled mane.

"No!" I screamed and fell to the ground, the apple rolling away.

I covered my head as his hooves flashed out. My padrino had told me that a horse's hooves could slice a man's flesh, break his skull with one blow.

I was only a small heap of bones and skin, cowering on the wet grass.

The stallion chuffed a snort of rage. Not dead, I dared to peek and saw the white star blazing his forehead as it dipped and surfaced in the dim light.

Tempesta! The black stallion.

I rolled to my feet and balled up my fists. His nostrils flared. He whinnied in fury, a shriek that registered in my stomach.

He reared above me, black as death.

"Santa Caterina!" I implored. "Save me!"

There was a shrieking call from another horse right beside us.

The stallion snorted, rolling back on his haunches. He shook his head, throwing his mane left and right, distracted. Rage pulled his eyes wide, making white rings in the darkness.

The snap of teeth, the thud of iron shoes hitting flesh.

I scrambled away, tripping on a root and sprawling headfirst onto the ground. I heard the galloping thud of hoofbeats charging away into the night.

Then I felt warm breath on my neck. I clapped my hand over my skin, terrified.

A nudge and the soft flesh of a horse's muzzle.

The colt's tiny teeth pulled the folds of my skirt. He chewed on the fabric, tearing at it as if were sweet grass.

The mare, Stella, stood above me majestically. Her sides heaved, her breath scattering the dried leaves on the ground. She gazed down at me, watching her colt nibble at my skirt.

I thought of the beating Zia Claudia would give me for the tear in my skirt. I could feel her whipping cane stinging the backs of my legs.

"Stop it!" I shouted. I swatted at the colt's nose.

He shied away, blinking at me in the moonlight.

"*Grazie mille*, Stella," I said. "You saved my life." My fingers searched the cool grass for the halter. "Now you will let me ride you, sì?"

The colt's whinny echoed, high-pitched and eerie, across the hills.

I had watched Brunelli put halters on horses for years. Still, when I tried it myself for the first time, I was clumsy.

"Steady now," I said to the mare.

She dipped her nose into the halter, her mouth still chomping my apple.

"Grazie," I told her, patting her neck. But the buckle was under her chin, the halter upside down.

It took several more tries before I could buckle the halter. I was certain it was still wrong—but it was good enough, I said to myself. I had never seen a brass buckle in my life.

I led the mare to the stone wall and clambered up the rock. My fingers worked, twisting the free end of the rope into a knot under the halter. Now I had a makeshift rein.

I held my breath.

I threw my right leg over her, my skirts hiked up to my underclothes, my bare legs dangling.

She moved off at a trot, and I came tumbling off.

"Oof!" I landed hard on my shoulder, then smacked my chin on the ground. I picked bits of cold mud and grass from between my teeth.

Stella stood a few paces away, eating grass, totally unconcerned.

Orione looked at me, perplexed. He nibbled at the hem of my skirt.

Again, I tried. Then again. I fell half a dozen more times, but each time I stayed on her back a few strides more.

"That's a difficult way to learn," said a voice in the darkness as I hauled myself up onto Stella's back yet again. "You will be black and blue by dawn."

CHAPTER 16

Siena, Pugna Hills

APRIL 1573

Giorgio stepped out of the shadows, his leather boots creaking, a wool hood pulled over his head. Stella shied away, snorting. I held on tight to the rope.

"Madonna!" I gasped. Stella took two more quick steps sideways and I spilled off her, hitting the ground hard.

I tasted salty blood from my lip and earth in my teeth. But it was my shoulder that hurt the most. I struggled to my feet, screaming at him. "What are you doing, spying on me? *Bastardo! Divoratore di stronzi!*"

Bastard! Shit eater!

"You curse like a Brindisi sailor, shepherdess," he said, laughing. "I knew you would come here. I am certain the duchessa told you that Stella would be pastured here just to tempt you. Sending you that collo—"

"It is none of your business," I shot back. "You just wanted to see me make a fool of myself. To see me fall, to see—"

"*Basta!* You have no idea—"

"You hate me. Admit it! I see you stare at me in the stables. You think a girl cannot ride—"

"Virginia Tacci. Never have you been so wrong," he said, shaking his head. "Why should a girl not ride?"

Giorgio caught me off guard. I struggled to compose my thoughts. "Then why are you here, spying on me?"

He remained silent.

"Why? Answer me!" I shouted.

He shrugged and looked up at the stars.

"And you just happened to come here to our lambing sheds and the horse pastures?"

He looked at Orione, nuzzling against my arm. "Yes, I am often here. I paint."

I looked at him in the moonlight. He carried a leather satchel that I supposed could contain his paints.

"I paint because I cannot sleep. I have not been able to sleep since I returned from art school in Florence."

He turned his gaze from Orione to me.

"What is wrong with you?" I asked him. "What do you want?"

"I can help you, Virginia. Let me."

I brushed the dirt from my skirts. "How can you help me?"

"Riding a horse is a skill that must be mastered. It would take you years to learn by yourself. And at the rate you are going, you will probably break a few bones—or your neck."

I glared at him. The moonlight caught his eyes, reflecting back at me. He approached, coming within striking distance. I winced, tightening my fist.

"I think I shall call you *Rompicollo*," he said. Breakneck. "It suits you."

My shoulder hurt where I had landed on it hard.

"The mare will not stand still," I spat.

"Why should she?" he said. "You have given her no command to do so."

"I have told her, *'Fermati, fermati!'* Instead she trots off."

"Don't be foolish. Horses don't speak Italian, or they would be at the taverna drinking *vino rosso* and laughing with the village drunks."

"She trusts me, I know—"

"Do not lose her trust. First you must learn to ride properly, how to talk to her in a language she understands. Then you will not insult her by rolling off her back like a circus clown."

I wiped angry tears from my eyes. The moon shone bright enough that I noticed his stare. His eyes studied me, taking in every feature of my face.

"I want to ride," I said, sniffling.

"And you shall," he said, the trancelike stare broken. "But you are not ready to ride a Palio horse. Let us choose a different mount to begin with."

Giorgio whispered soothing words to Stella and caught her lead rope. He unbuckled the Palio halter, patting her on the neck. "What a mess you made of this halter, Rompicollo!"

I glared at him. His eyes glittered, full of mirth.

"It is an honor to touch such an impressive mare," he murmured as he quickly sorted out the halter. He handed it to me, and we walked deeper into the pasture where we could see the horses all awakened now, grazing on the spring grass.

"That one," he said. "The bay gelding. I have seen him under saddle for many years. He is gentle to a fault."

He took the halter from me, walking toward the horse. I snatched it back. "No," I said. "I want to halter the horse. Let me!"

Giorgio threw up his hands. "Fine," he said. "Do as you like."

I clucked my tongue against the roof of my mouth, calling to the gelding. I stretched out my hand with a remaining chunk of apple from my apron pocket. The other horses trotted away, but he stood, curious.

His soft muzzle brushed against my outstretched hand.

"Ouch!" I screamed as the gelding caught my thumb in his teeth. I stuck my smarting thumb in my mouth. The old gelding contemplated me, still chewing the apple.

Giorgio laughed. I was glad for the darkness—he could not see my color rise, burning my cheeks.

"Don't you know enough to tuck your thumb under your fingers when feeding a horse?" he asked.

"No," I said. "I love horses, but I tend sheep. How would I know such things?"

Giorgio sighed, rolling his eyes.

"There is so much you do not know," I heard him whisper.

I struggled to slide the halter over the horse's ears. The old gelding withstood my fumbling hands as I stood on tiptoe.

"Do you want me to show you?" he asked. "You can learn a hundred times more quickly, you know. Otherwise you will be an old woman, wizened and gray, before you can even trot a horse."

I chewed the inside of my mouth. My thumb stung, my shoulder ached, and I wasn't one step closer to learning to ride.

"I put it on the mare myself," I said. "Did you see that?"

"Yes. I thought it would take you all night. And you got it all wrong, twisted."

"I only know the rope halters used in the stables that slip over the nose. I have watched your father—"

"Let me show you the right way. Just once."

"All right," I said finally. "But then take it off again, so I can do it myself."

"Watch me. Slide it up like this. Everything buckles or ties on the left side, remember that. That is the side you mount and dismount on. It has been a tradition for centuries, warriors carrying their lances in their right hand—"

"Wouldn't it be more convenient to use both sides?"

He shook his head.

"Do not argue. Just listen."

"It just seems easier—"

"You are very stubborn, Virginia Tacci. Look at how you thrust out your chin—it is quite muddy, by the way."

"Sì, sì! I understand now," I said, seizing the halter. "Let me do it."

The gelding, patient and gentle as he was, dipped his head into the halter. After I had put it on and taken it off half a dozen times, I said, "I want to get on now. I have to start riding, or I will never be able to win the Palio."

"Ah, is it *win* the Palio now?"

I threw my hands in the air, exasperated. "What is the point of riding the Palio if you do not win?"

"The point, my little Virginia, is that it is a great honor even to ride. Not everyone rides the Palio, only a chosen few. Anyone who rides the Palio has accomplished much."

"Never mind that. I mean to win. Now help me up," I said, bending my leg as I had seen other riders do at my padrino's stables.

Giorgio approached me, bending down to grab my leg.

"Do not dare look at my underclothes, Brunelli."

He laughed, dropping my leg. He doubled over laughing.

"Ha!"

"What is so funny?"

"Virginia Tacci, I do not have any desire to see the underclothes of a skinny little girl."

"Do not insult me, *etrusco*!"

"So now it's Etruscan?" he said. "Grazie for the compliment, shepherdess."

He slipped his hand under my foot, boosting me atop the horse and holding the halter in his other hand.

"Now sit up straight. Do not hold on to his mane, it will only pull you forward. Sit straight and tall, as if you are trying to reach the ground with your spine, your legs. Pull back slightly with the reins."

"Rope," I said. "This is only a rope."

"In your hand, they become reins. Pull back, sit up straight."

He let go of the rope. The gelding stood motionless.

"*Va bene*. Now squeeze ever so slightly, urging him to take a step. Then sit up straight again."

The gelding walked forward. I could feel him considering a trot. I pitched forward, clutching his mane.

"No! No!" shouted Giorgio. "Sit up straight. With dignity. Sit up like a queen, a centaur."

"What is a centaur?"

He shook his head. "Direct your backbone into him."

"My backbone?"

"Like a roman column, erect and solid. That is where your energy is. Speak to him through your body. Make him feel your command, your will."

The horse forgot about trotting. He was content to walk.

"See? If you give false signals to a horse as sensitive as Stella, she will gallop the Palio course around this pasture. You will never stay on."

I smiled so broadly, I knew my teeth were reflecting the moonlight.

I did not care.

"Teach me more," I said. "Per favore, Giorgio. Teach me more. Teach me everything."

CHAPTER 17

Siena, Palazzo d' Elci

JUNE 1573

"Have you given up sleep?" admonished the maestro, watching Giorgio's mouth stretch wide in a yawn.

Giorgio clamped his jaw shut, blushing. He looked around at the other students, who were grinning at him.

"Forgive me, maestro," he said.

"You are sucking all the air from the room, villano," said di Torreforte, his brush poised in midair.

"Open a window," added the young noble peevishly. He frowned at the last few brushstrokes on his canvas. "The villano's stink of garlic and peasant wine suffocates me." A smirk twisted his face as he tossed a casual glance in Giorgio's direction.

A servant opened the windows. A burst of fresh air blew in, carrying with it the vendors' calls, the commotion and bickering in the open market below.

Di Torreforte wrinkled his nose. The sounds of Il Campo displeased him, but he was struggling even more to finish his rendering of the Beccafumi. The maestro had told the students to repeat the lesson to see how much they had improved over the past months.

Insults being easier than painting, di Torreforte turned to Giorgio again.

"Your body reeks of the barnyard. Perhaps you have encountered an ignorant milkmaid to throw down in the hayloft for a quick roll. Peasants rut like goats in the spring, do they not?"

"Florentines prefer mud to girls, I hear," Riccardo De' Luca said before Giorgio could respond to di Torreforte. "Or a handful of sculpting clay in a pinch."

Giorgio covered his mouth, stifling his laugh. A hot beam of admiration filled his chest for his good friend.

"Basta!" shouted the Maestro. "This is a school of art. Art is divine grace, not a dirty brothel. You will speak as gentlemen, or you will be dismissed!"

Enraged, the maestro moved around the room. He leaned close to the canvases, inspecting his pupils' work.

"Federico! What graceless shoulders you have given Clelia—did you mean to cripple her in your depiction?"

"No, maestro—"

"Then cure the poor girl."

He moved to the next canvas.

"Bartolomeo . . . the Tiber River does not have the cross-stream current you have painted—"

"I was enhancing the light with spots of white—"

"—and if it did, Clelia and the virgins would have been carried downstream from Rome all the way to Ostia's shipyards. Calm the waters!"

The artists bowed their heads, too ashamed to lift their eyes.

The maestro moved toward Giorgio and stood still behind the young artist's canvas.

He said nothing. His jaw relaxed. He drew deep breaths, audible in the still room.

Di Torreforte grew restless in the silence. He recognized that the maestro's lack of comment was the highest compliment.

The Florentine strode over to Giorgio's easel, scowling.

"Maestro!" he said, his hand gesturing dismissively. "Look how he has painted the horses! Not the slightest likeness to Beccafumi's!"

The old maestro was shaken from his reverie.

Giorgio watched a resigned bitterness cross his teacher's face where deep satisfaction had shined only an eyeblink before.

"See there!" di Torreforte insisted. "An insult to your Senese master. See what he has done to the horses. Look! There is nothing of Beccafumi's style whatsoever."

The color drained from the maestro's face, but he did not look at di Torreforte or Giorgio.

"It cannot be fixed. Start—start over," said the maestro, turning away from his pupil.

"But maestro," pleaded Giorgio. He had worked for months painting studies in secret, knowing they would repeat the lesson. Today he had hoped the maestro would praise his work, for it was his best yet.

Di Torreforte's face lit up with boyish pleasure.

"Are you deaf as well as incompetent?" he demanded. "The maestro said, 'Start over!'"

Giorgio tasted bitterness in his mouth. He carefully removed the canvas, laying it on the marble floor to dry.

He drew a new canvas from his supply bag and began to tack it down. His mouth soured as he thought of the many hours ahead of him sketching the stuffed, stiff horses of Beccafumi.

The maestro looked down wistfully at the unfinished painting. He turned and walked silently to the windows overlooking Il Campo. His old eyes gazed down blindly at the busy marketplace, where the Senese carried on with their lives as they had for centuries.

CHAPTER 18

Siena, Pugna Hills

MARCH 1574

There were riding lessons a few nights every week. I quickly learned to communicate with my horses, working my way up from the fat old gelding to gentle ladies-in-waiting mounts, and finally to the retired hunting horses of the nobili.

All the while, Orione trotted beside us, occasionally wheeling around and kicking the air inches from my face. He would not leave my side.

"Va via!" I would shout, waving the tree branch I used as a crop. "Get out of here, you pest!"

I stole sleep while watching the sheep, dozing in the grass or high in the branches of olive trees. When the sheep were pastured among the horses, I took my naps near the lambing shed.

Often Stella would walk to stand near me. One day, I heard the clip-clop of tiny hooves.

I opened my eyes in time to see Orione's knobby knees buckle as he lay down next to me in the straw. He, too, was exhausted. For children and colts alike, it was unnatural to run and play in the hours after midnight. We napped side by side, nestled in the straw.

Flies buzzed around us, lazy in the heat. I watched his skin twitch when they lighted on him, even though he was deeply asleep.

My hand reached out to him, entwining my fingers in his nubby mane. For once, he did not nip me. I drew in his warm horse smell, the heady scent of manure and fermented hay, young and pure.

————

Giorgio worked hard with me. My thirst to learn conquered my need to question.

"Talk to them," Giorgio urged. "It doesn't matter what words you use. Speak from the heart. Speak from your strong will."

"What do you mean?"

"Horses feel your strength, your fears, your love. Words are gibberish to them. The strength of your will—*volontà*—that is what they feel. They are herd animals. They long for a clear leader, a confident leader, one they can trust."

Each lesson took me deeper into Giorgio's world of intuition. If I was afraid, my horse would sense it and take advantage. If I was sure and clear, the authority of my movements was respected immediately.

"Move steadily, firmly," he instructed. "If you don't doubt yourself, the horse will not doubt your judgment. She's ten times your size, but she welcomes a steady hand. This was sanctioned by God—otherwise why would a beast so mighty succumb to being ridden by a creature so inferior in weight and strength?"

I loved to hear Giorgio talk of horses. Sometimes when I was riding, he would take out parchment from his satchel and draw.

"Why do you not aspire to ride the Palio, Giorgio?" I called down to him one night from a new mare, Adela. She was a gray dapple. Her trot was easy, with a long stride.

I used my leg—my bare calf—to turn her around, facing Giorgio. She pranced under me, feeling my leg. I released the pressure, calming her. I sighed, wanting to canter, but Giorgio would not permit it yet.

"That is all for tonight. We will not ride tomorrow or for the next week. The moon has waned."

"I can ride in the pitch-black," I argued. "I do not have to see. I feel the horse under me, so—"

"No! Riding blind, you will betray its trust. He will stumble against a tree root or fall into a hole. And a horse will never forget."

I bent over my mare's neck, stroking her long mane.

"I will not betray you, Adela," I said to my new favorite. Orione, sensing I had abandoned him for the moment, nipped hard at my bare legs.

"Ouch!"

I swatted him away. He snorted, rearing beside me.

"If I had ridden you in the Palio, you would have won," I whispered to Adela. "We would have won together."

I saw Giorgio's white teeth gleaming in the moonlight. He chuckled to himself.

"Come along, Rompicollo. It is time you return to your bed. You are dreaming aloud to the stars and the night sky."

CHAPTER 19

Siena, Contrada della Giraffa, Palazzo Dei

MARCH 1574

For the fourth time, Giacomo di Torreforte straightened the linen cloth veiling his painting.

Father promised he would be here before pranzo. *When Mother was alive, he would never dare to be late for our family meal.*

He caught a rank odor of sweat from his stiff brocade.

I smell like a criminal awaiting sentence, awaiting the verdict of my father. Why do I suffer like this?

He reached for the cloth one more time, then stopped himself. He heard the scuff of leather boots on the staircase.

"*Mi dispiace,*" said his father. "I was making a visit to the orphans of Maria della Scala."

Di Torreforte noticed his father's proud smile.

He is not sorry at all!

"Well, figlio mio," said Signor di Torreforte. "Show me what pretty picture you have painted."

Di Torreforte swallowed.

Pretty picture!

"Ecco!" he said, plucking the cloth from the canvas. He watched his father's face, hungry for his reaction.

The scene was in Florence, the Arno River at sunset. The Ponte Vecchio was rendered in buttery tones, the river dark and moody, the stonework of the arched bridge a perfect replica of the ancient Roman foundation. Di Torreforte had a well-schooled technique.

"Pretty colors," his father said. "Although they could be brighter, my son. More cheerful."

Di Torreforte felt his chest collapse. He could barely draw a breath.

"Pity you chose a Florentine image," said his father. "There is such beauty to be found here in Siena."

"Father, we are Florentine! Look, I painted the corner of our palazzo here, at the edge. I crossed to the far side of the river to get the perspective to include both the Ponte Vecchio and our palazzo—"

"Yes, I see," said Signor di Torreforte. "Of course I was born and raised there, in Palazzo Tornabuoni. Your painting evokes those memories."

Giacomo di Torreforte held his breath. Was his father complimenting him?

"My nursemaid would take my hand, walking the riverbanks each morning," said Signor di Torreforte wistfully. "We would watch the boats. I remember . . . " His voice trailed off into an almost tender silence.

Di Torreforte began to breathe again. His father—did he find joy in his painting?

"It seems so—distant now," concluded Signor di Torreforte abruptly. "Like a dream or an old garment folded away in a cedar chest. I have no time or spirit for those Florentine memories." He clapped his hands together. The subject was finished.

"Come, son," he said. "Let us descend to lunch. I hear the *cuoca* has prepared *pici con la lepre*. She marinated the hare an extra day in red wine. Ah, *che apetito ho!*"

Di Torreforte thought of the thick strands of pici pasta, glistening with olive oil and chunks of potted hare. He suddenly felt ill.

"Sì, signore," he answered.

The young man picked up the linen cloth and shrouded his painting. He turned and descended the stairs, following his father in silence.

In Florence, the servants of Palazzo Buontalenti bit their lips, weathering one of their mistress's worst tirades. They bowed their heads in respect as the granduca entered the grand *sala* to address his mistress.

"Me? Not allowed at Court!" snapped Bianca. "I have been the granduchessa's lady-in-waiting for years. Her favorite!"

"Mia cara," said the granduca. "She has only just learned of our relationship. It is a shock, you must realize. You may have been her confidante, her most favored, but not anymore. You cannot return to Court now that she knows we are lovers."

Francesco shook his head, marveling that his mistress could not understand his wife's outrage.

"Giovanna is a silly cow—an overbred Habsburg idiot!"

"Bianca, *mia amore*—the servants!" whispered Francesco.

"I am to be banished from Court because she has been blind for all these years? All Florence, all Venezia, knows I am your lover."

"Protocol demands—"

"I come from a respectable, noble family myself. In Venezia! Never forget that!"

Francesco bit his tongue. He looked at Bianca's servants, blank-faced as statues.

Bianca pulled at a strand of blond hair that had tumbled down on her neck. Her ample white bosom heaved above the confines of her corset.

"Privacy, please," said Francesco, sending a searing glance at the servants.

"Servants—leave at once!" commanded Bianca. "You, Anna, stay and loosen my corset. I feel dizzy. I think I shall faint."

The other servants bowed, scurrying out of the room.

Once Anna had loosened the stays on her mistress's garment, she, too, left, latching the door behind her.

"Was it not enough to murder my husband?" cried Bianca, her white face turning crimson. "I see his ghost each night as I sleep. His blood stains the walls of Santa Trinita for all eternity—"

"Stop, Bianca! He was a traitor, blackmailing me. Treating me as if he were an equal, instead of merely a greedy cuckold. He cared nothing for you!"

Bianca covered her face with her hands, sobbing.

"But now, Granduchessa Giovanna! She will destroy everything. The Florentines already dare to call me *puttana*. While they call her 'our queen,' the withered old stick!"

Francesco ground his teeth, thinking of his lover's humiliation. He loved Bianca Cappello above anything on Earth, including his reputation and that of the de' Medici family.

"I shall go mad if I am not allowed at Court!" said Bianca. "I cannot be a caged bird. I must laugh and entertain. I must dance! Remember when we celebrated my twenty-fourth birthday? You pledged your undying love—"

Francesco took his mistress in his arms, smelling the sweet powder and Venetian soap lingering on her white skin.

His finger strayed, toying with her ivory bosom, freed from its restraints.

"The granduchessa has approached Cosimo, asking that you be banned from Court. He has told her to let things run their course, that I will return to her—"

"You bastard!" she said, striking at him with her fists.

He caught her hands in his, kissing them. His lips lingered on an emerald the size of a sparrow's egg.

"No, my darling. My father understands our love and my needs. He has told my wife that he will not ban you permanently. He does send word that a hiatus would be beneficial to all concerned."

Bianca smiled, sniffing back her tears. She directed his hands toward her nipples.

"Your father has always understood affairs of the heart. Dare I think he is fond of me?"

Francesco snorted. He looked into her eyes, the color of the Adriatic Sea.

"He understands women," he said. "And he understands me."

CHAPTER 20

Siena, Pugna Hills

Midnight riding lessons carried on into the crisp nights of early spring. I crept in the window to my pallet a few hours before dawn. Never had the straw felt so delicious, the scratchy wool blankets so comforting.

I slept like the dead until the first light of daybreak.

Zia Claudia complained I was a lazy girl, wanting to sleep past dawn every morning. She shook my shoulder hard, grumbling that I was useless if I would not wake earlier to start the morning fire and fetch water.

The chilly dawn air stung my face as I drew water from the well. I cranked the bucket to the rim, the rope beaded with ice, glistening in the sunrise.

All day, I watched our fields for signs of the de' Medici hunt. I craved the vision of Isabella galloping over the hills, jumping fallen trees and stone fences.

"The de' Medici will not return to hunt here again," said Giorgio when I confessed my hopes.

"Why not? There are plenty of wild boar in our hills, deer that linger in the meadows."

"They prefer their own land in Florence to that of Siena. I doubt we will see them here again, unless for the Palio."

I felt a rush of disappointment.

"I would like to show Duchessa Isabella I can ride now."

Giorgio smiled.

"You have a lot of learning to do before you impress that horsewoman, Rompicollo. She has ridden the best horses—and had the best horsemasters—all her life. She would only laugh at you, villanella."

I turned Adela, cantering away from him, the three-beat rhythm of the hooves resonating deep within me. The low stone wall caught my eye, and I directed Adela toward the rocky barrier.

"No, Virginia!" I heard Giorgio shout.

The wind whipped against my cheek, filling my ears with its roar. My hands slid up the mare's neck with the rein, my fingers entwined tight in her mane.

The white stone shone luminous in the moonlight.

"No! Stop!" he screamed.

"Come on, Adela," I whispered. "Take it!"

Her haunches bunched under me, jolting us into the air.

It was not as smooth as I had imagined.

But for a moment, we were airborne. Together. Then we landed.

Slipping to one side, I pulled desperately at her mane, trying to right myself.

She broke into a trot and I tumbled off, landing flat and hard on my chest, my chin knocked back.

I lay crumpled in a ball, trying to breathe. I could not draw air into my lungs. My fingers dug at the muddy ground, panicked.

I heard the footfall of running strides.

"Virginia! Are you all right?"

I couldn't speak, only gasp.

"You're all right. Be calm, take little breaths," Giorgio said, pulling me to a sitting position.

My eyes widened. I felt as if a horse were standing on my chest.

I was dying. Surely no one could survive without breathing.

"It's all right. It will take a minute before your lungs get over the shock of the fall."

I nodded my head, desperate to believe him.

He rocked back his head on his shoulders. I saw his white throat, his eyes cast straight up at the moon like a wolf's.

"*Santo cielo!*" he cried. "Give me strength!'"

He looked back at me, furious. "You scared the holy spirit out of me!" he said.

"I'm sorry—" I gasped.

"What were you thinking? You could have broken your fool neck. When you begin to jump, we will start with a wooden rail. And a saddle!"

"I do not want a saddle," I managed to say. "In the Palio, the *fantini* ride bareback, always bareback. So shall I."

He was right. I was beginning to breathe normally again. I would live.

Giorgio shook his head.

"The Palio! There are no obstacles to jump in the Palio. And Virginia, you may learn to ride and ride well. But your dream of the Palio is—is—"

"What?" I asked, my hand against my heaving chest. "What?"

I dare you to say it!

"Is it not enough to learn to ride well?" he said, lifting his shoulders in an exaggerated shrug. He turned his palms out at his sides in utter frustration.

I looked at him as if I did not know him. I spat mud from my mouth.

"No," I said, struggling to my feet. "No, it certainly is not enough."

PART II

The Death of Casimo de' Medici

ANNI 1574–1576

CHAPTER 21

Firenze, Pitti Palace
APRIL 1574

On the evening of April 20, 1574, Cosimo de' Medici breathed his last. His final gesture was to raise his left arm and take the hand of his wife, Camilla.

As the news of his death spread, Florentines mourned the old granduca and feared for their own future. They forgot his failings and remembered his victories and accomplishments.

Cosimo had made his beloved Firenze a great military power, defeating the ferocious Turks in battles at sea and sending his armies to fight against the Ottoman invaders. He had drained the malarial swamps of Pisa, banishing the disease that killed two of his sons and his wife, Eleonora di Toledo. He built aqueducts to carry fresh water to Florence—and the city glittered with fountains. He commissioned frescoes for the cupola of the Duomo, acquired priceless works of art for the royal palaces, expanded the magnificent Uffizi, and used all his courage and political wile to protect his city from the power of the Vatican, which sought endlessly to extend its tyranny.

Cosimo had made his city a center of power and culture and beauty and, perhaps above all, he had conquered its ancient enemy and rival, Siena.

He had defeated the Senese, the most fiercely independent of Tuscan people.

Florence wept at the passing of their great Granduca of Tuscany. Throngs mourned outside San Lorenzo chapel as Cosimo was laid to rest under the floor of the church alongside his ancestors.

But most of all, the Florentines mourned because they feared that with Cosimo gone, his son, Granduca Francesco, would become a brutal, pitiless ruler.

They were correct. Francesco cared about only one human being on Earth—his mistress, Bianca Cappello.

As the bells tolled the death of Cosimo, his eldest son wasted no time in seizing power. Before his father's body was cold, he had his stepmother, Camilla, locked away in a convent, ordering that she be sequestered for the rest of her life.

Because Cosimo's will had never been properly formalized, Francesco chose not to recognize it. While he could not take Villa Baroncelli from his sister, Isabella, he ignored provisions in the will for her and her children.

The reign of Francesco de' Medici had begun.

CHAPTER 22

Siena, Pugna Hills

MAY 1574

When the moon waned to a sliver in the night sky each month, Giorgio insisted it was too dangerous to ride under the dim starlight. And each month, I grew restless as we waited until the moon fattened once more.

After a year of lessons, the gnawing hunger to ride had not diminished. The more I rode, the keener the urge.

Even when I wasn't riding, I was practicing, imagining the world around me filled with horses. The bean pods I shelled became reins in my hand; my stride walking the grassy hills became the movement of a horse. I caressed the sheep as if they were Orione, Stella, and Adela. I wound my fingers tight around their wool. The skin of my rough hands grew soft and supple from their oil; the dirt and straw clung to my skin.

My posture improved so markedly, Zia Claudia noticed my height.

"The girl is growing quickly," she said to Zio Giovanni. "We should talk to the tanner soon and begin marriage bartering."

"I will not marry the tanner's son!" I snapped. "And you cannot make me."

Zia Claudia strode toward me, her hand poised in midair to slap my face. Zio Giovanni caught her by the wrist.

"Leave the child in peace!"

"You!" she said, looking at me over her husband's shoulder. She struggled against him, swinging her weight to break his hold. "You are a penniless orphan! You should thank the Virgin for anyone who would have you."

"Tranquilla," said Zio, holding her arm.

"Let go of me!" spat Zia.

"Leave the girl in peace."

Claudia glared at her husband, challenging him.

"If you want her to marry, do not bruise her face," he said. "She is of great value, Claudia. Can you not see that? Do not damage her assets."

Zio stepped back, gazing at me. His face took on an expression he wore when appraising a lamb or ewe to add to our flock.

"She has her mother's looks," said Zio. "Have you noticed how her face has hollowed with those same high cheekbones, how her eyes flash? A Senese beauty."

My hands touched my face. We had no mirrors in the house— these were costly luxuries—so how was I to know I was changing?

Zia Claudia snorted. "I doubt she can do better than the tanner. His wares fetch a pretty florin."

"We will see," mused Zio. "But she has caught the eye of several villagers as we walk through the lane. And I cannot say I relish the smell of dog dung and piss on a member of my family."

"It is the smell of money, you fool!" said Claudia.

But she looked at me differently now, as if she had not considered that I might have some value until that moment.

"She will need some fattening," said Zia, her eyes taking in my bony arms and flat bosom. "Then we will take her to market."

I could not wait for the late afternoon, when I would leave for the sheepfold. My cheeks burned with shame as I felt the appraising look from Zia. I ran to the hills, desperate to find Orione. I gathered the old ewes into the pen and whistled for the colt.

He nickered, racing to me from his mother's side. I sat in the grass, and within seconds he buckled his long legs, settling next to me.

I kneaded my fingers into his baby mane, drawing in the warm scent of colt. The sun set, coloring the Tuscan hillside molten gold. Together we watched the evening star appear.

"I will never marry the tanner's son!" I whispered, stroking his neck. I pressed my lips against his black coat.

"I love you alone, Orione."

His brown eyes focused on me in the twilight. I traced the white constellation of stars that formed his blaze, sealing my vow.

———

Old Brunelli's hands reached over a bay mare's withers, his lips murmuring a curse. His fingers traced the edges of a flesh wound.

The mare jumped back, pulling out of his grasp.

"Hold this mare." My padrino handed me the lead rope.

He limped over to his worktable, where bottles and bowls of potions lined the shelves, trusty soldiers ready for battle.

Brunelli returned with a bowl of white powder.

"What is it?" I wanted—no, I needed—to know everything about horses. How to cure them as well as how to ride them.

"Sugar," he said. "The finest, from a noble's kitchen pantry. Payment for shoeing a lame horse. One of a matched pair they could not do without." He chuckled.

His hands traced the backbone of the mare, sending a quiver up her spine. He stopped at the festering wound.

"A whore-born fool rode this good mare. Look how the saddle pinched her!"

The sore gaped open, oozing yellow pus.

He wiped the wound with wool dampened in sour red wine. The mare jumped away at first, but between the two of us, we calmed her down.

"Easy now, tranquilla," I murmured, stroking her neck.

My padrino caught my eye and smiled as the mare responded to my calming voice and touch.

He sprinkled sugar into the wound. The mare's skin twitched, trying to shake off the precious grains like flies. With his fingertips, Brunelli pressed the sweetness into the open flesh.

He stood back, wiping his hands on a rag mottled with stains.

"A week from now, that wound will close."

I kissed the mare's velvet nose.

"See there. You will be all better," I told her.

My padrino studied me.

"You seem so much more confident around horses now, ciccia," he said. "How you handle them, anticipate their approval."

I ducked my head. I loved when he called me by that nickname, although I was as skinny as a stick.

He smiled at me, almost as if he knew about my moonlight rides.

CHAPTER 23

Siena, Palazzo d' Elci

JUNE 1574

After the Beccafumi incident, Maestro Lungo was careful never to choose an equestrian scene again for his students.

He could not forgive himself for asking Giorgio Brunelli to destroy his brilliant painting, and for criticizing his work in front of the other students—especially di Torreforte.

But a study was a study—those were the strict rules of the academy. The objective was to copy and learn from the great masters, not to alter their work.

Any attempt to improve on the masters was considered an insult, hubris. And hadn't he warned Brunelli of the consequences? But the truth was, the maestro was haunted by his decision.

Maestro Lungo not only taught art at the academy but also procured paintings for some of the richest and most discerning men. His art dealings could easily sustain a comfortable lifestyle, but he refused to leave the studio. He dedicated the last years of his life to teaching other artists, hoping to find among them a Senese Da Vinci. That discovery would be his legacy.

The old maestro's choice for the newest study had been a closely guarded secret. Now a black carriage, discreetly displaying the emblem of the House of Ferrara, drew up to the doors of Palazzo d'Elci. Met by the duca's doormen, a cadre of guards whisked a carefully wrapped painting upstairs into the marble hall.

Di Torreforte's complaints about the paintings their teacher had selected for them to copy had etched deep in the heart of the maestro.

"All Senese, old and musty, devoid of talent! I smell their old men's breath, sour and aged. Bones in their graves before Florence came with all her glory, dragging the stagnant backwater of Siena forward toward a glimpse of renaissance. Why cannot Lungo recognize this fact and give us art of our times?"

"Too old and decrepit himself, I suppose," mocked another Florentine.

Though the maestro's eyes were veiled in cataracts, his hearing remained sharp as a hound's. He clenched his arthritic fingers. He would prove the arrogant Florentines wrong.

Antonio Lungo worked hard to procure a canvas so shocking—so sweeping in lust and carnality, passion and skill—that it would leave his students gasping.

Especially di Torreforte.

The June sun, already cresting the Torre del Mangia, spun glittering pools of light on the white marble. The maestro instructed his attendants to set up the easel and masterpiece in the far interior corner of the room.

"The canvas you have the honor of copying is of tempera paints, its nuances subtle," said the maestro. "It is best studied in low light."

"Tempera! Another Senese dark master," groaned di Torreforte. "I cannot bear any more—"

"On the contrary, Signor di Torreforte—this is by one of your fellow Florentines and quite contemporary. I think his reputation precedes him. The Duca Alfonso d'Este helped me to procure it from the house of Ferrara for a few months."

"The Duca di Ferrara—a foul adversary of Florence!" said di Torreforte.

"Hmm," mused the maestro. "In this particular case, I think you Florentines will forgive me."

The maestro drew back the satin cover. Several students gasped.

Di Torreforte stared, dumbfounded.

"Michelangelo," he whispered.

Giorgio stared, unable to blink. His lips curved in delight, his hands itching for his brushes and paints.

The studio buzzed with a thrilled murmur.

The most controversial work in Michelangelo's oeuvre stood before the students. It was rumored that the Duca di Ferrara had already sent it to a castle in France to avoid the fury of the Pope, who had demanded that this obscenity of a painting be destroyed.

Not yet.

The students crowded around the canvas, silent.

A tempera painting of a sleeping Leda, the swan between her legs, climbing to her breasts, his black beak posed just above her parted lips. Her naked body reclined against a crimson cushion in an elaborate curve, her bare thigh thrown around the swan.

Leda's fingers flickered, dreamily aware of sexual pleasure. Ecstasy.

"Enough passion for you, Signor di Torreforte?" asked the maestro.

Di Torreforte turned toward him, stunned. "How did you—"

"A little tactful respect and complete dedication to art brings good fortune, Signor di Torreforte. You should investigate that posture. It may profit you in the future. Students—to your posts. Begin your ink sketches at once."

The old teacher smiled over the bowed heads of his students. His dim eyes sought the light of Il Campo, just beyond the leaded windows.

CHAPTER 24

Florence, Palazzo Vecchio
JUNE 1574

Francesco de' Medici's personal secretary, Antonio Serguidi, finished his morning wine as the early light slanted through the windows of Palazzo Vecchio. He brushed the crumbs of breakfast bread from his tunic as his attendant entered.

"Buongiorno, Signor Serguidi."

"Buongiorno, Alessandro. What have you brought me?"

"A letter for the granduca, signore."

Serguidi turned the letter over in his hand, the red wax seal bright against the ivory parchment.

He examined the seal—a five-petal rose.

"Orsini," he muttered.

"A rider from Rome arrived a quarter of an hour ago," said the servant. "If the duca wishes to reply, he will carry the letter himself."

Serguidi raised his eyebrows.

"A bit of a rush, do you not think, Alessandro? That I should be inconvenienced at such an early hour of the morning to do Orsini's bidding."

Alessandro produced a leather pouch jingling with florins.

"The rider said Paolo Orsini sends this token of his apprecia-tion and hopes to hasten the reply."

Antonio Serguidi plucked the bag from the manservant's hand. He smiled, pocketing the bag without inspecting its contents.

"*Bene*. I shall deliver it immediately to the granduca. Please see that the messenger is comfortably lodged until it is decided whether a response is warranted."

The servant nodded and left.

Serguidi wiped his fingertips on a linen napkin, inspecting them carefully before touching the missive. He frowned, knowing the granduca would be working in his studiolo that morning.

The studiolo was a barrel-vaulted room that combined a lab-oratory for Francesco's alchemy experiments, a library, and space for contemplation. Its walls were jammed with paintings by Italy's most prestigious artists, although mostly not their best work. The gilded frames were crowded together, creating—for Serguidi, at least—a nightmarish kaleidoscope of colors and mythical figures.

Even the cabinets for storing the elements used in alchemical experiments were obscured by oval paintings with keyholes drilled through the canvases.

The space was windowless. The only entrance was through the granduca's bedroom. The four walls represented the four elements: air, fire, earth, and water. Chemicals, artifacts, and oddities were arranged in cabinets according to their nearest corresponding ele-ment. Pieces of coral, pearls, mandrake root, witches' potions, and poisons were shelved following Francesco's interpretation.

To Serguidi, entering the studiolo was akin to walking into an ornate sarcophagus. And as the granduca spent more and more time entombed there—away from the responsibility of running the business of Florence—his secretary wondered if it would not indeed be de' Medici's tomb.

He knocked on the door, sucking in his breath. Francesco de' Medici would be perturbed at any disruption that did not involve his mistress, Bianca Cappello.

As Serguidi entered, Granduca Francesco was bent over a small beaker. A tube ran into it from a larger glass vessel, over a small flame.

"Yes. Yes! Serguidi!" The granduca pulled a linen kerchief down from around his nose and mouth. "I assume you have a magnificent reason for disturbing me."

"Sì, Serenissimo—"

"First, come and see the distillation I am performing."

Serguidi coughed, the fumes from the granduca's apparatus irritating his throat. He often worried that the fumes were poisonous. "Yes, Your Majesty. With pleasure."

"Quicksilver," pronounced the duca with satisfaction. "The manuscripts suggest that under just the right conditions, heat and mercury can produce gold."

"A recipe from Prague, I assume," said Serguidi, trying hard to disguise his contempt for Holy Roman Emperor Rudolf II's stable of alchemical swindlers.

"Yes!" said Francesco, a smile spreading over his face. "Decoded from an ancient manuscript. Egyptian, Arabic. I cannot remember the source."

Serguidi gave a curt nod.

"And what do you bring me? A letter from my beloved?"

"I am distressed to reply in the negative," said Serguidi. "It is a letter just delivered from Signor Orsini, Duca di Bracciano, in Rome."

Francesco took the letter, moving away from the alchemical apparatus. He read the letter, blinking away tears from the experiment's fumes.

"Hmmmm," he muttered. "The miserable swine."

"Bad *notizie*, Your Majesty?"

"He begs to borrow more money to finance his naval operation. Such a huge sow of a man, how can a ship not sink into the sea with him onboard?"

"The Duca of Bracciano does seem overly fond of what he finds on his plate," agreed Serguidi.

Of all the de' Medici family, Paolo Orsini was the most repugnant. Corpulent and greedy, the husband of the elegant Isabella was a disgrace to the family name—both Orsini and Medici.

Orsini regularly pleaded for money to finance his estate in Bracciano—the family manor Isabella had visited only once—and his magnificent palazzo in Rome. The old Granduca Cosimo had often lent his son-in-law money to keep him happy and isolated in Rome. Now Paolo Orsini was attempting to ingratiate himself with Felipe II of Spain by creating his own naval fleet.

"The Duca di Bracciano has decided rather late in life to become a naval commander," observed Serguidi.

"Still, it rids me of his miserable presence at Court," said Francesco. "And Felipe will see it as augmenting his navy with our support. Yes, yes, grant him the money with choice land in Bracciano as collateral, as in the past."

"Very good, Your Majesty. I will draw up the contracts."

Francesco held up a finger, hesitating.

"The only issue that concerns me is how my sister Isabella will comport herself when her husband is not in Rome but far off at sea, fighting the Ottomans. I do not trust Paolo's cousin Troilo. Or my sister."

The granduca covered his scowl with the linen kerchief, turning back to his experiment.

Serguidi lingered. He cleared his throat.

"With your permission, Granduca," said Serguidi. "Your instincts are correct, as always. My sources indicate that Troilo Orsini is very much taken with your sister. And she with him."

Francesco looked up from the beaker. He straightened his back, yanking off his kerchief.

"I can confirm that Troilo has arranged trysts with the Duchessa di Bracciano, Your Majesty," said the secretary, his eyes lowered.

The granduca gnawed at the hairs of his mustache, his eyes ardent with hate.

"A bitch in heat!"

Serguido bowed his head, his eyes studying the polished tiles of the studiolo.

"What can I do? My sister takes lovers as if she were a man, with no discretion. She soils the de' Medici name."

Serguidi nodded. He chased away the fleeting image of Francesco's mistress.

"Perhaps to avoid a jealous confrontation, Duca Paolo is best occupied at sea," suggested the secretary. "Then you can reason with the duchessa."

"Reason!" said Francesco. "As if my sister would ever respond to reason!"

"If Your Majesty were to find an opportunity to talk privately with the Duchessa di Bracciano, perhaps you could—strongly convey—the danger of her—alliances."

Francesco raised his finger to his upper lip, stroking his mustache.

"Yes! As usual your counsel is invaluable, Antonio. Write the contract and send Paolo Orsini packing."

Serguidi hurried out the door of the studiolo, drawing a deep breath as he entered the hallway of the Palazzo Vecchio.

CHAPTER 25

Siena, Pugna Hills
JULY 1574

He could tell by her restless hands, the way she rubbed the horses furiously with the rag, and from her fidgeting stance, that something was not right. It was as if she were about to jump out of her own skin.

"I must ride," Virginia whispered to Giorgio. She held the rope of a horse he was doctoring, twisting the end with her fingers. Her Uncle Giovanni and his friends knelt several yards away, throwing dice. Their eyes were riveted on the game.

"Two weeks a month is not enough," she said. "I cannot bear it any longer."

"I have told you," Giorgio said, still looking at the hoof he cradled in his hand. "To ride in the dark is to injure yourself—or worse, your horse. And do not forget, Rompicollo, these horses are not yours."

The girl stamped her foot. "I cannot control this urge—"

Giorgio stifled a laugh. He looked at her from under the horse's belly. His soft brown eyes glittered, amused. Virginia looked away, annoyed when she heard a chuckle deep in his throat.

"You do not take me seriously, Giorgio," Virginia hissed. "I cannot sleep. I have to ride—and I will, whether you—"

"Hand me the tincture of violet oil from the shelf," said Giorgio, digging packed manure and stones from the horse's hoof with a blunt-tipped knife. He carefully avoided the soft triangle of flesh, the island of sensitivity in a horse's foot.

"Do not fret, Rompi," he said, dousing the hoof with the solution. The pigment etched deep into his cuticles, coloring his fingers a deep purple. "I will find a way."

He slipped the halter off the horse and walked to the doorway of the stable. The skies had cleared after the hard morning rain, and the air was fresh with the scent of crushed grass.

She is seized by passion, the urgent need to ride. It is no different from my need to paint. But it is dangerous to ride in the pitch-dark the way she rides now, with complete abandon. A galloping horse could easily stumble on a root, put its foot in a hole. . .

But for her, I will find a way.

Giorgio had asked me to meet him at the field on the night of the new moon. I stumbled through the fields, my feet catching on roots.

He was right. It was foolhardy to ride in the dark. I stared up at the sliver of moon, barely a fingernail paring. Fragile and white.

I thought of white bone, the fragile vertebrae of a lamb carcass, picked clean by wolves. I remembered my fall from Adela, taking the stone fence. The panic when I could not breathe, rendering my blood as cold as icy water from the well.

I could indeed kill myself or my horse. He was right to call me Rompicollo.

At the crest of the hill, I looked down toward the stand of olive trees where the horses pastured for the night. I sucked in my breath.

A circle of light flickered in the darkness. Giorgio had created a small track, outlined in the glow of lanterns, a butter-yellow halo in the night.

At the edge of the circle, I saw the silhouettes of horses, dark shadows mesmerized by the lighted world at midnight. A colt ran erratic laps in the moonlight, racing an invisible rival.

Chapter 26

Florence, Villa Baroncelli

July 1574

Leonora di Toledo de' Medici had spent several months living at Baroncelli with her cousin and sister-in-law, Isabella de' Medici Orsini, Duchessa di Bracciano.

The beautiful estate in the Arcetri Hills, near Florence's Porta Romana, had been a gift to Isabella from her father, Cosimo, before his death. The vineyards and property stretched down the hill, meeting the Boboli Gardens of the Pitti Palace.

Isabella had spared no expense in creating a country estate to rival any in Tuscany. She embellished the property with fountains and formal gardens. Beyond the gardens were fruit and olive trees and a roadway she had built leading into Florence.

With its magical gardens and stables, Baroncelli was a world of wonders, the perfect place for the frail Leonora to regain her health and strength.

Isabella carefully supervised all the meals, nourishing Leonora back to health. She was certain poison-laced wine or food had been responsible for her young cousin's poor health. Just enough poison to make her ill, killing her slowly, because a precipitous death would be suspect.

Letters from Pietro in Spain were infrequent—he seemed to care little where his wife and young son lived or how they fared.

Leonora gradually grew stronger, taking in the sunshine of the country, embraced by the cheery yellow-stucco villa.

In the absence of both their husbands, the two cousins flourished, laughing and sharing secrets as they had when Isabella was a teenager and Leonora her five-year-old constant companion. Their days and nights were filled with activities and entertainment, appealing to the cousins' voracious appetites for sport and intellectual activity.

Accomplished riders from childhood, they would head out on hunts, daring each other to jump obstacles, cheering encouragement for their feats. They recalled the days of Cosimo, how proud he had been of his two fearless girls—the ponies and hunters he had purchased over the years for each of them.

The good scent of horses brought Leonora vivid memories of better times. She dismounted at the end of the day, tired and happy, stroking her mare's neck.

"My dear father said there was no tragedy that could not be made better by a good gallop in the hills," said Isabella.

"Your father was the wisest, kindest man," said Leonora, wistfully. "I miss him more than you know."

Isabella smiled. "I am so pleased to see the change in you," she said. "You are blossoming."

Leonora pressed her lips to the mare's salty neck. She breathed in the comfort of childhood, of being the coddled Spanish niece of Granduca Cosimo.

"If only we could remain together at Baroncelli forever," she said. She relinquished the reins to a waiting groom. As the horse's shoes rang across the stableyard, she whispered, "Without our damnable husbands!"

They both laughed, but the laughter soon wore thin as they locked eyes, recognizing the fear in each other's gaze.

Every night, Isabella de' Medici planned diversions. She reveled in the theater, concerts, and literary events. She hosted the Accademia della Lingua Toscana. She scoured Tuscany for the brightest, wittiest company in the land.

Isabella sat in the cool shade of an arbor at a little desk, making out her guest list and addressing invitations. A shriek of delight rose from the gardens. Isabella looked up from her parchment, smiling at her cousin, who sat by a fountain, reading.

Children's laughter rang out again from deep in the garden. Leonora's little son, Cosimo, delighted in following his cousins around the vast grounds of Villa Baroncelli. The two-year-old toddled after Isabella's children, Virginio, three, and Nora, four, shrieking gleefully among the cool shadows of cypress trees.

Leonora sat in the sunshine, her eye straying to the hills north toward Florence. Isabella glanced up at a leaf tumbling down from the arbor. She brushed it away. She watched her cousin's smile fade and two faint lines etch across her brow.

"You are thinking of Pietro. Stop it."

Leonora sighed, her fingertips touching her mouth.

"I cannot help it. Everything here is so peaceful, so . . . perfect."

"We did have fun last night," mused Isabella. "What a heavenly voice you have. And Troilo gave you the perfect nickname! *Ardente*—with your flashing eyes and passion, so Spanish—"

"Oh, Troilo! The story you told last night of dressing as a boy and visiting the taverns of Florence with him. Was it really true?"

"Of course. He did not tell you the night we sneaked a common girl—as ugly as she was flea-infested—into the *Ferrarese* ambassador's bed! He thought the peasant was his beautiful mistress and got under the covers with her, groping for his lover. Once he touched her, he knew he'd been deceived and he shot out of bed, cursing. We laughed so hard! He slept in another bed that night and burned the mattresses the next day to rid his bed of fleas."

"The de' Medici have such a terrible relationship with Ferrara," laughed Leonora. "I have often marveled at the hatred your father and brothers had for Duca Alfonso. Yet I remember his kindness to me when I was five years old in his court."

Isabella's eyes narrowed.

"Our enmity goes back centuries, Leonora. Do not forget that the Duca d'Este poisoned my sister—his dear wife!"

"The man I knew would never—"

"You were a child! What could you know? The d'Estes backed the Senese against my father. They will always remain our enemies."

Leonora pressed her lips together, lowering her eyes. She cast about for another topic.

"What a handsome signore, your Troilo—so gallant!" she said in a moment. "I can see why he is a favorite in the French court. How could one not admire him?"

Isabella sniffed. She did not like thinking of Francesco's sending him away as an emissary to France.

"Troilo resembles nothing of his cousin, my husband," she said.

"And," Leonora said, lifting her chin, "your father, Cosimo, God rest his soul, reminds me nothing of his son."

Isabella put down her pen.

"When does Pietro return from Spain?"

"Next month," said Leonora. She looked down the long hill in the direction of Florence. "I must ready the apartments, return to the Pitti Palace."

"I want you to take my assistant cook with you. He will—"

"That will surely upset Giovanna and Francesco! The palace cooks—"

"Leave that to me. I will accompany you for the first few days of Pietro's return. He may hesitate to do you harm if he knows I am watching. I shall say you are on a special diet for your delicate health."

A breeze blew through the branches of the cypress trees, knocking a few cones to the ground. Little Cosimo waddled over to pick one up. The sharp points pricked him as he clutched the cone in his baby fist.

He dropped it, his eyes filling with tears. He held out his finger to his mother.

A shiver shook Leonora's body. She embraced her son, kissing his finger. Isabella could see she was crying.

Isabella hurried to her cousin's side. She stretched her arm around Leonora, pulling the red-haired young woman against her shoulder.

"It will be all right."

"I do not know what is to become of us, Isabella. He frightens me, and he despises his son."

"I know," said Isabella, tightening her embrace. "Pietro frightens everyone in the family. He was born not quite . . . right in the head."

"Will Francesco protect me? As his father, my uncle, did?"

Isabella bit her lip, pulling the frightened young woman closer. She thought she could smell the sharp scent of fear mingling with the perfumed satin of her cousin's bodice.

Then she wondered if it was her own fear she sensed.

"I do not know. Will he protect *me*?"

CHAPTER 27

Ferrara, Castello d' Este

AUGUST 1574

The late-afternoon light crawled up the interior walls of Palazzo d'Este. Alfonso, Duca di Ferrara, sat plucking at his beard as he listened to Ambassador Ercole Cortile's report from the de' Medici Court.

"According to my sources," said Cortile, "two years after the wedding, Pietro de' Medici was finally forced to consummate the marriage with his bride."

Alfonso grimaced, his hand waving a fly away from a golden fruit bowl. A particularly fat fly, it moved only inches, from an apple to a cluster of purple grapes.

"Despicable fool," muttered the duca. "What justice is there in the world when a half-wit should have such a lovely flower to pluck? And need to have his hand forced to grasp its beauty."

"More than his hand, my duca," whispered Cortile. He looked at his master, arching an eyebrow. "Pietro de' Medici was coerced—by force—to penetrate his wife."

The duca grimaced. He swatted savagely at the fly.

"Gah! Ercole, such an image! Tell me, is she still as beautiful as she was as a child?"

"Leonora inspires poetry, Duca. Yet Pietro despises his cousin-wife. He threatens her, making her life miserable. He disowns their son—grumbling drunkenly to anyone who will listen that the child is not his."

"Cosimo's, then?" asked Alfonso, plucking an orange from the fruit bowl. He turned the fruit in his hand, hunting for blemishes.

"That is the gossip in Florence, my duca. But Florentines are known for their lively imaginations."

Alfonso put down the orange and stood up, smoothing his velvet tunic. He walked to the window, looking down at the green waters surrounding Palazzo d'Este.

"I knew her as a child, after she lost her mother at the age of five," he said. "She was like a songbird, filling my wife's heart. They were inseparable. I remember her playing under the orange trees."

He breathed in the fragrance from the fruit trees.

"Cosimo sent her a white pony. Leonora hounded me mercilessly to let her ride every day."

The duca grew silent. He thought of his wife, now dead more than a decade, and the young Leonora. The grinding mechanical scream of a rising drawbridge broke his reverie.

"Lady Isabella has taken young Leonora under her wing," said Cortile. "Together they hunt and ride the hills of Florence, a bucolic life."

Ercole's eyes glittered, a sign he had more to report. The duca nodded.

"And?"

"And their sexual escapades do not escape the notice of Granduca Francesco. He is enraged by their conduct."

"What does he intend to do?"

"He, of course, withholds money, their allowances. Even inheritance rightly destined for Isabella and her children. My sources say he tried to take her estate of Baroncelli from her, but it was legally impossible."

"Laws rarely interfere with a de' Medici's will. I am surprised."

The duca took up the orange again. With an ivory-handled fruit knife, he peeled it in a delicate, continuous spiral.

"I have always hated the de' Medici," said Alfonso, turning toward his ambassador. "But Francesco is by far the worst. He would crush—nay, strangle—everything of beauty in his world."

The duca looked at the perfect spiral of orange peel, catching the last of the light. It reminded him of a tempera still life.

"The little bird Leonora, with her bright eyes that gleam like twinkling stars. To be spurned in her own marriage bed? My heart grieves for her. My mind—my mind sees a de' Medici web of evil that threatens her life."

His sharp knife severed the white curl of fruit skin. It missed the fruit plate and fell to the floor at the duca's feet.

He stared at it, pondering. Then he kicked it out of sight with the toe of his boot.

"Francesco has already murdered once to rid himself of his whore's husband."

"But, my duca. Do you truly believe he would allow harm to come to his own cousin?"

"His cousin and a relative of the Spanish king. But yes. I think the young granduca is capable of such evil and folly. I do not put it past him to murder his own blood to make his life easier. Leonora and Isabella have won the hearts of Florence. He will not stand by idly, watching their adoration."

He popped a segment of orange in his mouth.

"The women disobeyed the granduca by taking lovers and showing independence. He will make them pay. He cares more about his revenge than the fate of the House of de' Medici."

Cortile leaned forward and whispered, though there were no servants in the vaulted room. "Isabella fears he has tried already to poison the fair Leonora."

Alfonso spat two orange seeds to the tiled floor.

"Bastardo! And they accuse *me* of poisoning my de' Medici wife!"

Tiny beads of sweat stood out on Cortile's forehead. The haunting memory of Lucrezia di Cosimo de' Medici's death flashed through his mind: painful, lingering fevers and a bloody cough. He chased away this ghost, as he always did. He would never know whether the duchessa had been poisoned by his master, the Duca d'Este, or had died of natural causes.

"Francesco's darkness is untempered by reason or politics." Alfonso filled the silence without a moment's reflection. "Perhaps he has poisoned his brain with his alchemical experiments. He does not have the temperament nor the wisdom of a ruler."

Cortile gave an emphatic nod, glad to have the conversation steered into safer waters.

"He spends more time locked away in his windowless studiolo than he does at council or Court. An alchemist, they call him, but others swear he works on poisons to murder his enemies."

The duca grimaced. "De' Medici and Borgia! Gold and power breed a venomous sting."

Alfonso always demanded a thorough report after his ambassador's stay in Florence. The way this interview was proceeding, thought Cortile, he would probably be sent back south within days. He was already saddle-sore from the ride to Ferrara.

"A granduca who dabbles in the occult, while giving little regard to his allies," growled Alfonso. "He utterly lacks decorum, or he would have given up his Venetian whore long ago."

The duca wiped his hands clean on an embroidered linen cloth. He wrinkled his nose, catching a whiff of sweat from the silks of his Florentine ambassador.

"I want you back in Florence as soon as possible."

CHAPTER 28

Florence, Villa Baroncelli

AUGUST 1574

Morgante, the de' Medici Court dwarf, drew a deep breath, his barrel chest filling with the good hill air. Time away from the Court in Firenze soothed his nerves. The droning of the bees amid the villa's flowers eased him into a pleasant calm, which helped him to forget the cruelty of the Pitti Palace.

He could not entertain Francesco's children as well as he did Isabella's. They quickly became bored, calling him ugly and small, throwing toys and food at him as he shielded his face with his hands. Elenora, Marie, Anna, and Filippo preferred the antics of the feral children captured from the wilds of the Americas to his juggling, funny faces, and squeaky voice.

Isabella's Virgino and Nora, on the other hand, adored the dwarf, taking his hand, chattering about their ponies, pets, and lessons. Morgante knew their devotion mirrored the love their mother bestowed on him. The dwarf traveled with the duchessa, entertaining the children, but most of all acting as a faithful servant and confidant.

He was born in a poor village near Pisa, but both mother and father turned their eyes toward Firenze as soon as they saw the deformed infant, knowing that Granduca Cosimo de' Medici's family paid handsomely for unnatural children. The de' Medici ministers scoured the land for deformed children and *uomoni selvatici*—"wild men"—for entertainment. The favorite Christmas gifts of the de' Medici children—in particular Francesco—were aberrant people who fascinated their imaginations.

He was the de' Medici's second Morgante. The original was a fierce hunter known not only as a Court entertainer, but also as a skilled falconer. In 1550, Bronzino, the de' Medici court artist, had painted his likeness, naked and posed minutes after a hunt, an owl perched on his shoulder. On the back of the canvas, the feathered kill was thrown over his back, spilling behind his chubby buttocks. Cosimo delighted in walking his guests around clockwise, viewing the front and back of the standing portrait.

This new Morgante was nothing like his predecessor. The owls and falcons terrified him, pecking at his face and hands. But this Morgante adored horses, so Cosimo bought him a fat pony, thinking it hilarious to see the dwarf's short legs sticking straight out from the pony's back.

At first, Morgante took the most spectacular falls, his body so ill suited to the roundness of his mount. The hunting party laughed at the dwarf, lying on the ground like a sack of turnips spilt from a wagon.

Still, Morgante climbed back into the saddle, desperate to ride.

"Papa. We must give Morgante a horse," said Isabella. "He will kill himself one day riding that wicked pony."

"Why? Does it not amuse you? I laugh until my sides ache," said the granduca, his eyes crinkling.

"No," said Isabella. "I think he should have a horse and learn to ride properly."

"If he learns to ride that cantankerous pony, he will master equitation. Ponies are harder to ride than horses," said the granduca. "And what fun would it be to see him perched atop a horse?"

Isabella thought.

"A tall horse, an enormous one, like the ones the Germans ride. Now that would be a ridiculous sight, Papa. And far less dangerous than this mean little pony."

The next week, Morgante was given the tallest horse in the de' Medici stable, a chestnut mare. He fell in love at first sight, calling her Carissima. Anytime he was not engaged at Court, he could be found in the stables, grooming his new mount and braiding her mane and tail.

"How can I ever thank you, princess?" he asked, bowing to his mistress.

"You shall be my personal servant," she told him. "Never mind the Court, and especially never mind my brother Francesco. Whenever I can, I will take you traveling with me."

Now here at Baroncelli, Morgante watched his beloved mistress care for the beautiful lady Leonora. The lazy summer days at Baroncelli without the granduca's ugly humors and spoiled children made him happy.

He saw Leonora regain her health and beauty day by day. Like so many of the courtiers, he had been certain that the young red-haired mother was being poisoned.

What a lovely sight, he thought, *this fairy-tale world*. Two beautiful women, two cousins, growing strong and healthy together in the paradise of Baroncelli. As he watched Isabella stroke her cousin's arm absently, a shiver shook Morgante's spine, despite the heat of the summer afternoon.

He knew the fairy tale would end.

CHAPTER 29

Florence, Pitti Palace

SEPTEMBER 1574

Leonora watched the thick candles melt in her bedchamber as she waited for the arrival of Pietro.

The unbearable heat of late summer lingered into the evening, the cobblestones of the streets radiating warmth long after sundown. Despite the jasmine-scented gardens, the summer brought wafts of fetid sewage, even here.

Echoes of tension from the piazzas beyond the Pitti Palace haunted the hot night. Foul-tempered shopkeepers drove hard bargains, often ending their negotiations by spitting curses as their lettuces wilted, milk soured, and sugar pastries melted in the cruel Tuscan heat.

Leonora looked out over the city, a flickering nightscape with the black glitter of the Arno cutting across its breast.

Maria, her faithful Spanish maid, sat across from her, knitting.

"Come away from the window, my lady," she said, dropping the yarn and needles in her lap. "I hear thunder in the distance. Come away."

"Your hearing is remarkable," said Leonora. "I smell the wetness of stone. You are right, a storm approaches."

"When il duca comes, he comes," said her old maid, sighing.

"I want it to be over with," said Leonora, biting her lip. It quivered like a bird trying to escape a trap. "The homecoming. The disappointment that will wash over his face, his impatience to leave me. It is always the same, no matter how I prepare."

Her face crumpled. She raised her hand to cover her mouth.

Maria rose to her feet, her knees creaking.

"There, there," she said, taking the young woman in her arms.

"It is just—it is just I have been so happy with Isabella in Baroncelli. It was just as if I were a little girl again, loved and coddled by her hands, or by Lucrezia at the di Ferrara Court when I was much younger."

"You must try to please your husband."

"I do try, Maria. Am I any safer? And what of Isabella?"

"She trifles with Troilo," sniffed Maria. "All Florence shares this knowledge. She risks too much."

"While her husband keeps his mistresses in his villa in Rome, sending the de' Medici the bills?" said Leonora.

"He is a most disreputable gentleman," said Maria. "But still he is her husband."

"A fat, womanizing ogre!" said Leonora. "Why should Isabella not seek companionship?"

"He is a duca," said Maria, sighing, "and she is his wife. It is dangerous."

"She is a de' Medici! I am a di Toledo *and* a de' Medici. Have I not even more royal blood than my husband?"

"Of course, my treasure," said Maria. "But they are men."

"And what of my poor sister-in-law Giovanna, the granduchessa? She is sister to the Emperor of the Holy Roman Empire. And Francesco, parading about with the Cappello whore!"

A clap of thunder rumbled in the night. Leonora gasped.

"Come away from the window, my beautiful mistress. Come away, *bella*," implored her maid, taking the young woman in her arms.

———

Pietro de' Medici wasted no time once the Spanish frigate landed in Piombino. His coach was ready and waiting just beyond the docks, with two fine matched gray mares harnessed in de' Medici livery of red and gold.

"Fetch my trunks at once," he said to the driver and footman. "I will wait in the carriage. I cannot abide to breathe the stinking air of Piombino. It murdered my brothers. It is thick with fever."

Pietro pulled a lace kerchief from his sleeve, clasping it over his nose and mouth as he climbed into the black lacquered coach. Inside was a wicker basket of food Leonora had sent for him, filled with Tuscan sausages, hams, smoked cheeses, and fresh bread.

My darling Pietro, husband and father of our dearest son. Benvenuto!

Welcome, your own Leonora.

He kicked the basket, breaking the crystal glass meant for the fine red wine from Isabella's vineyard at Baroncelli.

———

As the coach descended the Tuscan hills into the Arno Valley, Pietro's face puckered in disgust. Already he missed the Spanish mistress he had left behind in Madrid.

And now I must return to the bed of the wife I married under duress. My cousin! Are the rumors of her unfaithfulness true? What could she see in another when she has a de' Medici as a husband?

He looked down, seeing the redbrick cupola of the Duomo, ribbed in white plaster.

Florence loves Leonora. They laugh behind their hands at me.

The young de' Medici prince rapped hard on the carriage roof. "Driver! Ascend to Fiesole at once."

High above the city of Florence, in the hills of Fiesole, stood a small villa tucked away in the woods. A brook rippled past, fed by a spring in a grotto formed by slabs of blue-gray sandstone—pietra serena, coveted by Brunelleschi, Vasari, Michelangelo, and Cellini. There lived Carlotta Spessa, Pietro de' Medici's mistress.

Carlotta had everything Leonora did not: tresses the color of wet coal, bright green eyes. A tigress in bed. The villagers whispered that Carlotta was a witch who fed on the vapors from the ancient grotto—and before they even whispered, they looked over their shoulder and spat, for they were terrified of Carlotta Spessa.

The Spessa name had belonged exclusively to women for generations—and they had been feared for centuries. But their beauty and passion had attracted men who found them irresistible despite—or because of—the peril. But the men who visited didn't stay. Villagers had never known a man to dwell in the villa.

It was no wonder Pietro was infatuated with her. His throat thickened as he thought of her, the carriage bumping over the rutted road toward Fiesole.

CHAPTER 30

Siena, Palazzo d'Elci
OCTOBER 1574

Rain sluiced against the crystal windowpanes of Palazzo d'Elci. A fire blazed in the hearth, but it was the brazier that warmed the Duchessa d'Elci, her feet and legs under a woolen mantle to absorb the heat of the coals.

She had invited her stablemaster to the palazzo to discuss business. She looked up from her ledger and handed it to her private secretary.

"Ernesto Battelli," she said, rising to meet her horsemaster. "So good of you to join me. What a malevolent day!"

"Thank you, good duchessa," he said, kissing her hand. "I fear it will turn to snow before nightfall."

"Come, sit by the fire, Ernesto," she said. "I have business to discuss."

Bowing, the horsemaster took his chair.

"I think it is time to begin training Stella's colt."

Ernesto nodded. "You are right, of course."

A twinkle grew in the duchessa's eye.

"Orione may be difficult," she said. "Tempesta's blood is in his veins."

"Yes, but the dam is Stella," said Ernesto. He thought of how the duchessa had insisted on breeding the mare to the fiery stallion. "My sincerest hope is that he will not have the ill temper of his sire."

"I do not know," said the duchessa. "I have driven out several times to see the colt. He snorts at me, runs away kicking. He is not exactly . . . settled."

"Carlo is the best trainer we have. He will gentle him in no time."

"Carlo?" said the duchessa. "He is rather rough with colts, isn't he?"

Ernesto felt the duchessa's eyes steady on him.

"Duchessa mia, I think he has just the right firmness to train Tempesta's colt."

The duchessa gazed toward the window, watching the raindrops warp the world outside.

"Drink some wine, Ernesto. This is a vintage from my husband's vineyards," she said. "If you do not object to drinking from a Selva cellar."

Ernesto smiled. The duchessa had married into the ancient family whose palazzo was built in the Selva contrada, but that was irrelevant. Like her horsemaster, she was an Oca through and through.

"I suppose I could sip just a little," he said. "The Goose in me does not object."

"Have you heard anything from the little villanella who saved my colt? Virginia Tacci?"

"There have been rumors," he said, taking the proffered glass.

"What is that?"

"Only rumors, Duchessa. Fanciful visions—"

"Tell me."

"Shepherds near Vignano have seen strange lights in the dark of the moon. When they moved closer, they thought they saw your villanella riding Stella."

The duchessa caught her breath and stared straight ahead.

"But how queer their visions are," said Ernesto, dismissing the idea with a wave of his hand. "A shepherdess riding a Palio horse!"

The Duchessa d'Elci brought her fingers to her open lips.

"Mia duchessa?" said Ernesto, rising. He poured a draught of wine into her crystal glass.

"She rides!" whispered the duchessa. Her old eyes shone, glittering with tears.

"Drink, good duchessa. Per favore."

The duchessa sipped the wine. Her hand fluttered to her heart. "You say she rides. My mare?"

"It is foolish talk of ignorant shepherds. They compete for grazing with the Tacci family, they may invent stories—"

"No!" gasped the duchessa. "I want this dream to be true. You must take me to her, tonight!"

"But my duchessa! It is only—"

"I will witness for myself this apparition," she said. "Please tell my footman to fetch the coach immediately."

———

It was cold and dark when the d'Elci coach arrived at the crest of the hill above the lambing sheds. The lanterns on either side of the coach swung side to side, throwing erratic pools of light as they jolted over the muddy track to the foot of Quattro Torra.

Ernesto pulled back the velvet curtain that blocked the rain and wind.

"It saddens me to see not a single candle lit in Quattro Torra," said Duchessa d'Elci, looking across at the horsemaster. "Before the siege . . ." Her voice trailed off.

"Are you warm enough, my duchessa?" he asked.

"I am fine, Ernesto," she said, gazing out at the dark sky.

The horses nickered quietly in the darkness, sensing something below.

The footman knocked. "My duchessa, we have arrived."

Ernesto and the footman helped the elderly lady descend from the carriage. Ernesto smelled the lemon verbena the duchessa always used on her neck and shoulders.

"Do you see the circle of flickering lights? Just there, below us," said Ernesto, pointing. "So it is true."

The Duchessa d'Elci squinted in the dark, just making out the shadow of a horse and rider sweeping past a man on foot, outlined against the lantern light.

Stella ran faster than she ever had that night. Giorgio timed our pace with the beat of his heart, his fingertips pressed against his wrist.

I leaned forward against the mare's mane, giving Stella more rein, my hands sliding along her neck as she contracted and exploded with each stride. My thighs and calves pressed tight against her barrel, clamped around the warmth of the mare.

I cast a quick glance behind me, smiling at what I saw.

Orione, his gangly legs not able to keep up with his mother, trailed behind, his ears plastered flat against his head.

"Brava, Virginia, brava!" called Giorgio. "You broke your record by five heartbeats!"

I pulled up the mare with gradual pressure on the bit, and Orione pranced neck to neck with his mother, snorting.

"Orione did a good job, too. Did you notice?" I said. I reached over to smooth his forelock between his eyes. "You will be a Palio horse someday, too, little one."

"I wonder," said Giorgio. "He is fast, yes, but looking at his legs and neck, I would say he is going to be a very big horse. He may not have the agility for the turns."

"I don't care. He is fast. And he has heart."

————————

"What audacity, riding your Palio mare!" stuttered Ernesto, his fists clenched in rage. "A girl, a shepherdess! Shall I arrest her this minute? And the stableman's son? I know him. Giorgio Brunelli, who paints at the academy. In your palazzo! What nerve!"

"Tranquillo," said the duchessa, resting her hand on his wrist.

"The driver will wait here while I find a soldier to detain him."

"You shall do nothing of the sort!" commanded the duchessa.

"But mia duchessa!"

"It seems both Stella and Orione are enjoying the exercise. I may run Stella one more time in the Palio. I consider this excellent training to have such a lightweight rider on her back. A bit extraordinary, but certainly a good workout."

The duchessa smiled in the dark. "This is my horse, and I will win on my terms. It will be a d'Elci victory, and our noble house will bring honor to all in the Contrada dell'Oca."

"I want you and the driver to forget what we have just witnessed," she said. "You must swear to me that you shall not whisper a word of this to anyone."

"Sì, mia duchessa. Sì."

"Now take me back to my warm fire. This hill mist will be the death of me. It is far too damp and cold for my old bones."

CHAPTER 31

Siena, Pugna Hills

NOVEMBER 1574

"Puttana!" shrieked Zia Claudia, her skin tight against her skull in anger.

She spat at me, sending a gob of phlegm shimmering on the grass.

"You whore!"

Whore?

I stared at her, not comprehending. I was still a child, but I knew full well what a puttana was: a painted woman who lurked in the shadows after dark, giving her body for money.

"You ingrate! After all we have done for you!"

My uncle restrained her, grabbing at her flailing hands, his body blocking her approach.

"Now the tanner's son will never want to marry you!" she screamed. "You—ruined by Brunelli's son! The red-haired demon who has no occupation but to spend his father's money on paints!"

I stared at her face, contorted with anger and bitterness. Slowly I realized her accusation. I was nothing to her but a prize ewe she could sell.

"Who told you?" was all I could say.

Zio answered, still engaged in subduing his wife.

"Your cousin Franco. He said he saw the two of you with the horses."

"But Zio, Franco is wrong," I said, pulling at his sleeve. "I ride. I ride the horses. Even Stella, the Palio winner."

Despite the effort to hold back my aunt, I saw a wave of pride cross Zio Giovanni's face.

"*You?*" he said, his eyes flashing open as if he saw me for the first time. "You—ride the Oca horses?"

He forgot about my zia and reached out to grab me by the shoulders.

"You *ride*, Virginia!" he said, emotion washing over his tired features. "Tell me—"

"Oh, Zio, how I have longed to share this with you! Sì, I have ridden Stella. She is faster than the wind. And Orione, he follows close behind—"

"Riding the duchessa's Palio mare!" Zia Claudia raised her arms to the heavens at this new outrage, this new terror. "A foolish girl astride a Palio horse? We must swear the boys to secrecy— bribe them if we must!"

I turned toward Zia.

"Oh, no," I said, standing firmly, facing her. "You are wrong. I want to show her. She shall be proud to see a girl on her mare."

Zia slumped to the ground, groaning.

"Help me get her to bed," said my uncle. "This is too much for her."

———

Once my zia knew of my nightly adventures, she forbade me to leave ever again after dark. I knew she would listen for me, sleeping lightly from then on to prevent my escape.

As I was thinking of the long nights that awaited me, with no horses to fill the minutes after midnight, I grew restless. Zia Claudia kept me busy scouring cooking pans with sand, ash, and ewe grease.

Zio Giovanni sat close to the hearth, poking the ember moodily.

"Harder," Zia said, watching me rub a pot's blackened bottom with a brush of red reeds.

As I bent my head closer to the pot, I saw a motion from the far end of the room.

"Wife, I have business to attend to," said Giovanni, rising to his feet. His voice was gruff.

"I will be back late tonight."

"Where do you go at this hour? What business—"

"*Basta*," he said, not answering her. "And leave the girl in peace!"

My uncle reached for his staff and cloak and disappeared into the falling darkness.

I spoke not a word to Zia Claudia in the hours after Zio left the house. She glowered at me, her eyes as hot and menacing as the burning embers in the fire.

Finally she spoke, her voice cutting through the hostile silence.

"You know what they say about horses and girls," said Zia, her eyes glittering. "Horses are for transport and necessity. A girl who loves to ride—"

"What? A girl who loves to ride, what?"

"A girl who loves to ride pleasures herself like a whore. What other enjoyment could there be?"

I stared at her, not understanding.

"You and that wicked red-haired devil. He put you up to this. To warm you up, to take you in the field, like a ram ruts a young ewe—"

Though I did not fully understand what Zia was saying that night, I felt the cold menace of her words, her shrunken heart. She could not see the beauty I felt when I was riding, the freedom and strength I gathered from galloping as the wind combed through my hair.

She cheapened my passion for horses to a whore's pleasure— something I could not even understand. Her words were ugly, destroying the magic I felt on a horse's back.

"You are a dirty, mean old woman!" I shouted. "I have always hated you!"

I ran out into the night, tears wet on my cheeks, chilling me.

I saw the silhouette of Zio walking up the hill. I raced down the path into his arms.

"Virginia!" he said. "What are you doing out in the night air? "

"I will leave, Zio!" I burst into tears again. I choked, and my nose began to run. "I will go live in the stables with my padrino."

Zio Giovanni took a rag from his sleeve.

"Blow," he said. "Clean that nose up and tell me what happened."

"Zia has said the most wicked things to me. She speaks of curses and dirty tales, she cannot understand the beauty of the horse—"

"Ah. We must convince her then, ciccia," he said, pulling me close. "Let us go into the house. I am chilled."

Inside, Zio Giovanni brought me next to the hearth. He sat next to me, stroking my hair. I felt Zia's spiteful stare boring into me. My zio pulled me close, sheltering me from her eyes.

His gentle touch, usually reserved for his favorite sheepdogs, calmed me.

"This is not the end of your training, Virginia," he whispered.

He tilted my chin up, forcing me to look at his brown eyes.

"On the contrary, it is only the beginning. I have talked to both Giorgio and your godfather. You start riding under your padrino's tutelage tomorrow. It is time to meet the true master. Cesare Brunelli shall instruct you himself."

"Davvero?"

I kissed my uncle on both cheeks, then kissed him again. Under the musk of hard work and sweat, he smelt warm, redolent of lambs and sweet grass.

"You are a Tacci," he whispered in my ear. "Let us see what the great horsemaster Brunelli can teach you."

CHAPTER 32

Siena, Brunelli Stables, Vignano

Once I began instruction under the famous Brunelli, everyone in Vignano and the Pugna Valley knew of my riding.

Villagers—and sometimes strangers from Siena—flanked the muddy field where my padrino gave me daily lessons.

Nobili from Siena drove out from the city in their lacquered coaches, waiting near the field where I rode. Even Siena's governor, Federigo di Montauto—a de' Medici official—came to watch me train. The noblemen raised their hands in animated gestures as I rode, finding points to criticize.

"Drive your heels down," they would say. "Chin up, leg down."

But the *nobila*—the noble ladies—would beam with delight, as if I were their own sister or daughter. Their faces would transform from restrained nobility to animated youth as they shouted from their carriages:

"Brava, pastorella Virginia! Brava!"

No longer was I permitted to ride Stella or the Oca horses. Now I rode mounts Brunelli selected for me—often as many as seven horses a day.

I ate, drank, and slept with horses. Never was there a minute I was parted from them.

"A fantino must know as many horses as possible in his education," said my godfather. "Each horse will teach you a different lesson. Only then will you be a true fantino."

"A fantina," I insisted, reining in the skittish mare he had selected that morning. The cold air made her shake with energy.

"I cannot change the Italian language. A jockey is a jockey. A fantino. Masculine," he insisted. He paused to think. "*Ragazza-fantino*," he said at last, compromising. A girl-jockey.

His mouth puckered at the strange word he had created.

"Now pay attention, do not talk back. "

"Sì, signore."

"Good," he said, watching me calm down the mare, who snorted and shied at the gathering of spectators.

"Do they have to be here?" I said. "Staring at me."

"And you are the girl who wants to ride the Palio? Get used to it, ciccia. There will always be an audience from now on. Ignore them. Only you and your horse exist."

As I rode out of the courtyard into the fenced pasture, a flock of little birds flew up from the pile of manure. The young mare Margherita jumped sideways as quickly as a thunderclap. I clamped my legs tight, barely able to stay on. I clung to her mane, pulling myself up straight again. I cooed soft words to her, calming the green filly.

"Yes, you look secure on a well-trained horse," said Padrino. "But I will put you on some wild ones. Then you will truly learn to ride."

"This mare is skittish enough, do you not think?"

"Ha!" he said. "Margherita is a child's pony compared to the horses you will ride soon!"

Someone in the crowd around the field shouted my name, and the mare shied sideways again as quickly as a bolt of lightning. She jumped in the air, skittering half a dozen steps sideways. I held tight, soothing her with my voice as I recovered my seat.

I knew the ground below me was frozen hard as stone. I had fallen off so many times in the last year, my legs and hips seemed permanently plum-colored. Only in the last few months had they started to turn pink again.

"Yes," he said. "Stretch your leg down the horse—even farther!—as if you were trying to reach the meadow grass with your feet. Pretend it is tickling your soles."

I smiled, stretching my thin legs down as far as they would reach. I heard the murmur of the village boys.

"Look at her skinny calves. More a scarecrow than a girl!"

"Silence!" shouted Brunelli. "If any man insults this girl, I shall thrash you myself."

Giorgio, on the edge of the field, shouted, "But not before I pummel you!" He rolled up his sleeves above his freckled arms.

A couple of young bucks sniggered at Giorgio's threat.

"Your bony fists can only hold paintbrushes, Michelangeletto!" said one.

"I could beat you into mush, you faggot!" said the other brawny youth.

But the crowd quickly silenced them. "Zitti! Shut your mouths! How dare you insult the girl, our ragazza-fantino!"

The two farmers' sons clenched their fists so their muscles bunched under their skin. They spat on the ground but held their tongues.

My padrino sucked in his breath, glowering at the boys.

"This is my goddaughter," he said, his voice loud but steady. "Do not forget this. An insult to her is an insult to me. And I will deal with you personally."

"And you, Rompicollo," said my padrino, "shall show all Italy what a Senese girl with a brave heart can accomplish on a horse."

A raucous cheer erupted, causing the two youths to drop their heads in shame. The sudden sound made Margherita jump sideways with me clinging to her back, my skinny legs clamped around her.

CHAPTER 33

Siena, Palazzo d' Elci

DECEMBER 1574

The day Giorgio saw Michelangelo's *Leda and the Swan*, a piece of his soul clicked into place.

He had always loved to draw horses—he had found passion in their instinct, majesty, and intuition. But they were beasts. He had never found perfect beauty and wild passion in humans, though he searched for it, an incessant thirst urging him on.

Except for one human subject: Virginia Tacci.

He had traveled to Florence once and felt his blood simmer as he stood before the statue of *David* in the Piazza della Signoria. He stood for hours taking in the curve of the muscle and curl of David's hair rendered in marble. The flawless white skin of a god-like creature emerging from the stone.

But that was perfection, not passion, he decided. And Michelangelo's *Pièta*, too, was perfection. Perfection of sorrow, the human condition. Yet still not passion. But *Leda and the Swan* was much more than mere perfection. The curve of Leda's thigh draped over the swan. The beast's beak reaching for her lips. The undulation of the swan's neck resting on Leda's breast. He had found erotic passion at last, between woman and animal, in the rendering of a myth.

He was aroused as he stood gazing at the canvas.

Giorgio was no stranger to the whorehouses of Siena. He had tried to find satisfaction between the legs of prostitutes, who kept a bucket and rag at the ready next to the musky straw pallets in the brothels.

But never had he seen the look of ecstasy that imbued the features of Leda. Never had he seen this transformation.

"Why do you stare at my face?" complained his favorite whore one night, catching sight of his glittering eyes. She reached out her long arm to snuff the candle, but he caught her by the wrist.

"Let me look at you," he pleaded. "Just a moment, let me study you."

"You look as if you lost a florin, the way you search. Close your eyes, signore. Then I can best perform my duties."

Giorgio was shaken from his reverie by the maestro's voice.

"Enjoy it, young Brunelli," he said. "You are one of the few Italians who will ever see her face, our Leda. Michelangelo himself is sending the painting to France for safekeeping. The Duke of Ferrara's envoy insulted it as salacious. Michelangelo has taken offense and will not send it to Castello d'Este, despite the duke's pleading."

"An authentic tragedy," Giorgio whispered. "For Italians not to see such beauty."

"More a tragedy should it be destroyed by the Pope," said the maestro. "Michelangelo fears the painting would not be safe in the Italian states."

Giorgio bowed his head. He returned to his work, dabbing the merest hint of hematite on the flesh of his Leda's lips. Then he set his eyes once more on the masterpiece before him.

"Look how smooth the gesso is on the wood panel," he said.

The maestro nodded. "Without a perfect foundation, the artist's skill is wasted. I suspect Michelangelo has legions of apprentices who would rather die than deliver a flawed panel to their master."

"I cannot begin to match even the preparation of the paints and canvas, let alone imitate his skill." Again Giorgio gazed at Leda's face. "I have never seen such a look of human divinity—"

"Of ecstasy, Giorgio. The transportation of the soul is hardly something a man would witness . . ." The maestro shrugged.

"In a brothel?" said Giorgio. He looked up at the old man. "That is what you were going to say, was it not?"

"Sì. I suspect at your age and station in life," said the maestro, smiling indulgently, "it is not an emotion you have encountered. Yet."

Giorgio blushed, studying the bristles on his paintbrush.

"As always, maestro, your wisdom far exceeds my knowledge. But there is something in this piece that won't release me. The artist has pulled back the curtain, we are voyeurs. It gives me— *brividi.* Look at the prickled flesh on my arm!" he said, extending his arm and pulling up his sleeve.

"Yes," said the maestro, nodding. He dragged a knuckle across his moist eye. "Despite my age, I feel those same shivers." He stepped closer to the painting. "A ghost of my youth. But it is the transformation, the nudity not just of the body, but of the soul. A masterpiece."

Giorgio set down his brush. "It is enough for me to give up painting forever. I could never capture that magic."

The maestro shifted his eyes to his pupil.

"Do not be so sure, Brunelli. I believe you have a gift, *mio studente.*" He put his hand on the youth's shoulder.

"Your horses," whispered the maestro. "Perhaps you do not have a Leda in your life, but your horses are imbued with a divine strength, Giorgio. There is something rebellious, magnificent about your renderings. Passion is not only sexual. Follow your vision."

Giorgio looked into his teacher's eyes.

"Yet in class, in front of di Torreforte and all the Florentines—"

"I had to. But that did not mean your work was not magnificent. I trust that you, as an artist, could not bear to destroy such a painting."

Giorgio raised his chin.

"An artist must find his medium. And his muse," said the maestro, inspecting his student's canvas. He put on his spectacles and leaned so close, Giorgio expected his maestro's nose to come away smudged with paint.

"And your muse is not Leda, nor is it a swan."

CHAPTER 34

Siena, Pugna Hills

In spite of the lessons and work with the horses at my padrino's, I still had to guard the old and fallow ewes at night. I preferred the company of the sheep to my aunt. There was a soothing quality to the rhythmic sound of the old girls chewing their cuds.

Even though I was still a pastorella, spending half my life with sheep, I noticed the village of Vignano began to treat me differently.

Shepherd boys who had never looked my way found an excuse to move their flocks nearer my ewes on the hills. When I brought the washing down by the stream, girls argued over who would take the rock next to mine to scrub their clothes.

"What is it like to ride a horse?" they asked, their eyes gleaming with excitement.

"How do you keep from falling off? Does the wind whistle in your ears as you gallop?"

But not everyone was pleased.

Nothing I did could please my aunt, of course, but I soon discovered Zia Claudia had an ally in the church, Father Alfredo, an emaciated old priest whose dry skin clung tightly to his skull like a corpse's.

Watching him from the pew, I could see the veins stand out on his forehead when he got angry. He shook his skeletal finger at the congregation, threatening us with God's wrath.

He especially cursed the pagan Brunelli, "a horse sorcerer amongst our Vignano flock."

One Sunday, the priest delivered a sermon on the responsibilities of women and our duties—given that we were made from the rib of Adam.

"Girls and women should serve God and Man, in that order, which was prescribed in the Bible." His mouth was wrinkled so tight, it was a wonder he could spit the words out. "Shepherding is a noble profession." He switched his focus, as if my zia had written the sermon for him. "Though some may think it beneath them."

"Pay attention, ragazza," said my zia, pinching me.

"Stories of shepherds are woven throughout the Bible," said the priest.

The congregation nodded their heads, the motion sending the scent of greasy hair and rarely washed bodies through the close, damp air of the tiny church.

"Who were the first visitors to the manger in Bethlehem? Is God the Lord not likened to a shepherd? Are we as innocents not referred to as his lambs?"

"Amen," whispered Zia. She slid her eyes toward me.

"A shepherd's livelihood gives time for reflection and prayer," said the priest. "Those hours can either be spent in devotion or idled away contemplating the devil's own ambition."

Franco, my cousin, sat directly in front of me, for he alternated Sundays with his brother, one always with the flock. My cousin smelled of sheep dung mixed with lye soap. A foamy crust still clung to his right ear where his mother had made him wash. Now he turned around, casting an accusatory look at me.

"Look away," I hissed. "Your ugly face makes my breakfast leap into my throat."

His mother tugged him by the ear, making him look back up at the priest.

"Shh!" Zia Claudia admonished.

"Give thanks for your profession, be content with your lot," said the priest. "To reach beyond the station God has assigned us is a serious sin indeed. It is the devil who urges us to reach our greedy hands up, trying to grasp the stars that belong to God alone!"

The priest fixed his eyes on me. I stared back defiantly, itching to get on a horse and ride far away from the dried-up old clergyman, my vicious zia, the smell of the congregation. Most of us were shepherds. The wet sheep dung clinging to the soles of their boots sickened me.

Time for reflection, yes.

And every moment I thought of horses.

I toted a bucket to the stables from the well. The water sloshed over the warped wooden sides. My padrino was tacking the last nail of a horseshoe into a mare's hoof.

"The thrush is better," he said. "It's the power of a new moon."

"What?"

"*Una luna piena* excites nature," he said. "What is growing will grow faster. What is good, better. What is bad, worse."

"What do you mean, Padrino?"

"Say a mare has thrush, rotting at her foot. If she is on the mend as the moon swells, her flesh will heal until it is sweet as a colt's. But a horse who has not responded to treatment? As the moon fills, the stink of its putrid hoof will fill the air."

He nodded sharply to underline the message.

"Never start a colt under a full moon. You invite the devil."

The devil? I looked up at him, thinking of what my zia had said, how my padrino would never cross the threshold of a church.

"A moon enhances. Only fools fight the moon," said Padrino, giving the mare a pat on the rump.

"Padrino," I asked. "What is a pagan?"

He removed the nail from his mouth and pounded it into the perforation in the iron shoe. He set down the horse's hoof, straightening his back with a wince.

"Your zia has been talking to you again about me?"

I shrugged. "The priest talked about pagans."

"Ah! The priest. Yes, of course. If we were all pagans, the nasty bastard would be out of a job."

"So what is it?"

Padrino untied the horse from the iron ring by the anvil. He led her to the stable highline where he tied the horses.

"She walks fine," he grunted. "Her new shoes suit her."

"A pagan. What is a pagan?" I insisted.

His fingers fashioned a quick slipknot while he answered. "A pagan is anyone who does not worship the way you do."

Yes. That would describe il mio padrino in the priest's eyes.

"But . . . then will that soul not enter the gates of heaven?"

"Heaven?" he scoffed. "My Virginia, cara. I do not presume to know where I will go after this life. When I die, I have only one wish. I want to be buried in Corsano, where I was born. Under the cypress tree near our stone stable, where my father and I buried so many horses in my youth. Beyond that . . . well, I will not pretend I know what happens after death. All I can try is to do good here on Earth. Healing and training horses. Horses are my connection to the sacred."

I nodded my head, drinking in the smell of horse and straw. I had always loved the majestic cypress trees lining the road to Quattro Torra. And the connection to horses—

"Padrino," I said. "I think I will be a pagan, too."

CHAPTER 35

Siena, Palazzo d' Elci

MAY 1576

Giorgio Brunelli watched the men wrap the painting in velvet and secure it in a trunk.

It was the last time anyone in Italy would see *Leda and the Swan*.

As they carried the trunk away, Giorgio felt a hollowness in his chest. He swallowed hard, watching the coach drive away with the painting.

"I know," said the maestro, cupping his hand around the young man's shoulder.

Giorgio was astonished to find his eyes hot with tears. He blinked them away.

"Michelangelo has touched your soul," said the maestro. "Keep that feeling, keep searching for that emotion in your art, my young Brunelli. Discover what haunts you. Then you will be a true artist."

Giorgio sighed, his breath catching in his throat.

"How can I ever forget this painting? And yet, maestro, my greatest fear is that I *will* forget. I will forget the perfect lines, the emotion in Leda's face and body. I am terrified it will become a smudge in my memory."

The maestro shook his head. Then he took Giorgio's hand in his. He held it gently.

"Not with this hand of yours," he said. "Our fickle minds may forget dignity and beauty, but the hand of a true artist will never forget."

CHAPTER 36

Fiesole

JUNE 1576

Firelight played on skin beaded in sweat.

Pietro looked up from between his mistress's moist thighs. He wiped his mouth, smiling with pride. He glimpsed the slightest flicker of her black lashes, a glimmer of light from her green eyes.

"Did I pleasure you, my lady?" he asked, climbing up her body and kissing her parted lips. He drew back his head to study her reaction.

Carlotta arched an eyebrow, her hand crossing her brow languidly.

"It was gratifying. And did you receive pleasure in turn?" she whispered. She gently pushed the de' Medici prince off her body.

The linen sheets were damp and tangled around Carlotta. She sat up and unwound them.

Pietro frowned. "Lie back down with me," he commanded.

"Not until I remove these fetters," she said. "I feel as if I am in bondage."

She kicked free of the sheets, and her face relaxed in victorious relief. When she lay down beside Pietro, she saw the mean glitter in his eye.

"I asked, my dearest, if I pleasured you?" said Pietro.

"Of course." Carlotta raked her fingers through her tangled hair.

"Of course?" he said. "Is that all you can say? Did I not send you into ecstasy with my tongue?"

Carlotta laughed.

"It is a very useful tongue indeed. Perhaps not meant for poetry and wooing, but it serves quite well as you have employed it."

Pietro set his lips in a sour pout.

"My mistresses in Spain glow with my touch. They beg me for more, worship—"

"Ah," said Carlotta. "You are speaking of the Spanish whores, my lord?"

Pietro sat up abruptly.

"Not at all!" he said, scowling. "Courtesans of the highest breeding."

Carlotta shrugged, continuing to comb her long hair with her fingers, plucking at a knot, tangled from their lovemaking.

Pietro grabbed her neck passionately. He threw her against the mattress, covering her throat and the tops of her breasts with kisses.

"You drive me into a frenzy of lust, Carlotta. I cannot think of anyone, of anything but you. These months in Madrid have made me wild with desire—"

He loosened his grip on her neck, kissing her large, plum-colored nipples.

"And your wife?" she whispered. "Did you not miss her? Your son?"

Pietro's lips lingered above hers just long enough to answer.

"I love only you. Would that I be rid of them both!"

Pietro washed in the basin of water set out for him in the kitchen. He shivered as he doused his face with icy water, drops dripping through his cupped hands.

Carlotta could see by his distracted motions that he was scheming. A quick shiver seized her, a dark cloud obliterating the sun. He dried himself with a linen cloth and looked up at her.

"I want poison. Poison that will kill, leaving no trace."

Carlotta flinched.

"And why do you ask me, amore?"

Pietro glanced at the herbs that dangled from the rafters above her head. Carlotta's kitchen was an upside-down garden with bunches of dried flowers and brittle leaves sprouting from the beams, growing top-down.

"My little prince," she purred, "I hear it is your brother the granduca who concocts the most potent poisons in Italy. Far more subtle than the Borgias', it is rumored."

Pietro's face buckled in an ugly frown. He grabbed her wrist, swinging her around to face him.

"It is treason to speak of the granduca in such a manner!"

"Ah, now you accuse me of treason. Such lovely compliments. Let go of my hand, Pietro de' Medici."

Pietro tightened his grip on her hand. For a moment they glared at one another, then he dropped it.

"That is better," she said, her nostrils pinching as if she smelled something rotten. She turned away from him.

"Carlotta—you *do* have poisons, do you not? Everyone says you are a witch!"

Carlotta turned again to regard him, a furious smile half-born on her face.

"And you, my lord, believe them?"

"The Strega of Fiesole, they call you. Your cures heal those who are sick."

"And my poisons?"

"Kill without trace," whispered Pietro, looking over his shoulder, though they were always alone in the house. "That is the potion I am in need of now. Give it to me!"

Carlotta pinched herbs from overhead, hurling them in the boiling cauldron. She whirled around to face the de' Medici prince, her face red and beaded with sweat.

"Well, you are wrong, Pietro de' Medici. You think because I share my bed with you that I will help you to murder an innocent."

Pietro stared at her, perplexed.

"How dare you address a de' Medici thus!"

"How dare I? I dare indeed. That and more. Maybe it is time for you to visit your wife and child at Palazzo Pitti." Carlotta stared down at the bubbling liquid in the cauldron. "I shall send a boy to the stable to bring your horse at once."

PART III

Murder in Tuscany

ANNI 1576–1578

CHAPTER 37

Tuscany
JULY 1576

Cafaggiolio, the most ancient of the de' Medici villas, lay several hours' travel north of Florence. With its crenellated walls and tower, the villa looked remarkably like the Palazzo Vecchio in Florence.

As the coach rumbled north from Florence, Leonora dabbed her eyes with her kerchief. The summer dust of the road penetrated the silk curtains of the carriage, coating her clothes and skin.

Pietro sat across from her, his face rigid and sullen. His expression never changed, despite the rocking and sudden jolts as the carriage ran over the rutted road.

Little Cosimo, usually so mobile and curious, sat motionless. He stared at the stitching of his mother's skirts rather than lift his eyes to his father's face.

"How fine we should have time together," said Leonora, stroking little Cosimo's head. "Just the three of us, away from the Court and the heat of Florence."

Pietro did not answer but pulled the curtains wide to watch the progress along the road.

Both Leonora and Cosimo moved away from the window, coughing, as dust blew into the coach.

Peasants walking along the road stared, wide-eyed, at the de' Medici coach. Leonora caught sight of an old woman with a bundle of fagots strapped to her back. The woman's face was a map of creases, her gray head covered with a black shawl. Leonora's last glimpse out the window was the woman mouthing words to her, making the sign of the cross with her gnarled hand.

Leonora shuddered, pulling Cosimo close to her, despite his sticky dampness.

Her mind flew to the latest missives from Naples. Both her father, Garza, and her uncle Luigi begged her to leave Florence at once and come directly to the kingdom of Napoli.

Leonora, now more de' Medici than di Toledo, was troubled by their concern. Surely they must have reason to want her to leave her husband. She wondered what secrets and what gossip had prompted them to demand she return to Naples.

What did they know in Naples that she did not?

———

The de' Medici retinue had arrived at Cafaggiolio the day before to ready the villa for their master and mistress.

Maria took little Cosimo in her arms, kissing his cheeks while murmuring endearments in Spanish. She turned and handed the boy to an Italian maid, with instructions to take him directly into the kitchen to be fed his luncheon.

"Madonna," said Maria, her old knees creaking under the burden of a curtsy. "How was the trip from Florence?"

"Get out of our way!" snapped Pietro, nearly pushing his wife out of the carriage.

A footman stepped forward, taking Leonora's hand so she did not stumble and fall.

"Grazie, Simone," said Leonora with relief. She swallowed quickly, regaining her composure. But her cheeks burned with humiliation.

"I have a great need to make water," Pietro said, bolting from the coach. "You and the lady can make your hen cluckings in her chambers, beyond my earshot. Such chatter gives me a headache."

As he strode toward a manicured shrub, Leonora caught her breath. She struggled to remain calm.

"Cafaggiolio is looking grand under your expert care," she said to the servants clustered around her. "I commend your efforts. I am sure we will be most pleased with our stay here."

"All the arrangements for tonight's dinner party and dancing have been made," said Pietro's secretary. He cast a quick look at the bush and his master. Seeing him ill disposed, he turned to Leonora.

"I am sure you will find a sufficiency of gaieties planned, my duchessa. And the hunting is said to be superb this year. We have your two favorite horses awaiting you in the stable."

"Perfetto!" said Leonora, smiling. She breathed in the scent of freshly cropped hay in the fields. "What a relief to leave Florence for the wholesome goodness of the countryside. Sweet Cafaggiolio has never looked so lovely in my eyes."

As Leonora picked up her skirts to walk in the villa, a black crow flew from the cypress trees to the high wall, cawing harshly in the sunshine.

———

The evening's guests included nobili who had summer homes in the north and who were gladdened by the de' Medici invitation to dine.

"She is truly a beauty," said a neighboring nobleman, Signor Mignone, gesturing with his wine goblet to Leonora on the dance floor. "Duca, you certainly have the most beautiful woman in all Tuscany."

"Shut up," said Pietro, gulping what was left in his goblet.

The nobleman gasped at the insult. Before he could reply, Pietro added, "See how she dances without a care as to how tired I am. I loathe the air she breathes, the—"

A servant with an accent from Romagna, to the east, poured the de' Medici prince more wine.

"Excuse me, sir," he said, his dark eyes gleaming. "Shall I inform the lady you would like to retire?"

Signor Mignone watched Pietro exchange looks with the servant. How strange he should import a servant from Romagna when his Florentine retinue had accompanied him.

Pietro de' Medici was a strange being, Mignone thought, and never remotely equal to his enchanting wife.

———

"What a fine reception to Cafaggiolo!" said Leonora, lifting her arms so that the maids could remove her linen chemise. "I am afraid I have dampened all my clothes with my dancing. Such dashing men—"

"Will you wear the beaded nightdress, my lady? With the lace-work at the neckline?"

A frown flickered over Leonora's face. She did not wish a conjugal visit from her husband, but the way he had watched her with hungry eyes that night had made the event a possibility.

Leonora exchanged a look with Maria, who nodded, lowering her eyes. It was her signal that the duca had requested that his wife visit his chambers.

"Yes, please, Maria. And my perfumed oil, please. I will have you scent my clothes, please."

Leonora sat down at her dressing table as Maria, tired and wan, brushed her mistress's long red hair.

"I wish you would take my invitation to forgo these late nights, Maria," said Leonora, catching the old woman's eyes in her looking glass. "It is far too late for you to be up."

"Whenever you need me, I shall be here," said Maria, her smiling eyes crinkling with crow's-feet. But she stifled a yawn, born from fatigue deep in her bones. "And who else can untangle your hair as well as I? Have I not cared for you since you were a baby?"

Leonora's heart ached suddenly for her dead mother.

"I love you, Maria," she said. "Dearly."

Maria stopped the brush halfway down her mistress's tresses. She sought Leonora's eyes in the mirror.

"That is the dearest gift you could ever give me," said the servant. "I have loved you since the day you were born." Her eyes misted.

A ferocious rap at the door made them both jump. A second later, three men rushed into the room.

Leonora started to scream when a hand was clapped over her mouth.

"Your husband, Pietro de' Medici, commanded us to prepare you for his visit."

A bearded man pushed Leonora's old maid along the red tiled corridor to her small bedchamber.

"Go, old woman. Gather your belongings," he snarled. "You will have only a minute to take what you can carry."

Maria stumbled in the dim light, the flickering sconces casting pools of moving shadows in the dark hall. She was too shocked to cry, too shaken to protest.

In her room, Maria's hands fumbled among her few belongings. She took the crucifix given to her on her Saint's Day by her mother, and a locket with a strand of red hair from her beloved mistress.

She wrapped her gray hair in a black woolen shawl. Furtively she made the sign of the cross, and then kissed her fingertips.

"Adesso!" said the guard. Now! "The coach is waiting."

The old servant stared in bewilderment.

The guard pushed her toward the stone staircase. Pietro appeared above, his bulging eyes staring down the flight of stairs. His mouth was twisted in rage.

"Get rid of her!"

The guard pushed the old woman again, making her stumble and grasp the marble banister.

Above her, she could hear Leonora's sobbing.

"But. My mistress—"

"Get in the coach, you old Spanish cow," hissed the guard, "before he commands me to break your neck."

CHAPTER 38

Florence, Palazzo de' Medici, Via Larga
JULY 1576

Isabella opened her window wide, despite the street noise of the Florentine night. Midsummer, it was nearly impossible to sleep. She could smell the approach of rain, a mineral tang in the first cooling breeze of the season. The dampness would bring the deer out from the woods, making for good hunting.

Still, Isabella shuddered, thinking ahead to the next few weeks with her husband, Paolo Orsini.

"Come away from the window," whispered her lover. "I cannot bear your absence. There has been too much of that."

The de' Medici princess smiled, studying Troilo Orsini's body twisted in the sheets. His left flank was naked, and she could make out the strong riding muscles in his buttocks and thighs. His jousting arm was sculpted with sinewy tendons and hard muscle, born from carrying and thrusting the heavy lance. His aquiline nose, aristocratic and thoroughly Orsini, tilted toward her, eager to nuzzle her neck. No wonder he was a favorite in the Court of Catherine de' Medici.

She thought of the thick bands of fat that circled the waist of Troilo's cousin, her husband, Paolo. Next week, Paolo would take her to the de' Medici estate of Cerreto Guidi for time together as man and wife.

His sudden affectionate letters made her skin prickle with fear. She began counting Paolo's mistresses, slowly touching her fingertips in the dark.

Isabella, deep in thought, jumped when she heard Troilo's voice from the bed.

"Why do you torture me? Come back to my arms, Isabella."

Isabella gave a last look out the window, her eyes searching in the blackness of the clouds.

"It is going to storm," she said, sliding back into her lover's arms.

"All the better to mask your screams of pleasure," said Troilo, sliding his lips down her neck.

The first clap of thunder struck. Isabella shuddered.

"Is that from the thunder or my kisses?" said Troilo.

A rap on the door made them both freeze.

"Quickly," said Isabella. "Into my dressing room."

She donned her chemise and robe.

"Who is it?"

One of her ladies-in-waiting entered the chamber.

"Forgive me, my lady," she said. "I would not disturb you—"

"Speak!"

"The Spanish maid, Maria, Leonora's servant, begs to speak to you in private. She says it is a matter of life or death."

"Show her in immediately!"

Old Maria, wet as a ship rat and smelling of damp wool, entered Isabella's bedchamber. Her clothes were splattered in mud, her face white as chalk.

"Come in, Maria. What has happened? Here, sit in a chair before you collapse."

The maidservant helped the old woman to a chair, then began lighting candles around the room.

"Lucia, send for some wine to revive her."

When the door closed, Isabella knelt beside the old servant. She took her hand.

"What has happened? Why are you not with Leonora?"

"Oh, my lady! They dragged me from her bedchamber. Your brother Pietro. I have never seen his face more bedeviled."

"Why did you take your leave?"

"The guards forced me, shoving me into the coach. They left me on a wet, muddied road outside Florence's gates."

"Leonora? How fares she?"

"In great danger, my lady. I fear for her life. We waited in the courtyard a few moments before the coach drove away—there was some problem with the horse, the driver was shouting. The lights were still ablaze in the master's chamber. And I saw her silhouette in the window, her hand raised, fending off someone. The Duca de' Medici, if I dare say so."

"And then?"

"I heard him scream in pain, in agony. A screech to raise the devil!"

"And then?"

"Then two large silhouettes blocked the window."

Maria broke into sobs, her face in her hands.

"My lady, forgive me. They were pulling her away."

CHAPTER 39

Florence, Palazzo Vecchio
JULY 12, 1576

The first light of dawn brought out the street sweepers, their red reed brushes scraping rhythmically at the wet cobblestones of the Piazza della Signoria.

The half dozen men raised their eyes at the clatter of Isabella's coach, approaching the Palazzo Vecchio at a full gallop.

"Mala fortuna," said a grizzled old man, resting on his broomstick.

The other men grunted, shaking their heads in the pale light.

———

"Francesco, I think Pietro has plotted to murder our cousin!"

Francesco sipped his morning tea as his sister stood before him, white-faced.

He set down his cup with a clatter, his fingertips flying to his burnt lip.

"This is too damned hot," he snapped to the servant.

"Francesco!" said Isabella, grabbing his shoulder and shaking it. "You must send the guards at once! Leonora's servant informed me an hour ago. It may be too late already!"

"My sister, you must calm yourself," he said, removing her hand from his shoulder.

"I will not!"

"I am sure the maidservant is suffering delusions. I found her Spanish prejudice against our family to be insulting—I am glad she was finally dismissed."

"Your Highness," said Serguidi. "I am sorry to interrupt. But I have a letter."

"It must be an important letter for you to interrupt a conversation between us!" said Isabella.

Serguidi bowed.

"I fear it is . . . most important."

Francesco broke the seal and unfolded the letter. His eyes raced across the words. He called, "Servant. Bring grappa for the duchessa at once."

Then he passed the letter to his sister.

Isabella reached for the letter, seeking her brother's eyes. He drew a long breath and refused to look at her.

With trembling hands, she held the letter.

"*Last night, at seven o'clock, an accidental death came to my wife. I beg you to write and instruct me what I should do, if I should come home or not.*"

Isabella crumpled into herself, her body shrinking in her chair.

"Your grappa, my lady," said the manservant. He looked nervously from the granduca to the duchessa.

"Drink it, Isabella," said Francesco without emotion, not moving from his chair. "You need it. You must compose yourself, sister. Do not forget you are a de' Medici."

CHAPTER 40

Florence, Palazzo d' Este

JULY 1576

The Duca di Ferrara set down his goblet of wine, his ringed fingers unfolding the encrypted letter from his ambassador at the Florentine court.

"Scribe!" he called. "Interpret this letter."

The scribe rushed to his desk to find the tablet with the key to Cortile's code.

"Read it at once!" snapped the duca.

The scribe fixed his spectacle on his nose, bending over the soft vellum.

"It seems Lady Elenora di Toledo de' Medici has been murdered, duca mio," said the scribe.

"What?" gasped the duke. "Leonora? Murdered?"

"Yes, it seems so. I—"

"Read the details!"

"She was strangled with a dog leash by Don Pietro."

The scribe looked up from the cryptogram, his eyes blinking behind the glass lenses.

"Go on!" shouted the Duca di Ferrara.

"*And died after a great deal of struggle. Don Pietro bears the sign, having two fingers injured from the bite of the lady.*"

The scribe paused to study the encrypted message, then read on.

"*He might have come off worse were it not that he called for help from two villains from Romagna, who, it is said, had been brought to the villa for that purpose.*"

"That *purpose*? The swine could not murder his young wife without the help of two brutes? From our provinces?"

The scribe, befuddled and frightened, said nothing. He bent his head once more over the letter, his index finger searching on the key for the appropriate letters.

"*The poor lady, it is understood, put up the greatest defense, as was seen from the state of the bed, found all tumbled, and from the voices heard throughout the house.*"

"Good God!" said the duca, running a finger through his hair. "Are there swine anywhere more vile than the de' Medici?"

CHAPTER 41

Siena, Pugna Hills

JULY 1576

Despite my tutelage in riding, Padrino would not teach me to jump.

"No Palio rider needs to jump a horse except to mount him!" he scoffed. "Put that idea out of your head."

But the image of Isabella de' Medici soaring over the fallen olive tree danced in my memory, in my dreams.

My padrino insisted we work on the basics of riding.

If I was not to be taught to jump a horse by Brunelli, I would teach myself. But first, there was a colt that needed to be broken. Then we would jump.

I slipped out of the stables with an old bridle that was never used, the iron rusty, the leather reins chewed by rats. In the cold lambing shed on winter nights, I filed away the rust until the bit was smooth and the iron shining once more. Then I hid the bridle in the hay pile.

———

Orione galloped to the stone wall, snorting. The muscles under his neck bunched and curled like a snake, waiting to spring. He had grown to be a solid three-year-old, big-boned like his father, with a glossy black coat.

His star gleamed bright in the full moonlight, dancing around erratically as he shook his head at my approach.

"Good boy," I said. "You and I are going to learn to jump together."

I did not realize how foolish I was. I was too blinded by my love for Orione to see the danger. And I had forgotten what my padrino had told me about the danger of a full moon.

"We will do what the de' Medici princess did, but we will do it even better, because we are both Senese, you and I," I said, rubbing his star. "Senese always do things better than Florentines."

Orione threw his head, pushing away my hand.

I tried again.

"Now. First you must hold very still. I will put something in your mouth. Yes, caro, it will feel hard against your mouth. But you must not worry."

Orione looked at me dubiously.

"Here," I said, hovering the bridle above his head. "We will just slip my thumb in here, and you will take the bit like this—"

The cool iron of the bit touched his teeth and tongue. I sensed raw anger in the air, like an electrical storm. He reared up next to me, the whites of his eyes shining in the dark.

"Orione! It's me, *la tua* Virginia!"

His hooves sliced the night as I covered my face. He came down hard against me, banging my shoulder and knocking me to the ground. A copper taste filled my mouth. I realized I had bitten my tongue.

The whites of his eyes shone in the moonlight. He backed up a few steps, snorting.

Bits of spittle flecked my bodice.

"No, you brute," I said, slapping the spit off my clothes. "We are going to prove them wrong. You will be ridden. You will not become another Tempesta, locked away for life."

As I approached him, he reared again, high off the ground. He shook his head, menacing me. I caught my breath, chasing away the memory of Tempesta nearly killing me. "No, caro. We must do this."

I took a step closer. "Here," I said, hovering the bridle above his head. "Slowly, now—"

He reared up next to me, spinning on his hind legs. He knocked me to the ground once more.

"Figlio di puttana!" I screamed. "Bastardo!"

Scrambling to my feet, I shook my fist in his face.

"If you cannot be ridden, they will wall you up someplace or even shoot you. You must—"

Orione took a step toward me and bit my arm. His teeth clamped hard and fast, striking like a viper.

"Ow!" I screamed. "Ow! Stronzo! *Testa di cazzo!*"

I swung my leg up from under my skirt and kicked him as hard as I could in the belly. He grunted in pain, galloping away.

I crouched over, holding my arm. I pulled up my sleeve and saw the teethmarks where Orione had miraculously not broken the skin, but pinched deep into my muscle.

"I hate you!" I screamed, my cry echoing across the hills. "Do you hear me? I am sorry I ever saved your life, you wretched horse!"

I crawled over the stone wall, clutching my arm.

———

In the nights that followed, I tried other ways of persuading Orione to take the bridle. I rubbed the bit in crushed apple to sweeten the taste. I hummed "Per Forza e Amore" to him, the song I had sung the night he was born.

He would mouth the bit, curious at the taste of apple. But time and time again, he threw his head, refusing to let me bridle him. He had grown strong and broad across his chest and muscled in the neck, and he looked more like the stallion he was.

Still, he followed me whenever I was near the pasture. He paralleled the stone wall as I moved with the sheep, racing back and forth, shaking his head. He wanted to be near me. But he would not let me place a bit in his mouth.

My cousin Franco caught my sleeve one afternoon as I was working with the dog, dividing my ewes from the herd.

"That colt needs cutting," he said, gesturing down the hill to the pasture.

I pushed away the memory of Orione's slamming against my shoulder when I tried to bridle him.

"As if you knew anything about horses," I retorted over the backs of my sheep. "Tend to your flock and stay out of my business."

I turned away from my cousin. I leveled my staff over the sheep I wanted cut from the herd, drawing an invisible line among them. The dog picked them out one by one.

"I know about uncastrated males," said Franco, spitting thickly on the grass. "You can see the danger in that one. No matter whether you saved his life or not. That stallion has Tempesta in him. If they don't cut him, his *coglioni* will rule him. His father killed two men. He looks just like his father did at his age. They should castrate him now before he kills you."

"Shut up, Franco. Come on, Dog!" I shouted.

———

I developed a plan. If Orione could not abide the taste of iron in his mouth, I would not fight him.

The collo di cavallo now hung in the Brunelli stables in a place of prominence, near the entry. I had insisted it belonged to my padrino as much as me. Also, I did not trust Zia Claudia with such a treasure.

While rubbing down a horse I had just ridden, I took the collo from its hook, folding it in the shepherd's bag I wore slung across my chest when I wandered the hills.

"What are you doing with that?" asked Giorgio.

I whirled around, gasping, my hand to my heart.

"You always appear from nowhere! Why are you always spying on me?"

"I asked a simple question. The collo."

"I need it. La duchessa gave it to me. I can do what I want with it."

"I never questioned that. What are you going to do with it?"

"Never you mind," I said, turning away to rub my horse's steaming back. "Go back to your painting and leave me alone."

———

Now, with the collo di cavallo, I was ready to try again. But the night before I planned to ride, when the moon was only a sliver, I heard galloping hooves.

I rose from the straw and lit the lantern. I ran out, trying desperately to see in the darkness. I heard a whinny, high-pitched and raw.

In the night, I saw his star beyond the stone wall. He galloped toward me, smelling my scent as the wind changed direction.

"No, Orione. *No!*"

The paddock meant to contain him had been built more than two *braccia* high, the height of my shoulder. He would break a leg.

I heard more than I saw. The drum of his hooves churning up the turf, nearing the wall. And the silence.

The silence as Orione lifted off the ground, soaring over the stone barrier.

A two-beat thud and the hoofbeats resuming.

His star danced in the dim light as he approached me. He trotted the last few paces, dropping his head. He stood before me in the pool of light cast by the lantern.

I buried my head in his mane, breathing in the warm, salty horse scent.

"You jumped," I said. "You! You did it without me. What kind of friend are you, *ingrato*?"

Orione snorted and his lips stretched out, gently searching my apron for apples.

"Wait here," I said.

But of course, he didn't. He followed me right into the lambing sheds where he had been born.

Under the straw, I had buried some apples in a wooden box so the mice would not find them. I opened the lid and felt Orione's head on my shoulder, looking on. I chose the biggest and fed him, the weight of his head comforting me.

He took the apple tenderly.

We stood together for a moment. I looked at the corner of the lambing sheds, remembering the day he was born.

"What do you think, Orione?"

He chewed on the apple, regarding me in the lantern light.

"Tonight, I will ride you. But not with the bit. You have won that battle."

I gently pushed his head away and walked to the cot where I had stored the collo.

"Isn't it beautiful?" I said to him. "This was your mother's. The day she won the Palio."

Orione looked wary. But as I fingered the ribbons, feeling their silky touch, he grew more interested.

He approached me. His lips stretched out to nibble the ribbons.

"Not to eat," I warned him, pulling away. "It is the souvenir of your mother's victory."

I stroked his neck, feeling the warm life under my fingers. I looked back at the straw-strewn corner where he was born.

"I wonder if you can remember," I said, reaching both arms around his neck. "How far back can horses recall?"

The stars twinkled beyond the open shed. My eyes searched for the constellation, his namesake.

High above us, it sparkled bright.

I must be pazza, *crazy, to ride an unbroken colt on a dark winter night. I could end up lying on the frozen ground with broken bones.*

Rompicollo.

A broken neck. My cousins would not find me until morning.

"Easy, now," I said. I showed Orione the collo. I rubbed it against his neck, his lips, his muzzle. He sniffed, pulling in its scent. He curled his lip up, showing his teeth in the comical way horses do.

"Do not insult the collo, Orione," I said. "It represents great honor."

He backed up, his nostrils flaring.

"See how beautiful it is, Orione."

I slipped the collo over my own neck. I held the rope in my hand, twisting the end into a knot. Now I had two reins to hold.

I rubbed his muzzle, my hand flat against his lips.

"You see! No iron bit. You will be as free as the day you were born. Just the two of us. See how I wear it?"

I put the halter around my head, the leather cavesson against my nose. Orione flared his nostrils, his breath warm against my check as he sniffed the collo. He shook his head, retreating.

"With this, we can jump the way she did, Orione. You and me. Together."

Turning my back on Orione, I walked out into the inky darkness. He followed close behind me. I walked to the stone wall.

When I turned again, he stood with his ears alert and forward. "You want to try?"

We touched heads, the crown of my head against his star. Slowly, ever so slowly, I lifted the collo over my head. I let the weight of it rest against his forelock.

He did not pull back. When I lifted my head, he stood his ground.

"Now," I said, unbuckling the left strap. "Let me do this, Orione. Come on, boy."

I slipped the collo below his nose.

"That's my good boy. Bravo, ragazzo!" I whispered as I pulled it up.

He stood, it seemed, almost against his will. I saw his flesh twitch as I buckled the strap. My hand stroked his neck.

"Bravo, bravo," I cooed.

He mouthed the remains of the apple. He bobbed his head, the halter buckle clinking.

"No bit, Orione. No iron against your lips."

I let go of the rope tied to both sides of the cheekpieces. My hands searched for a purchase in the stone wall. I tried to climb up, tripping on my skirt.

"This will not do," I explained to Orione. I looked out into the darkness. My fingers searched for my apron tie and the hook for my overskirt. I peeled off the layers of clothing, laying them across the stones.

I shivered in my linen shift, despite the warmth of the summer night. Should I go back for my leggings or, wiser yet, crawl into the straw of the lambing shed and forget this? Perhaps I should wait to have Giorgio at my side. When there was a little more moonlight, when . . .

Pazza, Virginia, pazza. You crazy girl.

I forgot the danger. I trusted my intuition, I trusted my horse. This was the moment. I could not dwell on the risk, only seize this chance. As Orione sidled next to me along the wall, I slid my right leg over his back, knotting my fingers in his mane. My little finger hooked the rope shank, keeping it high on his neck.

I made the transfer of weight as gently as I could. I waited for him to buck, to rear. I waited for him to bolt, to gallop.

He swung his head toward my leg, sniffing it. Then he straightened up again, looking off into the distance.

If I did not know better, I would swear he was looking at the thin slice of moon, balancing open-ended in the night sky.

———————

That night, I sat on the colt's back for only a few minutes. I knew better than to move too far too quickly. In a low whistle, I breathed the tune of "Per Forza o per Amore." I felt his muscles relax under me, his ears swiveling to catch the melody he had heard since birth.

From that night on, he would follow me anywhere—no fence could keep him away. He stood near the stone wall for me to mount him, though before long, I could swing up on him like a Palio fantino.

The first time he felt pressure from my legs, he broke into a trot. The makeshift reins on his halter frustrated him, and he threw his head, threatening to rear.

I dropped the reins on his withers. With his head free, I used my calf and inner thigh to direct him. He responded more quickly to the pressure of my seat to halt than he did to my hands. I soon realized I didn't need the halter at all.

But I kept it on him, hoping one day he would accept a bit and bridle. Besides, the fluttering rosette blew in the wind, making us both feel like champions in the night.

It was only in the morning, when the mares whinnied from the far pasture, that he would leap the fence again back into the paddock, galloping to the far end to be near the mares.

He would stand there in the dark before the sun rose, before my cousins would descend to gather up the flock.

CHAPTER 42

Morgante flared his nostrils like a beast smelling death. The simple wood coffin of Leonora lay open in the nave of the San Lorenzo chapel, and Morgante smelled the rancid fear and hatred in the clammy air of the small room.

The rainy weather makes the silks of the mourners stink like wet curs. No matter how costly the cloth might be.

A handful of candles, a paucity unknown at a de' Medici funeral, cast capricious light and shadow over the faces of the family.

The granduca was burying his first cousin and sister-in-law with virtually no ceremony. And the de' Medici vault under the floors of San Lorenzo would not be opened to receive Leonora de' Medici's body.

Who knows where her body will be interred? And where is the murderous fiend, Duca Pietro?

Morgante's eyes darted between the grief-stricken Isabella and the expressionless face of her brother Francesco.

The little man swallowed hard, watching the cruelty hardening the granduca's features. Morgante recalled the petulant look in Francesco's eyes as a boy when he did not get his way. He remembered how Cosimo's son would sooner break a toy than share it with his siblings.

Morgante did not approach any closer. His legs planted like roots in the dark corner where the feeble candlelight did not reach, he silently watched the funeral of Leonora di Toledo de' Medici, remembering her tinkling laughter.

Tears welled in his dark eyes, splashing over rims of chubby flesh.

He felt the cold of the stone church on his wet cheeks and wiped away his tears with a knuckle.

Tears at this funeral were risky. Morgante knew better than to demonstrate his sentiments in front of Granduca Francesco de' Medici.

The granduca gave a curt nod, dispatching the priest when the last word of benediction still rang in the cold air. It was a hasty service, a ceremony fit for a pauper, but Francesco would permit no more. There was to be no public display of Leonora's body, no mourners to grieve her death except the most intimate members of the de' Medici family.

A summer shower darkened the lead-cased windows of the church as Isabella lay a red rose across her sister-in-law's breast. She bent over the dead young mother, whispering in her ear.

Morgante watched the silver and ivory brocade of Isabella's gown shudder as she cried silently.

"Basta!" Francesco pulled her away from the coffin. "Comport yourself with dignity, sister."

Morgante saw Isabella, her face white with horror, unable to speak to the granduca.

"We will return to the Pitti now for luncheon," he said, turning to walk out the door.

"But Francesco—"

"The funeral is finished. Her life, her treacherous infidelity, is finished. I will not tolerate her name spoken again in our Court!"

Francesco walked to the door, ordering the carriages to be brought at once. As the granduca's servant opened the portal and ushered his master out, Morgante saw the crescent moon hanging over Francesco's shoulder. The lunar sickle cupped to the left, waxing.

Isabella returned to her cousin's coffin.

"*Madonna, aiutami!*" she implored. Mother of God, please help me!

Morgante watched as Isabella's finger traced the cold forehead, sweeping an errant strand of red hair back behind the dead woman's ear.

Isabella gasped as she examined the bruises on her neck, the signs of struggle.

"*Principessa,*" whispered Morgante, the last of the mourners.

Isabella's hand flew off the corpse, covering her mouth.

She stared at the little man, her shoulders relaxing enough to make the embroidered material of her dress rustle.

"Remember how I could make you laugh when you were a child," he said, approaching her, his legs swinging from side to side. "You laughed at my antics—your father—"

"I am not a little girl anymore, Morgante. And my father would kill both my brothers were he alive still. His heart would break to see this beauty buried at such a tender age. She was his favorite. Not me, not my sisters. Leonora, always his favorite."

Morgante took Isabella's hand in his. Few people could presume such intimacy, but Morgante was as much part of the de' Medici family as a courtier could be.

"I know, Principessa. I know. Your father's ghost will haunt your brothers. I have dreamt as much."

"Have you, Morgante?" She smiled grimly. "That gives me comfort."

The dwarf looked around, judging the distance of the last mourners waiting for the coaches to take them to the Pitti Palace.

"I worry. I fear for *your* life, Donna Isabella."

Isabella sniffed back her tears.

"My life? Why ever would you fear for me?"

"If the granduca condones the murder of his own cousin, he is mad. And madness knows no limits. You must be careful, my lady."

Isabella looked over her shoulder at the simple wood coffin.

"Go to France," said Morgante. "Your cousin Catherine will protect you!"

Isabella straightened. The flickering candles illuminated her white skin and long forehead.

"The thought of escaping Firenze has crossed my mind more than once in the past few days," she whispered. "But my husband has planned a trip—"

Francesco's secretary, Serguido, entered the church. He gave a startled look, seeing Morgante at Isabella's side.

"The last coach is ready, my lady."

"I am coming," she said. She gave a curt nod to the dwarf and turned to leave. Her stiff brocaded skirts brushed over the marble floors of the church.

The absolute silence of San Lorenzo returned. The dwarf breathed in the heavy air, redolent of melting beeswax and ancient stones.

Morgante finally allowed himself to cry. Without restraint.

Chapter 43

Florence, Pitti Palace

July 1576

At the funeral meal, Francesco's wife, the Granduchessa Giovanna, sought the company of her sister-in-law. The two noblewomen consoled one another, wet cheeks pressed together.

"Be careful, dear sister," whispered Giovanna. "I beg of you! I do not trust—"

Francesco pulled his wife away from his grieving sister. The Austrian ladies-in-waiting gasped to see the duke's rough hand on Emperor Maximilian's sister.

"Leonora was not a good wife—she disgraced the de' Medici name," hissed Francesco. "A marriage between two first cousins should never have been permitted!"

His head pivoted, looking around the room.

"Giovanna, tend to the children. They are quarreling again. Make them stop immediately!"

Giovanna picked up her skirts and walked away, her hand covering her mouth to stanch a sob.

When his wife was out of earshot, the granduca gave Isabella an icy look.

"Do you now comprehend what happens to those who disgrace the de' Medici name, sister?"

————————

Florence learned quickly there had been no formal ceremony for their beloved Leonora. They heard that the Granduca de' Medici demanded a *damnatio memoriae* of his young cousin—her memory was to be erased. Any trace of Leonora was removed. Portraits, poetry, references of any kind were forbidden. Even the mention of her name was forbidden.

The people of Florence mourned the loss of their beautiful princess. They heard servants' reports of her bruised body, the signs of struggle, and the injured hand of the hated Pietro de' Medici, her husband, her murderer.

Paolo Girodano Orsini wrote to Isabella that he was en route to Florence. He had heard of the terrible accident. He would come to comfort his beloved wife. A few weeks hunting in the countryside would do her good.

————————

Isabella was ill for five days. She lay in her bed, her eyes swollen with crying. She could not eat. The Granduchessa Giovanna, not knowing what else to do, sent the dwarf Morgante to Palazzo Medici to cheer her up.

He approached Isabella's bed, waddling on his short legs, listing like a little boat against a current.

"To think Francesco and Pietro both have Leonora's blood on their hands," Isabella whispered to the little man she had known since birth.

Morgante blinked back his own tears.

"Your father told me to beware the duca's moodiness, the darkness of his nature," he whispered in return.

"My father is uneasy in his grave now," said Isabella. She covered her face with her hands, weeping.

"You must leave Firenze, my lady," said Morgante.

"Stay by my side, Morgante," she said. "I implore you."

"Ah, my duchessa, I am but a silly jester. I have no power to help you."

"You are wrong," said Isabella, looking into Morgante's eyes. She remembered how she had once watched him wrestle a monkey in her father's court. The first Morgante had killed one such monkey brutally, much to the amusement of the Court. This second Morgante only played with the monkey, ending the match with the creature perched on his shoulder, taking grapes from his fingers.

"You have the gift of friendship," she said. "And what I need now is a friend."

Isabella took the dwarf's hand in hers. She pressed the man's palm to her cheek and thought of her father.

———

The day he arrived in Florence, Paolo Orsini informed his wife that they would be leaving immediately for the Cerreto Guidi, a favorite de' Medici hunting villa.

He had written to the Duca d'Urbino days before, asking for special hounds and harriers. He had invited his Roman neighbor and good friend Massimo, a Knight of Malta, to join them at Cerreto. Paolo made plans for a grand party but allowed Isabella to bring only a few of her ladies-in-waiting. Reluctantly, he agreed that the dwarf Morgante could accompany them.

Because the de' Medici princess was still overcome with grief from Leonora's death, Paolo made arrangements for her to be transported on a *lettuccio*—a small cot.

Isabella, relieved that her husband was not forcing her to return with him to the hated castle in Bracciano, agreed to the trip to Cerreto, where she and her father had spent so many pleasant days hunting. She was desperate to leave Florence and escape the sight of her brother Francesco.

———————

Morgante rode in a coach with Isabella's ladies-in-waiting. Usually the journey with Isabella's women was festive. Morgante had always entertained the ladies with his antics, filling the coach with the sweet titter of saucy gossip. But not on this day.

This day, the 16th of July, 1576, there was no lively chatter. Instead the ladies spoke in hushed voices of Leonora's death, obsessively repeating stories the way children repeat ghost tales that terrify them.

"She had no chance to escape," said the youngest handmaiden. "Her ladies say the room was in great disorder. She put up a great fight."

"She nearly bit off his fingers."

"Did blood stain the sheets? Surely that would be evidence," said Madonna Lorenza.

"Who would dare bring evidence against a de' Medici?" said Elicona, Isabella's court poet. She dabbed her eyes with an embroidered handkerchief and looked at Morgante.

Morgante said nothing. He turned away, pulling back the curtain of the carriage, watching the Tuscan countryside slide past. Women in white kerchiefs tended the grapevines, pulling up the ever-grasping weeds. A wizened farmer with a load of ripe melons goaded his donkey forward, coughing in the cloud of dust the de' Medici carriages raised. Children ran alongside the coaches, jabbering in Tuscan dialect so thick, he could barely make sense of what they were saying.

Morgante had kissed Nora and Virginio good-bye, explaining to them that their mother was sick with grief. This was a hunting expedition, he said. The children knew how much their mother loved her horses and hoped the hunt would cheer her.

Her husband, Paolo Orsini, had insisted a stay at Cerreto Guido would be the solution for her grief and illness.

Morgante had never known Paolo to be concerned with Isabella's health, and he strongly disliked the tall, brooding Signor Massimo, who accompanied Paolo.

Morgante rubbed his mouth with his pudgy hand, a sour taste in his mouth.

They would not dare. Not six days after Leonora's death—

"Stop talking about death," he snapped at the ladies. "I cannot stomach any more!"

Morgante looked out the window at the throngs of peasant children, running alongside, crying, "Le Palle! Le Palle!"

The de' Medici emblem: red balls on a gold shield.

———

The fresh air of Cerreto and the smell of the horse stable revived Isabella.

"I want to get up, Madonna Lorenza," she called to her main lady-in-waiting. "I want to ride."

"Oh, Your Highness! Do you think it a good idea to ride a horse in your weakened condition?"

"If anything on Earth can restore me, it is a horse," said Isabella. "The Duchessa Leonora will ride with me in spirit. Her spirit needs to escape from the miserable funeral in San Lorenzo. Escape that unmarked grave."

Madonna Lorenza bit her lip, even as she nodded.

"Sì, Your Highness. I will inquire about the horses immediately."

"Yes. Help me to the window."

"I beg you sit on the edge of the bed for a minute to regain your strength. You might faint—"

Isabella sat up with her servant's help, dangling her legs over the bed. Madonna Lorenza fetched her satin slippers.

"There," she said. "Lean on me."

"I am too much weight for you. Ask Morgante to assist."

Madonna Lorenza opened the adjacent door to a room between Paolo's bedroom and Isabella's. There, two ladies were unpacking their mistress's clothes and Elicona was working on a poem to raise her spirits. Morgante sat, sniffing the air like a hound.

"I saw the Roman Signor Massimo walking the grounds with the Duca di Bracciano," said the poetess. "He dresses in the Roman style, a fine moss green hunting coat. Perhaps I shall write a poem and sing it at dinner tonight."

She noticed Morgante was not paying attention. He paced the room, distracted.

"Whatever is the matter, Morgante?"

"I do not care for the air here," he said, looking at Elicona.

"The air?" asked the poet. "Ah, but it is fresh with nature! What a relief after the stagnant Arno in the heat of July."

Morgante continued to sniff, his face contorting with apprehension.

"Morgante, I need your assistance with our lady," interrupted Madonna Lorenza. "She wants to look out the window. We need to steady her. I fear she may fall."

Morgante hoisted himself up on his stubby legs. "Did she mention riding?"

"Yes, can you believe it? She can hardly stand," said the maidservant.

He smiled and clapped his hands together with glee.

"It is a good sign. She should get out of this house. I smell something—something evil—in the air," he said. "A horse will take her away from the bad air and revive her spirit."

The poetess Elicona regarded the dwarf, her soft blue eyes registering his fear. She knew Morgante's strange ways of thinking. There was something bestial about his mind, instinctive as a feral dog's. She also knew that he hated Duca Paolo as much as Isabella did. Perhaps the Orsini's presence here had affected Morgante's senses.

Isabella had already stood up by the time Morgante entered the room.

"Let us help you!" said Madonna Lorenza.

"Grazie. I believe I am all right." Isabella took a wobbly step.

Morgante seized her arm. "The trip from Florence has tired you, my lady," he said. "Far more than you realize."

"Morgante. I want to ride. I must ride," she pleaded.

Morgante pressed her hand in his. "I understand, my princess. No one understands better than I! You need fresh air to clear your mind and your heart. But perhaps it would be better to wait a day, and walk about the gardens to regain your strength and equilibrium."

Isabella drew a deep breath.

"If I could only ride. I know I could recover my heart."

Morgante nodded.

"I, too, want you to leave this house. But you do not want to fall from your horse. Let us walk and inspect the estate. We can pay a visit to the stables now, before dinner. You can see your horses and give the grooms your orders for the morning."

"But—I must ride!"

"I understand," said Morgante. "A horse will cure you, the wind in your face. But it is almost time for the midday meal. After you eat, I will escort you to the stables."

———

Isabella refused to descend for the midday meal. She sent a letter to her husband, begging him to forgive her absence at the dining table and apologizing to their guest, Signor Massimo.

Isabella's note was answered in person only a short time later. Paolo Orsini's heavy footfall on the stairs heralded his approach. He saw the small cluster of Duchessa Isabella's entourage gathered in the hall outside her bedroom.

"Out of the way!" growled Paolo. "Should you not be attending your mistress within her bedroom?"

"She is sleeping, my lord," said Madonna Lorenza. "She tried to rise to ride her horse but was too fatigued after the journey from Florence."

"Horses!" he spat. "Always horses! She and her cousin."

Morgante kept his eyes lowered to the floor.

"Tell her she must visit my chambers at once. I do not care if she is tired. I have a gift for her to raise her spirit. A halter for her favorite horse."

A deep drumming began in Morgante's ears. He felt as if he were swimming underwater.

When no one moved, Paolo's jaw tightened. "Bid my wife come to my room!"

Morgante's eyes widened, his nostrils flared. No one moved. Lorenza and Elicona turned pale, frozen in place like statues.

"Are you deaf?" said Paolo. "Send her at once!" He turned his back on the stunned servants, slamming the door.

"But my duca—she is sleeping," said Madonna Lorenza to the closed door.

"Let us all go together," said Elicona. "Is she only in her chemise?"

"Yes."

"We will wrap her in her robe," said Lorenza. "Then the three of us will walk in—surely nothing could—"

The trio could hear stirrings in Paolo Orsini's chamber.

"I must fetch her," said Madonna Lorenza. "If I do not, it will make Master Orsini even angrier."

She and Elicona slipped into Isabella's bedchamber, leaving Morgante shocked with despair.

Morgante could hear the slip of leather soles approaching the door.

I must think. I must protect her. I must—

The door creaked open, and Isabella appeared, refusing the support of her female servants.

"I will go alone," the Duchessa di Bracciano said, shrugging her shoulders, as if she had resigned herself to what lay beyond the door.

Morgante stood paralyzed. "No" was all he whispered.

Madonna Lorenza and Elicona joined arms, standing behind Isabella as she walked through the door. Morgante shook his head, still dazed, and pushed in with them.

"I asked for my wife!" shouted Paolo. "Not a traveling circus. Out, all of you!"

The women lingered. Morgante stood firm, his hands clenched in fists at his waist. But with one push from the big man, angry and rough, the three fell out of the doorway like bowling pins.

A double click of the lock secured the door.

They heard a muffled cry from across the hall, behind the closed door.

Morgante sank to his knees.

———

Half an hour later, Paolo threw open the door.

"Come quickly!" he shouted. "Your lady has had a fainting spell. Bring vinegar."

Madonna Lorenza did not search for vinegar but rushed into the room, falling to the floor beside her mistress, who lay on the stones, her mouth agape, tongue protruding.

"The vinegar!" shouted Paolo.

Morgante pushed into the room. He fell to his knees, cradling Isabella's head. Under his fingers he saw the blue marks of strangulation. Her eyes bulged hideously from their sockets.

"I ordered vinegar!" shouted Paolo. "Can you not see my wife is ailing? Witness her condition!"

"She is dead," said Morgante.

"You have brought her to her death, signore!" cried Madonna Lorenza. "What do you need with vinegar or anything else?"

Elicona stood staring from the doorway, unable to move. Her eyes played over the bulging eyes of her dead mistress. Under the bed, she saw the moss green sleeve of a man hidden from sight.

Paolo yanked the poetess into the chamber along with the others and locked the door. His brow was beaded with sweat, his hair matted and tangled.

"Listen well, you servants. If any of you dare to utter any suspicions, I will have you killed. Worse yet, thrown into a de' Medici dungeon in Firenze," he snarled. "Do you understand?"

They nodded.

"You will simply say she died," Orsini said, pointing a stout finger at all three. "Because . . . well, you all are witnesses to her delicate condition. She has been sick for months! Sì, you are witnesses and will bear testimony to her frail health. She drank cool liquid on this hot day. A grave mistake for one so ill."

The ladies-in-waiting and the poet blinked.

Is that the best he can do?

The dwarf's foot struck something just at the edge under the bed. He looked down.

A leather horse halter.

When Morgante looked up again, his eyes met Paolo's. Morgante puckered his mouth, despising the murderer who stood before him. But he was not even worth the dwarf's spit.

"Now go!" roared Paolo. "You are all dismissed. I must write to the granduca immediately. He will want to make the appropriate funeral arrangements at once."

The granduca!

Morgante swallowed hard. Paolo shot a look at him.

Now the dwarf was sure.

Granduca Francesco's hand was behind this murder. This murder and Leonora's.

CHAPTER 44

Siena, Brunelli Stables, Vignano

JULY 1576

As I entered the stable, leading a three-year-old colt from the morning's training, I heard a snatch of conversation.

". . . the devil's own ill-born litter," said the cobbler.

"And that fat Orsini?" said the baker. "I curse the dirty sow who gave him birth."

"A disgrace," said the cooper. "But he would never have dared if the granduca had not given approval."

"*Certo.* The deed stinks worse than the tanner's vats. Surely the King of Spain . . ."

The men looked up, hearing the colt's iron shoes on the cobblestone.

"Buongiorno, Virginia," they said. They looked down at their feet sheepishly.

I noticed they were not gambling, but sharing a jug of wine and a loaf of bread. The cobbler swallowed his mouthful, swabbing his lips with the back of his hand.

"Are you not throwing your dice this morning?" I asked, tying up the colt for a rubdown.

The men looked at the ground, studying the bits of straw and dry shreds of manure.

"What is the matter?" I asked them, picking up a rag to rub the colt's back. "Has the cat snatched all your tongues? I would think her too busy with all the barn mice."

Brunelli entered the barn, limping because a mare in heat had kicked him the day before. He wiped the sweat from his eyes and turned to me.

"How did Principe run this morning?"

"Bene," I said. "Though I had to rein him in quite a bit in the fields."

Brunelli noticed the men were still, with no dice in their hands. "No gambling?" he said.

"Something troubles them," I said. "And they will not tell me."

"It is not a topic for young ladies such as yourself," said the baker, wringing his cap in his hand.

"Ha!" I said, rubbing hard at the salt and sweat. "Training colts is not appropriate for girls either. But here I am, signori."

Padrino Brunelli glanced at me and shrugged his shoulders. "Go ahead, tell her. She will learn anyway from the gossips in the village—or worse, from her zia Claudia."

The men nodded solemnly.

They looked at the cobbler, signaling him to be their spokesman.

"The two de' Medici princesses were murdered. Leonora and Isabella de' Medici."

The rag hung tight in my fist, poised above the horse. I noticed how the sunlight entered the stable door, catching the spinning motes of dust. I heard the throbbing of my heart in my ears, like it did the time Giorgio held my head underwater in the horse trough as a joke, and I thought I would drown.

I felt I was looking at the world from underwater and would never reach the bright surface again.

"Isabella?" I whispered. "Murdered?"

"La Princessa Isabella and Donna Leonora de' Medici. Both."

I could hardly will my lips to move.

"How? *Why?* But when—"

"Leonora's death was said to be an accident, but her Spanish servants have let the truth spread. Her husband strangled her with a dog leash. She bit and fought, leaving the marks of her teeth on his hand, scratches on his neck—"

"And she would have broken free, but Pietro had henchmen from Romagna in the bedchamber to help him finish the job."

"What of Isabella?" I asked. "What happened to her?"

"Strangled with a horse halter. Never could I imagine a collo di cavallo—"

"A halter?" I said. I marveled at the word, as if I had never heard it before in my life.

"By that brute Orsini husband of hers."

"Oh!"

I dropped to my knees in the filth, my kneecaps striking hard on the stones. My godfather limped to my side.

"Virginia, Virginia," he said, sliding his arms around me. "These are the cruelties of the nobili of Florence," he whispered. "They have nothing to do with the Senese, with us. The de' Medici are our enemies! Forget them, ciccia!"

"I will never forget her," I said. "Isabella. Her horse leaping over the olive tree—"

"They are Florentines! De' Medici! Our sworn enemies—"

"No! You do not understand. *She*—she was not my enemy!"

I pulled the halter off the young horse and, standing on my tiptoes, slipped on his bridle again.

"Ciccia! Where are you going?"

I swung up on his back and galloped out of the stables without another word.

I headed the colt straight to the Porta dei Pispini of Siena. The muddy road changed to stone as I rode through the Contradas del Nicchio, del Leocorno, della Civitta, to della Selva—straight to the heart of town.

Women and men alike stared at me, their mouths dropped open.

"Una ragazza!" they shouted. "Look at the ragazza!"

I had never ridden the city streets before, and my horse—accustomed only to the paddocks and fields around Vignano—shied at every creaking wheelbarrow, every hawking street peddler, every braying donkey. He jumped at the flapping laundry and the colorful banners of the contradas.

I held tight, reaching my legs down deep as Brunelli had taught me.

Melt your body over the horse until you become one.

The sound of hooves clattering on pietra serena echoed through the streets: Via di Pantaneto, Banchi di Sotto, and Via di Città, until I reined in my horse in front of Palazzo d'Elci.

"Per favore!" I screamed to the guards. "I must see the duchessa at once! Tell her it is Virginia Tacci."

"La duchessa knows you?" said the guard, doubt scrawled across his face.

"Sì! It is of the utmost importance—"

By this time, a small crowd had gathered.

Among them were the artists, coming out of the hall from their morning lesson in the palazzo.

My horse danced and reared, not accustomed to the bustling crowd.

"Virginia!" shouted a voice I recognized.

Giorgio had his paints in a leather satchel under his arm. Beside him was a black-haired youth with the most startling blue eyes I had ever seen.

"What are you doing riding Principe in the city?" said Giorgio. He handed his satchel to the blue-eyed companion, who stared at me, wide-mouthed.

"How dare you gallop that colt over the cobblestones! Did you not think of his tender feet, the stone bruises? He may be lame—"

I swung off the horse, burying my head in Giorgio's chest.

"Isabella de' Medici was murdered!"

A d'Elci servant took the reins from my hand. He recognized Giorgio from the art classes held in the d'Elci Palazzo. "Shall I take this horse to the stables?"

"Per favore," Giorgio answered. He held me tight in his arms.

"I know, I know," he said, comforting me.

He whispered in my ear, his breath warm.

"But careful what you say, Virginia. She was a de' Medici, and you are surrounded by Senese."

"But the granduca had her murdered!" I whispered back. "He murdered her—"

"Careful," he murmured. "There are also Florentines in the street. Your words could be treason."

"Treason!" I said, pulling back to look at his face. I wiped my eyes with the back of my hand. "Treason?" I shouted. "She was a woman! She rode like an angel. I do not care if she was a de' Medici! She was brave—"

At that moment, I felt a soft touch on my shoulder blade.

"The duchessa has asked me to escort you," said a gentle-woman dressed in blue.

I raised my eyes. Looking high above, I saw a figure standing by the window. A pale hand beckoned me.

I nodded and kissed Giorgio on the cheek.

"I am sorry I galloped Principe over the stones," I said. "I was not thinking—I pray I did not lame him. Forgive me."

"Do not worry. I will care for his feet," said Giorgio. "We will not ride him for a week. Now, go! Give my best regards to the duchessa."

The lady-in-waiting took my arm, leading me through the crowd.

Giorgio's blue-eyed companion stared at me, unblinking. I felt his eyes follow me through the wrought-iron gates of the palazzo and up the polished marble staircase.

CHAPTER 45

Siena, Palazzo d' Elci

"Who is she?" asked Riccardo, still looking through the wrought-iron gates of Palazzo d'Elci as Virginia was escorted up the marble stairs.

Giorgio slid the palm of his hand across his forehead. He barely heard his friend's question.

What was she thinking? Crying for a de' Medici? Galloping an unshod colt over cobblestones?

"Hmm? *Cosa?*"

"I said, 'Who is she?' This, this young goddess of the horse."

For the first time, Giorgio noticed his friend's rapt attention.

"Her name is Virginia Tacci," he said, tugging at his companion's sleeve. "Come on, I need to look after the horse. It is one of my father's best colts."

The two artists walked to the stables, tucked into a little passageway off Via di Città. Ancient brickwork curved over their heads, darkened with age and smoke from the night torches.

"But how did she learn to ride—"

"It is not important," Giorgio said, waving away his friend's question. "What is important is whether this colt comes up lame." They approached the Selva stable, where the servant had taken the horse.

"Ragazzo, show me the horse just brought in from Palazzo d'Elci," said Giorgio.

The stable boy eyed Giorgio warily.

"He belongs to my father, Cesare Brunelli. I want to make sure he is all right. He has never been ridden on cobblestones. His feet are unshod—"

Riccardo said, "He is with me, ragazzo. Show us the horse."

Everyone in Siena knew the De' Luca family of Contrada del Drago. The groom nodded. He led Giorgio to a roped stall, where the colt pranced, weaving back and forth in excitement.

"She should not have ridden him into the city," muttered Giorgio.

He calmed the horse, clucking to him, muttering sweet nothings. One by one, he picked up the horse's hooves, checking for stone bruises or swelling.

"He looks all right, grazie a Dio," said Giorgio. "Still, she had no business—"

"Basta, Giorgio! Who is she?"

Giorgio looked at his friend, finally noting the hungry look in his eye.

"Riccardo! She is a shepherdess, as poor as a bone. She is the girl I was telling you about who trains horses for my father."

"Ah, but how incredible, her control of that horse! Did you see how she sat its rearing? Did you see how he shied away from the donkey cart like a bolt of lightning? She sat bareback as if she were a part of the horse."

"She is getting better at horsemanship," said Giorgio, rubbing his chin. "Still, she should not have taken—"

"Giorgio! You act as if we see *una donna,* a young woman, ride like that every day! She astonished everyone in Via di Città. Did you not notice?"

Giorgio shook his head vigorously. "I was busy. Besides, she is not a woman. She is a little girl. Ten years old, if that!"

"Why was she—"

"Never mind," snapped Giorgio.

Why was he annoyed at Riccardo's interest in Virginia?

"Let us go to the taverna and have some wine and dinner," said Giorgio. "I am famished."

"Will you tell me more about the girl?" asked Riccardo.

"What?" said Giorgio, shrugging his shoulders while lifting his open palms in supplication. "Do you not have young *ragazze* in Contrada del Drago?"

"Not like her, you idiot! Not who can sit a horse like that! I do not know a man who can sit a horse bareback while it is rearing like that."

"She has developed a good seat," admitted Giorgio. "With enough tumbles to break every bone in her body!"

Riccardo stopped midstride. He grasped his friend's shoulder.

"Come, you will dine at our palazzo. I insist!" He collared a peasant boy in the street.

"I will give you a lira if you will run to Piazza Mateotti. To Palazzo De' Luca, in front of the Carmelite convent. Knock on the door and tell the maid that Signor Riccardo brings home a guest for the midday meal."

The boy's grubby hand stretched out for the coin, nodding his head eagerly.

"Thank you, Riccardo," said Giorgio. "I suppose I shall accept your invitation. Although you did not wait to hear my acceptance."

Riccardo clapped his friend on the back.

"Forgive me for not giving you the opportunity to refuse."

Giorgio smiled.

"It will be an honor."

"Come." Riccardo gestured up Bianchi di Sopra. "But you must tell me more about this astonishing girl."

CHAPTER 46

Siena, Palazzo d' Elci
JULY 1576

I collapsed in the arms of the duchessa, and though she was old, she supported me. Her hands stroked my hair, tangled from the wind.

"Oh, Virginia," she said. "Do not cry anymore. Isabella is in heaven now, surely riding the best horses that have ever lived. Jumping clouds, ciccia! Imagine how beautiful!"

I shook my head bitterly. Then I looked at her through blurring tears.

"You do not hate her, do you, Duchessa? She was a de' Medici. Everyone tells me I should hate her!"

"No. No," said the duchessa, shaking her gray head.

"But all the others, everyone in Siena. They all despise her."

"Of course. She is a de' Medici. They are Senesi. It is only natural."

"But if it is natural, how do you forgive her?" I asked. "You have suffered as much as anyone. Why do you not hate her like all Senesi?"

The duchessa cast her clouded gaze into the distance. "I think of Isabella as a woman of great courage and spirit. A woman who defied her brother . . . no! She defied all men. How could I hate her?"

"Giorgio said I should not shed tears over her. My zia Claudia said it was treasonous that I should admire a de' Medici. That I should have learned to hate her from birth."

"Yes, we all have good reason to hate the Florentines, especially the de' Medici. But not Isabella. She was a rebel. Like the Senesi. She could not be dominated. Not even by the Granduca Francesco de' Medici himself. She was murdered because she did not obey his wishes."

The duchessa gave me a *fazzoletto* to blow my nose. When I had done so and cleaned my face, I looked up at her.

"I knew you would understand. I do not understand why, but I knew you would. That is why I rode here."

She studied my face.

"I understand what you saw in Isabella. You recognized her as a kindred spirit, with her love of horses and independence. You did not judge. Only the innocent have such a facility."

"But how do you understand? You must hate the de' Medici as much as anyone. You lived through the siege! Do you not despise them all?"

The duchessa pulled me close again, patting my back. She rocked me in her arms, kissing the top of my head. She smelled of sweet powder.

She released me, lifting my chin with her finger.

"Not all is black-and-white, Virginia. There is more in this world than simple evil and good."

The duchessa took my hand. "Come, sit with me in the library. We will have some tea and panforte. The best baker in Siena makes panforte for the d'Elci family with a secret recipe that has been in our family for centuries. Long before the siege."

Despite my sorrow, my traitorous stomach growled at the thought of panforte studded with fruits and nuts.

"And then, ciccia, I will tell you a story about the war with Florence. You will see that the de' Medici are a complicated family."

I nodded.

"Then maybe you will understand why I can forgive your admiring a de' Medici. You should know: I, too, have de' Medici blood in my veins, though I despise it."

"You?" I said, pulling back to examine her face. "You are a de' Medici?"

"Generations ago. All nobili are intermarried, Virginia. But I am Senese, through and through."

The duchessa poured our tea from a beautiful ceramic pot. Everything was so delicate. I cradled my cup like a baby bird.

"This is de' Medici paste porcelain," she said. "The cup was a gift from a Florentine nobleman at the de' Medici court."

I closed my eyes, savoring the flavor of the panforte, letting the honey sweetness slowly dissolve in my mouth.

"You know, at the very start of the siege, we made as much panforte as we could. It gave us strength through many long days of war. But it couldn't outlast the de' Medici armies.

"It was a sad day when we ate the last of the panforte." She turned her face toward the window, but her eyes were unfocused. "We ate the pigeons and even the bony swallows that swooped over our heads in Il Campo. Then the skies were empty, and we understood dark times were upon us."

She turned back to me again.

"You cannot understand what we felt. Every day, we awoke to hunger, if we were able to sleep at all. My stomach felt as if it were eating itself, cramping and grinding. I am surprised I could give birth to children after starvation had ravaged my body.

"No thought was as keen as finding food. The noble hope of withstanding the siege, a show of Senese pride, dulled each day as the urge to eat overwhelmed everything.

"We could not feed anyone. Jesus could make three fishes and three loaves nourish the multitudes, but we had no divine power, despite our dedication of the city to the Virgin.

"There was no difference between the nobili and the most common beggar. We were all beggars together, all committed to the cause. We became, for those eighteen months, a true republic once again.

"We ladies of the nobili and the merchants' matrons banded together. We formed three divisions. The first led by Signora Forteguerra, dressed in violet cloth. The second by Signora Piccolomini, in red satin. The third by Signora Livia Fausta, in the white of angels. We were three thousand ladies—now soldiers in the defense and succor of Siena. I was with the first division, and my violet gown was soon filthy and torn.

"We carried pikes and spades. We dressed soldiers' wounds, fed the hundreds of children housed in Maria della Scala." The duchessa dropped her eyes. "Until there was no more food to give.

"The French soldiers, as well as our Senesi troops, starved along with us. When our stores of grain ran out, and with no bread to feed them, we sent one hundred and fifty children, and the old and infirm, from Maria della Scala—" She swallowed, looking away. "We sent them out the gates of Siena, begging the enemy for mercy on the innocents. Instead, they were attacked by the Spanish.

"The Spanish slew many, even the youngest. At dawn, the houses at the perimeter of the city were awakened by the wailing of children. Beyond the gates were children crying to be let back into the city. Others lay dead in the frosty grass.

"We had no food to give them, but we took them back in to die within our walls. We had never expected that our enemies would kill the innocents, waving white flags in their baby hands."

The duchessa took a deep breath and stared into my eyes, her own eyes shining beneath the cloudy haze of age.

"We few who still had horses that had not been butchered rode into the surrounding hills, searching for lost children. But I thought of how the children, along with all of us, were condemned to the agonizing death of starvation, and I turned my horse toward the north, riding where I knew I would find the encampment of Cosimo de' Medici.

"My horse, painfully thin, like all of us, galloped bravely across the hills. I felt its sharp ribs digging into my legs. When I saw smoke billowing from the campfires in the distance, I stopped and ripped the hem of my white undershift, putting it in my right hand, tight to the rein.

"As I drew closer to the encampment, a mounted guard raced down the slope to take me prisoner. I waved my tattered white cloth and shouted, 'I am Lucrezia d'Elci. I come to speak to Duca Cosimo de' Medici.'

"The guard looked at my dirty violet uniform, my spiked helmet, my worn boots, and the dagger at my side. 'Do all the noble ladies of Siena dress in such a peculiar style?' he asked.

"'Spain and Florence have fashioned our apparel,' I said bitterly. 'And have slain our orphans and left them to rot on unhallowed ground!'

"I spat at the ground beside his horse's hooves.

"'It was not our army, but the Spanish,' he said. He was unable to look me in the eye. He lifted his chin, pointing toward the campfires. 'Come. You will find Duca Cosimo de' Medici over there. Allow me to accompany you.'"

The duchessa stopped again and closed her eyes. I wondered what she was thinking, what horrible visions she was reliving in her mind's eye. After a long pause, she spoke again.

"Cosimo was standing in front of his tent when we reached the camp. He looked much like his portraits, clad in armor, gallant in his military garb.

"And I hated him more than any soul on Earth.

"He studied me, his hands on his hips.

"In my younger day, I was considered a great beauty, but that was before the siege had stolen the blossom of my youth, carving deep hollows in my face, reducing my body to bones.

"I straightened in my saddle, knowing that on my skinny horse, dressed in my tattered gown, I appeared pathetic to the duca.

"But somehow he recognized me. I saw the light in his eyes. He laughed.

"'What a surprise, Duchessa. May I offer you tea? Or perhaps a draught of something stronger?'

"The aroma of fried pancetta, bread, and roasted meats made me weak. I tried to control my trembling, but it was impossible. I quaked like a leaf.

"His face fell, all the levity vanished. He hurried to help me off my horse.

"'Forgive me, brave lady. I do not treat you with the respect you merit. Come to my tent and partake in a meal as my honored guest.'

"After more than a year of starvation, I accepted my enemy's invitation.

"How I wanted to turn away. But I challenge anyone to resist such a meal after eighteen months of siege. Had Our Lord Jesus Christ himself faced such temptation in the desert, I wonder if he could have resisted.

"But still, I could not allow myself to forget why I was there. 'The children,' I said straight away. 'We sent them out Siena's gates, and they were butchered by the Spanish.'

"An attendant placed a plate in front of me, laden with roasted partridge—oh, I remember it so well, glistening with olive oil.

"'Eat, my good lady,' said the duca.

"'No! The children!' My voice cracked.

"'We will speak of the children once you have eaten. I swear to you.'

"I twisted my fingers around and around in my lap, my eyes never moving from the plate. I could not betray my weakness with too much eagerness.

"'Will you not join me, Duca de' Medici, in my repast?' I said, swallowing back the juices in my mouth.

"'No, I have eaten. Please, go ahead. Buon appetito. But take care you do not eat too much.'

"As I picked up the silver fork, my hand trembled.

"'You are truly a most remarkable woman,' said the duca quietly. 'I do not know when I have seen more bravery.'

"I said nothing, but began to eat, closing my eyes, my whole body shaking as I tasted the roasted partridge. One bite, and I felt my stomach rebel, unaccustomed to real food.

"As Cosimo had warned, I could not eat much at all. I stared at the plate of food, pushing it away before I had eaten even half. I could not make myself ill and forget my task.

"'May I speak honestly to you, Duca?' I said. 'As one noble to another?'

"He nodded, his eyes seeking mine, as if we were lovers instead of mortal enemies.

"'You are a Tuscan!' I said. "How can you treat other Tuscans so cruelly?'

"'Duchessa, I shall do you the honor of speaking candidly. I shall tell you the truth, a favor I extend to the few who merit it.' Again he sought my eyes, his look deep with meaning.

"'I mean to make Siena part of my Tuscan empire. I shall be granduca of all Tuscany one day. I will protect us all from invaders . . . and from Rome. We will be Tuscan brothers and sisters—'

"'You are indeed a fool!' I said. 'Florence will never rule the Senesi.'

"The duca studied me, subduing his laughter.

"'See how brightly your blue eyes glitter when you have enjoyed good Tuscan fare. You Senesi are a marvelous people.'"

"'You will never, *ever* control us.'

"'Never?'

"'Never! We will never accept a de' Medici.'

"The duke bit his lip.

"'I see,' he said. 'Did you know we are cousins? Ah, but of course you do. We are all related in one way or another, we nobili.'

"I shook with anger, digging my dirty fingernails into the palms of my hand.

"'I was born a Senese and will remain faithful until I die. My family has lived in Siena for hundreds of years. If I have a drop of de' Medici blood, may it be squeezed from my veins!'

"Cosimo chuckled ruefully, studying my face.

"'Well, my cousin. I can tell you a few things that might be useful to know for your proud Senese. For example, your General Strozzi lies to you.'

"'You lie! General Strozzi is our hero!'

"'No, Lucrezia. Think what he has promised you. He lies.'"

The duchessa stopped again and looked at me, almost as if she were surprised to see me there, surprised to find she wasn't talking to the Granduca de' Medici. She sighed.

"The truth is, Virginia, doubts had lurked in my mind. Our people died one by one of starvation, as time after time General Strozzi promised our victory was near.

"'What do you mean?' I asked the granduca.

"'Ah! You do me the honor of listening and lending credence. Let me ask you: How many times have you heard that the French armies are on the way to protect Siena?'

"I looked down at my greasy hands. I had forgotten my table manners and seized a leg of goose in my fist just minutes before. I wiped my hands on my napkin, distracted. We had been told over and over again that the French were coming. We had only to hold out a little longer. We mixed sawdust into our panforte. We stripped the bark from our fruit trees. And yes, we ate dogs.

"And no one came to our salvation.

"'What do you know, Duca?' I forced myself to ask.

"'I know that Strozzi will continue to lie to you. He hates me, and he will do anything to stop me. But he will fail. And he treats Siena as a pawn in the European wars.'

"'No,' I said. I shook my head, trying to rid myself of the thought.

"'He cares only about his own ambition. He will escape Siena and leave the Senese to deal with the Spanish . . . and with me, good lady.'

"I tried to ponder all he had said. Too much truth had made me light-headed. It seemed as if all we had suffered for was lost. The only personal favor I received from Duca de' Medici was that he agreed to take my starving horse.

"When we were drawing close to the gates of Siena, I begged him, 'I know it is only a matter of days before we are forced to eat my horse, Bruschi. Please, take him. He will make a good saddle horse for your children. He is brave of heart on the hunt field, if he can recover his strength.'

"He may have been a villain, but his smile was soft. 'I have a twelve-year-old daughter who adores the hunt. I shall bring your Bruschi as a gift. And I promise I will take excellent care of him and fatten him the way I would like to indulge you, my lady.'

"I could not smile at him, but my hatred for him dimmed its bright fire.

"'And,' he added, 'I will see that he never is ridden into battle against the Senesi. Or enters the gates in the triumphant colors of Firenze.'

"His face grew serious. 'I shall discuss matters of mercy for the children with the King of Spain. Do not let any more of them beyond the gates until you hear from me expressly. Else they return with their noses and ears cut off.'

"I winced.

"'Now, Duchessa, I have done your favor for you. Expect no more. We are at war.'

"I dismounted my faithful horse, giving him the reins.

"'Grazie,' I said. 'For the children's sake.'

"'*Piacere.* But just once will this happen, my good duchessa.'

"He took my hand and kissed it. I snatched it away, hurrying down the hill. I could feel his eyes on my back, watching. But I did not turn around until I was safe within the city walls."

The duchessa closed her eyes, her blue-veined lids fluttering. I said nothing, letting her return to the present. The silence stretched so long, I thought perhaps I should leave.

Finally, she spoke.

"His daughter, Isabella, was very much like him. She had the bravery, the curiosity, the appreciation of the arts. She was indomitable."

"She inherited your horse?" I said.

"Yes," said the duchessa. "Though you hardly met her, just those few minutes in the field, you saw the essence. She rode as well as any man. You recognized the spirit of the woman and the horse."

"And now she is dead," I said, my eyes smarting again with tears. "What justice is that?"

The duchessa drew a deep breath.

"Yes. Francesco de' Medici leaves his mark. The fangs of a rabid dog. But you must remember Isabella as you saw her that once, the way you told me. Soaring, boundless, defying her brother." Her voice sounded young for a brief moment. "Defying everyone's expectations. Laughing as she did so."

She reached over and took my hand, pressing it.

"She was a de' Medici. But she was not the enemy. Our enemies are the power-drunk tyrants who bend our spirits into ugly forms. Politics and age-old hatred blind us to the goodness of others."

She held my hand in hers and gave it a squeeze.

"There is *forza* in her memory. Remember her on the day when you ride the Palio."

Forza—strength. A good word to remember Isabella de' Medici by. And, now I knew, a good word for the Duchessa d'Elci.

CHAPTER 47

Siena, Palazzo De' Luca

AUGUST 1576

The De' Luca family home had an ancient scent of cedar chests, beeswax, and centuries-old furnishings. The unmistakable aroma of wealth and nobility greeted Giorgio Brunelli as he entered the palazzo.

Riccardo had chosen Giorgio over any other student in the Accademia dell'Arte as his constant companion. Though they were mismatched in social class, Riccardo admired both Giorgio's brilliant artistic talent and the fierce ardor with which he challenged the Florentines, despite the danger. But this was the first time Giorgio had entered the Palazzo De' Luca.

The De' Lucas were an equestrian family. Although their wealth had been destroyed during the Florentine War, they had rebuilt their fortune, returning once more to banking.

The first florins they earned were spent bringing horses back to the De' Luca stables so that they could race in the Palio again.

"Per favore, Giorgio," said Signora De' Luca. "You must sit next to me so I can hear your stories of art."

"Papa, you must hear—" Riccardo started, but his father was intent on their guest.

"And we must talk about horses," said Signor De' Luca, gesturing to Giorgio to take his seat. "Your father's stables and horsemanship are legendary. I took one of my own colts there a few years ago to be trained."

"Davvero?" said Giorgio. "What was his name?"

"Zucchero," said Signor De' Luca. "We sold him to the Gonzaga family in Mantua. He was a bay colt with a broken blaze running down his face."

Giorgio smiled, losing his nervousness at dining with the nobili.

"I trained him myself," he said. He took a sip of wine, savoring the fine vintage.

"Davvero?" said Signora De' Luca. "Well, you did a magnificent job. The Gonzaga family has him as a stud now."

"Mamma, Babbo, the most extraordinary—"

"With the profit from selling Zucchero, we were able to augment our stable once more."

"You have beautiful horses," said Giorgio. "I have seen them run the Palio."

"Grazie, grazie. We are proud of our horses. I have another filly—a beautiful chestnut—who is two now," mused Signor De' Luca.

"She is three already, Papa," corrected Riccardo. "And has already developed some bad habits."

Signor De' Luca waved away his son's words.

"Tell me, Giorgio. Would you work with her, train her as you did Zucchero?"

Giorgio wiped his lips on his linen napkin, hesitating.

"I am dedicating my time to art now," he said. "I wish I could say yes, but—"

When he saw Signor De' Luca's face fall in disappointment, he quickly added, "But I have an idea. There is a girl named Virginia Tacci who has the lightest hands and most secure seat of any—"

"That is what I have been trying to say!" exploded Riccardo. "This girl, this magnificent girl—"

"Did you say a girl?" said Signora De' Luca.

"She is ten," said Giorgio, then squinted, thinking. "Well. Maybe she has turned eleven now—"

Riccardo smiled.

"I told you. She is a young donna, not a little girl."

"Of course she is a little girl," said Giorgio, his face coloring. "Certo!"

"How extraordinary," said Signor De' Luca. "A *girl* rider?"

"She rides like a goddess!" exploded Riccardo. "This is what I have been trying to tell you."

"Yes," said Giorgio, looking at his best friend. There was something in Riccardo's voice that startled him.

No, it annoyed him.

"My father has her working all his two-year-olds. She is as light as a feather, especially as she insists on riding bareback."

"Incredible," murmured Signor De' Luca. "Truly *incredibile*."

He snapped his fingers.

"I must see her. Can you arrange that, Giorgio? I may call you Giorgio, yes?"

"Per favore," said Giorgio. "Of course. We will arrange it right away."

"Papa, when you see this girl ride, you will not believe your eyes."

Giorgio stared down at his plate. He clutched his fork hard, trying to sort out his feelings.

Signora De' Luca motioned to her family to be quiet. She nodded to her guest, still staring at his pasta.

"*Mangia*, Giorgio. Mangia!" she said, waving her forkful of pici in midair. The thick red sauce glistened, and her motion carried the delicious aroma of a lamb ragù.

"Enough with the horses," she said. "There is good food in front of you. Do not let it get cold. Remember the siege, and you will not soon forget your appetite."

CHAPTER 48

Siena, Pugna Hills

SEPTEMBER 1576

I lowered the bucket into the village well. My cousin Franco stood next to me, having come into Vignano for weekly supplies.

"The Oca's *capitano* attempts to train Tempesta's colt," he said. "The devil attacks him, rearing and biting."

I let the bucket splash into the well's depths.

"What do you mean, he is training him?"

Franco straightened his neck, sensing my interest.

"Carlo Ruffino comes every morning when you leave the ewes for the stables. We see him from atop the hills. He ropes up the colt, tries to handle him. The devil—"

"Damn you, his name is Orione!"

"The devil slashes out with his hooves, rears. The capitano cannot even place a light blanket on his back," said Franco.

I bit my knuckle, thinking.

"It is only a matter of time until the colt is pronounced useless and put to death," said Franco, jutting out his jaw. "He would make a good dinner for the village of Vignano, tasty—ummph!"

My riding boot sank into his gut.

"*Zitto!* Shut up, you ignorant fool! No one is going to touch Orione."

Franco clutched his abdomen, groaning in pain.

I stood panting, then spat at him through the gap in my teeth. "Next time, I will kick you lower. In the coglioni, cousin."

I turned away from the stupid fool and went back to the well. My arm worked furiously, cranking the bucket up from far below. I felt the warmth and fatigue in my muscles as I drew the water to the surface.

Franco cursed at me, stumbling away.

"Horsemeat!" he called, out of striking distance. "Only a matter of time, *cugina mia!*"

"Do not call me 'cousin,' you lout. You must be a bastard child, son of a shit gatherer! No Tacci would be so mean and ignorant!"

A small cluster of villagers gathered, watching us.

"Brava, Virginia, brava!" shouted the tavern owner.

"Cat got your coglioni, sheepherder?"

I poured the contents of the bucket into my water pail, lugging it back to the stable to clean Brunelli's tack.

What would become of Orione? He was too spirited for his own good.

The image of horsemeat hanging in a butcher's window haunted me.

CHAPTER 49

Siena, Palazzo d' Elci

Carlo Ruffino was summoned to Palazzo d'Elci.

"How goes the training of Orione?" asked the duchessa.

Carlo bowed deeply.

"I must report, with regret, that I have not made much progress," said Carlo. "The colt will not take the bit, no matter how I sweeten it. Honey, crushed apple. He rears and lashes out."

The duchessa's eyes hooded in dismay.

"Not all horses can be tamed," he said quietly. "Tempesta was his sire."

The duchessa looked up at the horsemaster. "I have an idea, Capitano Ruffino. I ask that you follow it faithfully."

Carlo took a deep breath. "Of course, my duchessa."

"The girl, the pastorella. The one at Orione's birth who trains horses in Vignano for Cesare Brunelli."

"Virginia? Virginia Tacci?" said Carlo.

"I want her to train Orione."

"The girl? But she would break her neck!"

The duchessa tried to hide her smile.

"I remember Orione's birth, watching her that night," said the duchessa. "She has a connection with this colt that no one else possesses. Let us see what she can do."

Carlo bowed his head.

"I have watched her break colts," he said. "She was pitched to the ground more than once, but she is young. Her bones bend like spring willow branches. She just climbs back on the horse, like a monkey swinging up a tree limb."

"Ah," sighed the duchessa. "To be young again."

She looked out the window, studying the Torre del Mangia. Then, slowly, she nodded. "If anyone can ride Orione, it will be Virginia Tacci."

CHAPTER 50

Siena, Pugna Hills

SEPTEMBER 1576

Carlo, horsemaster of Oca; his son, Marcello; and Giorgio rode with me to the hilly pasture near the lambing sheds. I rode Caramella, the De' Luca filly, though I dismounted downwind over a crested hill.

"You all ride geldings. A mare will make Orione crazy with distraction," I said, tying the mare to a scrub oak, near a ravine. I grabbed Stella's halter out of my saddlebag and put out a hand for Giorgio to pull me up on his gelding, behind the saddle. I wrapped my arms around his skinny frame, and I could feel his muscles relax.

My added weight was nothing on the gelding's back, and we cantered the rest of the distance over the rolling hills toward the lambing shed.

Orione roared a nicker, his nostrils flaring. He reared at the sight of new horses approaching him, then charged down the hill toward us.

Carlo chewed his lip.

"Are you sure you want to do this, Virginia?"

"Of course," I said. "But I will ask you to keep your horses at a distance."

They did not know that I had been riding Orione alone in the dark several nights a week.

I slid off the gelding at the rock wall and walked the rest of the distance to the pasture. Stella's halter rested on my shoulder as I dug in my apron for the apples I had brought.

Orione trotted toward me, eager for his apples.

I took off my apron, spilling the apples on the muddy spring grass. I twisted the hems of my chemise, skirt, and overskirt into a single strand, then used the apron as a sash to tie all the hems to my waist. I stood in my leggings, ignoring the men around me.

"Come on, ragazzo," I said. "Let's go, boy. It is time to show them what you can do. You must prove to them you are not Tempesta, a horse to be imprisoned or killed."

Orione raised his head from the last apple. His ears worked back and forth as he crunched the fruit, slobbered bits of apple spilling from his mouth. I slipped the halter over his nose, fastening the buckle. The Oca rosette gleamed in the sun.

"Brava!" I heard Giorgio call. "Brava, Virginia!"

I did not wait for further comments, as I knew they would only distract me. Clutching a fist full of Orione's mane, I swung up on his back.

He stood still until I gave him pressure with my leg. Then Orione broke into a canter, circling the pasture.

I urged him into a gallop. The wind filled my ears, so I could not hear their cheering.

"Just you and me," I said to him. "That is the way it will be forever."

CHAPTER 51

Florence, Palazzo Vecchio
SEPTEMBER 1576

The Granduca Francesco de' Medici was not finished. The murder of his sister was not enough to slake his rage. He was determined to obliterate any trace of her, removing her portraits from the walls of the residences, arresting her friends and even merchants who had served the de' Medici princess.

The Florentine merchant Bernardo di Giovannbattista was imprisoned and beheaded. Isabella's coach attendant was imprisoned, as was her gardener at Baroncelli. Even the *votapozzo*—the man who cleaned her cesspool—was whisked away. Gossips whispered that Isabella had delivered a baby conceived of Troilo's seed. They said the baby was born dead, and the votapozzo had disposed of the tiny corpse—as he was now disposed of himself. Her surgeon, Maestro Paolo, was thrown in the dungeons, as was Signora Arditi, an occasional nanny to Isabella's children.

In his fury to annihilate any trace of his sister, no one was safe. The granduca seized most of his sister's possessions, selling them immediately.

Bianca Cappello fingered the pearl seeds embroidered into her camisole.

"That woman certainly had the finest seamstresses. This piece rivals anything I have in my own wardrobe. It is exquisite even by Venetian standards."

The little maid blinked her eyes, holding back tears.

"The Principessa Isabella was meticulous about her clothes, my lady—"

"Oh, no! You mustn't call her a principessa," said Bianca. "Help me with my bodice, girl."

The servant was grateful to stand behind her mistress, for a few tears had spilled from her eyes. She tightened the laces on Bianca's bodice as her mistress chattered on.

"A damnatio memoriae is quite serious. You could be whipped for even referring to her, especially as a princess."

"Sì, Madonna. I thank you for reminding me of my error," the handmaiden said, closing her eyes tight. Her fingers trembled as she pulled on the laces of the bodice.

"Yes, well, I must remind all of my staff. I have heard her name uttered elsewhere. The granduca will not stand for it."

Bianca moved to her looking glass, posing this way and that.

"Margherita, do I look too plump in this skirt? I think it does not flatter me at all."

Margherita swallowed her tears. How she longed to stick a pin in the ever-englarging balloon that was Bianca Cappello.

"No, madam. I find the color enchanting. The gold brocade on peacock blue is quite stunning. It flatters your figure."

Bianca glanced in the mirror to see her maid's eyes. She knew she had fattened over the years. Her figure had become quite matronly, with a double chin that pouched downward, meeting her thickening neck.

"Your eyes," said Bianca, picking up a painted fan that had been Isabella's. She tapped her chin with it thoughtfully. "Your eyes appear quite red, Margherita."

"Niente," said the maid. Nothing. She picked up the comb to finish off her mistress's coiffure. "Something in the air," she said, blinking back a tear. "Lately, the climate has been torturing me."

CHAPTER 52

Florence, Via de' Pecori

APRIL 1578

The Viennese handmaiden lifted the Granduchessa Giovanna's chin up toward the priest.

"I beg of you, Highness," she said in German. "Open your mouth to take the holy sacrament."

The granduchessa's lips trembled as she opened her jaw just enough to accept the host. The priest gave the wafer a little shove, like a child launching a paper boat into the water.

Giovanna let the wafer dissolve on her tongue, accepting the blessing as the priest gave her last rites.

"But I cannot die now!" she said, her face crumpling in pain as another birth pang constricted her uterus. A gush of blood stained the sheets.

"I will bear a son, I know it!" she cried. "The granduca must have thought I would bear another daughter. He would never have wanted me to die—"

The Viennese maid tightened her lips in fury. She exchanged looks with the priest and the doctors gathered just beyond him.

"It was an accident, Serenissima. Lie back, good granduchessa. I will care for the baby myself. And you have already given Florence a young duca—your son Filippo."

Giovanna had not the strength to stay upright without support. The maid lowered her back into the snowy white pillows. The doctors moved the priest out of the way to resume their position between the granduchessa's legs.

"Filippo is so weak," said the dying woman. "I must make sure . . . make certain! That . . . that the Venetian traitor never usurps my children's right. A Habsburg-Medici shall rule Florence."

"Rest, Giovanna. All is in God's hands now," said the maid, stroking her mistress's long, thin forehead. The skin under her fingertips had turned clammy and as white as marble.

"You have been his faithful servant all the days of your life."

———

While Giovanna de' Medici, wife of Granduca Francesco, had not ever been comfortable or loved in the de' Medici Court, her early death came as a great shock to the people of Florence. She was the sister of a Habsburg emperor and the aunt of Rudolf II, and Florence had taken great pride in their Habsburg princess.

"He pushed her down the stairs," whispered the royal butcher to a palace kitchen maid, his current mistress. She lay exhausted on his bed. He leaned on his elbow, his head in his hand.

"Is that not the rumor in the Pitti Palace?" he said, teasing a strand of hair from her braid, loosened from lovemaking.

"The granduca?" she said, raising her head from the pillow. "No, not when the princess was about to deliver another male heir."

"Dead, too, the baby boy. And Filippo, the other son, is such a weakling! He will never live to be an adult."

"But it was not the granduca's doing, these deaths. Why would he jeopardize the birth of a male heir?"

The butcher twisted the ends of his mustache. "That whore, Bianca Cappello. He did it for her, so the changeling Antonio could take the dukedom."

"You are mad!" retorted the girl. She sat up in bed, kicking the twisted sheets from around her ankles. "No matter how much the granduca adores Donna Cappello, he would not murder his own blood."

The butcher was not convinced, but he wanted to keep his pretty mistress in his bed that night. He did not pursue the point, even though the rumors ran rampant in the streets of Florence.

Granduca Francesco did himself no favors when he tipped his hat to Bianca Cappello as he passed her balcony in Giovanna's funeral procession.

PART IV

The Heroine of Siena

ANNI 1579–1581

CHAPTER 53

Siena, Brunelli Stables, Vignano

JANUARY 1580

"Why does the *presidente* of Aquila ask you to join him, Papa?" asked Giorgio, saddling his father's horse. "We belong to no contrada here in Vignano."

"The meeting must have to do with horses," said Brunelli. "Why else would they invite me?"

"Perhaps some new Florentine tax imposed on our horse trade," said Giorgio, slipping the bridle's throatlatch into the buckle.

"Son, I can tell you nothing. Only that the meeting is a secret."

"Florence would not dare meddle with the Palio," mused Giorgio. "Governor di Montauto—"

"Bah!" said Cesare Brunelli, adjusting his stirrup leather. "I did not raise my son to be a fool. The de' Medici will meddle in any business they care to." He tightened the girth with a quick grunt. "They don't care about the Senese governor."

He slapped down the iron stirrup on the leather, making a fierce crack. "Federigo Barbolani di Montauto may love Siena after living here all these years, but he will always be a Florentine and a servant of the de' Medici. He has no choice."

Giorgio cupped his hands to give his aging father a boost up into the saddle. Giorgio winced, noticing his father's legs were like thin sticks rattling in his boots.

Simone Uccello, presidente of the Contrada dell'Aquila, had called the meeting with haste, hardly letting the scribe's ink dry on parchment as he sent out the messages to the heads of the other sixteen contradas. Faithful Aquila messengers scurried through the streets, urgently imploring attendance the following morning.

Signor Uccello did not want the Florentine spies to hear of the contradas all meeting under one roof. His dream would be crushed if Francesco de' Medici learned of it.

As the bell atop the Torre del Mangia struck nine, the presidenti of the contradas arrived by foot from all corners of the city, hurrying down the Casato di Sotto from the Piazza del Campo into Aquila's narrow streets, festooned with hanging laundry, the snap of half-frozen clothes keeping the ever-present pigeons away. Glancing over their shoulders, the men slipped into the ancient Chiesa di San Pietro alle Scale.

The small brick church was modest and unremarkable with its single nave, but to the contradaioli, it was the beating heart of Aquila. The presidenti of the contradas removed their caps and genuflected before the Virgin, surrounded by candles of smoking tallow.

Brunelli entered the darkened church, the scent of incense prickling his nose. His eyes slowly adjusted to the dusky gloom. It had been years since he had set foot in a church.

He recognized the members of the seventeen contradas kneeling, heads inclined in prayer. There were no other worshippers in the church.

One by one, a priest gestured to the men. Each ended his prayers with a quick sign of the cross and followed the priest through a small door off the nave.

Finally, only Brunelli was left. The clergyman pressed his lips tight as he stood in front of the old horse witch. Unlike the others, Cesare Brunelli sat upright in the wooden pew, his arms folded stubbornly.

"Buongiorno, Cesare Brunelli," whispered the priest.

"Buongiorno," grunted Brunelli.

"I see I do not interrupt your prayers," said the priest.

"I see you are not blind," said Brunelli.

The priest tightened his lips, saying nothing.

"I do not pray, priest, because I was summoned to a meeting of the contradas, not an ecclesiastical affair," snapped Brunelli. "You would do well to tend to God's business, and keep your nose out of man's."

Cold air chilled Brunelli's face as the priest led him to a winding passage and down the marble stairs to the crypt.

In the antechamber of the crypt, the men stood bundled against the cold. Arms folded tight around their cloaks, they hugged their bodies, stamping their feet.

"By God, how do the dead stand it?" said the presidente of Contrada del Nicchio. "You would think they would wake just to ask for a blanket."

"Let us begin," said Uccello of Aquila. "I will make my proposal brief."

"Are we plotting a rebellion after all these years?" ventured the presidente of Torre, half-joking.

The expression on the faces of the contradaioli stiffened. Several shifted their weight, making their leather boots creak.

"A revolt of the spirit only," said Signor Uccello. "To put it simply: we of the Contrada dell'Aquila will host a Palio."

The men exchanged looks, astonished.

"We are Siena, heart and soul," Signor Uccello continued. "We, the contradas, can show our unity, our independence, by racing one another. A race without the banners of d'Este, the de' Medici, the Sforza, Piccolomini, and Pannocchieschi. Imagine our city without their banners obscuring the Senese. Only the fair flags of our contradas."

Most of the men nodded.

"The nobili run their race on horseback through our city." Uccello raised his voice in anger. "Then we have donkey races, and they laugh at our antics."

"Signor Uccello is correct," said Brunelli, leaning against a marble tomb. "I see the nobili from Cortona, Arezzo, and especially Florence heave belly laughs. They jeer at us on our donkeys, as we fight each other and drag the beasts across the finish line."

"Davvero!" said Selva's red-haired presidente, Signor Caretto. He scowled as he looked at his fellow Senese. "I hear them in the balconies above the piazza, drunk with our red wines. The terraces are raucous with insults and jeers. They love to see us pitted against each other, pummeling our neighbors' faces. We are buffoons in their eyes."

"Our young bucks enjoy it well enough," argued the presidente of Pantera, Signor Manetti. "The youth yearn to fight in the piazza and prove their strength and bravery. It is in the Senese blood."

"Bah," said the presidente of Drago, Signor De' Luca. "Pulling an ass across a finish line is not a noble fight." His contrada was allied with Aquila, and he had a personal dislike for Manetti. "As long as the nobili can laugh at us, they regard us as unworthy rivals. But the glory of a horse race among contradas. That would unite us and celebrate the glory of Siena!"

"Yes! Signor De' Luca is exactly right." Signor Uccello pressed the point. "This is what I suggest: on the 15th of August, Day of the Assumption, Aquila, with the help of the other contradas, will stage a Palio on a course from Porta Romana at Santuccio, up

Via di Pantera, and over Via di Città and Via del Capitano to the Duomo."

Several contrada presidenti nodded.

"And," continued Uccello, "this shall be exclusively for contradas, with no participation from nobili whatsoever unless they join us as equals, as contradaioli. Each contrada competes against the others, mortaring together the bond of brotherhood of Siena."

"But what of horses?" said the man from Leocorno. "Our contrada does not have the lire to buy fine thoroughbreds as do the nobili families. We cannot afford such a luxury."

"We will race what we have, what we can afford. This is about our hearts—not our horses."

More heads nodded.

"The granduca will never permit it," said Signor Manetti, a sour set to his jaw.

"On the contrary. I have spoken to our ally in these matters—"

"If you are referring to Governor di Montauto, he is a puppet of the de' Medici," snapped Manetti. "One grumble from Granduca Francesco, and di Montauto will run with his tail between his legs."

"Manetti is right. I know of your friendship with di Montauto, but you can never trust a Florentine," said Cesare Brunelli.

"On the contrary, the governor has offered to present the proposition to the granduca next month, if the contradas are willing," said Uccello. "I believe he is a true Drago contradaiolo."

Several men grudgingly nodded their heads. The Medici-appointed governor loved his contrada.

"The Contrada dell'Aquila will request permission from the Balia," said Ucello, referring to the city's autonomous governing council set up under Cosimo. "If the Balia approves our request—and why should they not, they are contradaioli of Siena—the Palio will have legal sanction.

"Then the governor will invite the granduca to attend as our honored guest." Uccello allowed himself a sly smile. "It would be politically uncomfortable for him to turn down an invitation from the City of Siena to such a celebrated event."

"You have thought this out quite carefully," said the Civetta representative, Signor Nonne. He blinked his bulging eyes, looking very much like the owl for which his contrada was named. "All Europe eyes Tuscany, yearning for an excuse to attack. Francesco cannot afford even the slightest misstep. If he refuses an invitation to be our honored guest, he will look petty and fearful. If he over-turns the Balia ruling that allows an event of civic pride, he will show his doubts in his own power as ruler of Tuscany."

Nonne's sly smile mirrored Uccello's.

The men grunted their assent, knowing how all Europe despised the de' Medici granduca, especially after the murders of the two de' Medici princesses.

"The Day of the Assumption is dedicated to our city's saint and protector, the most Holy Mary. The contradas' Palio will be a sign of our pride in Siena," said Signor De' Luca. He didn't add "and our glorious republic"—nor did he need to.

He clapped his hands together. The sound echoed in the cold air of the stony vault like a clap of thunder.

"Drago will join our brothers of Aquila in the first true Senese Palio."

"What say you then, men of the contradas?" asked Signor Uccello. "Will you of Siena accept Aquila's invitation of a contrada Palio on the Day of the Assumption? A Palio for the contradas, and only the contradas?"

The chorus of "Sì!" filled the crypt, ringing in the ears of the frozen dead.

CHAPTER 54

Siena, Brunelli Stables, Vignano

APRIL 1581

"You must learn to ride the Palio by racing one," said Brunelli. "It is one thing to control a horse in an open field. It is quite another in narrow streets with screaming mobs, neck and neck with other horses and fantinos. We will take you to race in the small-town Palio."

I said nothing, excited at the thought. A Palio!

"I have made arrangements for you to race Signor De' Luca's Caramella at Monteroni d'Arbia," said my padrino.

"Monteroni?" My zio had taken me to their market to sell our wool.

"It hosts a Palio," he said. "And you can get the feel of the tight corners, compete against other racers, learn to maneuver—"

"I am going to race De' Luca's horse? Really?"

"He wants the horse trained for the Palio. I think she is too young to race, but Caramella is his property, not mine. And at least you will be only a feather on her back."

I threw my arms around my padrino's neck.

"You trust me? Signor De' Luca trusts me?"

"I think his son might have some influence," said my padrino, clearing his throat. He looked down at me solemnly.

"The blue-eyed one? Giorgio's friend?" I said, running my thumbnail between the gap in my teeth.

My godfather smiled. "Ah, you have noticed his eyes, have you?"

"Per favore! He doesn't even know I am alive," I said.

"Do not tell me you have not noticed how he hangs around, watching you ride. Contrada del Drago is a long way from Vignano. Surely he does not come here just for the scenery."

"I do not care why he comes if it means I can ride Caramella in a Palio!"

"You must be careful," said my godfather. "If anything happens to that filly, you may lose your support . . . and your admirer. To a De' Luca, a horse is more important than a rider."

"I shall never betray the De' Lucas' trust," I promised. "I love Caramella."

I smiled so wide, I could feel the bright sun warming my teeth. I reached down and stroked Caramella's tawny coat, glistening chestnut in the afternoon light.

"A Palio, Caramella," I told her. "Not Siena's Palio, but a Palio just the same."

We were ready, Caramella and I. She had had two days' rest after making the ride from Siena to Monteroni, on the banks of the Arbia where it joined the Ombrone. When we got to the town, my padrino had insisted I stand her in the cold waters of the Arbia.

"She is still a baby," he said. "Babies need care. This was a long ride for a filly who has now to run a Palio."

Now we stood by the edge of the course, the four of us: my padrino, Giorgio, Caramella, and I.

The track, made of the good *tufo* earth carried into Monteroni from the countryside around the town, had been packed by the villagers' feet. Although compressed, it made an ample cushion on the cobblestones.

Monteroni's course started and finished at the piazza. The course ran clear through town, *alla lunga*, like that of Siena. But it ended with one final lap *alla tonda*, a circuit around the piazza, where the crowd could watch the finish.

"Are you ready for this, Virginia?" asked my godfather. Despite the crowd's raucous laughter and festive chatter, his voice flew to my ear clear as an arrowshot.

"More than ready," I said. "Caramella can beat any horse here."

His forehead creased.

"Too much confidence can lose a race, cara. These are all experienced horses—and experienced riders. You must respect them. They know many tricks to win—and to make another jockey lose."

"I am not afraid," I said.

My padrino grunted.

"Maybe you should be. Just a little, ciccia."

I made a face. Why should I be frightened when I knew I could best them? I had worked hard to blot out any shadow of doubt.

"Caramella is a headstrong filly," said my padrino, as he adjusted the *spennacchiera* on her headstall. The little mirror, rimmed with yellow, green, and red satin ribbons, flashed in the sunlight. If Caramella were to lose this precious ornament, she would not be qualified to win the race. She could cross the finish line without me on her back and still win, but without the spennacchiera, all was lost. I would have to fight to keep her head away from the snatching hands of another fantino.

"Guide her carefully into the turns. Monitor her speed. Otherwise she will take the bit in her teeth and use her strength, not her wits. The corners in this village are even tighter than Siena's."

"Not as tight as our Siena finish," I insisted, "the turn onto the final stretch to the Duomo, Via del Capitano." I wanted to show him how much I already knew.

"No," he said. "Not that tight. But there are more of them, and a young horse like this could easily take a fall. And the final lap around the piazza can throw off the best horse and rider."

We had walked the course together, and now he reminded me—yet again—of the landmarks I had already memorized and dreamed of all night.

"Watch for the market corners. Both of them! And then the chiesa. The three pillars. And then let her run!"

He patted my knee.

"Use the gifts you have, feel the horse under you. Stay centered, Virginia. But do not forget, you are *la testa*, the head that guides this horse. Guide her wisely."

"Sì, Padrino."

"Up you go," he said, boosting me up.

My linen skirt whispered as it creased under me. I tugged material away from my legs, leaving my skin bare against the filly's body.

"What do you think?" I said.

His face creased in a smile.

Giorgio spoke for the first time since we had made our way to the track. "I think you look like a ragazza-fantino. I never would have imagined it. You look like you were born on the horse's back."

I dipped my chin in gratitude. I gave the slightest pressure with my right leg. Caramella danced forward, bobbing toward the *mossa*, the starting area.

"Virginia!"

"Sì, Padrino?"

"Do not let anything distract you. Forget your pride, forget everything but the race."

"Of course, Padrino," I said. "But we will win, you will see."

Brunelli pulled off his cap, rubbing his gray head. He cast a look around at the other riders.

Five other horses and riders—two from Siena houses of nobili, and three from Florentine nobili—lined up at the rope, inside the mossa. A sixth horse—the *rincorsa*, the starter horse—and rider from Arezzo took a position outside the mossa. When the rincorsa entered the mossa at a full gallop, the rope would drop and the race would be on. That is the way of the Palio. That last fantino controls the start completely. He can wait as long as he wants until he sees an advantage—perhaps a rival is distracted—and then he starts.

I maneuvered Caramella into the line at the rope. The filly reared, squealing at the scent of the other horses, especially a stallion right beside us.

"Be careful, ragazza," shouted the fantino, not much older than I. His horse was black, a glossy sheen reflecting the morning sun.

He reminded me of Orione. I swallowed hard, seeing the sculpted muscles prancing under the fantino. I was riding a novice filly who had not the strength and weight of that horse.

If I were on Orione . . . but, no, Orione would not do well in the flats. He would be impossible to control. Only running uphill—

An older fantino on my other side muttered, "This is no pony ride, *ragazzina*." Little girl. I scowled at him. He had a Tuscan accent but a coastal look: the salty look of a sailor. His thin face was creased and scarred, the skin pulled tight over his skull.

Probably from the Maremma—the wild west of Tuscany—raised to ride Palios in Florence.

"Stay out of my way. I do not have time to watch out for little girls," he snarled.

A laugh rippled through the crowd, pressing close to watch the start of the race. I saw the glint of a silver flask tipped to the sun as a young nobleman dressed in silk brocades took a draught. He lowered the flask and stared right at me.

I stared back, not recognizing him. The nobleman pointed at me and pushed his way closer to the mossa. In the intensity of that moment, waiting for the race to start, I saw everything with a fierce clarity. A few drops of red wine stained the young nobleman's lips, colored his teeth purple. I saw Giorgio turn toward the stranger and his eyes widened. He shouted something, but the noise of the crowd covered his voice. Then he pointed to the nobleman and back to the Maremma jockey.

Now I could hear him as he stabbed his finger at the older fantino. "Stay away from him, Virginia!"

The young nobleman turned. "Outrageous, Brunelli! A girl riding a Palio?"

"Next we will have pregnant women riding!" said a jockey.

"Or worse, the whores of Siena," taunted another.

The oldest jockey laughed wildly. "At least I ride for Signor di Torreforte, who can tell the sex of a rider. Where are your coglioni, girl?"

I screwed up my mouth, preparing to spit at the fantino. Caramella sensed my agitation and danced, rubbing her chest hard against the taut rope of the mossa.

Just as I let the spit fly from the gap in my teeth, I saw a movement from the corner of my eye.

The start horse galloped into the mossa. The rope dropped in front of us.

The oldest jockey had kept his eye on the rope, using his laughter to distract the rest of us. He was first across the start line, with the others close behind.

Caramella leapt forward, her herd instinct attuned to the other horses. I was pitched backward, then flung to the left side, my hand grasping for her mane.

As I fought not to fall, that fierce clarity returned, and I was certain I could hear my padrino's voice.

"*Tieni duro*, Virginia!" Hold on!

I pulled myself upright as Caramella flew down the street.

Bits of mud from the other horses' hooves splattered my eyes and face. I leaned down low, my chin touching Caramella's mane, my hands pumping the reins as the filly surged forward.

"Diabolo domine!" spat Giorgio as the horses disappeared into the city streets.

"She was distracted," muttered his father. "Her pride lost her the advantage."

"She can still make it up, Papa," said Giorgio, his fists clenched.

"She must learn to control her temper, or she will never be a fantino."

"Fantina," mumbled Giorgio under his breath. "The first fantina."

Virginia's light weight allowed Caramella to fly through the course. Together they passed several riders, recovering time lost at the start.

The small, twisting streets of Monteroni offered few straightaways. Her padrino's words and the sight of the landmarks filled her mind. The market's two sharp twists. Yes. The Chiesa di San Fabiano's three pillars. And now! The one long straight leading to the piazza, her chance to let the filly stretch out her stride.

The black stallion came into view. As Virginia rode past the boy, he whipped his horse wildly. The fantino's teeth clenched white against his dark skin as his lips pulled back, desperate not to let Virginia pass him.

Ahead of her by two lengths was the Maremma fantino. He looked over his shoulder as the course bent around the last turn and spilled out into the piazza.

His eyes widened as he saw Virginia's skirts.

To a roar from the crowd, they entered the piazza—the Maremma fantino and Virginia far ahead of the rest.

The young nobleman with the wine-stained teeth leaned forward, cupped his hands around his mouth, and shouted at the Maremma rider.

"Dai! Dai!" Come on! Come on!

Standing near him, Giorgio's eyes narrowed to slits. His mouth stretched into a smile.

"Babbo! She's gaining!"

"Dai, Virginia. Dai, dai!"

As Virginia and the Maremma jockey galloped neck and neck, the fantino raised his whip in an arc. He lashed out at Caramella, slashing at her neck.

"No!" screamed Virginia.

Caramella wavered, then regained her stride. The fantino raised his whip again and Virginia, without a thought, slashed out with her whip, striking the fantino hard in the face.

The jockey raised his hands, protecting his eyes. The horse slowed, confused by the tension on the bit.

Caramella surged forward, Virginia clamped her torso flat against the filly's mane, and they crossed the finish line half a length ahead, to the delight of the roaring crowd.

The young nobleman—Giacomo di Torreforte—spat in disgust. He kicked at the wooden barrier set up along the course.

"Maledizione!" he cursed and turned away, elbowing through the crowd of well-wishers swarming to congratulate Virginia.

Riccardo and his father, Signor De' Luca, approached her. Signor De' Luca's stroked his mare's neck, then nodded his head.

"You have made the House of De' Luca proud this day, Virginia Tacci," he said. Riccardo stared up at Virginia saying nothing, but his face radiated joy.

"Will you, Virginia Tacci, do the Contrada del Drago the honor of riding the Siena Palio on Caramella in August?"

Virginia's mouth opened in a gasp of joy. She sought Giorgio's eyes, then her padrino's.

"Sì," she said, clasping Caramella around the neck. She buried her face in the mare's mane, drinking in the warm smell of horse. Then she heard her padrino clear his throat.

Virginia straightened up, sitting tall, the way she had been taught to ride from that first night in the hills of Vignano.

"It would be the greatest honor of my life to ride Siena's Palio for Drago," she said.

CHAPTER 55

Florence, Palazzo Vecchio
MAY 1581

Francesco de' Medici slit the wax seal and unfolded the parchment. Governor di Montauto's letter reached from the granduca's eyes to his waist.

"Too wordy, this di Montauto fellow," said the granduca to his secretary.

He hurried through the document, then handed it to Serguido.

"It seems I am invited to a Palio in Siena. In August."

"Serenissimo, of course. As the Granduca of Tuscany, you are always invited to the Palio," said Serguido. His forehead creased as he strained to make out di Montauto's exuberant handwriting.

"But this is a special Palio. Only the contradas will run. Not a single nobile house. It seems that Siena's Balia has given permission. Damn my father for granting them their own government! The scoundrels shall not have my approval."

"What do the commoners know of staging a Palio? Where will they get the horses, the money? Preposterous!" said Serguido.

"He does not say. Only that the Contrada dell'Aquila is hosting the event for the Assumption in August. You will write immediately, insisting Palios are a reserved right of the nobili. We cannot let Senese contradas think they are our equals."

The granduca clenched his fist. "A Palio for the commoners. It would only foster rebellion."

The secretary looked down at the letter again.

"Why does di Montauto not use his scribe?" said the granduca. "His handwriting is like a drunken poet. All flourishes and ridiculous squiggles. I can barely make it out."

Serguido stood with the letter in his hand. His dark eyes darted left to right. Then his jaw dropped open, like a turtle drinking raindrops.

"My granduca," he said. "I fear you did not finish the letter."

"Full of Senese gas, this signore," said the granduca. "I have not the patience. Tell me what he says. I have work to do."

"There is to be a special entry in this race of the contradas. A girl."

"*Una ragazza?*"

"A fourteen year-old girl, Granduca. Representing Drago contrada."

"Let me see!"

The granduca snatched back the letter. Serguido pointed his fine manicured finger at the offending sentence.

"A ragazza! A girl riding among men? In a Palio?"

"Yes, Your Highness. A girl. And it seems the race is dedicated to *tutte le donne*." All the women of Siena.

"And who is this ragazza?"

"I will inquire immediately. Might I see the letter again?"

"Are there not . . . laws?" stormed the granduca, rising to his feet. "These Senese are insufferable and . . . sublimely treacherous. Are they doing this to draw attention to themselves? To shame Tuscany? To shame *me*? Letting a girl race a Palio!"

"Might I see the letter again, Your Highness?" asked Serguido once more.

The granduca flung the parchment to his secretary.

"We must find a law!" Francesco thumped his fist against Serguido's writing desk, making the inkpot erupt in a black spurt. "This is against all moral decency. A virgin, I would assume. Riding astride, bareback! We shall write to the Pope, to my brother the cardinal. Women astride on horseback, acting as if they had a *cazzo* between their legs."

The granduca crossed his arms over his chest. Serguido scanned the letter. He cast a quick glance at his master, wondering if he was thinking of his dead sister.

"It seems," said Serguido, "the girl's name is Virginia Tacci. She is of di Montauto's own contrada, the Drago. And . . . she is a shepherdess."

"A shepherdess! He is joking, yes?"

"No, Your Majesty. Already there are poets who write sonnets to her talents, according to di Montauto."

"A girl riding the Palio? A shepherdess, at that? Find a law, Serguido. Or create one, damn it, subito!" This minute!

Serguido dipped his head, acknowledging the granduca's instruction.

"Might I offer counsel, Granduca?"

Francesco expelled his breath so fiercely, Serguido could smell the red wine and garlic from his noonday repast.

"Speak!"

"I will look to see if there is such a law, but I doubt there is. My counsel to you would be to accept the invitation. I think it is a challenge. I think the Senese mean to make you look weak, threatened by a mere shepherdess."

Francesco glared, but said nothing.

"If you write to Governor di Montauto and forbid this girl from riding the race, it will only bring back memories of—forgive me, Your Highness—"

"Speak, damn you!"

"Memories of Princess Isabella and Lady Leonora. Everyone knew how you despised Isabella's independence, including her riding and hunting."

Francesco shot a look at his secretary.

Serguido paused. When the granduca remained silent, he continued. "Let the Senese do as they please, I beg you, Granduca. Permit the Palio. The Contrada dell'Aquila will soon see that the expense of hosting such a race is ruinous. And the girl will most likely fall off early in the race, humiliating herself. Then you can justly amend the law to forbid girl fantini forever. For their safety and well-being, of course."

Francesco pulled at his mustache. He looked across the room where the Bronzino painting of Isabella used to hang.

"The Senese fling sand in my eyes. But damn it! Yes, as always, your counsel is wise. I shall sidestep their trap, damn them to hell! But I shall have some words for the loquacious di Montauto. Clearly he needs to straighten his mast, for it leans windward toward Siena."

CHAPTER 56

Siena, Palazzo d' Elci
JUNE 1581

The dark interior of Palazzo d'Elci was a cool marble refuge from the heat of the Siena summer. Giorgio drank in the chilled air, lingering to enjoy its refreshing embrace before mounting the stairs.

A clatter of horse hooves and the creak of wooden wheels rushed into the dark quiet of Via di Città.

The great door behind him opened again, the heat spilling over the threshold. He could hear di Torreforte speaking to his coachman in gruff tones.

"Push past the other coaches, then! I expect you to be right here in front when I descend. The street is dusty, the street cleaner shirks his duty. It sullies my clothes to walk so far from the entrance of the palazzo."

Di Torreforte entered the dark foyer. His eyes momentarily blinded, he stood blinking in the transition.

Giorgio studied his features, committing them to memory.

"Who's there?" said di Torreforte, reaching to the sheath where his dagger should be.

"Do not fear," chuckled Giorgio. "I have no weapon either."

"Ah, it is you," said di Torreforte. He pushed past Giorgio and up the travertine steps.

Giorgio called up to him, his voice echoing up the stairwell.

"Did you enjoy the Palio in Monteroni d'Arbia?"

Other art students above them stopped on the stairs, even coming from the open hall of the art studio. Heads hung over the railing, ears cocked to hear. Word of Virginia Tacci's victory and di Torreforte's defeat had spread quickly.

Di Torreforte stopped at the landing in front of a marble bust. He let out a disgusted grunt.

"Yes, I saw your ragazza-fantino race, Brunelli, if that is your meaning. Disgusting display."

"Ah," said Giorgio, crossing his arms. "Then you saw how she was victorious. Impressive, wouldn't you say? A girl astride a horse."

Voices echoed above in the stairwell. A low, approving whistle from a Senese floated down. Di Torreforte jerked his head up, searching in vain for the culprit.

The stairwell filled with laughter.

"Not a true victory!" said di Torreforte. "A fluke, entirely. My fantino said his horse's tendons were swollen at the start of the race. Otherwise he assures me he would have beaten her by ten strides. She did not know how to rate her horse, she took the corners with dangerous imprecision—"

"Is that so?" said Giorgio, taking a step closer to the staircase to meet di Torreforte's eyes in the dim light. "Because it certainly looked as if your fantino struggled at the end of the race. As if he couldn't fend off Virginia's whip to his ugly face."

Di Torreforte's nose pinched down, his entire countenance narrowing like water through a funnel.

"Monteroni is meaningless. The Siena Palio is a different race. A filly might win on a level course like Monteroni, but never in the ascent from the Porta Romana to the Duomo. A filly—"

"Are you referring to the filly Caramella or to Virginia?" taunted Giorgio. "Both would beat any match."

"Damn you, Brunelli, you *pezzo di merda*!" Piece of shit.

Giorgio basked in the echoing curse. He heard shrill whistles of appreciation echo down the stairwell.

"You listen to me, bastardo," said di Torreforte. "If you care about that girl, you will keep her from riding next month in your foolish contradas' Palio. There is a distinct possibility she might get hurt. Or worse."

The young nobile pivoted and continued up the stairs toward the painting hall. The students hurried away from the banisters to the easels overlooking Il Campo.

Giorgio suddenly felt the air chill his bones, despite the heat of a Tuscan summer.

————

Di Torreforte was not blind. He had seen Virginia Tacci's shining dark hair fly out from under her racing cap, the gleam of determination in her eye. Those dark eyes against her skin tanned by the Tuscan sun had not escaped his notice.

But he did not see her as a beautiful girl.

She was the essence of Siena, descended from ancient bloodlines that were Roman, perhaps even Etruscan. As he watched her ride, he recognized the strength of a people raised from time immemorial on the grapes and grains of the ocher soils, a ferocity of spirit that was unmatched.

He knew how the surging Senese pride had enraged the granduca.

Di Torreforte would use that rage to his advantage.

Granduca Francesco was a distant relative—the di Torrefortes had married into the de' Medici family during Lorenzo the Magnificent's reign. Di Torreforte's grandfather had distinguished himself, battling the Turks as a naval commander. He was richly rewarded with tracts of land in southern Tuscany as a result of his faithful service to Cosimo.

Di Torreforte's father had done nothing to burnish the family's military honor, but he had done quite well in Senese banking when the de' Medici had seized Monte dei Paschi, Siena's ancient financial institution.

His father's financial triumph had enabled young di Torreforte to pursue painting. He would eventually inherit his father's money and lands, so there was no need to seek his own fortunes.

It pleased him greatly to paint, to dine in Florence with art collectors and hold forth, discussing art. He sold canvases to Florentine merchants who wished to curry his family's favor. He loved their flattery and their shiny florins for his artwork.

But one person—another artist—soured his joyful pursuit: that damned Senese horse trainer whose talent far outshone di Torreforte's efforts.

And that was where Virginia Tacci entered his plans.

Di Torreforte had seen the gleam of pride in Giorgio Brunelli's eyes when he watched Virginia Tacci ride. He had never seen Giorgio as proud of his art as he was of the Senese girl.

The key to Giorgio's soul was this shepherdess. To destroy her would destroy his rival.

CHAPTER 57

Siena, Crete Hills

JUNE 1581

After the Palio at Monteroni d'Arbia, I felt I could fly. News of my victory reached Siena and Vignano before I did.

Riccardo De' Luca accompanied us, never speaking to me but riding alongside as if he were a servant. When I turned to speak to Giorgio, I caught Riccardo's eyes glowing.

"Did you want to say something?" I asked him.

"No. Sì—" he said. His flesh took on the color of a toad's belly. His blue eyes blinked at me.

"Sì? What is it, Signor De' Luca?"

"I want—I want you to call me Riccardo," he said. His lips were rigid, as if a fish were talking to me.

"Va bene. Riccardo," I said, finding the sound pleasant in my mouth.

"You—Virginia. You rode very well. My father was pleased. Caramella does well under you."

He turned from white to red in a blink of an eye, and looked away toward Siena in the distance.

Giorgio shrugged, looking disgusted with his companion. He gestured toward the city on the high hills.

"Nearly home."

"She is *bella*," I said. The Duomo tower and the Torre del Mangia were visible, rising before us.

"Bella," croaked Riccardo. "Bellissima!"

"But I love the Crete just as much," I confided, looking at the fields of grain that had turned golden in the last few weeks. The undulations of gold and green comforted me.

My padrino was strangely silent during our ride. I considered this to be a sign of his advancing age, for it had been a long few days.

———

I was between sets of horses the next day when my padrino took me aside.

"Virginia, I want to talk to you," he said. Because he did not call me ciccia, I suspected something.

"Did I not ride the new colt well today?"

"It is not that. It is about Monteroni d'Arbia."

I relaxed, beaming at him. I could never get enough of praise. "Sì?"

"You made a terrific error in the race."

My smile fell.

"I won, Padrino! I won!"

"That is not enough. You were lucky," he said. "You let your temper control you, and your horse was left abandoned."

"What do you mean? When I whipped the jockey on the course?"

"Not that. That was good, in fact. Brava! I'm referring to the start, at the mossa. You were more interested in emotions around you than in communicating a sense of calm to your horse. She felt it. When the rope dropped, she left you because she felt only a senseless weight on her back, like a sack of barley. You are lucky you had the strength to pull yourself up and stay mounted.

"That was a serious error in judgment, not worthy of a Palio fantino."

Ugly words flooded my head, puckered my lips. I loved my padrino more than anyone else in the world.

"But—"

"No! Listen to me, Virginia Tacci. You listen to me, because what I say could be the determining point of the Palio. Before the race, there is only one thing to focus on: keeping calm. Your horse. And yourself."

"But I must maneuver at the rope, find the right position."

"That is second. First, you communicate with your horse—your legs, your seat, your hands—but most of all, your head, la testa. La testa is the most important part of a Palio for both the horse and the rider. If you keep a cool head, you will allow your horse to conserve his strength for the race."

I listened. I listened as if I were back again in those first years of riding. That was what Giorgio always taught me. Then I thought again, for a moment, about la testa. My Padrino was using that word to refer to my head, my mind, that I had to think for both myself and the horse. But every time I thought about the Palio and la testa, I thought about the other meaning of that same word: the head of the race, the rider in the lead.

Yes, Padrino, I will be la testa—and I will be in la testa, too. I will be in the lead. I will win the Palio!

My padrino laid a hand on my shoulder. "Be the rider the horse can trust. Then the two will become one."

"Yes, Padrino," I said, my eyes lowered. "Forgive me. Until the rope dropped and the race started, I was no rider."

I felt his strong arm around my back in a hug.

"Yes, remember this," he said, pulling me close. He kissed the top of my head. "Then we will see a winner at the Palio."

———————

Riccardo could no longer sleep at night. He wandered the streets of Siena.

The de' Medici guards nodded to him—at first suspiciously, but after several weeks of following him down Banchi di Sopra or Via Termini or Via Terme, they learned his routes and, more important, his destination.

Riccardo would ultimately make his way to the Piazza del Campo and stand gazing silently at the Torre del Mangia in the moonlight.

Lovesick, they said. Riccardo De' Luca has the *mal d'amore*.

The night watchmen in Contrada del Drago would give a two-tone whistle to let the Contrada della Civetta guards further down the street know that Riccardo was approaching.

No danger, advised the whistle. Only the nightly visitor.

Riccardo leaned against the cool stone arch of Vicolo San Pietro that led into the piazza. He watched the moon ascend to the left of the Torre del Mangia.

Virginia.

Has there ever been a more beautiful girl?

Yes, she is young. Fourteen, perhaps. But not too young to ensnare my heart.

Her grace on a horse, her determined face. The iron of a shepherdess raised in the Crete, hard as flint. The essence of Siena.

And the gap between her two front teeth. Enchanting.

He had noticed more and more young men—and older signori—had made the journey from the city to watch Virginia ride. Indeed, Riccardo did not know it, but even the elderly Florentine governor, Federigo Barbolani De' Conti di Montauto, had fallen a little in love with the girl. He had written letters to his friends in Florence, even to the granduca, praising her virtues of both beauty and horsemanship.

But as he stood at night, under the sparkling stars forming a dome over the piazza, Riccardo did not think of other suitors for the young Virginia. It was he, and he alone, who was her love, even if he found himself tongue-tied for the first time in his life when he watched her ride.

He stood babbling as she dismounted one colt and swung up like a boy from the wilds of Maremma onto the next.

She barely nodded to him; her focus was always on the horse. She ignored the growing throngs of spectators, the cheering, the popping of corks as her admirers toasted her skills. Peasants watched the shepherdess fling herself up on the backs of wild colts. Old men picked their teeth with their fingernails as they gaped in astonishment.

"Guarda! La villanella . . . guarda!"

Look at the villanella, look!

When Virginia galloped her horse out into the fields and hills surrounding Vignano, Riccardo felt as if she carried off his soul as hostage.

"Thinking of a ragazza?" asked a guard as Riccardo blinked up at the stars.

Riccardo pulled out abruptly from his reverie, straightened his posture. He composed himself, his face regaining a semblance of dignity.

But the Florentine guard only chuckled and clapped his hand on the younger man's back. At first De' Luca resisted, hating the touch of a Florentine. But the warmth of the gesture was genuine.

"You were far away, signore. Surely you are in love."

Riccardo shrugged.

"How do you know?"

"It is obvious," whispered the guard. "I have been in love quite a few times in my life."

"I shall never be in love again as I am now. There is no other girl—"

"Ah, but that is what we all say. No one like this one."

"No, you do not understand. Truly, there is no girl like this one. Davvero!"

"Arrivederci," said the guard, moving on. "Do not drink up too much of the moonlight, or it will make you pazzo."

CHAPTER 58

Florence, Pitti Palace

JUNE 1581

"Will we attend Siena's Palio?" Bianca's brocade dress rustled as she sashayed this way and that, admiring her velvet slippers, a gift from the Venetian Court. "I must have new dresses for my appearance on the balcony of the Palazzo Pubblico. I cannot let the Senesi see me in anything less than splendor—"

"What do you know of Siena's Palio?" asked the granduca. He stroked her arm as if trying to erase her thoughts. "Why would you want to travel the dusty roads when you have Boboli Gardens and our country estates?

"It will be a grand festival," she said. "Or so say our courtiers who bring news from Siena." She smoothed his fingers under her own.

He dropped her hand, frowning.

He is in a foul mood. No matter.

Bianca's white hand reached for a ripe fig on a blue ceramic fruit tray. As she bit into the fruit, the folds of her double chin trembled.

"I am told the contradas will race against each other as if they were nobili houses. And there is a twelve-year-old villanella riding! Delicious! This is a spectacle I must see, Francesco. Imagine, a little girl—"

"Who told you this?" he snapped.

Bianca pulled in a breath. She knew how to handle Francesco de' Medici. Had she not managed to marry him secretly only months after Giovanna's death?

"I heard it from Governor di Montauto at dinner last night. He praises this girl as if she were a goddess. He says she is given the most difficult colts and, despite their rearing and bucking, clings to their back—"

"Like a trick monkey!" said Francesco. "And she is fourteen, not twelve."

Bianca swallowed the last juicy mouthful of fig. *Basta! I am the Granduchessa of Tuscany now. I will not endure rudeness!* She cocked her head at her husband.

"Francesco, why does this girl disturb you? I should think it is entertaining to see the best horsemen of Tuscany look like fools—racing against a shepherdess."

"Because that shepherdess is a Senese!" said Francesco. "You do not understand the Senese, or you would not be so flippant! They will make her into some kind of symbol of rebellion."

Bianca laughed, dabbing her lips with a linen napkin.

"Oh, really, Francesco! She is not going to *win* the Palio. She is simply a delightful diversion. And I should like to see a girl race the streets of Siena in her skirts. Please?"

Francesco glared at the granduchessa as if she were mad.

"You do not understand politics, Bianca. This is not for your amusement. You cannot understand the significance of this for Siena and Florence."

"Oh, really, Francesco—"

He snatched her linen napkin and threw it to the floor.

"And stop devouring everything in sight!"

CHAPTER 59

Siena, Pugna Hills

JUNE 1581

My zio Giovanni came as often as he could to watch me ride. He especially liked to watch the training of Orione. But I noticed his fits of coughing as he bent low over his knees in spasms.

At first I thought it was the dust that kicked up from the tufa in the arena. But then I saw that no one else was coughing, no one else bending over to spit, leaning against the post like an old man.

I rode up into the hills where we kept our flocks to visit him. I never went by our cottage, for I had vowed never to see Zia Claudia again as long as I lived.

Zio Giovanni and I developed a stronger bond than we ever had when I was a baby or young girl. I was nearly fourteen now, and though still considered a ragazza, I knew that other girls my age in the village had already married and were young mothers.

"Virginia!" cried my uncle. He was using his staff more and more to support his weight. "What beauty do you ride today?"

I was on a particularly skittish horse named Nero, who reared when I brought him closer to smell Zio's hand.

I leaned forward to keep my seat. My skirt flew back, ballooning behind me. Nero heard the flap, rearing all the more.

"Tranquillo! Easy, boy. Easy, boy," I called to him.

"Brava, Virginia, brava!"

When the colt had settled enough that only a thin white ring shone in his eyes, I spoke again, through my seat and hands, communicating calm.

"This is good for him," I said. "He needs to see more, get away from the stable. He has no experience beyond his paddock."

"You will need that skill at the mossa," said my uncle, nodding. "So many accidents happen there. Too many fantini have fallen before even crossing the rope."

"I will not let Caramella sweat," I said. "I am riding her now in the streets of Siena. She sees the city's hawkers, the ox carts, the splash of the chamber pots, the crush of people. I have ridden her among the stalls of the market, past the tanner's vats, between the fishmonger's stand and wine casks. Everywhere there is confusion, noise, and excitement.

"She will not sweat at the mossa, Zio, I swear it. I will be one with her."

I slid off the colt's back.

"He needs to have a new experience. Let's take him among the sheep."

We walked side by side toward the sheepfold. I caught my uncle looking from me to the horse.

"Cosa?" I asked. "What?"

"I cannot believe that our little shepherdess has grown up to be a fantino. Look at this magnificent creature."

"He is a beauty," I said, admiring the colt.

"And Orione?" asked Zio.

I smiled.

"My heart will always belong to Orione. But Carlo Ruffino thinks he is too tempestuous to be a Palio horse. He still will not take a bit—I always ride him in Stella's collo di cavallo."

"To forever ride the stallion in a halter? No, you would never be able to control him in the turns of the Palio."

"It is the only way to ride him. He fights iron in his mouth. And I am the only rider he has had on his back. But you should see how he gallops up hills! That is the time I can truly control him. Coming down, he is wild. He takes me for quite a ride!"

Zio raised his hand to my head. He let his hand slip down my hair in a caress.

"You must know how proud I am of you, ciccia. And how proud your babbo and mamma would be," he said, pulling me close. "Yes, you would make your parents proud."

"Carlo says Orione does not have the testa for the Palio," I said, chattering on. "And it is the head that is most important. To stay calm, to focus, says Padrino."

One of the ewes that I had raised from a bottle caught my scent. She *maaa*-ed and bounded up to me.

The colt reared, pulling the reins from my hand. He stood snorting, his nostrils so wide I could see the red flesh far inside his nose.

"Easy, tranquillo, tranquillo," I cooed, my fingers hooking the loose reins.

I brought colt and ewe together slowly. *Poco a poco.*

"There now, Nero," I said. "This is Petra. She is a good friend. She used to keep me warm at night."

I remembered the years when the tangy odor of the grass in Petra's cud was the smell that accompanied sleep. I would entwine my fingers deep in her wool, the way I would later do with Orione's mane. Before Orione, Petra and Dog were my only companions, night after lonely night.

"There, much better. Friends now, no?"

"You are still a shepherdess, Virginia," my zio said, laughing. Then he began to cough.

"I am a horse trainer, Zio! I—" The coughing became choking.

"Are you all right?" I asked.

He waved me away. "Nothing," he said.

But then he bent over, the way I had seen him do at Vignano. I watched him spit bloody sputum.

"Zio, you are not well!"

"Nothing, niente!" he repeated between spasms.

"We must go speak with Padrino Brunelli. He can make you a tonic to cure your ailment. Come!"

"I cannot—leave—the sheep."

"I will stay here with Nero. I will spend the night. You must go!"

Zio nodded to make me stop nagging, but it meant nothing. Then he collapsed in the grass, his hand clutching his chest.

"Zio!"

He groaned, his cheek mashed down into the grassy loam.

I galloped Nero as hard as he could run to Brunelli's stable. Nero ran all the faster, knowing where we were headed.

Giorgio set down the bucket in his hand, seeing something was wrong.

"It's Zio Giovanni!" I said, swinging down off the colt. He reared back, the hem of my skirt frightening him.

"I have left him in the hillside with the sheep. He—he—"

Giorgio called out, "Babbo! Giovanni Tacci is ill! I will fetch your bag."

He turned to a stable boy leading a mare into the barn for a rubdown.

"Hitch up the wagon with the young roan at once!"

Padrino drove the wagon while Giorgio and I raced ahead to the hillside.

The sheep were scattered along the grassy banks, while Zio's two dogs chased them toward the lower pasture. I saw Zio's body in the exact same position.

The wind lifted a tuft of his graying hair.

————————

My zio Giovanni lived, but God had taken his speech. He could walk with the help of a cane, but only stumbling steps. He moved his eyes slowly, like a baby trying to focus.

One morning when he awoke, he could not even raise his hand. He lay in bed, paralyzed.

I visited the house daily, though my zia did not acknowledge my existence. Still, she did not chase me from the cottage, as she knew that she and my zio needed me more than ever to help with the sheep.

"I promise I will tend to the ewes and help the cousins as much as I can. Do not worry, zio," I said, pressing my cheek to his. "Do not worry, I will take care of you."

I could see by the desperate light in his eye he understood.

CHAPTER 60

Siena to Vignano

MAY 1581

Governor di Montauto breathed in the fresh air of the country-side. It was still cold enough in Siena for wood fires to burn in the hearths, choking the city with the lingering smoke of winter.

Only beyond the great walls, in the country, was one able to see and taste the first signs of a late spring. Birdsong filled his ears as he rode his mare along the muddy road, through pastures where the red poppies patched the green with brilliant swatches of crimson.

Di Montauto pulled up his mare, leaning on the pommel of his saddle. His weight made the leather creak.

"Beautiful," he sighed as he surveyed the rolling hills. By his side, his stablemaster, Fausto, nodded silently.

The governor of Siena insisted on riding, rather than taking the ornate governor's coach. At heart, di Montauto was a horse-man, and Siena's passion for the Palio had fanned his own ardor over the years. There was nothing he loved more than the Palio—and he was excited that this year, the contradas would host their own horse race for the first time.

Despite being a de' Medici pick for governor, Federigo di Montauto had been seduced by Siena's charms. It was not a popular sentiment at the de' Medici Court, and the governor had to contain his enthusiasm for Siena and its people when talking to the granduca.

But sometimes, despite di Montauto's best efforts, his affection for the Senese spilled over into his conversations and letters. It was then he would notice the sour look on the granduca's face, as if he had sipped bad wine.

Gazing out at the beauty of the Senese hills, di Montauto knew he would have to do a better job of controlling his passion for his new home—lest he lose his position, his privilege, perhaps his life.

"Over there," said his stablemaster, breaking into the governor's thoughts. "The girl—you can see her. See, just there, on the crest of the hill. Virginia Tacci."

Governor di Montauto lifted his hand to his brow, shading his eyes from the sun.

"Dio mio!" he whispered. "She has grown. No longer such a little child perched on top of her mount. Look how she commands her horse now. She truly rides like"—he was going to say angel, but there were no horses in heaven for angels to ride, were there?—"a goddess," he finished, resolutely. "This girl rides like a goddess. And the horse! Look at the horse she rides."

Di Montauto studied the bulging lines of the horse's neck, the muscled torso and haunches.

"It is a stallion! Look how she is one with him as he gallops. What a horse!"

"I believe it may be Oca contrada's stallion, from the d'Elci dam Stella."

"Stella?" said di Montauto. "I watched her win the Palio twice! He does not resemble her. He looks more like—an Arabian horse, but much larger, sturdier of bone."

The stableman said, "Stella was bred to a wild Maremma horse, Tempesta. Tempesta has never been ridden. Too pazzo—crazy and dangerous! The Duchessa d'Elci insisted she wanted an Oca foal from him."

Di Montauto smiled slowly, watching the girl gallop the stallion across the poppy fields, cutting a swath through the pools of red.

"What a horse," he said, then he whispered it yet again. "What a horse!"

When Carlo came to the stables, Giorgio stood in the stall with Virginia.

"I am sorry, Virginia," said Carlo, leaning over the boards. His voice was soft and gentle. "The Duchessa d'Elci sends her apologies as well. It is for the Palio we do this, you realize. We must keep the governor's favor."

Virginia's fingers entwined around Orione's mane and neck. "Please let me have a few minutes to say good-bye to him."

Giorgio nodded to Carlo.

"We will bring out the stallion in just a minute, Carlo."

"Sì, signore."

"How could they?" spat Virginia. "How could the duchessa do such a thing? I am the only one who can ride him. The only one!"

"Listen, Virginia. Governor di Montauto is all that stands between Siena and the tyranny of the granduca. If the duchessa refuses to sell Orione to him, it could be disastrous. If di Montauto said one word to Florence against us, Francesco would forbid our Contradas' Palio. With joy."

"But Giorgio, Orione is mine, I saved his life!" She choked back tears, tears that Giorgio had never seen before, despite the many falls and injuries of learning to ride, despite hunger and loss, the lonely childhood of an orphan, the cruelties of a hateful aunt.

Never had he seen Virginia Tacci cry.

Outside the stable door, they heard Florentine accents. Hooves clattered on the paving stones. Carlo, waiting respectfully at a distance from Orione's stall, went out to greet Governor di Montauto's horsemen.

Giorgio pushed back her hair, wet with tears. He whispered in her ear.

"In spirit, he will always be yours. But one girl's love for a horse cannot stand in the way of Siena's Palio. Think of the contradas! Think of Siena—"

"But it is Orione!" Virginia sobbed. "Giorgio—it's Orione!"

"The Palio," said Giorgio, shaking Virginia's shoulders. He pulled her arms away from the horse to make her look at him. She struggled, twisting away, but he held her tightly by the shoulders.

"This is bigger than your love for a horse, Virginia. Listen to me. It is the *Palio*, our Palio—the way it always should be. The contradas of Siena. This is our chance to see Siena united and proud again."

He shook her.

"Look at me, Virginia. You will ride Caramella for Drago. A shepherd girl, a poor villanella—the impossible! If you do anything that interferes with Governor di Montauto's pleasure, there will be no Palio to ride."

She stopped crying. He knew she was listening at last.

"If you do not let Orione go, people will laugh forever at your dream—*our* dream, Virginia. You do this for Siena."

He let go of her shoulders and tied the leather lead to Orione's halter. She shook, holding back sobs, but in her shaking, she nodded her head.

Yes.

CHAPTER 61

Siena, Santuccio Church

AUGUST 1581

My padrino and I rode to Porta Romana one last time before the running of the Palio.

Time and again, day after day, we had walked or ridden our horses the length of the course, from outside Porta Romana at the ancient church of Santuccio to the steps of the Duomo. Over and over again, my padrino pointed out the difficult sections, places where I might falter, places where I might fall. Dangers I had never considered. And he suggested strategies, tricks I could never have thought of.

Today, as we neared the gate, children ran alongside us, pointing and cheering. One little girl, her face smeared with dirt, plunged her fingers in her mouth. She stared, transfixed, as I rode bareback.

I lifted my reins and wiggled my fingers at her. The girl stood stunned. Her brother shoved her, waving back at me.

"Wave to the villanella, you idiot. Wave to her!"

The girl moved her hand, her black eyes riveted on Caramella, then on me.

As we approached the redbrick church of Santuccio, Padrino Cesare halted his horse at a spot where the road widened for carriages to turn around.

"The mossa will be right here." As if I didn't know. "Unless you are the rincorsa—the starting horse and rider—you will press your horse against the rope to feel the drop. But if you are not in control, and your horse jumps forward before the rope drops completely, the rope will trip your horse and you both could fall." As if he hadn't warned me a hundred times already.

I stroked Caramella's neck. The children pressed closer. My padrino's horse flared his nostrils, prancing.

"Move away, ragazzi!" said Cesare, his voice gruff. He flung his arm in the air to shoo them away. His horse jumped. Despite his age, my padrino stayed centered in his saddle.

Then he winked at me. "Look how Caramella accepts the crowd and confusion. You have done well with her, ciccia."

"Rompicollo! Rompicollo!" chanted the children. "*Viva la villanella!*"

My padrino frowned. "Do not call her Rompicollo!"

"What's wrong, Padrino?"

He shook his head. "Villanella is all right. Not Rompicollo."

I looked down at the chastened children.

He does not want to think of me lying on the cobblestones with a broken neck.

"It is all right, Padrino. They mean no harm," I said.

"Basta! *Vai via!*" Go! He chewed his lip. "They are brats. Fine. Let them shout. Come the Palio, the crowds will wave flags in her face, shout, and scream. You and the horse must focus only on the race. You must focus on the course, on the streets, on the turns—on the most treacherous turn, from Via di Città onto Via del Capitano. Many hopes have died at that turn."

I know the turn, Padrino. I see it in my sleep!

"And then—only then!—you must focus on the banner, the *drappellone* at the finish."

We were standing at the starting line, and he was already imagining the finish. And standing there with him, I could see my hand reaching out and grabbing the drappellone, the sign of victory.

Caramella took a little side step under me, imagining victory right along with us.

————

As we rode the course, my padrino's every word was an echo of words he had spoken so many times already.

"Here at San Giorgio, Caramella will be heaving, for you will have galloped a long way uphill. And here the *discesa* begins. You must control your horse, or she could stumble when she hits the downhill pitch. Prepare her. Tickle her bit with some pressure to let her know you expect her to listen. Collect her just enough to shorten her stride.

"Her legs will still be expecting to climb. I have seen other horses falter here. They run down the hill splay-footed, dangerously. Your horse must be nimble, ready for the descent."

I nodded.

If I were riding Orione, that would be a problem. But with Caramella, I can control her gait with a light hand.

"In the late afternoon, the downhill section is shadowed like a canyon," said Padrino, his brow creasing. "But then, as it rises again on Via di Pantaneto, there will be patches of bright sun and shadow."

I nodded, because I had to—as he warned me for the hundredth time, because he had to.

"These shadows are the devil! If it is a bright, hot day like today, your eyes, your horse's eyes, will not adjust to the darkness quickly enough. You could miss a turn or a narrowing of the street. I have seen both horses and fantini die smashing into a wall."

My linen blouse stuck to my back. The divided skirt that the Drago seamstress had designed for me was soaked in horse sweat. *Better to feel the horse's back.*

Via di Pantaneto became Banchi di Sotto, and we walked the long, gradual curve of the streets past the palazzos that circled the outside of the Piazza del Campo, past the point where Sotto joined Sopra and the two streets together became Via di Città, the lower end being the old Via di Galgaria, where cobblers sold their wares.

Every step of the way, my padrino pointed out corners, arches, doorways, balconies, windows where contradaioli might cheer or jeer—or throw something—places for speed, places for caution.

We moved aside for a procession of creaking wagons loaded with dirt. The contadini were bringing more *tufo*, Senese earth, the color of yellow dust. They stopped up ahead, where half a dozen other wagons were shoveling their loads onto the pietra serena. Women and children stomped the sandy dirt, packing it down onto the stone. They were followed by two wagons with barrels of water. Men doused the tufa to harden it more.

My padrino's horse snorted at the commotion.

"*Buon lavoro, signori!*" called my godfather.

The men looked up from their labor. They doffed their caps. "Long live la villanella," they cried. "Virginia Tacci, la villanella!"

"The footing should be good—unless we have rain," said a man dressed better than the others. He nodded to me and winked. "But we'll see to it the *tufo* is set well. For you, villanella. For you."

I stared up into the deep blue sky. Today, at least, there was no sign of rain clouds, the traitors against a Palio.

"Buon lavoro," said Padrino, nodding to him. Good work.

"Buon Palio!" answered several of the men with gap-toothed smiles.

"There may be scraps of trash underfoot," said Padrino as we continued on the tufa-covered track. "Usually the children prowl the streets, gobbling up any edible scraps they can find. But watch for anything that might make Caramella lose her footing."

I nodded, thinking of the children we saw lingering at the Porta Romana, arms and legs as thin as sticks. They looked as I did only a few years before, on the day I saw Isabella de' Medici jump the fallen olive tree. I wondered what the little girl with the jam-smeared face thought when she saw me ride Caramella. She could not speak nor move.

"Those children at the Porta Romana," I asked. "There are so many. Do they have family?"

Padrino shook his head. "If they had family, they would be working alongside them. The ones at the gates, begging for scraps, are orphans. They must sleep at night in the Maria della Scala."

My mind shot back to the months I lived in the orphanage opposite the Duomo. After my parents' death, Zia Claudia was certain I had the contagion, marsh fever, and would not let me enter her house.

Santa Maria della Scala—a great church and orphanage—was heaven and hell.

The frescoes on its ceilings filled with saints and angels. The graves in its catacombs filled with the bones of the ancient dead. Above us, the singing of the nuns, the deafening clanging of the great bell of the Duomo. Below us, the moans of the damned.

Night after night, I woke screaming. Not even the kind nun in our nursery could chase away the fear, though she rocked me in her arms, kissing my head. "It is all right, Virginia," she whispered. "Santa Caterina's spirit lingers here, even amongst the dead. She worked here many years, tending to the sick and abandoned children, just like you."

"Virginia!" said Padrino.

I was yanked out of my reverie.

"Pay attention. Study the landmarks. Forgetting one could mean defeat—or death. Right here! Where Via Fontebranda meets Via di Città. Remember! This means you are coming to a very dangerous place, where Via dei Pellegrini joins La Città. The shadows can hide the curve, and here on your right, Palazzo Cervini protrudes out into the street. A horse I dearly loved died right here, Virginia. Listen to me! When you see Via Fontebranda on your right and the Costarella dei Barbieri on your left, it is almost too late. Gather up Caramella. Remember! Here! Left rein and pressure on your right leg to hold the turn. Stay well to the left, *capisci*?"

"Sì, Padrino. I understand."

We walked on, past the Palazzo d'Elci to where the street curved back to the right at the white limestone of Palazzo di Chigi. Then the final, sharpest turn: Via del Capitano, leading to the Duomo.

"There are sure to be many nobili here," said Padrino. "You must not be distracted by them. The ladies will wave silk banners and scarves, men will shout. Even if they don't frighten Caramella, they could make another horse shy or balk. Be ready for a spooked horse to jump in front of you or hit you from the side in its fright."

"Sì, Padrino. But I will be in the testa, I am sure."

Padrino chewed his lip again. "The horses who are in the testa are the first to encounter any obstacles. Do not be a fool, Virginia. If you think you will be at the head of this race the entire time, you know nothing about winning a Palio. Victory goes to the rider and horse who use the shadows and their knowledge of the course to slip by their opponents. And disaster comes to the fantino who does not know where a palazzo juts out into the road, where a widening becomes a narrowing."

At last we came to the Via del Capitano. My godfather took off his cap.

I looked at the rolls of canvas in donkey carts. Canvas barriers lined the turns of the course, blocking off side streets so that a *scosso* horse—a horse without a rider—would be directed into the piazza of the Duomo.

"Quattro Cantoni," said my godfather with a nod. "It will be packed with signori from the nobili houses, pushing against the canvas to see the horses negotiate the turn. The last turn. The worst turn."

Yet again, he told me because he had to. I nodded, yet again, because I had to. This was our ritual.

"The canvas can reflect the sun, blinding the horse. And the nobili will be mobbing this corner to see the riders negotiate the turn. By now, you will be tired. Caramella will be tired. Here, above all, you must be careful."

I pulled up Caramella, staring at the open square, the Piazza di Postierla. The last of the evening sunlight glanced off the roof tiles, leaving a pool of shadow on the gray stones. The nobili strolling the piazzetta stopped dead in their tracks, transfixed at the sight of me bareback on a horse.

Caramella whinnied, the high shriek from her lungs vibrating against my legs, shaking my spine.

"Come on," said my padrino, making the turn into Via del Capitano.

In the light at the end of the street, I could make out the Duomo's façade past the Palazzo de' Medici and the archbishop's palace. On the corner of the façade reared my white marble horse, and in the piazza directly below it, the single column that marked the end of the race.

———

The night before the Palio, Signor De' Luca insisted I sleep at their palazzo. It was only a few minutes from Drago's stable, where Caramella was kept. While I preferred to sleep in the straw next to the mare for the night, I was persuaded to show some decorum for my host and patron.

"Tonight you belong to us," his wife said, kissing me on both cheeks. "Perhaps to all Siena, but especially to Drago."

A blazing parade of candles lit the night as Siena prepared for the Day of the Assumption. Required by law to bring candles to the Duomo—the wax that would illuminate the cathedral for the rest of the year—every citizen of Siena entered the arched doorway carrying his contribution to the Virgin.

The cathedral filled with flickering light, then the thunder, as each contrada sent flag bearers and drummers. Ricocheting in my rib cage, pounding in the deepest cavity of my body, the reverberation stirred my spirit. I looked up to the golden stars cut in the midnight blue sky of the Duomo.

Giorgio stood at my side. He touched my elbow to draw me close.

"The stars?" he whispered in reverence.

"Sì," I said, still looking up. *"Le stelle."* I found myself thinking of Orione.

Giorgio took my hand and squeezed it.

"The drappellone is painted to match. It is my maestro's gift to the city of Siena. Here it comes!"

Aquila's contrada marched behind the great banner, stretched high on gilded poles, ten braccia high. Celestial blue brocade fringed in silk, fur, and pearls gleamed in the candlelight of the great cathedral.

Gazing down on us from the linen was the Virgin of the Assumption, wearing a lapis blue veil, with the gold crown of heaven upon her head. Seven golden stars, representing the seven contradas that would race the Palio, floated over the Virgin's crown. Gold and silver embroidered rays lifted her up to a heaven of blue-white clouds.

My eyes were riveted on the Virgin's downcast glance as she bid farewell to the mortal world below.

"Look, there," whispered Giorgio. "At that man."

I could not move my eyes from the splendor before me. The candlelight from the thousands of offerings blazed, bathing the Virgin in light.

Giorgio shook my elbow, insisting. "Look, Virginia!"

I reluctantly shifted my stare.

A man dressed elegantly in black silk taffeta stared back at me, his eyes glittering in the blazing candlelight.

"That is di Torreforte," said Giorgio in my ear. "Make sure you know him."

I felt a chill, but I stared at him in the flickering candlelight, absorbing his features.

"If you see him near you, you are in danger," said Giorgio. "He is my enemy. He will stop at nothing to see us fail."

I did not shift my eyes away from the man's stare, but met it with my own.

The drappellone came between us, a mob of Aquila contrada-ioli marching solemnly behind.

When the crowd had cleared, di Torreforte had disappeared.

———

The night before the Palio of the Assumption, Aquila invited all the contradas to a feast in the Piazza del Campo. The heart of the city—already stifling from the mid-August heat—was choked with wood smoke from Aquila's ovens. The streets were clogged with merchants bringing salamis, sausages, and vegetables from the countryside, wagons groaning with casks of red wine from the surrounding vineyards.

The piazza had been swept and washed clean, the stones slick and gleaming in the evening light. Tables stretched the length of the piazza, and even the meanest beggar was given a place to break bread and drink a jar of wine.

La Signora De' Luca had dressed me in a brocade dress of crimson with a bodice of emerald green. The cuffs, made of red silk, were slashed with a brilliant gold. Together they represented the colors of Drago. Red, green, and yellow ribbons were braided into my hair, capped with a pearl-seeded headpiece.

I was given a seat of honor next to the capitano of Drago, Signor De' Luca. I fidgeted, twisting my braided hair around my fingers, until Signora De' Luca gently pulled my hands to my lap.

"All eyes are on you, carina. Let them see you proud and dignified, as befitting a dragaiola."

She was right. All eyes were on me.

I avoided those eyes, looking up instead at the lavender sky of the summer evening. Clouds of *rondini,* the swallows of Siena, flew in erratic circles above us, black soot caught in a capricious wind. The flapping of the de' Medici banner on the balcony of the Palazzo Pubblico caught my eye. The entire second floor was ablaze with candelabra.

A blast of trumpets startled me. The granduca and granduchessa walked hand in hand onto the balcony. The granduchessa wore a braccia e braccia of green taffeta, molded over her wide hips, squeezed tight against her full bosom.

She looks like a stuffed olive.

The presidente dell'Aquila stood, and all of Siena rose.

"On this feast of the Assumption," he said, looking not at Granduca Francesco but at the contradaioli packed in the piazza, "we ask the Santa Madonna del Voto for her blessing as we begin our festivities. Bless our city, the glorious Siena, our brave fantini and their magnificent horses, who will run tomorrow with the blessing of the Madonna in the Palio of the contradas. We ask her blessing in memory of the Republic of Siena and its faithful contradas."

Everyone at the table opened their eyes to exchange glances, their heads still bowed.

"He dares to leave the granduca out of the blessing!" whispered a woman to my left.

"Is he mad?" whispered a nobleman across from us.

I looked up and saw the granduca had lifted his head, his red lips pressed tight together, staring down at the speaker.

"And . . . ," continued the presidente after an endless moment of silence, "finally, we ask for a special blessing upon our granduca, Francesco of Tuscany; his wife, the granduchessa; and their blessed children. Amen."

Governor di Montauto, seated next to the presidente dell'Aquila, rose quickly.

"Indeed, it is the greatest honor to have our granduca and granduchessa here to witness our Palio," said the governor, bowing to Francesco. "I am sure all Siena joins me in extending a special Senese welcome."

The crowd applauded dutifully, the Florentines among us cheering.

I heard Giorgio to my left. "A special Senese welcome indeed," he muttered. "His words have double meaning. He does not like the granduca any more than we do."

The governor continued. "Tonight we salute the magnificent horses and the brave men—and one girl—who will ride the Palio tomorrow."

"Brava! Virginia Tacci!" called a Drago contradaiolo at our table.

"Brava, Virginia Tacci! Brava, Siena!" echoed Contrada della Torre, adjacent to us.

Then all the contradas—those who were running and those who weren't—erupted.

"Brava! Brava! Brava!"

Governor di Montauto beamed as the contradaioli of Siena beat their fists against the tables, the sound echoing in the piazza.

"Brava! Brava!"

An attendant whispered in the governor's ear. Di Montauto turned to see the granduca glaring down at him from the balcony.

The smile slid from the governor's face.

"Wait, wait!" he said, waving his arms to arrest the cheer. In the silence, he struggled to find something to say. Then he smiled. "Now we will have poetry! The best poets of Siena will speak to honor our granduca and granduchessa."

"Yes," said Aquila's president, rising. "We shall hear the voices of each contrada in poetry."

One by one, the contradas extolled the virtue of their neighborhoods, of their camaraderie, and of their devotion to the Virgin.

When Drago's turn came, Riccardo pulled out a scrolled parchment from his coat. His hand shook as he unrolled the paper. He stood, clearing his throat. He did not look at me but spoke clearly to the hundreds who filled Il Campo.

Virginia Tacci, the virgin shepherdess
Born and bred in the Senese country, among the flocks
To poor parents with no fanfare or notice
but so strong-hearted is she
her courage has quieted the swaggering braggarts
she races the Palio bravely, without wile or deception.
You holy goddess, may your beautiful mantle protect
This girl who keeps her virginal flower

I swallowed hard. "My virginal flower? How dare he refer to my virg—"

"Silenzio!" hissed Giorgio. I noticed his cheeks burning as much as mine at the words.

Come and rescue me from my burning ardor
I long to be sheltered in your glorious temple
To which I devote all my heart

that sings of my desire.

There was a moment of silence in the piazza.

"*Grazie a tutti.* Thank you, signore e signori," said Riccardo, finishing.

"Bravo!" Contrada del Drago erupted in cheers. The tables rumbled with the pounding of fists. All the campo joined in, cheering for the poet, cheering for me. For me! Virginia Tacci.

Riccardo bowed to me, his blue eyes seeking mine. "Every word I say is true, Virginia Tacci," he said. He sat down beside his mother, whose eyes were shining with tears.

Is this man in love with me?

I stared down at the wine stains on the tablecloth, unable to speak. Then a woman at our table stood up. Her hair was uncovered, braided in strands of pearls. She was elegantly tall, strong, and calm. Until now, all the poetry had been read by men. There was a murmur around the piazza.

The poetess took a deep breath and began, her voice clear in the suddenly quiet night.

No better courage could be shown,
No better skill.
It could not be foretold from her humble origins
That from the ancients such high passion
As Bradamante and Marfisa
Should show themselves in her.

Il Campo shook with the applause, cheers, the pounding of fists on the table.

"Who are Bradamante and Marfisa?" I asked, looking at the cups of wine raised in my honor.

"They were women, warriors who fought during Charlemagne's time to save Christianity from the Saracens," said Signora De'

Luca. She saw my bewildered look. "She compares you to them as a liberator for Siena."

"A liberator? From whom?" I asked.

Signora De' Luca raised an eyebrow, then lifted her chin up toward the blazing lights and the de' Medici above us.

Giorgio squeezed my shoulder, whispering in my ear. "It is very dangerous, these words this poet has chosen. Stay close to me when we leave the piazza. Do not speak to any Florentines."

Again I looked up at the balcony of the Palazzo Publicco. The granduca stared down at me, not applauding. He rubbed his open palm over his beard.

"Viva Virginia Tacci!" shouted a voice from Aquila's contrada.

"Viva Virginia Tacci e Siena!"

I sat stunned at hearing my name echo around the piazza. I lifted my eyes to the Torre del Mangia. When did I become a liberator for Siena? My dream was to ride—and win—the Palio. Now all Siena had fastened their hopes on me.

My dream and Siena's had become one.

I thought of my father and mother. How I wished they could hear the voices of Siena shout our family name to the heavens. I watched the pigeons burst from their roosts in the bell tower of the Torre del Mangia and circle into the sky.

Maybe my parents could hear after all.

Chapter 62

Siena, Contrada del Drago
Midnight, August 15, 1581

"Virginia Tacci! Wake up!"

In the guttering candlelight, I saw the maid's face puckered with horror.

"Signor De' Luca waits downstairs. Hurry!"

———

When I burst into the Stalla di Contrada del Drago, the two grooms wouldn't lift their eyes from the straw-covered ground, stained with blood.

"How could this happen? Were you asleep? Drunk? What?"

I grabbed one by his tunic, pulling his face close to mine.

"Look at me!"

The boy, about nineteen, flicked his eyes at me, his eyelashes laced with hay dust.

"I am . . . sorry."

"Sorry! You . . . !"

Giorgio pulled my wrist.

"Let him go, Virginia."

When I didn't let go, Giorgio yanked me away.

"Virginia!" he whispered harshly. "Leave him alone."

A crowd pressed in the open doors. The small space was packed. I felt their eyes on me—on me and on their horse, who lay bandaged in the stall.

I crumpled to my knees beside Caramella.

"She will heal, Virginia," said my padrino, wiping his hands on a purple-stained cloth. "The knife did not cut so deeply as to cripple her. But she will never again run a Palio."

"How could this happen?" I cried. "How could anyone—"

"The guards said they saw no one until after the deed was done. The scoundrel took off running down Via Sapienza," said Giorgio.

"Guards! What kind of guards are they?"

"They are grooms, Virginia. Only grooms."

"Virginia," said the other boy, who was only a year or two older than me. "I slept in the straw of the stall, never leaving. I heard no one, nothing, until the squeal of the mare—"

My eyes widened, my throat constricting.

"Basta!" snapped the older boy, cuffing his companion on the ear. "Do you not know when to keep still?"

The smaller boy clapped a hand on his ear and ran out of the *stalla*, crying.

"We failed you, we failed the contrada," said the older boy. "Most of all, we failed this good mare. I will bear the shame for the rest of my life."

I heard a murmur from the crowd.

"What is your name?" said Giorgio.

"Bastiono," he said, hanging his head.

Giorgio laid a hand on his shoulder.

"Whoever did this was practiced in stealth. A paid assailant. You are expected to sleep next to the mare and observe her health, feed, and water. But no one expected an intruder with a knife."

"It was another contrada," growled the butcher from Via Terme.

"A Goose," muttered another.

"Or Aquila itself, wanting to win—"

"Stop!" said my padrino. "Listen to you all, flinging accusations at our brothers. No Senese would have done this!"

"He is right," shouted the wheel maker. "No Senese would hurt a Palio horse."

"It was an outsider, someone who was determined that this mare would not run the Palio," said Brunelli. My padrino stopped for a moment, then said, more quietly, "Determined that this mare wouldn't run . . . or Virginia!"

———

Governor di Montauto arrived in the cool of the morning, his carriage rattling down the cobblestones, scattering the crowd that had gathered beyond the stalls, spilling out to the entrance of the old university.

"Clear the way!" shouted the driver as he turned the carriage into the mouth of the tiny Vicolo della Palla a Corda.

The mob of Drago contradaioli parted to let the de' Medici governor into the stalls. Under the brick-arched ceiling, the chestnut mare stood awkwardly, holding the weight off her bandaged foreleg. Beside her stood Virginia, stroking the horse's neck.

"Governor di Montauto, buongiorno," said Signor De' Luca quietly.

The girl turned toward the governor, her face etched with grief. He had seen her in Il Campo dressed in a brocade gown, her hair caught up in ribbons. Now she looked vulnerable and pale, just a little girl, her hair covered in a kerchief, stroking a badly injured horse.

A memory of his granddaughter flashed in his mind.

Just a girl. Not an Amazon or a goddess—a girl. A girl who loves a horse.

"I came as soon as I heard the news. How badly wounded is the mare?"

Signor De' Luca turned. Cesare Brunelli appeared from the shadows.

"She will walk again, perhaps even gallop, governor. But run a Palio—never. The knife cut through the first bands of sinew."

Governor di Montauto saw the girl flinch.

"Do you have any idea who the assailant was?" asked the governor.

Several people murmured, then a ripple of hostile sounds spread out of the stall to Via della Sapienza, but no one answered.

"No," said Signor De' Luca, his voice firm, silencing the crowd.

Di Montauto looked around. The despairing faces of the Drago contradaioli made him think of Siena's defeat in the siege twenty-six years before. The bright, spirited flame of last night's celebrations had been extinguished. Bad fortune had robbed these people of their chance to compete in the Palio, maybe to win.

Governor di Montauto knew in his heart it had to have been a Florentine who did this. A sour taste welled up in his mouth, matched by a twinge of guilt.

Now the girl—this Virginia Tacci, celebrated just hours before in poetry and toasts, the star of the celebration—would not ride.

But was that not exactly the motive for this barbaric attack? This cannot stand. I cannot allow it!

"I have a horse," said Governor di Montauto. "He is not accustomed to the streets of Siena—but he is one of the finest horses in my stable. Bred in the Crete hills, a black stallion. I believe you know him."

Virginia stared at the Florentine governor, unblinking.

Orione!

"Virginia Tacci," said Governor di Montauto. "He is yours. For today and always."

Virginia opened her mouth. Her kerchief slipped back, exposing the waves of dark hair.

"I give him to you, Virginia Tacci. A present. You shall ride the Palio today for Contrada del Drago."

CHAPTER 63

Siena, Contrada del Drago

AUGUST 1581

Orione was led to the Drago stall behind a chanting crowd. The stallion, having been confined to a stable in recent weeks, was unaccustomed to the city and to the shouting people who surrounded him.

Orione reared and snorted, nearly pulling the rider who led him from his horse.

"Get back, Drago!" he shouted, spurring his gelding around to face the stallion. He yanked hard on the lead.

The rider behind him flicked a whip at the stallion.

"Get up there, devil," he said. His horse pranced and spun around, spooked by the whip.

They had galloped the streets, despite the hard cobblestone, to keep the stallion moving. From the Piazza del Duomo to the heart of Drago was only a matter of minutes—descending the hill, crossing in front of the blessed home of Santa Caterina, and climbing up through the little streets near San Domenico.

Drago banners waved, their green, red, and yellow the most intense colors of any contrada. The cheering roused the rest of Siena, robbing them of the few hours' sleep before Palio day.

Orione jumped sideways at each wave of a flag, each shout of a Drago contradaiolo.

"The girl is sure to break her neck riding this stallion!" said the lead rider.

The grooms ran out to Via della Sapienza to take Orione.

"Get him into the stall," said di Montauto's groom. "He is going to kill himself or a Senese in the street."

"*No!*"

Virginia Tacci raced out.

"He must learn the Palio course. We have only a few hours."

Orione roared, smelling her. She held Stella's collo di cavallo in her hand. Instead of the rosettes of Oca, the browband and cheek-straps were woven with the green, red, and yellow of Drago.

She gave a pulsing whistle. Orione pricked his ears and gave a violent jerk of his head, breaking free of the handler. He trotted to Virginia, whinnying.

"I will take him now," she said.

The stallion tossed his massive head. He lowered his muzzle into her arms, sheltering his eyes from the riotous scene.

"Orione," she murmured, pressing her lips against his blaze.

The crowd quieted. Di Montauto's men withdrew their horses, looking over their shoulder at the girl and the horse.

"You have a lot to learn in the next few hours," she said. "You will run the Palio, as we have always dreamed."

Brunelli limped over to her. He pulled her close. For the moment, it was just the three of them: the man, the girl, and the stallion.

"Do not ride him now, Virginia."

"What do you mean?"

"He cannot be accustomed to the streets of Siena in the few hours remaining. It is impossible."

"But, Padrino! He will balk at everything. The banners, the shouting crowds, the flag bearers, the children—"

"It would take months to acquaint him with the kind of turmoil he will face today. Think of the training you have done with Caramella. You do not have that luxury of time."

"But—"

"Listen, ciccia. There is only one way to ride him in the Palio. Ride him as wild and as free as his spirit. He was bred to run. Do not hold him back, let him burn bright."

He stared fiercely into Virginia's eyes.

"He will feel your urgency through your legs, your hands, your seat. Through your being, Virginia. Ah! Via di Sotto and Via di Città. Via dei Pelligrini and Via di Città. Madonna! Via del Capitano—"

He stopped himself and closed his eyes. When he spoke again, he said, "Virginia. Urge him to run as fast as he can. Then he will see and feel nothing but you."

An old man with firewood strapped to his back entered the crowded street.

The stallion reared high on his back legs at the sight, pulling the halter out of Virginia's hands, scattering the contradaioli like pigeons in the piazza.

Signor De' Luca rushed over to Virginia and her padrino. "He will be a disaster on the Palio course. I cannot permit you to ride him, Virginia."

Her heart sank. But then Orione returned to her and nuzzled her again.

"He will quiet down with me, you will see."

"And he was quiet just now—until that woodcutter walked by. How do you expect to control him in the pack? How will you control him in the streets, in the noise, the flags? How?"

Virginia swallowed, stroking Orione's muzzle.

"Signore, I do not know how. But I will."

I put Stella's collo di cavallo on Orione myself, after the Drago *barbaresco* fastened the spennacchiera on the halter.

The barbaresco's face was sour, his mouth drawn up in a crooked line. He tied the ends of a long leather band under Orione's chin.

"Stand, you gruesome devil," he said, snapping the collo hard to test the knot. "The least we can do is give you reins."

"Leave him alone. What is wrong with you?" I said. "A barbaresco on the day of the Palio should rejoice, not wear an ugly face—"

His hand sliced the air with a disgusted gesture.

"Our first chance to race against the contradas of Siena," he said. "And we throw it away on a girl. A girl and an untamed horse!"

He spat on the stone floor. "Drago will be a laughingstock," he said, wiping his mouth with the back of his hand. "You know nothing of a true Palio. There are dozens of others who have experience. You rob us of victory, you skinny little shepherdess!"

I opened my mouth to curse him. The ugly words formed deep in my throat, bubbling to my lips like venom to be spat.

"Figlio di troia maiale."

"Virginia!" shouted my padrino. "We must ride to the mossa now!"

"Give him to me!" I said. "You are not fit to touch this horse."

I yanked the reins from the barbaresco. "Orione and I will make Drago proud, you mean bastard son of a whore!"

The crowd surged forward as we descended Via di Pantaneto to Via Roma, then out through the Porta Romana. As we passed through the city walls, I looked up at the emblem of the de' Medici palle above.

I swallowed back spit and hatred. I cleared my head.

La testa! La testa!

The mossa was set in front of the ancient Santuccio church—one rope clear across the street at a horse's chest level and one shorter rope behind, leaving the gap where the rincorsa would enter at a gallop, officially starting the race.

Governor di Montauto had assigned a representative to draw the starting positions. The crowd was silent in anticipation of the drawing, although with the confusion of the mossa—horses and fantini fighting for space and control—the actual starting positions would be far from exact. Except for the rincorsa, who would stay clear of the struggle until he charged through the opening and started the race. The governor's representative turned an iron and crystal vessel with a crank handle, withdrawing a little tube containing a name of a contrada.

"L'Oca! Posizione UNO!"

The Geese roared. Orione pranced under me. We watched as the fantino in green, white, and red took his position.

"Leofante. Posizione due!"

"Lupa. Posizione tre!"

I watched Padrino wipe the sweat from his eyes. He exchanged a worried look with Giorgio.

"Drago. Posizione quattro!"

I heard the dragaioli groan. I was in the middle of the pack.

If I were on the inside. Or even the outside. But squeezed between two horses—

"Take your position, Virginia. Do not lose your head. Don't worry too much about where you start. There is a long race ahead. Focus on your horse, you and Orione as one. Remember! La testa!"

"Sì, Padrino," I said, moving Orione past the attendant, who handed me my *nerbo,* my whip. I urged Orione forward through the opening and into the lineup at the front rope.

"*Onda. Posizione cinque.*"

"*Montone. Posizione sei.*"

The contradaioli from Giraffa roared. Giraffa was left as the *rincorsa,* the rider who would control the start of the race.

As the other horses jostled near us, Orione snorted, making short bolts under me as I tightened my legs and seat.

"Stop it!" I said.

The fantino from Onda said, "Get that horse under control." He waved his nerbo at us.

Orione reared, his nostrils flared. I wove my fingers deep into his mane with my legs clamped around him.

He smells a mare in the pack.

"Here!" said the Lupa fantino, moving his horse to make room. "Turn him toward me, villanella."

I dipped my head to acknowledge his kindness.

I maneuvered Orione sideways, his head toward the Lupa gelding. His flank brushed the taut rope, and he balked.

"It is all right," said Lupa. "Keep him sideways. The rope is too much for him."

"Grazie," I said. Orione skittered sideways. As I worked to control him, I saw an arched gate, framing the hills beyond Siena, a flash of green and brown—

Testa, Virginia, testa!

"Get that stallion out of my way!" shouted the Onda fantino. He smacked Orione's flank, making him jump under me. Out of the corner of my eye, I saw a movement of Giraffa, the rincorsa, felt the subtle charge shuddering through all the horses.

I swung Orione around and pressed him into the rope just as it dropped.

We catapulted into a full gallop up the hill toward the Porta Romana. Onda was left behind in a moment.

In the wild confusion of the charge, I narrowed my focus. For the moment, there was nothing but Orione and me. Flying. I pumped my hands with the movement of his neck. Then I raised my eyes to the Porta Romana. The first test would be the shadows of the thick city walls as we raced through the gate and into Siena.

Santa Caterina!

Orione did not falter. His heart told him he must lead the pack, and there were other horses in front. He could not allow that. We tore through the archway, through the darkness, into the light of the city.

The uphill was to our advantage. The street curved to the left, giving me room to slip past Lupa. I glimpsed a flash of white marble on my right: the Refugio di Santa Chiara.

Orione surged ahead, his strength forged from running the hills of Vignano. We passed Leofante.

The green-and-white tunic of L'Oca's fantino was just ahead on my right. We were nearing the gate through the original city walls from centuries ago. The street narrowed there, and L'Oca would have to crowd closer to me as we raced through the arches.

I let Orione have his head, depending on my legs and seat to control him. No strategy now, just speed. The hill crested at the ancient gate, and once we plunged into the mottled shadows of the downhill stretch toward the church of San Giorgio, there would be no place to pass.

I felt Orione under me. I was galloping too fast to talk to him. Everything was feeling, pressure, and touch. I did not see anything now except L'Oca close on my right and Giraffa and Montone on my left.

We reached the crest, racing past the statue of the she-wolf and the two human children she suckled. I knew that statue. I saw it. I didn't see it. I sensed it fly past, Orione still pounding below me.

Tranquillo, Orione, tranquillo.

And down we plunged. I tucked my seat under me, sitting down hard on Orione's back and pulling the reins in short tugs, hoping he would recognize the movement.

His stride shortened, but his pace did not. He hammered out a faster staccato. I could do nothing to control his speed.

L'Oca had pulled ahead, his horse accustomed to the transition onto the downhill course. The road narrowed, barely allowing our pack to pass. Squeezed together with Giraffa and Montone, I fell behind, but we were still in the race.

Now came more dark shadows and the Church of San Giorgio at the bottom of the hill. Just beyond that, the street narrowed sharply, and then the course would begin to climb again.

"Attenzione!" shouted L'Oca.

He swerved left to avoid the buildings jutting out onto the course ahead. Now Orione and I were trapped to his right on the outside, close to the buildings lining the edge of the street.

Orione hated being behind. He was born to race, born to win. I felt him surge toward the opening L'Oca had left.

The other riders knew I would have to give way to get through the narrow section. But Orione didn't want to slow down, and I didn't want to force him. For the last few strides before the narrows, there was a widening at the entrance to San Giorgio. If we did not get back into place, Orione and I would ride straight into the wall to our death.

As we met the final stretch of the downhill, I let go of my seat muscles and leaned forward, flattening on Orione's mane. We galloped beside L'Oca. The jutting building was right there, just ahead, there was no way . . .

And then, with a final impossible surge, Orione bolted past L'Oca, threaded his way through the vanishing slice of clear space, and we were still alive.

Alive and in the lead.

La testa!

I saw only the road rising ahead of us and the cheering crowds pressed flat against the walls, risking their lives and ours.

We veered to the right. Hoofbeats thundered in my ears, close behind.

But we were in la testa!

Now the road climbed up toward Le Logge del Papa and the curve left onto Via di Città and into the last third of the race.

We were embraced by the pounding thunder of hoofbeats, surrounded by the cheering of the crowds above us, beside us, all around us. And amid all that, I heard the shattering of crockery, a flowerpot, on the street behind me. Was that an accident, or was it aimed at someone? It didn't matter. All thought was lost in the thunder as we battled through the turn onto Via di Città. I caught a glimpse of the tower of the Duomo rising above the city's roofs.

Focus, Virginia!

A sharp whistle. The repeated thwack of a whip.

L'Oca on the right! He pushed next to me, his nerbo smacking his horse and then Orione. Then I felt the whip across my hands and the reins.

All is fair in the Palio.

"No!" I shouted.

I saw the buildings flashing by, a glimpse of Via Fontebranda. I heard my Padrino's voice, "Almost too late!" We were at the fatal curve, the shadowed corner where the Palazzo Cervini jutted out into Via di Città.

A horse I dearly loved died right here.

L'Oca was on my right, still lashing at me with his whip. Montone was hard on my left, shoulder to shoulder.

"Narrows!" I screamed.

I kicked Orione with my right foot, pulling sharply on my left rein. We ran hard against Montone, making him bounce away, staggering for a stride.

L'Oca slipped into the space I had occupied a blink of an eye before. The fantino screamed in agony as his arm and leg scraped the wall.

I had let him live. But now I saw the light blue and white of Onda on my left—where had he come from!—forcing his way between Montone and me.

The road to the Palazzo Chigi was a hard uphill. Orione heaved ragged breaths under me. I could hear the roaring breath of L'Oca and Onda as we galloped toward the gleaming white palace.

A riderless horse came up on our left side. Montone's fantino had come off in the battle with Onda.

We made the sweeping right toward the last stretch of uphill, toward the final corner. The hard right turn onto Via del Capitano, then the final sprint to the Duomo.

The afternoon sun was fierce, beating down on the white marble of the Duomo and the crowds at the finish line. Just above, on the terraces of the de' Medici Palazzo, looking out over the Piazza del Duomo, sat the granduca and granduchessa. Bianca Cappello tried in vain to cool herself, her fan beating the air with the velocity of a hummingbird's wing.

"Bring me another glass of wine," she snapped to her lady-in-waiting. "This heat is barbaric."

Secretary Serguido slipped out onto the balcony.

"The horses should be approaching any moment, my granduca."

"Are we ready?" asked the granduca, his voice low.

"Sì," said Serguido. They both stared down Via del Capitano to the sharp curve, the late sunlight casting a pool of shadow.

Giacomo di Torreforte was among the nobili gathered at Piazza di Postierla, at the corner of Via del Capitano. He stood as close as he dared to the canvas barricade. He heard the hoofbeats an instant before the horses came into sight.

The villanella was in the lead!

L'Oca and Onda were riding hard, close behind on either side. But as they fought their way up Via di Città, the black stallion pulled ahead.

Out of the corner of his eye, di Torreforte saw two men on the flag-draped balcony of the building at the apex of the turn. Their heads disappeared as they quickly crouched out of sight. As Orione entered the hard right corner, the men reappeared, their shoulders working in unison.

Three large planks sailed down, clattering into the street.

"No!" di Torreforte shouted.

The men disappeared inside the dark room behind the balcony.

———————

Later, I thanked God. But right then there was no time to pray, no time to think. Orione raised his head. I caught a glimpse of the nobility—the ladies in finery under the shade of fluttering awnings; the men crowded tight, cheering their contradas.

Then I saw something. There! What? Boards! Just in front of me! Clattering to the street. I clung to Orione's mane as he leapt. I felt the two of us lift up and over, flying, weightless.

We cleared the first two boards. There was no room for a stride before the third.

Orione fought to keep his footing, then lost that battle. I went down with Orione, clinging to his back as he stumbled on his forehand.

Women screamed. Men shouted. And somehow in that swirl of noise and panic and color and fear, I saw one single face clear in the crowd: Giacomo di Torreforte standing close enough to touch. And in that same instant, I heard Giorgio's voice. *"He will stop at nothing to see us fail."*

Faces and voices disappeared as Orione scrambled to his feet in the instant that L'Oca and Onda raced past. We pushed on, galloping toward the piazza and the towering marble Duomo. But I felt the change in his gait, and my gut sank.

The shadows of Via del Capitano were a tunnel between what could have been and what now had to happen. In the distance, I could hear the roaring crowd, see the sun dazzling on the marble cathedral, glimpse the flap of the drappellone just ahead. I pressed my face close to Orione's mane, letting his head free to gallop the last strides of the race.

We emerged into the bright light of the piazza and the roar of the crowds, the flap of banners, the whistles and cheers. We raced hard to catch the sweating flanks of L'Oca, never reaching Onda. Onda had come out of nowhere to take first, L'Oca second. I pulled Orione into a circle, trying to avoid running down a Senese. I slid off Orione, my hands already on his left fetlock as my boots hit the ground.

He flinched at my touch, raising his foot. A Drago contradaiolo took his reins.

"We will take care of him, Virginia. We will treat him like a king."

"Soak his foot in cold water. Send for Cesare Brunelli. I think he broke a bone—he—"

The next thing I knew, I was raised above the ground on the hands and shoulders of a throng of dragaioli.

"La villanella! La villanella!"

"But she lost!" exploded Granduca Francesco, dashing his crystal wine goblet to the ground. An attendant scurried to pick up the shards.

"These Senese morons!" roared the granduca. "Why this jubilation? The shepherdess did not win!"

He looked down at the girl, lifted in the air above the crowd as they roared.

"La villanella! La villanella!"

He saw Drago's barbaresco lead the limping Orione away, surrounded by dragaioli.

"Serguidi! Summon di Torreforte at once," snapped the granduca.

"Sì, Serenissimo!"

"Where did she get that horse?" said the granduca, turning to Governor di Montauto, thinking he already knew the answer.

"I believe that horse has always belonged to her, Granduca," the governor said, watching the girl be jostled in the waning sun of the afternoon. "They were born for each other."

CHAPTER 64

Siena, Pugna Hills
AUGUST 1581

I sat on a stool beside Zio's pallet, stroking his hand as I recounted the Palio. He was too weak to move, and he could not speak. But he hung on every word I said, the flickering candle reflecting in his eyes.

"We would have won, Orione and I. He was so bold, so swift and nimble. You should have seen him move past L'Oca, charging ahead!"

Zio could not smile, but I saw the glint of light move in the shadow of his eyes like a bright fish.

"Ah! But the boards spooked him. Such treachery. I know who did it. I am certain—"

I stopped, hearing a commotion at the door and the sound of a carriage outside our hovel.

"She is in there," I heard Zia Claudia say. "She will not go willingly, mind you!"

A spark of fear widened Zio's eyes. He opened his mouth, but no word came. Only the silent echo of a scream.

Giacomo di Torreforte ducked his head to avoid the low beam as he entered the house. He was accompanied by a big man in coachman's garb. I saw Zia Claudia beyond him, shaking a bag that sounded with the heavy clink of gold coins in her sooty hands.

"Forgive me, Giovanni," she said, her fingers clutching the bag. She pushed past the two men. "I cannot raise this wild girl alone."

Zio struggled to rise, to speak. But he lay paralyzed, his eyes blinking.

The coachman grabbed me, tossing me over his shoulder. I pounded my fists against his back, my feet kicking hard until he pinned them tight against his chest.

"Tie her up," said Signor di Torreforte. "Put her in the coach facing backward. I will sit opposite."

As the big man turned to carry me out the door, I heard di Torreforte address my zio. "You will never know what a favor I do here today, Giovanni Tacci," he said. "She will always be Siena's heroine. Not even the de' Medici can take away that honor. Not ever."

I couldn't scream. I couldn't cry. I couldn't breathe.

The world went black.

PART V

Ferrara

ANNI 1581–1582

CHAPTER 65

Tuscan Countryside
AUGUST 1581

"We have never been formally introduced, Virginia Tacci," he said. "I am Giacomo Giovanni di Torreforte," he said, bowing in the cramped quarters of the coach. "We are about to make a very long journey together."

I was sore and dusty, choking on the gag in my mouth. The straps on my arms and legs bit into my skin as I struggled. And struggle I did. The gag was soaked with my saliva as I tried to scream.

To curse Giacomo di Torreforte, my kidnapper.

The coach drove for two days, bumping along dusty roads. Fat flies clung to the linen curtains, light brown dust gathering on their wings. Between my sweat and my captor's, the cabin stunk.

Giacomo di Torreforte sat across from me, dressed in expensive traveling clothes. He darted glances at me but would not look me in the eye.

I tried to kick him, but my legs were secured to the coach seat.

"Stop struggling," he said. "It will do you no good. We are now beyond Siena's old territories, even beyond Florence's. No one knows you. You'd best learn to accept your fate."

Of course I could not answer him. More saliva soaked the gag.

"If you calm down, I will allow you to eat and drink. I had some particularly good Chianti wine, but I drank it all, I am afraid. But we still have salami, cheeses, and bread, all from excellent sources."

I tried to kick again at him.

"You mustn't kick me. I have to appear fresh when I go about my business on our arrival. I am negotiating your future, Virginia."

I opened my eyes wide.

"Ah, I have your attention. Yes, my business concerns you. And believe me or not, you should be grateful. You are still alive because of my intervention."

I stared at him with hatred. A crow cawed outside, and I saw it launch heavily from its perch on a plane tree into the air.

My future? Where was he taking me?

I had heard of women sold to the Ottoman sultans to become part of their harem. Was I kidnapped to be bartered among the foreign savages?

What enemies did I have?

I heard a hard thumping on the back of the coach. The coachman pulled to an abrupt stop. Billowing dust engulfed the coach.

"What the devil?" shouted di Torreforte. He pulled a lace-trimmed handkerchief over his nose to block the dust.

"The stones and ruts in the road have bounced the dowry chest loose. I must lash it down again."

Dowry chest?

I shook my head, my eyes wide.

"There is business we could discuss if you were not so agitated and savage, Virginia."

He bent forward to untie my gag. His face grew disgusted with the effort. He took a dagger from his waistband. The metal flashed near my cheek.

Di Torreforte saw my eyes follow the blade. He let the knife linger there.

"Just so we understand each other, Virginia," he said. "I come on the granduca's business. I follow orders—had the de' Medici henchmen taken you themselves, I doubt you would have survived."

If Granduca Francesco could murder his own family, he would think nothing of ridding himself of a Senese peasant.

"No one knows where we are traveling. You could be easily disposed of here and now. Death leaves no wagging tongues. But, thanks to my insistence, the granduca has other more . . . Christian . . . plans for you."

He slipped the knife through the knot of the gag. The wet linen fell to my lap. My mouth moved like a fish's gasping for air.

I struggled to speak, but words wouldn't come.

Di Torreforte turned his attention to the hamper of food.

"Where are you taking me?" I finally managed to say.

"It is best you do not know. Somewhere you will be safe, but where no one will find you."

"Safe? How could I ever be safe in your hands?" I said. "Or the granduca's?"

Di Torreforte shook his head. "You do not understand, Virginia. When we reach our destination, not even de' Medici hands can reach you."

I eyed him, still working my sore mouth and jaw.

"A cup of wine, Virginia? The wines of Ferrara may not be up to Tuscan standards, but that is what the village had to offer us."

"Ferrara? Why are we here?"

"Later you will have time to contemplate that. You will have an abundance of time to . . ." He looked away. ". . . reflect," he said at last.

"Please give me wine—and water. *Acqua!* I am so thirsty."

"Water? I will have to stop the coachman for water. He has buckets for the horses." He gestured at the stream that ran beside road. "You do not mind sharing your drink with horses?"

How many times had I bent over the water troughs, drinking beside horses?

"It does not matter. Per favore. Water," I pleaded, my voice raspy with thirst.

"You are indeed a horsewoman."

Di Torreforte rapped his fist against the roof of the coach. The horses slowed to a stop.

"Sì, signore? Your desire?" said the footman, blinking in the swirling dust.

"I need to get out for a moment. Let the horses rest here. You may accompany our visitor to the trees if she needs to make water. Unbind her hands so that she may lift her skirt. But keep a tight grip on her arm. Never mind her precious modesty. I wager our little shepherdess could outrun you."

My captor descended from the coach, stretching his arms over his head languidly.

"And fill a jug with water from the stream. Virginia Tacci is thirsty."

He did not look back as he strode away from the coach, down to the stream to refresh himself from the choking dust.

We traveled until late at night, when di Torreforte rapped on the roof for the driver to stop.

I heard their conversation outside the coach.

"The horses must rest," di Torreforte said. "They need at least eight hours grazing and their fill of water before they are harnessed again.

"Daniele, stay here and keep an eye on the girl," he said. Taking one of the driving lanterns with him, he walked toward the horses. He ran his hand over their heads, neck, withers, legs. He picked up their hooves, inspecting them with an experienced eye.

"Daniele, where is the doctoring kit?" he asked, coming back to us. "I'll need the lamb's wool and camphor. Poggibonsi has a bad sore under her harness."

"Sì, signore. Everything is in the box. "

"Well, unharness the horses and lead them down to the stream. Only let them drink to the count of twenty-five. Then let them graze. After our repast, we will let them drink their fill. I do not want a case of colic, do you hear me?"

The footman nodded. "Sì, signore."

"Go ahead, then. Leave a good knife so I can cut the lamb's wool to fit the wound." He grabbed my arm. "You come with me, villanella." I stumbled down to the stream, lying flat on the bank and lowering my mouth to the sweet water.

"You drink like an animal," he said, looking down at me.

I finished drinking and wiped my mouth with the back of my wrist.

"You behave more bestially than any animal I have known," I said.

Except for your care with horses. How can a man who cares so much about horses be so cruel to humankind?

I thought of how his fingertips had traced the mare's withers, how he whispered to her.

What kind of man is he?

"Why has the granduca kidnapped me?" I asked.

He hesitated for a moment. The trill of the crickets filled the silence.

"Since you rode the Palio, you have become a symbol for Siena," he said at last. "A dangerous symbol. Your disappearance will cool the revolutionary fires. Your flame will flicker and die out."

"Will you then let me return to Siena?"

Di Torreforte looked away abruptly. "I do not know. These matters with the de' Medici are not so reversible. And your aunt, whose roof has sheltered you all these years, has given written permission to keep you where you will be safe. Away from revolutionaries, foolish men—"

"Away from horses?" I asked.

Again he turned away from me, looking out into the black night. I saw his throat move as he swallowed.

"Yes," he said. "Away from horses."

We passed the night on blankets under the oak trees. I listened to the water play over the rocks, soothing me.

I woke before dawn, thinking of a world without horses, without the Palio. Without Orione.

That world was unimaginable.

———

"Why Ferrara?" I asked him, as we jolted and rolled on over the rutted roads. I knew almost nothing of Ferrara. Why would I? I was Senese. Ferrara was nothing to me. They had sympathized with us as we fought the de' Medici during the siege. Cosimo and Alfonso of Ferrara had been the bitterest of enemies, each pursuing the title of granduca until Cosimo had won it from the Pope.

"The Senese will search all Tuscany, but Ferrara? Never! Not with de' Medici relations so tenuous with Duca Alfonso."

He handed me a cup of water mixed with wine. I drank it in one gulp, then made a face.

"Ah! You do not care for Ferrara's vintages?" he said.

"There was something else in the cup," I said, staring at the dregs in the bottom. I looked up in terror. "Have—have you poisoned me?"

"No, Virginia. Just something that will help you sleep. The de' Medici chemist prepared this. Here, eat something now while you still can."

The next thing I remember, di Torreforte was shaking my shoulder. It was night when I opened my eyes. The world spun around me.

I saw the driver hand a paper to a guard at a bridge across a slow-moving river. I gazed out at the deep red brickwork of a city wall.

The coach clattered across the bridge and through the gates. I felt the bone-rattling jolt of cobblestones beneath our wheels. Frantic curiosity kept my eyes open.

"Look at the sights of Ferrara," said di Torreforte. "Ah, there! The Este castle—a vain attempt to emulate the elegance of Palazzo Vecchio and the de' Medici. As if they could compete with Florence!"

I pulled myself up on the seat, staring at the crenellated castle built all in brick. I had never been to any city beyond Siena.

The castle was magnificent. Oil lamps around the piazza and torches on the walls flickered and leapt with each breath of wind, casting light and shadow across the stone and brick. People chatted and laughed as they walked arm in arm across the great square, filled with the sound of music floating down from the castle windows.

I caught a glimpse of green water sparkling in the moat. A man embraced a woman beside the water. She looked over her shoulder in a wash of shadow and light, and our eyes met.

The great marble cathedral gleamed in the moonlight, rose and white. But I could barely keep my eyes open.

Again, di Torreforte shook my shoulder hard. My eyes opened wide when I felt the sting of a slap on my cheek.

"Rouse yourself," he said. A cool rush of air flooded over me as he opened the door of the coach. I moved my feet and hands—he had slit my bonds with his knife. The coach had stopped in front of a church.

"You must walk through the doorway yourself," he said. "But remember, I walk behind you with my dagger under my cloak. Behave, or you will feel its blade in your back."

"You are indeed the devil," I spat.

"No," he said, shaking his head. "I am your savior. Even if you will never believe that."

I stumbled ahead of him into the church, my legs so unsteady I was sure I would fall.

A golden cross with our lord Jesus Christ crucified upon it shone in front of me. That is all I remember, except for the soft hands of two nuns, helping me to a straw pallet where I slept, dead to the world.

———

"Her uncle is deaf and dumb," said di Torreforte, taking a sip of wine. He looked down into the red liquid, reciting the story he was to tell on behalf of the granduca of Florence.

"Signor . . . Amaro, is it? Florentine name?" said the abbess.

"Sì, Madre."

"Signor Amaro. What of the aunt who signed permission for her admittance to our convent? Did she have a loving relationship with the girl?"

"Silvia's aunt cannot control her. Apparently she behaves provocatively with the village boys—"

The abbess blanched. She looked at Giacomo di Torreforte with severity.

"Is she with child?" asked the abbess, her patrician nose tipping down at the visitor. "I need to know now, signore."

"No, no. Not that, Holy Mother. But Silvia's benefactor—a distant cousin, really—is a very well-respected lady of good family in

Lucca. She simply cannot allow this girl to besmirch the family's reputation. It was all the talk of the village. Gossip travels great distances."

"I see. The patroness is from Lucca, you say?" said the abbess. She arched her brow, scrutinizing the man across from her. "The sisters have told me that she speaks with some Tuscan accent. Possibly Senese?"

Giacomo di Torreforte blinked. He had not counted on the nuns pinpointing the accent. He nodded.

"Your holy sisters are quite astute. Yes, abbess. An old noble family, I am not permitted to say more. Silvia is of a poor branch of the family, near . . . Asciano. They are shepherds, poor as the soil. But the good lady has taken pity upon her niece."

"I see. And the dowry you mentioned?"

"The family is offering one hundred ducats a year."

The mother superior straightened her back. Di Torreforte could already see her calculating what one hundred ducats could do for the convent. She caught him watching her face.

"And why has she not been sent to one of the many convents in Tuscany?" said the mother superior, narrowing her eyes.

Di Torreforte set his crystal glass of wine on the heavy oak table, taking a moment to remember what Secretary Serguido had instructed him to say.

"The Tuscan gossips, Mother Superior. They are notorious. In return for the hundred ducats, we ask that no one here in Ferrara ever learn of her whereabouts. There are some—brokenhearted swains—who may try to track the girl down, dragging her into disgrace."

"That simply could not happen," the abbess said. "No one can enter without my express permission. And the gates are locked with my key only, which I wear around my waist. One hundred ducats, you said? Annually?"

"Sì, Madre."

"There are conditions, of course, for such a rich dowry, abbess," said di Torreforte. "She must never see anyone but the nuns and priests."

"No one beyond these walls shall ever see her again if she stays within the San Antonio cloisters. Except for you, of course, and her family, when they wish to visit."

"There will be no visits," said Giacomo di Torreforte.

"No visits?"

"None at all," he said.

The abbess bowed her head.

"The family in Lucca selected this abbey, knowing your reputation for holiness and obedience in your order. We could, of course, take her to Convento Corpus Domini if you refuse."

"No, Signor Amaro," said the abbess, straightening her wimple with her restless fingers. "I think the girl will be better housed with us."

Di Torreforte watched her closely.

This abbess is of noble blood. Or very least a wealthy family. The elegance of her hands, her throat. The mannerisms of a duchessa. But a duchessa greedy to stroke coins of gold.

The abbess noticed his gaze.

"And I will share with you, Signor Amaro, in strictest confidence . . . there are other noble—extremely high-ranking noble—families whose members are housed within these walls, and not all from Ferrara. Now these sisters are brides of Christ. And they reside here in the most dignified matter, I assure you."

Di Torreforte looked startled. He set down his glass of wine, composing himself.

"These families . . . do they visit these sisters often? We must ensure that Silvia does not communicate with anyone. Her whereabouts must remain a secret."

The abbess cocked her head.

"Of course Silvia will see no visitors. I repeat, only her family. Our nuns are a strictly cloistered order."

Di Torreforte rubbed his fingernail against his chin, thinking. One more point Secretary Serguido had stressed.

"One other word of caution. Silvia has . . . a fantastic capacity to lie."

"A liar!" said the abbess, crossing herself. "Not a recommended quality for our vocation—"

"More of a fantasy, really." He bit his lip, rehearsing the story that would protect Virginia within the convent walls. "This poor shepherdess! She fancies herself to be an accomplished horse-woman. In fact, she believes she actually competed in the Palio of Siena, riding against men."

"What?" said the abbess, clapping her hand over her mouth.

"Yes, I know it is absurd, but . . . I am afraid while she is at heart a good girl, she suffers from these flights of fancy. Her mother married a scoundrel who gambled away her small inheritance. They were reduced to shepherding a small flock. But, yes, young Silvia imagines herself as a Palio rider!"

The abbess looked doubtful.

"Is she . . . mad? Signore, our convent is not an asylum."

"No, Madre! No. Not mad. Only—you know how feverish young girls are who desire boys. In Silvia's case, if she cannot have satisfaction with a man, she dreams of riding astride a horse."

"Santo cielo!" said the abbess, looking away.

Giacomo di Torreforte pulled at his tunic, suddenly uncomfortable in the heat of the fireplace.

Have I gone too far?

"That is why the family has asked me to be honest with you. We know that with strict instruction, you can purge her of these demons."

The abbess fluttered her eyelids.

"One year," she said finally. "She shall have no contact with anyone for one year's time. We will cleanse her of these demons."

Di Torreforte inwardly heaved a sigh of relief. He reached for his pouch, tied at his waist. Sparkling gold winked at the abbess.

"One hundred ducats," he said, counting out the coins. "And no contact with anyone. Especially men who might present themselves as family."

"She will never see a man again," pronounced the abbess. "She will never leave the confines of our convent walls as long as she lives."

He gave a curt nod. He could not manage anything more. He had achieved what he set out to procure. Virginia Tacci's safety.

But this abbess!

He had bribed her, but she had given in too easily, too eagerly. Too cruelly.

CHAPTER 66

Tuscan Countryside
AUGUST 1581

Riccardo De' Luca could neither eat nor sleep. He scoured the countryside for Virginia Tacci, devoting every hour to searching for the young shepherdess.

He had heard that her aunt had sold her for a handful of ducats.

"She will be a bride of Christ. We did not want a de' Medici assassin slipping his blade between her ribs," Claudia had told anyone who would listen, fending off the stones and insults from those who considered her the Judas of Siena.

The Senesi held their breath, praying that the granduca had not, in fact, simply murdered her, as he had his sister and cousin.

With the help of the churches of Siena, Riccardo and Giorgio Brunelli made a list of convents throughout Tuscany. There were hundreds of convents, though Riccardo narrowed the list down to those that had high walls as a means of confinement.

Virginia Tacci would never consent. Only walls, bars, or fetters could keep her from Siena.

Or from Orione.

He wished he could include himself in that list, but he knew her heart belonged to Siena and a horse.

But she is only a fourteen-year-old girl. With time, I shall prove my love. I will find her—

Riccardo was shaken from his reverie as his horse nickered. They were approaching the town of Montalcino. Above the town, perched on a hill was yet another convent. He turned his horse away from the main road, following the route to the abbey.

———

A small metal door slid open behind a grate. A woman's voice addressed Riccardo.

"Signore. May I help you?"

"I search for a fourteen-year-old girl who might be confined within your convent walls."

The abbess studied him, pressing her chapped lips tight together.

"Are you family?"

"No. A good friend."

"An *amante*, perhaps? A lover searching for a girl who will take Jesus Christ as her husband?"

"No. This girl is not my lover. All Siena seeks her—"

"Ah!" said the abbess, opening the door. "Come in, signore. I know the girl in question."

A cool rush of air greeted the weary traveler. Riccardo drank in the refreshing darkness of the vestibule.

"Virginia Tacci is not within our walls, signore," said the abbess.

"How did you know—"

"All the convents in Tuscany know of Siena's search for the villanella," said the abbess, a smile flitting across her face.

Riccardo dropped his head in his hands.

"Forgive me," he said. "I am weary from travel."

"Young man, let me counsel you. I am certain Virginia Tacci is not interned within a southern Tuscan convent. Despite our apparent isolation, news travels quickly amongst orders who serve Jesus Christ. A secret like this would be difficult to keep for very long in Tuscany. Virginia Tacci is already a legend."

"A lost legend, I fear."

The abbess joined her hands together in prayer. She pressed her fingertips against her lips.

"She will never be lost, signore. Not to us."

The abbess saw the young man turn his face away.

"I suppose you think it is possible that a northern Tuscan convent would keep such a secret as a favor to the de' Medici family and the granduca," said the abbess, touching the forlorn man's sleeve. "Especially one that he supports monetarily. Some convents are completely beholden to the de' Medici. But even the granduca's money and power could not keep Virginia Tacci's name from being whispered amongst the sisters."

"Where else should I search?"

"Ah! She could be anywhere. Spain, quite possibly. Venice—with the granduchessa Bianca Cappello's roots there, she could have been admitted as a mad relative of the granduchessa. The granduca's new wife might lack the royal Habsburg blood of her predecessor, but she is not without her own network of connections. The Venetian sisters would prepare her to take the orders."

Riccardo's face crumpled. He heard the bells toll for prayers.

"Then she could be anywhere," he said, his voice cracking in despair.

"Anywhere at all," said the abbess. She shook her head so that her veil trembled over her wimple. "I am sorry, signore."

Riccardo fingered his cap. He prepared to leave.

"Grazie," he said.

"One point I must make before you leave," said the abbess. "Montalcino, Montepulciano, Asciano, Grosseto—never! None of us would ever confine the villanella. No abbey in Siena's regions would permit such a crime. You waste your time searching here. Go home to Siena."

Riccardo bowed his head in respect. The abbess unbolted the door for him to leave.

"We are as proud of her here as you are in the city, my son," she said. "Do not forget that Montalcino suffered and sacrificed in the struggle against Florence. Virginia's image burns strong for the sisters here in Montalcino. As does the thought of our republic's independence, despite the de' Medici grip on our throats."

Then she added, her eyes gleaming, "Besides . . . Virginia Tacci would never make a good nun."

CHAPTER 67

Ferrara, Convento di Sant'Antonio, Polesine

AUGUST 1581

From my cell in the convent, I could see rows of grapevines, their leaves bright green, their sweet fruit swelling under the late summer sun. A lazy drone of bees entered my one small window, attracted to the white flowered vine clinging to the stone walls.

Below, I could see the outer cloisters and a patch of green land, a vegetable garden. The black-and-white magpies—that is what we called nuns in Siena—bent over the rows of plants, digging weeds with whittled sticks. I could not see the city of Ferrara from my cell, only the massive brick wall surrounding the convent.

Why had the granduca imprisoned me here? I rubbed my mouth and jaw, still sore from the gag. I had been here scarcely more than a day.

So far away. Had I been taken to a cloister in Siena, someone would gossip and word would get back to Giorgio and my padrino, or even Governor di Montauto. *Who would ever search for me in Ferrara?*

I felt a chill on my neck. Despite the rising heat of August, the stones were still somehow cold. I shivered, thinking of a winter within these walls.

The sackcloth robe I had been given smelled sharply of the last girl who had worn it. Her terror, tears, and sweat had soaked deep into the weave of the cloth through years of kneeling, nights lying on a cot, and those countless hours of chapel until she had finally been given the habit of a confirmed nun.

Who was she? Or had she perished of a broken heart or disease?

The sackcloth robe may have been washed and beaten on the rocks of the stream beyond the convent walls, but it still stank of a hard life . . . and of my future.

A nun with buckteeth brought me stale bread and water. When she spoke, I could see the flash of teeth, which I first had mistaken for a smile.

"Eat this, the mother superior commands it," she said, jabbing a finger at the bread. "You will need your strength. Our abbess wants you to work the gardens and hitch up the donkey to the little wagon."

I looked at her, stupefied. I was still emerging from my drugged haze. "Hitch up a donkey?"

"To carry the vegetables to the storehouse, girl. You will drive the cart."

"*Asino?*" I said. "*Sorella*, I know nothing of donkeys!"

"We hear you claim you rode the Palio," mocked the nun. Now I saw the mean spirit in the flash of her buckteeth. "You must know horses well. Surely you can manage a donkey," she said through her tight lips. "Let us pray to God for the bread you eat and your safe deliverance to his service here at Sant'Antonio."

I stared at the bread in my wooden trencher while she prayed aloud.

"Our Father, we give thanks for your bounty and mercy upon our new postulant, Silvia," she said, her eyes squeezed tight in piety.

Silvia? I thought. *Who is Silvia?*

"May this food sustain her this day so that she may serve you, our Lord." When she had finished, she looked to me to make the sign of the cross. My hands flew from my forehead to my breastbone, left and right. I seized the chunk of bread, ravenous with hunger. I tore savagely at the crust with my molars—it was too hard for my front teeth. Still I could not tear it.

"Dip it into water," said the nun. "It is easier."

I stared at her yellowed teeth. Maybe they were useful after all with bread this stale.

"I leave you to your repast. Recover your strength and wits. In our lord Jesus's name, and us to his service."

I rose from my straw pallet, smelling the cold, damp stones surrounding me. I used the terra-cotta chamber pot to relieve myself, squatting in the darkness. The rattle of my urine echoed in the tiny room.

I stumbled to the window, not much larger than an arrow slit, and pressed my face against the stone, breathing in the air of freedom beyond. I heard birdsong in the gardens. The potion di Torreforte had given me had worn off, and I was fully aware—and lost in despair.

"You are awake at last," said a voice.

I whirled around. It was not one of the magpies, dressed in black with a white wimple, but a *conversa*, a lay laborer at the convent. Her white head scarf was tied tight, hiding her hair. She carried a clay pitcher of water.

"I am Margherita, your serving girl. It is part of your dowry that I should serve you in order to better serve God."

"My dowry? I—no! I am not a postulant. I am a horse trainer!"

Margherita averted her eyes as if she were speaking to God.

"Give me patience to help serve you," I was sure she was saying.

"If we hurry with your ablutions, you will be groomed and ready for your audience with the abbess before Sext."

"Audience? Sext?"

"Of course you must speak to the abbess, who has graciously accepted you as a postulant at Convento Sant'Antonio. Sext is the noon prayer. There are eight prayer times when we cease our work in the convent. You shall learn them quickly."

"Eight? Santa Madonna!"

"Oh, no!" she whispered, her face tight in horror. "You mustn't use the Virgin Mary's name in vain. Ever again, I beg of you."

"Eight prayer services?"

"Yes, I shall teach them to you. But first, let me pour water in your basin."

Her hands gently tilted the spout of the pitcher toward the washbasin. The splash of water was strangely comforting.

"We will comb the knots from your hair and wash your face," she said, clucking her tongue against the roof of her mouth. "You must be clean and presentable for our abbess. I will fetch more water."

Margherita disappeared before I could say anything.

As soon as she was gone, the bucktoothed nun—her name was Adriana, I soon learned—appeared in the doorway.

"You were given a potent draught, Postulant Silvia. Your family must have good reason to deliver you to our convent."

"My name is Virginia Tacci. I was kidnapped!"

"You are in safe hands now, Postulant Silvia. You have been delivered into God's care. He will drive the demons from your soul."

"No! I must get back to Siena. My horse—he is lame. I must tend him."

"Postulant Silvia," said the suora, her voice cold and toneless. "You must learn to control these evil spirits that possess you. You are a girl, a shepherdess. Not a horse trainer. That is a man's profession. A woman astride a horse is—"

"I am most certainly a horse trainer. I rode the Palio just days ago!" For a moment I was almost struck speechless, even in my anger, as the memory of that ride, the memory of the Palio, filled my mind. The colors so bright, the noise so loud, the cheers still ringing so clearly in my memory. Though I had not won, I had ridden—and that was a triumph they could not take away from me. Except that they had. They had taken everything bright—my life, my horse, my triumph. They had taken it all and imprisoned me here in this cold, damp darkness. My anger flared, and I almost shouted.

"Do you not understand? I was kidnapped! Granduca Francesco of Florence had a hand in this! That man who brought me—he is a relative of the de' Medici. This is all a plot to keep me from riding another Palio."

Suor Adriana breathed deeply, consuming all the air in the room. She expelled it noisily from her flaring nostrils like a dragon. I waited for her to shout, but the toneless pronouncement was even more chilling.

"Here, under the holy roof of God, we will purge you of these devil dreams."

She turned on her heel, nearly upsetting the bucket of cold water Margherita was bringing to my cell. The conversa set the bucket on the floor.

Once the door was closed, she bent near my ear. I felt her warm breath on my face.

"Suor Adriana is prone to anger," she whispered, stroking my hair. "She can make your life miserable. Speak little in her presence. Your words are her weapons, sorella. She will be sure to use them against you to the abbess."

I raged, pleading with the conversa Margharita.

"I am held prisoner here! I am a free maiden, I earn my own keep. I train horses in a village just outside the walls of Siena. I belong to no one!"

The conversa continued brushing my hair. It was so dusty and matted from the long coach ride from Siena—and the dust from the Palio—that she could barely work a comb through it. She dampened her fingers in the basin of water, trying to free the knots with her hands.

Her silence infuriated me.

"Are you deaf? Have you no reaction? I am a prisoner. I was kidnapped by the Granduca of Tuscany!"

Margherita's fingers pried apart a particularly treacherous snag of hair.

"I am not knowledgeable in these matters," she said in a loud voice. "My mission is only to serve you and the convent. Here—lean over the bucket so I can rinse the dirt from your hair."

She beckoned me with a crooked finger. When I knelt beside her, she whispered in my ear.

"Let me teach you the prayer times, Postulant Silvia. They are listening for compliance. They assign spies who report to them. It will go better for both of us if you allow me to teach you, for they will punish me, too."

She straightened up and spoke loudly and clearly. "Lauds are the early morning prayer, before dawn." Margherita supported my head with the palm of her hand, lowering my hair into the bucket. "Prime will be an hour later. Terce are midmorning. Sext is at noon—the abbess will expect you to see you there today. Nones are the midafternoon. Vespers before dark. Compline are just after dark and before retiring to your cell in the evening."

She swirled my hair in the water.

"Then we sleep? We have spent the whole day praying!" I protested.

"You can sit up now. Allow me to dry your hair."

Margherita shook out a white cloth embroidered with a family crest I did not recognize. She patted my hair between the linen folds.

"Oh, no. There are chores to be done throughout the day. When you return to your cell, you will be tired, but you must spend time in contemplation and personal prayer. Then you will extinguish your candle and sleep until Matins."

"Matins?"

"I had not gotten to that yet. Matins are the eighth prayers of the day. At two hours past midnight." She smiled. And, despite the harsh thought of prayers at two in the morning, her smile was the first moment of real warmth I had felt in this cold stony place. "They are the hardest for young postulants. But you will grow used to them with time. And it is the quietest, most spiritual hour of prayer, when the rest of the world is asleep."

She moved the basin of water to me.

"Now please wash your face. Bring back the radiance that God has bestowed in your pure heart."

I did as I was told. I was beginning to understand the rules in the Convento di Sant'Antonio.

The morning breeze carried the sounds of Ferrara through the narrow slit of my window. I could hear the tolling of bells beyond the convent, the clip-clop of horses' hooves, and the rattle of carriages.

Margherita handed me another linen cloth, again embroidered with a family crest. I noticed it was stitched with the initial T and realized it was the *stemma* of the di Torreforte family. I flinched. But wiped my face on it just the same.

Then I blew my nose in it for good measure.

I learned the routine of prayer quickly. My conversa, Margherita, taught me the life of the convent, the manners befitting a novice.

And I broke every rule there was. My audience with the abbess was the first revolt.

"You come here under the auspices of your gracious aunt," began the abbess, who sat behind an enormous desk spread with correspondence in parchment and vellum. "Surely you must include her in your daily prayers."

"My aunt? My aunt is a sheep-breathed fool who has begrudged me every day of my life!"

"She is generous beyond measure giving you this opportunity—"

"Zia Claudia is poorer than the dirt she treads on. She hates me—"

"Postulant Silvia! You will learn not to speak until I ask your opinion."

"Silvia, who is Silvia? I am Virginia Tacci, and I will speak! I will shout until you give me my freedom! I am a horse trainer from Siena. I rode the Palio!"

The abbess gripped the edge of her desk. Like Adriana, she refused to raise her voice. But the low monotone of her utterance carried a lethal venom.

"We were warned of the demons that possess you, Postulant Silvia."

I stood up, kicking the chair over.

"My name is Virginia Tacci. You will release me at once!"

The abbess sat back, a smile tugging at her bloodless lips.

"That certainly will not be the case. I am the only one in this convent who has a key to the doors, Postulant Silvia. And they shall not be open to you. Ever again. May God forgive you your sins. Sorella Adriana, please escort our new postulant to her cell. See that she prays for forgiveness."

Suor Adriana put a hand on my arm. I slapped her away.

"Get away from me!"

The abbess rang a little bell with a fierce shake of her wrist. Adriana stepped outside, returning with four other nuns much larger than she. At once, they seized my arms.

"Leave me alone! Let go of me!" I screamed. I kicked, connecting with one, who buckled over in pain.

The others seized me even tighter, digging their short nails into my flesh. They dragged me from the abbess's office.

"I am a fantino! I rode the Palio—I will never, *ever* be a nun!"

Conversa Margherita was cleaning her mistress's cell while the young novice had her first meeting with the abbess. The servant shook out the dusty linen shift and overskirt, smoothing its folds with her hand. It was a coarse weave, not much different than Margherita's own.

How strange for the niece of such a wealthy patroness to wear simple linen verge! Especially on the day of her internment . . .

A scent, earthy and animal, rose up, greeting her nose. Margherita bent closer to inspect the cloth in the dim light of the cell, pulling the cloth tight to her face.

The scent was strong in the folds of the linen. She sniffed it, then rubbed her fingernail across the pale yellow-brown stains, encrusted with coarse animal hair.

"Santo cielo," she whispered. She scraped some of the bits of sticky hair into her palm to inspect it.

What is this?

She touched her tongue lightly to the cloth.

Salt.

The screams of her mistress, Silvia, being dragged across the convent courtyard made Margherita jump. She quickly pulled up the corner of her apron and brushed some of the hairs onto the fold of the cloth. She tied a knot in the hem, pulling the material tight with her teeth.

The nuns brought the girl into the cell, screaming and flailing.

"Get out of here, conversa!" Adriana commanded. "Take the clothes she wore last night and burn them at once. She will never need them again."

Margherita cast a look at the struggling girl, her face red with rage. She bundled up the clothes and leather boots.

"Now! Go and throw them in the kitchen's hearth!"

Margherita hurried out of the room just as the nuns pushed the young girl in, sending her sprawling to the stone floor.

"You will forever regret your behavior today!" said Adriana, heaving. Her hair, mousy brown and stringy, had been pulled out from beneath the wimple. The sister turned, pulling closed the door with a slam.

Margherita heard the key turn twice in the lock. With the scraping of metal, it seemed the new novice's fate was forever sealed.

———

As part of my penitence, I was forced to lie across the threshold to the refectory. The nuns walked upon my body as if I were a mat. The nuns who dragged me to my cell after the rebellious audience with the abbess trod on me the hardest. Suor Adriana ground her heel into the place where my neck met my spine, her full weight lingering there.

The floor smelt of vinegar and old women. As I contemplated the odors of the convent, the lingering stench of nightly chamber pots was not masked by the incense of the adjacent chapel. The conversas scrubbed the tiles and stones, but the stale odor of enclosure still clung to the air. It seemed as if the old nuns died and disintegrated, clinging desperately to the air and stone and brick of the convent, refusing freedom even in death.

The young novices chattered like excited starlings as they entered the refectory, for a few seconds chasing away the moldering spirits that haunted the convent.

"Silence!" snapped Suor Adriana. "You enter the refectory to nourish your body in order to sustain your spirit. Enter with reverence."

"Sì, Sorella Adriana," they murmured. "Forgive us."

Most stepped lightly over my prostrate body, barely the weight of a bird. They had heard my screams of pain.

"Brava," whispered a novice above me. "You disobeyed." I made a mental note of the lovely young voice above me.

I would find her, this kindred soul.

––––––––

Suor Maria had charge of all novices' education. She eyed me warily at our first audience, having heard of my rebellious nature.

"I trust the conversa has instructed you on the schedule of prayer. You must listen for the bell and not arrive late for the service, or you will pay penitence."

No, I will not be late. Until the day I find a way to escape.

As if she were reading my thoughts, Suor Maria said softly, "Do not try to escape, Postulant Silvia. Dozens of others have tried; there is no way out. The walls are too high to scale, and there is a watch night and day. I tell you this so that you will not harm yourself in a failed attempt to flee.

"Receive our holy savior Jesus here in our abbey. Only then shall you receive peace."

No, Sorella Maria. There will be no peace until I regain my freedom.

The little gray donkey was shaggy and docile. I buried my nose in his neck. Not quite the smell of horse, but an equine, a cousin at least. My eyes welled with tears as I breathed in his scent.

He turned to nuzzle me. My fingertips touched his velvety softness, felt the warm puff of his hay-sweet breath.

"His name is Fedele," said the old suora, sitting in the shade of a fruit tree. "Mine is Suor Loretta. He likes you, I think."

She raised her body slowly from the iron stool. I heard the creak and snap of her joints.

"I heard of your tale. You profess to love horses. As did I in my younger days, before I was interned in the convent. Nothing else existed for me."

"Davvero?" I said.

"Yes, but I had to forget all that," she said, looking at the donkey. "And so will you. You are here, Silvia, because I requested your assistance."

"I know nothing of donkeys," I said stubbornly. "I ride horses, large and beautiful. Not asses."

She looked at me as if I had slapped her. "Do not dare insult Fedele! He is a handsome fellow and earns his keep. So shall you, postulant."

"But I—"

"Come. I shall show you how to harness my donkey," she said, as if she did not hear me. "My arms have become too weak to lift the heavy yoke. I shall be grateful for your help. I will teach you what you need to know about the donkey and its care."

I nodded my head. A donkey was hardly a Palio horse, but I said nothing.

Suor Loretta was devoted to her four-legged charge, running her fingers through his scraggly mane as I had Orione's. She whispered in his long ears and kissed his donkey cheeks. I watched her harness and unharness the donkey. Her arms trembled with the weight. I stepped in and took that weight from her.

"Let me, Sorella Loretta. I am a quick learner."

"I can see that," she said, trying to recover her breath. She put a hand on my shoulder to steady herself. "Silvia, thank you."

I did not correct her. I wanted no confrontation here. The sweet hay and smell of golden oats in the tiny stable made me feel at home.

"I procure the best oats in Ferrara for Fedele," she said, pointing to string sacks.

I dipped my hands in the oats, letting them spill through my fingers. They rattled down like gold coins into the sack. I bit into one grain. Its sweet and plump meat had chewy goodness.

"They are indeed fine," I said. "Finer than any grain we fed our horses in Siena."

How can a simple suora procure such fine-grade oats for a mere donkey?

The suora looked at me, her old head nodding. But she said nothing.

CHAPTER 68

Florence, Pitti Palace

SEPTEMBER 1581

The dwarf Morgante had hoped he would be dismissed after the death of Isabella. The granduca would remember he was present at Isabella's death. Surely he would be banished from the de' Medici Court.

But he was wrong. A dwarf was a valuable commodity, and the de' Medici prided themselves on the few dwarves they could procure.

Morgante was assigned to the care and entertainment of Antonio, born to Bianca Cappello and Granduca Francesco.

Born to the granduchessa? Morgante knew better. Rumors had spread like wildfire throughout Florence that Bianca was barren and Antonio was a changeling.

Ha! Born to a scullery maid and passed off as a de' Medici heir.

There was nothing remotely de' Medici—or for that matter, Cappello—about the strange-looking boy. But he was not as unkind as the de' Medici girls and enjoyed the company of the little dwarf. Morgante took a reluctant liking to him.

One day, when Prince Antonio took a tumble from his pony, Morgante raced to the apartments of the granduca to inform him of the accident.

Being a member of the Court, the dwarf—shouting that there was an emergency—was admitted at once, though there was another visitor finishing his conversation with the granduca. Knowing better than to interrupt, despite his urgent news, Morgante listened outside the door to Francesco's interior study.

"I have followed your orders precisely, Granduca. She is safely interned. She is forbidden to see anyone from outside the convent."

"You have assurance of this?"

"I do."

"A hundred ducats a year! A small fortune. My original plan would have cost me nothing."

"Your magnanimous gesture ensures . . . God's blessing."

Morgante noticed the man's hesitation. He was searching for words.

"She has been assigned the duty of caring for a donkey, the abbess writes me."

"An ass?"

"A little donkey that is hitched to a cart to carry the convent's vegetables to the storeroom. The girl curries its coat, feeds the beast, and mucks its stall."

The granduca's hearty laugh spilled out into the hall. Morgante noted the malevolent tone.

"What a fine result!" said the granduca. "We rid Siena of her heroine, and we reduce her to caring for a donkey."

Again, the granduca laughed. The visitor kept silent.

What heroine is this?

Morgante rubbed the bridge of his nose. He knew nothing of Siena, only that it was one of Florence's greatest conquests under Granduca Cosimo.

"My lord . . . shall she be freed? In a few years, perhaps? When the danger of a Senese rebellion has passed?"

"What? No, never!" snapped the granduca. "The Senesi will always remember her. She poses too much danger to Florence. Let Ferrara have her!"

The private secretary Serguidi emerged from the antechamber. "Morgante! Why are you here?"

"The little prince has had a tumble from his pony. I have notified the physicians, but I come to give the news to the granduca."

"Subito!" said Serguido, ushering in Morgante.

The stranger was preparing to leave. He was dressed with a black scarf wrapped loosely around his neck.

Granduca Francesco frowned, his brow folding in angry puckers.

"I have a private audience with Signor di Torreforte, Secretary Serguido," he said, staring viciously at the dwarf.

"Excuse me, Granduca," stammered Morgante. "But your son Antonio has had an accident—"

"What?" gasped Francesco, rising. "Take me to him at once."

Morgante pressed himself against the frescoed wall as the granduca hurried out of his office. In Francesco's wake, the dwarf saw a wistful sadness in the visitor's face.

The visitor glared at Morgante. "Do not stare at me, little man."

He turned on his heel and left, the black scarf trailing behind his shoulder.

CHAPTER 69

Ferrara, Covento di Sant'Antonio, Polesine

SEPTEMBER 1581

I took my place among the novices on the wooden benches. To each side were the carved choir chairs for the nuns, inlaid with precious woods in intricate designs.

The wimpled heads swiveled to watch me as if I were a circus performer.

"Is it true you slapped Suor Adriana?" whispered a girl my age sitting next to me.

"I slapped her, yes. Then I punched her hard in her fat stomach," I said.

"No!" said a postulant on my other side. She leaned forward slightly so I could see her sharp cheekbone jutting out from her tight head scarf. "You struck the suora!"

"Good," said another from further beyond. The whispering had been passed down the line. "She is a mean witch of the devil. I would like to slap her myself!"

I recognized the voice. The one who had whispered "brava."

"*Shhhh, Anna Rosa!*" cried another. "Or we will all be on the floor of the refectory, the sisters dancing on our backs!"

I was deep in my dream world. I rode the swiftest horses. I fed Orione apples one after another, his lips searching my palm. We raced the Palio again, not to place third but *to win*.

Drago! Contrada del Drago wins!

"Wake up, Postulant Silvia!" said a voice.

I looked up to see the face with the rose-flushed cheeks.

"Who are you?"

"I am Anna Rosa, but there is no time to speak!" she said, pulling my arms. "We both will be late to Matins. I did not see you for the first bell, so I came to wake you. The abbess will be very angry if you are not there. They will tread across your back for another week!"

"Ooooh!" I groaned, wincing as she pulled me from my cot.

I could barely move. But Anna Rosa pulled me through the dark cloisters under the starlit night, and we made the second bell for Matins.

The conversa Margherita fingered the soft leather of the boot. As she had bent over the kitchen's hearth to burn the new novice's clothes, she had folded the boot into her apron pocket. It was small and soft. The styling was strange. Despite its soft folds, it looked too practical, too substantial to be a lady's shoe.

And it was heavily soiled. What lady would wear such a boot?

When she was safely home in the hovel where she lived with her mother, father, sisters, and brothers, she took out the boot.

Dried mud clung to the sole—mud and a speck of dung, threaded with grass.

She held the boot close to her nose, drawing in the smell of earth . . . and of horse manure.

CHAPTER 70

Siena, Brunelli Stables, Vignano

NOVEMBER 1581

Cesare Brunelli, the mighty smithy, his strength forged by the anvil and horse training, had turned gray and frail after the disappearance of his goddaughter, Virginia Tacci. Cesare Brunelli spent more and more time with Orione, petting the stallion with his raw, chapped hands. The old man brought treats, feeding him sweet-smelling grass by the handful.

He worked ceaselessly on Orione's fetlock, trying to mend the injury incurred at the Palio race. He spat, thinking back to the treachery of that day.

Cesare knew the horse would never run the Palio again, but he wanted to cure the painful swelling. Then he could let the stallion retire to the fields with a herd of mares. This horse that had almost carried Virginia to victory in the Palio deserved at least that much.

The stables smelled of camphor. Brunelli bent over his boiling pot, concocting liniments with mixtures of dried flowers, peppermint, and tree saps.

He kept a store of root vegetables packed in earth and straw in a small cellar under the stable. In the cold of winter, the carrots still shone bright orange through remnants of dark soil, a white lace-work of roots tangled about their flesh, their frilly stems yellowed and wilted.

He pulled out a few. Every day after doctoring Orione's fetlock, he would offer the stallion a reward. Orione pawed at the straw of his stall. His hoof dug deep, ringing against the stone beneath.

"Ah, beauty. You are impatient, just like our Virginia. Two impetuous fools."

He sighed, half-smiling in the perpetual twilight of the stable. He reached out the small bunch of carrots to Orione.

"You see what stubbornness gets you?" His voice trailed off. He could have said "kidnapping." He could have said "murder." He could have cried.

The men from the village had stopped their dice game in silent sympathy for Brunelli. If they could not quite share his pain, they understood it.

The stallion snatched the carrots greedily, crunching on the roots, the grinding of his teeth filling the cold stable air. The big horse tasted the earth still clinging to the roots. He made a bobbing motion with his head. Mud-colored froth spilled from his mouth.

"Buon appetito! A mouthful of good Senese soil." He patted the horse's neck. "You may not be fit to run the pastures, but our good earth will be in your belly, bringing your health back."

Cesare's eyes strayed upward. "And she will return one day to us, too. You cannot keep a Senese away from Siena."

Orione never accepted being locked in the stall or being tethered to the rope line strung from wall to wall. He kicked and reared, his neighs echoing in the stone stable.

"Do not fret, my beauty," said Brunelli soothingly. "You will gallop again. I am beginning to think that the little fetlock bone is not broken but just chipped. A little piece I can feel. And I feel scar tissue growing around it. You will be strong again."

Then he murmured, "It is good that you jumped the first boards. Otherwise you would have surely fallen hard by the last. You saved her life, Orione. Our precious Virginia."

"And who will ride him now?" said the cobbler, venturing to break the silence.

"Giorgio will ride him, you will see," said Cesare. "He will be in excellent shape when Virginia returns."

The men stared down. A mouse skittered across the stones, making a break for the open door.

A horse whinnied outside.

"Ho, now!" Giorgio entered the stable, leading a mare to be teased before breeding with the black stallion.

"What's this silence?" he said, leading the mare near Orione. "Why are you not busy gossiping and losing your wages to one another with the roll of the die?"

"Niente," said the cobbler. Nothing.

Orione nickered at the scent of the mare, stretching his neck over the stall door. The mare turned her rump to him and kicked hard. Orione reared back in his stall, his penis stiffening.

"That a girl!" Cesare said. "You have his interest."

The mare lifted her tail and kicked again, slamming her iron shoes against the wooden door.

"You are really going to breed him to that mare?" asked the baker.

Giorgio pulled at the rope, moving the mare away.

"Enough now!" Giorgio said to the mare. "Certo. Of course she will be bred to him. We will continue Orione's bloodline with our best brood mares. What other horse has the heart and strength of this stallion?"

"That is what I told them," said Cesare, smiling at his son. "The best blood of the Maremma mingled with the strongest of Siena. What foals he will sire! They shall be my legacy when my bones are turned to dust."

———————

Giorgio made as many trips as he could, searching for Virgnia, but he could not leave Brunelli's stables for long. Then it became impossible to leave at all.

His father was very ill.

He realized it one night when he returned from a journey to convents surrounding Florence. Giorgio led his storm-soaked horse into the stables, blinking away raindrops. He saw a wizened man bent over a pot, stirring its contents with a wooden spoon. White, wrinkled skin clung to the bones of the old man, the muscles loose and flaccid.

He heard the wretched cough of the stranger echo through the stable.

The old man turned. His face fell in sorrow.

"Ah, figlio," he said. "Son, you did not find her."

Giorgio couldn't speak. This ancient man was his father. He stood in silence, rainwater dripping from his coat.

"No, Babbo," he said at last. "I did not find her."

"Then I wonder if I shall ever see her again," whispered Cesare. "I am growing old. And weary of this world."

Chapter 71

I believe I would have died in the convent that first year, had I not remembered a story my mother had told me. It was the story of a six-year-old Senese—Santa Caterina—seeing a vision of God on the roof of San Domenico.

Santa Caterina's vision came to her on the brick road leading up from Fontebranda into the city of Siena. I had walked that same road, the raised brick steps on the steep incline making it possible for horses, donkeys, and oxen to enter the city. Just paces from her home, the little girl saw her first vision.

She froze, stunned, gazing at a vision no one else could see. In that moment, her life was forever changed.

I saw no vision of God or Jesus. When I closed my eyes to pray, I saw a horse—a black horse with a twisted white star—leading all the other horses in a race up Via di Città. I knew I had lived that vision, that dream. How many other souls could claim to have accomplished their life's ambition at age fourteen?

Orione recovered, stumbling to his feet over the boards thrown from a roof above us. We galloped toward the piazza and Siena's

towering marble Duomo. The shadows of Via del Capitano were a
tunnel between what could have been and what now had to happen.
In the distance, I could hear the roaring crowd, see the dazzling sun
on the marble cathedral, the flap of the drappellone just ahead. I
pressed my face close to Orione's mane, letting his head free to gallop
the last strides of the race.

We emerged into the bright light of the piazza and the roar of the
crowds, the flap of contrada banners, whistles, and cheers.

———————

Ferrara's Palio took place on the 23rd of April in honor of the city's
saint, San Giorgio. I gathered what information I could from the
nuns and novices.

"The course is along the river Po, just outside our walls," Suor
Loretta told me. "Fedele brays when he smells the horses."

I breathed deep.

"Can we see it?"

"Oh, no, child," said Suor Loretta. "But you can hear the excitement, the people gathered along the Via Grande. The best riders in
the world race our Palio."

"No," I said stubbornly. "The best riders in the world are the
Senese . . . and perhaps the horsemen of the Maremma."

The old nun shook her head.

"You are very proud of your homeland, Silvia," she said. "But
you must make room in your heart and head for the rest of us. Our
Ferrara Palio is the oldest. In 1259, horses ran this same course."

Three hundred years ago sounded like a long time, but was not
Siena's Palio even more ancient? I set my jaw to argue, but I could
not remember dates. What use would I have for them? I never
cared how old the Palio was . . . I only wanted to win it.

And I almost had.

I saw that Suor Loretta was growing weary, and I needed to harness the donkey before the other nuns complained I was behind in my work loading the vegetables.

As the day of Ferrara's Palio grew nearer, there were more visitors to the abbey. I, of course, had no one to visit me, but my friend Anna Rosa's family came to see her. I watched her visit with her family through the iron grille in the chapel. The abbess would not let me share in any of the other novices' visits.

It was not a joyous occasion, even though they brought a trunk of woolen blankets, fine linen, candlesticks, and beeswax candles. They were obviously a wealthy family from Ferrara. Blessed with twelve children, the faithful woman had dedicated one of the girls to be a bride of Christ.

Whether she liked it or not.

Anna Rosa kneeled at her mother's feet, weeping in her lap. I could see her shoulders shaking under her cloak.

"You must accept God," coaxed her mother. "For your sake and the family's. It would shame us were we not to keep our promise to the Holy Church."

Among the family members crowded into the visiting room was an elegantly dressed young man wearing riding boots. He was about the same age as Giorgio, tall and well built, his hair sandy blond. He kissed Anna Rosa on both cheeks and squeezed her hand. I realized he must be her brother.

Later, I questioned her. I did not stop to think that she was heartsore from the visit.

"Your brother, the fair one. He wore riding boots."

"Yes, he did not take the coach with the family. He rode his mare here. He is an accomplished horseman. He owns at least five Palio horses."

"*Palio* horses?"

"Yes. He could barely make time to see me, but the occasions I am allowed visitors are so few. The Feast of Saint Giorgio is an important one for us."

"But your brother. Perhaps since he knows the Palio, he might know me, have heard of me—"

Anna Rosa turned to me, her face questioning.

"Heard of you, Silvia?"

"No, of *me*. Virginia Tacci. The girl who rode the Palio."

"Basta!" she hissed, looking over her shoulder. "Enough!"

I thought no word had ever pierced my heart as sharply.

―――――――

Wounded at my friend's disbelief, I sought solace with Fedele the donkey. The old suora had obtained permission for me to sleep in the tiny stable with the beast. With the training for the Palio, the streets smelled of horse, and Fedele brayed constantly, keeping the nuns from the few hours of sleep they were allowed.

The sweet smell of hay comforted me, and my company stopped Fedele's braying. I stuck a blade of straw between the gap in my teeth, teasing it with the tip of my tongue, making it flick up and down.

Sometimes in Ferrara, I caught a whiff of the sea. It was miles away, but the salt flats encroached far enough inland that when a strong wind blew, it carried the salty aroma. I had never seen the sea, only heard tales of it, the blue waters beyond the Maremma in Tuscany. Once, when I sunk my nose into Orione's thick fur, the old cobbler from Vignano asked me, "What elixir draws you to bury your nose into that colt's neck?"

I could not describe the smell of a horse to one who does not know its power. I asked Giorgio later that evening.

"How can you describe the scent of a horse?"

He thought a moment, pausing as he curried a mare. "Warm animal in the sunshine mixed with the perfume of the sea."

The sea. Now I was closer to the sea than I was to Orione or Siena. I had no mooring; I was left adrift with a false name and no past. Sometimes I wondered whether I was mad, if I really knew my own identity, since no one believed me.

I flicked the piece of straw about in my mouth with the tip of my tongue.

Anna Rosa found me on my knees in Fedele's straw, remembering Orione and the night he was born.

"You look as if you are actually praying," she said, startling me. "Sincerely, I mean. Except for that piece of straw in your teeth. Do you move it with your tongue?"

"What are you doing here? You will be punished," I whispered.

"No, I will not. You will never see me punished. The abbess would not dare."

I did not reply, though looking back, I should have questioned her. But that night, I was too far down the deep well of my sorrow.

"I came to see you," said Anna Rosa. "I am—sorry—for what happened between us."

"You do not believe me!" I said, turning away from her. "I raced Siena's Palio of the Assumption. No one believes me—"

She grasped my hand, pulling me to face her. "I do, Virginia. I do believe you."

I looked up at her.

"I do, you know," she said. "It is just that you suffer so much at the hands of the abbess. I cannot bear to see you punished! But I believe you. You *are* Virginia Tacci. And I believe you rode the Palio, as impossible as it sounds."

I braced my hand against the donkey's shoulder and stood up.

"Why do you believe me when no else does? They think I am mad or a liar."

"Why should you lie? You are locked in here, the same as me. What good is a lie when you are a prisoner anyway?

"And," she added, "the bright spark in your eyes when you say your name. The defiance. The name suits you, Virginia. You do not look like a Silvia to me."

I sighed, closing my eyes. Outside I heard the shouts of the Palio crowd.

"They will be starting a practice run any moment," I said, my ear cocked to familiar sounds of horses snorting and nickering.

Fedele began to bray, forcing us to cover our ears. He kicked at the wall of his stall.

I slipped a halter over his head.

"Do you want to stand near the wall with me and listen?" I asked. "At least we can hear the hoofbeats."

Anna Rosa pressed close to me, and we waited long moments in silence. Our patience was rewarded with the roar from the crowd and the pounding of galloping hooves.

CHAPTER 72

Ferrara, Convento di Sant'Antonio, Polesine

NOVEMBER 1582

A new postulant's cries pierced the early morning dark after Matins. Suoras rushed to the girl's cell, praying and no doubt administering sleeping draughts. She was from a noble family in Modena. I heard the shattering of crockery.

Her suffering and outrage awakened a spark in me.

Tonight!

The moon cast bright light on the brick wall that held me prisoner. Far better had it been a new moon mantling the yard in darkness, but I would not wait another night. I dragged the wooden chest from my cell—emptied of its contents—across the courtyard. The nightwatch—the sharp-eyed Suor Claudia—was occupied with the new postulant, who still wailed pitifully.

I moved stealthily across the yard, hoping that there would be no other magpies out in the small hours of the morning.

I looked up. A wall at least three times my height. I remembered my brawn as a shepherd, as a horse trainer. Would I have that same strength now?

I had said good-bye to my friend Anna Rosa weeks ago, not knowing when the right moment would come.

"I must go with you," Anna Rosa had said, snatching at my hand. "You cannot leave me here!"

"Anna Rosa," I said, "you do not have the strength to scale a wall. I am not sure I do."

"But how shall I survive without you, Virginia?" Tears spilled down her freckled cheeks.

"Stop crying!" I hissed. "The suoras will notice. You will ruin everything."

"I am sorry. I did not mean to be selfish," she said, sniffling. She looked away.

We didn't talk again. I felt sorry for her, but I could not look back.

Now the frost glistened on the top bricks of the wall. I pulled the wooden chest up close to Fedele's shed. I heaved the empty box up on its side, and climbed onto the roof of the tiny stable.

Snowy slush had accumulated on the top of the slate roof of the shed from two nights of inclement weather. Now the slush was beginning to freeze, making my work treacherous. I leaned over and pulled the chest up. My feet slipped, and I fell back onto the roof, still grasping the chest. With a thud I was sure would wake the entire convent, the coffer landed beside me.

Fedele, startled from his sleep just below me, began to bray. I pressed myself against the slate tiles, hoping my sackcloth robe would shroud me in its darkness.

I waited. No one stirred.

"Good-bye, Fedele," I whispered.

I hauled the chest upright and pushed it flush against the brick wall at the back side of the shed. The chest was taller than I was. Scattered all around me were the flat stones I had heaved one by one on the roof over the past weeks. I set to work stacking the stones against the wall, building a pile I could climb to reach the top of the chest—and from there, I hoped, the top of the wall. How I would get down from the wall, I didn't know. But if I died in the fall, then at least I would die outside this cursed convent—free.

A shriek sounded across the courtyard. The postulant's door had been opened. Probably Suor Adriana had been sent in to quiet the girl with a threat—if the sedative didn't work.

The face of Suor Loretta, kind and gentle, flashed in my mind.

I cannot think about her. I cannot think about anything but escaping.

My hands were numb from stacking the icy rocks. Sooner or later, the nightwatch would resume her guard.

Now!

I climbed the pile of stones, feeling them shift precariously under my foot. Out of the corner of my eye, I saw the light of a lantern, the nightwatch in the corner of the yard, beyond the garden.

"Chi e'?" she shouted. "Who is it?"

This was my only chance. I thought of the world beyond this wall. I thought of Orione and Siena.

I tried to spring from the stones onto the chest, and I felt the stack collapsing. I grabbed the chest, but it was no use. The stones, chest, and I tumbled together from the roof of the stable onto the ground.

I heard the snap of a bone breaking.

For an instant, the pain of the broken bone blossomed in my arm, filling me with a savage fire that wiped away everything else in the world—it was almost a relief, because an instant later that first fire faded and was replaced with a deeper, darker, more savage pain. I had failed. I was still within the hated walls of the convent.

Perhaps an outsider might think that the simple brick walls of a convent would not be enough to stop an unwilling

postulant—especially one with the strength and will that I possessed as a girl. But that outsider would not have understood the
force of the locks, the height of the walls, or the fierce vigilance
of the sisters of the night guard. Many a soul was tamed by failed
attempts—and by the punishment the abbess inflicted upon them.

I had failed, and I was punished with cleaning floors and
chamber pots and lying prostrate on the floor of the refectory, but
I did not surrender. The dispensary nurse did not set my broken
bone properly, and for the rest of my life, I could not fully extend
my arm.

Still, I never gave up.

My solace was the donkey, Fedele. And I was his. Suor Loretta
was astonished that I knew to soak his hooves in cold salted water
to soothe his sore legs and how to pack sugared herbs in his hooves
to chase away thrush.

"But how did you learn such cures?" she asked me, her eyes
dimmed by a milky film.

"Sorella! I have sworn to you a thousand times, I rode Palio
horses!"

Suor Loretta looked over her shoulder.

"Mia cara! You mustn't speak of this again. The abbess will
punish you—she will take you away me and from Fedele."

I wanted to scream in protest, but I saw Suor Loretta's eyes fill
with tears.

"I have grown quite fond of you, Silvia," she said. "So has my
donkey."

A donkey! I have ridden the finest—

I saw the wet pink cheeks of the old suora, heard her labored
breathing, burdened with strong emotion. A rush of shame made
me bite my tongue.

"I will prove one day that what I say is true," I whispered. "But
until then, this work with Fedele and with you, Suor Loretta, is the

only thing that consoles me. For that, I will obey—even if you do not believe me."

"It would do you no good for me to believe you, Postulant Silvia," said the old nun, turning up her hands palm in a helpless gesture. "For there is nothing I or anyone else can do. I, too, was immured in this convent against my will. There is no way out. Acceptance will give you peace."

I buried my nose in Fedele's neck.

"I will never—ever—reconcile myself to this life! I do not want that kind of peace."

"Then your soul will always be in turmoil. Even when we are buried, our bones will not leave the convent. You have seen the cemetery."

"Sì," I said, choking back tears. I clung tighter to the donkey's neck. I thought of Orione, of Siena.

I felt a gentle touch on my shoulder. The old woman reached out a hand to comfort me. She stroked my back as I had often seen her caress the donkey. I melted under her touch.

"I will tell you a secret that comforts me. My beloved Fedele will be buried alongside me. I have secured a promise from the abbess to bury the donkey as close to my final resting place as possible."

A donkey in consecrated ground! Is Suor Loretta mad?

I did not question how this suora could hold such sway with the abbess.

Why did I not realize then who she was?

She was excused from certain prayers, had meals brought to the little shed that sheltered the donkey. These deviations from the convent routine were monumental. In a convent, everyone was treated the same. The one common goal was devoting our lives to Christ.

"You must learn there are blessings to our life here," said Suor Loretta. "Many girls would have been married to brutal men, forced into partnerships with those who detested them, who beat them."

I thought of the tanner's son.

Could I have been happy bedding a stinking simpleton who would never let me walk the streets and hills of Siena, let alone ride a horse? Every night he would have climbed into my bed, forcing his smelly body onto mine. Once married, I would have had to give up my freedom to be his wife.

"Have you looked carefully at the marvels of our convent? Have you seen the frescoes—the one of Jesus climbing up a ladder to the cross? Look at it during prayers. Jesus is not fettered or forced by the point of a sword. He willingly mounts the ladder as his followers watch."

Why do I care, you crazy old magpie? What difference does it make?

"Our Christ made a choice—willingly. Perhaps someday you will do the same."

"Never!" I said, my throat tight with anger.

Suor Loretta looked away from the scorn written on my face.

"Perhaps I can help you find some comfort in the convent, some advantages you have not recognized."

"What possible advantage could there be, locked away as a prisoner?"

Suor Loretta picked up a brush and stroked Fedele's back. He closed his long lashes, his ears swiveling back in pleasure.

"Would you like to learn to read and write, Silvia?" asked the nun, brushing the brown line down the donkey's back. "Because that is a gift I can bestow upon you."

I stared at her, astonished "*Me? Read? Write?*"

I remembered Giorgio pointing out my name in the letter from the Duchessa d'Elci when she sent me the collo di cavallo. I had traced the two words—Virginia Tacci—with reverence.

"That is one gift the convent can give you. It will open all the doors of the world to your mind . . . and quite possibly your soul."

For the first time since my incarceration in the convent, I smiled.

PART VI

The Art of Death

ANNI 1582–1586

CHAPTER 73

Siena, Brunelli Stables, Vignano

NOVEMBER 1582

Giorgio studied the stirrup leather in his hand. His weight had stretched the leather over the years. It was past time to shorten it.

He selected the correct punch, laid the strip on the bench, and with two taps of the hammer, the job was done. He sighed, looking around the stables.

Since Virginia's disappearance, there was double the work to be done. Giorgio had too many horses to train and care for alone. He would have to hire another groom to lug water from the well, rake the stable floors, and clean the paddocks. There were horses that needed doctoring and brushing, tack to be cleaned, hay to be pitched.

Alone in the stables, he found no time for his painting. Not since his father's illness.

Giorgio rubbed his open hand over his face.

He collapsed onto a pile of straw to rest. His left hand—his painting hand—massaged his tired shoulder muscles and neck. He drank in the toasty smell of straw, considering a nap for a few minutes.

He gazed at his hand. The paints that had embedded so deep in his cuticles had faded, replaced now with the soot of the smithy fires, the muck of the horses.

When would he paint again?

A clatter of hoofbeats.

Giorgio groaned, dusting himself off with a slap of his hand. He could not handle any more horses.

"Greetings. Are you Giorgio Brunelli?"

"Who wants to know?"

"You are summoned for an audience at the Palazzo de' Medici in Siena," said the rider, dismounting. He wore deep scarlet and gold.

The bright crimson of the de' Medici chased away Giorgio's fatigue. Medici meant trouble.

"I was dispatched to escort you at once," said the rider. "My name is Andrea Sopra."

"And who has summoned me?" said Giorgio, still slapping the bits of straw off his clothes. "I have paid all of our taxes. I am very busy—"

"The *cardinale* Ferdinando de' Medici bids you to come immediately, Brunelli."

Giorgio studied the rider's face. While his accent had the intonations of a Florentine, Giorgio recognized a countryman.

"You are Senese, are you not?" he asked.

The messenger shifted his weight.

"I am. Many generations. I know of your sorrow—the villanella is beloved by all of us. Her name is echoed throughout the streets of Siena, not just in Drago."

"Then tell me. Why does a de' Medici want to see me? I despise the name."

The messenger looked around quickly. His eyes darted to the dark corners of the stables.

"Do not worry," said Giorgio. "There are no de' Medici spies here, or they would have carried me away in chains long ago."

"I am not certain," said Sopra in a low voice. "But the *cardinale* is not his brother the granduca, I assure you. I beg you to come and hear what he has to say."

———

The de' Medici flags—with the five red palle—lifted languidly in desultory breezes in front of the palazzo in the Piazza del Duomo. Giorgio Brunelli and Andrea Sopra dismounted, and a small squadron of grooms took their horses away.

"I will search you for weapons," said a Florentine guard, holding up his hand. "Surrender any you might have now. If I find anything on your person, you will be arrested immediately."

Giorgio gave the guard his knife, an essential tool for any rider.

The guard nodded. Then he ran his hands down Giorgio's body, sweeping his fingers over the artist's crotch.

"Get your filthy hands off me, Fiorentino," said Brunelli, pushing him away. "You might fondle the palle of the de' Medici, but not mine."

The guard reached for his sword. Andrea Sopra leapt between them, grabbing Giorgio's tunic and yanking him away from the guard.

"No!" he shouted. "The cardinale wants to speak to this man. Leave him alone!

"Steady, Brunelli," he hissed. "No one sees the cardinale without a thorough search."

"He is clean," snarled the guard. His nostrils flared wide, and he gestured to Brunelli. "As clean as a shit shoveler can be."

"Basta!" said Sopra, plucking at Giorgio's sleeve. "Do not take his bait."

"What can I expect from a Fiorentino play soldier?" said Brunelli. "He has his mighty weapon in his hand. Senese have only wits, well-bred manners, and real palle between their legs, not on a flapping banner with painted balls!"

The guard took a step toward him.

Andrea Sopra whisked him away.

"You certainly do not make friends easily, Brunelli," said Sopra. "Your attitude could easily result in your death."

Inside, a guard escorted the two men to the private quarters of Cardinale Ferdinando de' Medici.

"When the cardinale speaks to you, bow your head or give some semblance of respect," warned Sopra. "Things will go better that way."

Giorgio's lip curled in disgust.

"I am Senese. The de' Medici—"

"I tell you this as another Senese. Study the floor when you enter. It will keep your head attached to your neck."

Giorgio gave a snort of disdain. The sound carried down the stone corridor of the palace. "You have lost your Senese heart, Sopra. I will look the cardinale in the eye, as an honest man should."

Andrea Sopra whirled around, looking to see who might have heard. He shook his head. "I should have had you wash. You have hay in your hair, soot and dirt on your face. The guard was right, you do stink of horse sweat and manure. In my haste—"

The heavy mahogany door swung open while they argued. A servant ushered them into the cardinale's office.

"My smell?" hissed Giorgio. "It is the perfume of brave horses!"

"Ah, Giorgio Brunelli," said the cardinale, his voice breaking into their argument. He sniffed the air as he looked up from his writing desk. "So . . . it is the perfume of brave horses I detect." Several parchment letters lay open on the desk, a gilded eagle paperweight taming their curl. An enormous tan leather Bible occupied the upper right corner of the desk, a red ribbon marking a passage. Giorgio strode forward, looking directly into the cardinale's eyes.

Ferdinando de' Medici was dressed in crimson satins; bright jewels adorned his fingers. His dark eyes looked out from under hooded lids, grown heavy like the rest of his body with too much rich food and drink.

"I had hoped you would accept my invitation."

The cardinale flicked his hand, dismissing his secretary and Andrea Sopra from the room.

"Your invitation, Cardinale de' Medici? I was summoned," said Giorgio. "And escorted here by an armed guard."

"Yes, I suppose you were," said the cardinale. "But please sit. I have some business to discuss with you."

Giorgio sat down cautiously, as if the chair might be pulled out from underneath him.

"Ah! You do not like me," said Ferdinando, raising his eyebrow.

"The de' Medici have given Siena reasons for our animosity."

Ferdinando glared back. "You are impertinent, Brunelli."

"I am honest, Cardinale."

The cardinale jutted out his thick lips, considering the young man across from him.

"May I tell you, Brunelli, that your attitude toward the de' Medici family could be easily construed as treason."

"Sì. I suppose it could be," said Giorgio meeting his eyes.

The cardinale did not answer right away. He walked to the window and looked out at the Duomo across the piazza.

"You despise my brother, the granduca, sì?" said the cardinale. He twisted the rings on his fingers.

Giorgio said nothing, but tightened his fists. To speak against the granduca would be treason.

"I understand Siena's frustration," said the cardinale. He lay a hand on Giorgio's shoulder for a brief instant. "You were once a free republic."

Giorgio sat up straighter in his chair, making the wooden frame squeak.

What is he saying? It must be a trick.

"Let me come to the point, Brunelli. We do not have to remain enemies, you and I. I know well your hatred for . . . the conquest. My Senese . . . friends have kept me well informed."

"Then there is nothing more I can tell you, Cardinale," said Giorgio, starting to rise from his seat.

"Sit down, Brunelli. Listen to what I have to say."

"As you command, Cardinale," said Giorgio.

The cardinale studied him as if he were contemplating a move on a chessboard. He poured himself a glass of wine, taking a sip.

"Siena is now and forever under Florentine rule. The sooner you come to terms with that, the better."

Giorgio stared hard at his hands. He longed to lunge at the cardinale and strangle him before he could say another word.

"I think, however, there is something I could do to help you," said the cardinale, setting down his glass. He sat down across from Giorgio. "That is, if I believed I could trust you unconditionally. Hardly a simple task given your feelings toward the de' Medici."

"Help me?" said Giorgio.

"Yes, I do believe I can. Help you."

The two sat for a moment, watching each other, controlling their breathing and emotions.

"We have a common interest, I believe," said the cardinale at last, flexing his ringed fingers. "I know of your search for Virginia Tacci—"

"What do you know of Virginia?" said Giorgio, half-rising.

"Sit down, Brunelli. Your constant buoyancy in your chair is most annoying."

Giorgio forced himself down to sit.

"I know very little. I believe she was, as you suspect, sent to a convent. I expect her name was changed to prevent you or any other Senese from finding her."

Giorgio's felt his throat tighten.

"Can she be found?"

The cardinale sat back in his chair. He looked out his window at the Duomo. "I am not certain, Brunelli. At least under the current circumstances."

"But—you could find her! You could question the granduca," said Giorgio. His hands stretched out in frustration. "She means everything to me, to Siena—"

"I need some assistance," said the cardinale, ignoring the emotional plea. "I understand you are a gifted painter. Especially of horses."

Giorgio looked up at the cardinale. "Yes, I paint. I am part of the accademia here in Siena."

What does this have to do with Virginia?

The cardinale leaned forward in his chair.

"If I were granduca—and quite clearly, I am not—I would use all of my power to search for la villanella."

Giorgio swallowed.

There was a moment of silence as the two men stared at one another.

"We have a great deal in common, I think," said the cardinale at last. "Am I correct?"

La villanella. Giorgio's mind lingered on the word. Its resonance still floated in the air.

La villanella.

"Yes, you are correct," he said looking back at the de' Medici prince, not quite certain if he were agreeing to something.

The cardinale sat back in his chair, a ghost of a smile spreading across his face.

If he were granduca? What can that mean to me? What could I—

"Good," said the cardinale. "My concern with you, Brunelli, is your temper and impatience. If we were to begin a course of action, a course of action that would require your participation, a course of action that would ultimately find Virginia Tacci, you would have to wait. And wait perhaps years. I am not sure you are capable of that."

"Years?" said Giorgio. "Why?"

"Because, you see, I am powerless in my present role to do anything to find the villanella. My hands are tied."

Giorgio felt his eyes sting. "I will do whatever I need to find Virginia Tacci and bring her home to Siena. Even if I have to sell my soul to the devil."

The cardinale sniffed. "I expect that will not be necessary. As I was saying earlier, I understand that you are an artist of extraordinary talent."

Giorgio stared at the cardinale. "What does my art have to do with Virginia?"

The cardinale didn't answer. He reached for the leather-bound Bible. "Brunelli. You will not hear from me for some time. The hour is not right . . . yet. But the first matter of business is to swear a holy oath of secrecy. To protect both you and me. And Virginia Tacci."

Giorgio hesitated. How could he possibly be in league with a de' Medici? In his mind's eye, he called up the memory of Virginia, riding Orione at full gallop through the streets of Siena.

He dipped his head, assenting. He lay his hand on the holy book.

"If I can find Virginia, I will swear anything," said Giorgio. He met the cardinale's eye.

"Even on a de' Medici Bible."

CHAPTER 74

Siena, Brunelli Stables, Vignano

JUNE 1585

For three years, day after day, month after month, Giorgio had watched the road to Siena, waiting for a messenger in de' Medici livery. And now Andrea Sopra was standing in front of him, waiting while Giorgio read the letter from Cardinale de' Medici.

The messenger watched Brunelli burn the missive in the smithy fire, and as the edges of the parchment curled and crumbled into black ash, he asked, "What response shall I give the cardinale?"

"Tell him sì," said Giorgio, his eyes still on the bright flame. "I will do it."

———

Giorgio rode up the winding road toward Fiesole, climbing the hills high above the red tile roofs of Florence. Soon his horse began to sweat, attracting horseflies whose buzz competed with the frenetic drone of the cicadas clinging to the tree branches. He let the gelding walk in the mottled shade of summer leaves. A stream gurgled alongside the road, spilling down the hillside.

When he reached the stone quarries of Borgunto, Giorgio dismounted and let his horse drink. He stared at the men hauling rocks on their backs, sweating in the sun, their faces encrusted with powdered rock, their linen tunics stained yellow-brown with sweat.

"You, traveler," said a foreman. "What do you want here?"

"Only water for my horse."

"And what else?" The foreman's face narrowed with suspicion.

Giorgio sized up the man approaching him—a man who surely recognized his Senese accent. He thought quickly.

"I am seeking help," Giorgio said, taking a step toward him. "My daughter is stricken with a high fever and cough. She has turned a mottled blue, with black splotches. I—"

The foreman jumped back.

"The pox! You must leave at once!"

"I will," said Giorgio, taking another step toward the man. "If only you will tell me where to find the healer Carlotta Spessa."

"La strega."

Giorgio frowned.

Witch? The cardinale has sent me to speak to a witch?

"I have been told she makes healing potions. To cure my daughter."

"Up there," said the foreman, jabbing a finger toward a dark opening in the rock wall in the slopes far above the quarry. "The de' Medici prince built her a villa over the grotto."

Giorgio made out the edge of a slate roofline above the quarry.

"Now be on your way at once!" said the foreman. "We do not want your contagion here."

———

Giorgio tied his horse to one of the iron hitching rings outside the doorway, bored into the ancient stone. The lower half of each ring was worn smooth, the leather chafing away the metal over the centuries.

A coal-tressed woman answered the door. Her eyes glittered like shards of emerald glass against her light brown skin. She studied him from foot to head, saying nothing.

"I am looking for a healer," said Giorgio, twisting his hat in his hands.

The young woman glanced over his head, her eyes searching for watchers.

"No, you are not," she said. She paused, this time staring straight into his eyes.

What deep green! Never have I seen eyes so piercing. Cat's eyes—

He felt his knees weaken. He shifted his weight to keep his balance.

"Healing is not your business with me. But you may come in anyway, stranger."

Giorgio stepped over the threshold. A wild onslaught of aromas—sweet, herbal, acrid, fetid—stopped him, paralyzing him midstep.

"You will get used to it," said the woman. "The smells—pungent and potent—are the tools of my craft."

She spun around to face him. "I am Carlotta Spessa."

"I am Antonio Martini," he answered. His eyes met her brilliant eyes.

She shook her head. Her black hair rippled around her shoulders. "If you continue to lie to me, I shall ask you to leave."

He dropped his gaze to the rush-covered floor. "All right," he said, eyes still lowered like a scolded child's.

"Speak," she said. "You have only one more chance to tell me the truth."

Giorgio hesitated for only a moment. "I come on a mission that persuaded me to disguise my name and my purpose. I am Giorgio Brunelli of Vignano, just outside the southeastern walls of Siena. I am a horse trainer," he said, his head bowed. "And an artist."

When he looked up again, her eyes were chipped emeralds, a fierce sparkling green. She smiled.

"Si. Sì, Giorgio Brunelli of Siena. That is much better." A fat black cat wove between her legs. "Now that I am hearing some truth, I shall ask you into my kitchen to sit by the hearth and have a cup of tea. Or wine, if you prefer."

"Grazie," said Giorgio.

He followed her into the interior of the house, her hair a black flag waving behind her.

———————

Giorgio had never met a more physically attractive woman than Carlota Spessa. Her smell, her simple presence, made his body tingle, the hairs stand up on his arms. The fact that she had invited him, a stranger, into her house, seemed to send a signal that filled him with desire.

He saw the curve of her breasts as she bent over the fire to retrieve a boiling pot of water. Her fingertips crushed herbs into two terra-cotta cups.

What lovely hands. I would use lime-white paint, bianco di San Giovanni, to capture the skin color—perhaps a minute grain of madder lake red. A bit of scrubbing on the canvas. But no. Completely wrong. There is that undertone of brown, earthiness. An umber or—

She interrupted his reverie.

"Why do you seek me?"

"You will be angry if I tell you."

"I shall be incensed if you do not. What do you want from me?" Carlotta handed him an earthenware cup of chamomile tea.

"Revenge," he answered. His eyes were still studying her skin. "And in the revenge, a reward. I seek a dear friend of mine."

Her eyes glowed back at him.

"Vengeance kills the avenger," she said, nodding to the cup. "Drink. You are agitated. It is filled with soothing flowers and sweet meadow honey. It will calm you."

Giorgio sipped the tea. He noticed Carlotta watching his throat and studying his hand on the teacup. When he set the cup down, she picked up his hand, admiring it.

"You have the hands of an artist," she said. "Look at the length of your fingers, the sensitivity in the fingertips."

She turned his palm over, to inspect it. He swallowed hard at her touch.

"But you have tragedy written in your hand. You have suffered."

"How—how do you know?"

"You told me, of course!" she said, laughing. Then her face turned serious, dark. "Yes. You seek revenge. And . . . I see the revenge you seek so clearly. What a pity."

"Where?" asked Giorgio, bending closer to his hand, to her.

She looked away from his hand, and up at his face.

"In your eyes," she said, her voice softening. "You come for vengeance. Justified vengeance, perhaps. You seek to right a wrong. But all revenge poisons the avenger."

He said nothing. His eyes met hers, not denying a word. He sensed a great depth before him, an abyss. And he didn't have time to wonder, to puzzle. Or to fear.

He could taste honey on her breath before his mouth met her lips. Giorgio drank deep of those lips, of that breath. He forgot completely why he had come to Fiesole.

But Carlotta had not.

The next morning, his body was damp and sore from lovemaking. He stretched out on the bed, still feeling the warmth left by

Carlotta, smelling her scent. He fingered the linen sheets, remembering. He closed his eyes, picturing the outline of her body in the moonlight, the black blanket of her hair spread over his chest.

The sun began to rise, shafts of crimson finding their way through the open doorway. He walked naked to the hearth, where she stirred a cauldron. He kissed the place where her shoulder met her neck, his tongue lingering there.

He closed his eyes, drinking in her earthy scent and the warmth of her skin.

"You will find what you seek there, on the plank," she said. He could feel the muscles in her shoulder work as she churned the wooden spoon.

There on an oak board lay nuggets of the most vibrant pigment he had ever seen.

———————

Carlotta cracked eggs into two bowls, separating the sunny yolk from the clear membrane in preparation for tempera.

"Let me do it," he said, setting his hand on her shoulder. "I have been doing this all my life."

She stiffened at his touch, shrugging off his hand. "No. Watch me."

"But Carlotta—"

"This is no ordinary paint," she said. "It is from a source unknown to you. Until you know how to handle it the way I do, I will not permit you to touch it. You must earn the paint's trust, its respect."

He dropped his hand, her words haunting him with a memory he could not retrieve.

"Watch the care I use in the paint's preparation. Never do I introduce a speck of my body oils, my flesh or fingernail. The color must not lick your skin, or . . . " She looked away.

"Or what?"

She turned back to him, the shine in her eyes vanished. Instead there was deadly matte green that reflected her warning. "The magic will be reversed. You may die as a consequence. Do you understand?"

"My fingernails have been stained with paint all my life! It is part of my technique to use my fingernail to etch fine detail. No artist—"

She set down her stone pestle with the greatest care.

"If you do not promise me to handle the paint as I instruct you, I will never permit you to use it. Never!" Giorgio saw the hard glint in her eyes. She would not tolerate treason. "There is magic here, and I will not allow you to insult it. Or endanger your life."

Giorgio opened his mouth to say something, but the words were stillborn. He watched her left hand grasp the pestle carefully, crushing the pigment into the white marble mortar.

She shifted the yolk to a piece of parchment, her fingers working with the delicacy of a spider spinning a web. The last of the clear membrane skated across the paper, soaking through.

When there was not a speck of white left, she pricked the skin of the yolk with a needle, releasing the pure yellow within.

"Now. Watch," she commanded.

Carlotta worked the finely ground pigment into the yolk with the urgency and care of a midwife delivering a child. First the green, then the blue.

When she was finished, Giorgio had never seen a more glorious color in all his life.

I would promise my firstborn son to paint with that color!

"I swear to you, I will follow your instructions," he said. "Just let me have that pigment!"

"Do not assume that every habitant of Firenze wishes Siena harm," said Carlotta as they lay in bed.

"I am thinking of love," Giorgio objected. "Don't bring politics into our bed!"

He kissed her neck, drinking in the warm scent of cloves and rosemary.

Carlotta traced his shoulder with her fingertip.

"We have also suffered from Francesco's rule. His taxes ruin our farms, our livelihood. Ask the merchants on the street. They would say the same—if they could tell the truth, which is impossible. Our money goes to embellish the Pitti Palace, to finance the homes of Bianca Cappello, her wardrobe, her horses, carriages, jewels, while we Florentines stew bare bones for broth. Parents go to bed without even a crust of bread in their bellies, trying to feed their children."

The memory of the siege of Siena flashed in Giorgio's mind.

"We are not all the enemy, Giorgio," she said.

Giorgio shook his head.

Of course the Fiorentinos are the enemy. And always will be.

"Ah, you are wrong, Giorgio Brunelli," said Carlotta, combing her hair between her fingers. "What a stubborn man, suckled on vengeance!"

He stared at her, startled. Had she really read his thoughts? His penis withered between his legs, lovemaking a distant memory.

"Especially the Florentine women," she continued. "Women everywhere want to see their children prosper, see their grandchildren grow fat on the cream of good fortune. They scorn the politics of the de' Medici. They believe in the prayers of Santa Caterina."

"Santa Caterina was our saint, born in Siena," scoffed Giorgio.

"She belongs to the world, not just Siena," she said, sitting up to face him. "Santa Caterina dedicated her life to the poor and sick, to peace and healing—and not only for Siena. Her letters begged for peace throughout our land. She implored all Europe to find peace through unity, a unity that would comfort its people. A faith that would render God more important than kingdoms here on earth."

"Carlotta Spessa. I had not taken you for a devout woman of the church," said Giorgio, wrapping a strand of her dark hair around his finger.

She caught his wrist, carefully unwinding her hair from his grasp. "I am not a religious woman, far from it. But I do believe ultimately in peace."

Giorgio stared at his mistress, who had climbed his body like a ladder only moments before, her kisses moistening his skin. What passion had suddenly stirred her blood to make her forget their lovemaking?

Never had he known a woman to speak of politics and religion in bed. And to speak of Santa Catarina while they were both wet from love—blasphemous.

"Many women want only to procure peace for the sake of their children," she continued. "We do not worship the de' Medici. Their wealth and power are not ours. As we of Firenze kneel at the altar for communion and taste the host, sip the cup of salvation, it is not Francesco de' Medici to whom we devote our souls. We pray only to make it through another day."

She paused for a moment, lost in thought.

"Your Virginia Tacci," she said, "is one of our kind. If she had learned the art of healing and potions, I am sure she would have made a potent cunning woman."

Giorgio pulled Carlotta close, shaking his head. His rough, unshaven face scraped the skin of her cheek, but she did not flinch. He was falling in love with this fiercely independent woman.

But she was wrong about Virginia.

"Virginia? Her heart was stamped with only one passion," he said. "To race the Palio—and to win."

CHAPTER 75

Siena, Brunelli Stables, Vignano

JULY 1586

Giorgio's left hand possessed its own special memory. His brush-stroke remembered the curve of her neck, the determination of her chin as she focused herself and her horse, preparing to break past the rope of the mossa the instant it dropped. The colors of Drago shone with preternatural pigments—green, yellow, and red—on her cap, her riding silks, on the mirrored spennachiera of the horse.

He watched as his brush painted the brown eyes of the Tuscan girl, her dark brown hair windblown, peeking out from her cap. The way she sat astride the horse, the inclination of her body, anticipating the leap forward, was hers alone. The quarter-turn of her hands on the reins—he had taught her that. She had the gentlest but most commanding hands of any rider he knew.

If I had not taught her to ride, would she have disappeared? She would not have caught the granduca's eye . . . or di Torreforte's.

He swallowed hard as the image emerged on his canvas, more real than if she were standing before him. Truer than his own memory could conjure.

The artist stepped back to gaze at her.

Where are you now, Virginia?

He stared down at his hand.

How does my hand remember more than my mind? When I close my eyes, I cannot see her as clearly as I do now, looking at my canvas. But if I leave my hand free to work, to see what memory lives there . . .

Giorgio did not sketch out a preliminary drawing. He applied the paint directly onto a blank canvas. He felt an urgency—and a clarity of vision that directed his hand.

He dipped his brush in *ultramarino* to paint the Tuscan blue sky. He remembered how he had acquired his first true ultramarine when his father had bartered with the Duchessa d'Elci—the day Virginia had saved Orione from death. No, the day Virginia had brought Orione to life!

A brilliant red and an emerald green were set aside from the other paints. He dipped a separate brush into these colors, painting with greater care. He built up the paint layers, red vermillion and emerald green, for the Drago colors of Virginia's jacket.

Working in egg tempera, he painted quickly.

Perhaps the quickness is the magic. No time to reflect.

He shook his head. Already he could see the telltale opaque sheen on his pallet. The paint would set soon and be ruined.

I cannot afford to waste these pigments. There may be no more.

Without thinking, he reached out with his finger, tracing his nail across the brilliant green, etching minute striations.

In his rapt attention to finish his work, he did not hear the heavy steps approaching as Cesare Brunelli thumped his way down to the stream, leaning heavily on his cane. He knew he would find his son there. Every hour he was not working with the horses, Giorgio would take the linen panels and his paints to the shade of the linden trees.

He stopped to watch his son stooped over his work. Giorgio's tunic was plastered to his back with sweat. Flies buzzed around the cast-off eggshells.

Cesare's sight had faded, but the startling green pierced his clouded eyes. Bright crimson and yellow contrasted vividly, the Drago colors. He stared at Virginia, blinking.

He has brought her home again!

"Who commissioned these?" gasped Cesare.

Giorgio whirled around, holding the paintbrush in the air.

"Babbo!" he said.

A blood-red drop flew from the bristles of the brush, landing in the brown dust. Giorgio stared at it as if it were a living creature. He retreated a step.

"Wait! I will help you down, Babbo."

He put down his brush carefully on the tree stump that served as his worktable and hurried to help his father down the little bank.

"These are the most magnificent paintings I have ever seen," rasped Brunelli, out of breath. "The colors, her face! My son, your work is fit for a king."

He tightened his grip on his son's arm. Giorgio winced, amazed at his father's strength despite his age.

"Who has paid the commission?" asked Cesare. "Where did you get such pigments?"

"It is a private commission."

"For whom, my son?"

With a flick of his eyes toward the palette, Giorgio hesitated.

"I am sworn to secrecy, Babbo."

Cesare tightened his hand on his cane.

"Take me closer," he said, reaching for Giorgio's arm. "I want to see these paints—"

"No, Babbo." Giorgio had never told his father "no" before in his life. "The colors are best appreciated from a distance," he said, holding his father back from the paintings.

"What do you mean, no? I want to see her again—let go of me!" Giorgio saw tears well in his father's eyes.

"Babbo. These colors are—magical. They possess great powers."

Cesare flung his son's hand from his arm. "*Magical?* Are you dabbling in the black arts?"

"Not I. But I have procured the pigments from someone who does."

The old smithy took his son by his shoulders, holding his face close to his own. "A witch?"

"I cannot say. She may be. In truth, I do not know."

Cesare blew out a breath noisily through his dry lips. "It has come to this. Perhaps because I never took you to church as your mother wanted."

"No, Babbo! You are the best father there is on Earth. It is because . . . "

Cesare looked off over the hills. "I wonder where she is. Our villanella. Is that what has driven you to . . . this?"

Giorgio nodded. He could hide little from his father. He, too, looked southeast toward the Crete, its golden hills bleaching under the fierce sun.

"Only a Pope could afford such luxuries as these," said Cesare, staring at Virginia's face on canvas. "Or worse. A de' Medici."

The old man eyed his son and turned away, looking up toward the stable.

"Help me up the bank. I want to see Orione."

Giorgio buried the paintbrushes and his pallet deep in the soil. He filled the narrow trench, watching the remaining paints color the soil bright red, green, and yellow.

He thought of the many generations who had lived and died in these hills, how their lives and their secrets were consumed by earth, pulled up into the roots of the ancient cypresses. The paintings were done, and he never wanted to think or look again upon the colors that had created the images of Virginia Tacci. Her exact likeness made his heart ache.

Giorgio packed the canvases carefully, swathing them in silken cloth that the cardinale had provided for their transport. He knew they were the best work he had ever produced, but he would never look upon them again. He wondered if Michelangelo's heart broke when he created Leda and sent her away forever.

As he was loading the wagon with his two paintings, another short wagon stirred the dust with its approach.

"Is this the Brunelli stables?" called the driver.

"It is."

The driver rubbed the grit from his eyes. He was dressed in a serge tunic, grimy and worn.

"I come from Fiesole with two packages for a gentleman. Giorgio Brunelli, do you know him?"

"That is me. I am Giorgio Brunelli."

The driver set the brake on the wagon and stepped down.

"I bring presents from Carlotta Spessa. She says only you know how to handle them. Two rolls of wallpaper that I am not to touch. As if I could not unload some colored paper! She packed them herself. And this letter," he added, handing Giorgio a sealed parchment.

"Wallpaper?" said Giorgio. The driver shrugged.

"Come into the stables, unhitch your horse," Giorgio said. "Water him and tie him in the shade. I will fetch some cheese and salami. You can refresh yourself with wine."

"Not until you unload these bedeviled packages I bring. She made me swear to unload the cargo into your care immediately. Then I rest."

Giorgio nodded. The gelding harnessed to the wagon snorted, pawing the earth at the smell of water, hay, and the other horses in the stable yard.

Giorgio climbed into the back of the wagon. With a knife blade, he lifted the corner of cloth to inspect. The packages were covered in sackcloth. He could not see color or design. He moved them carefully to the paint shed at the far corner of the stables.

He cast an eye at his own wagon, loaded with the cardinale's paintings. He squinted.

Better move my horse into shade, too. There may be more to bring the cardinale.

He led his horse under the shade of a linden tree, accompanied the driver to the stables, and settled him with food and drink. Then he broke the seal on the parchment.

Darling Giorgio,

I send these rolls of wallpaper to accompany the paintings you are creating. One is an ethereal green, the color of the grottos. It will appeal to her and remind her of the Adriatic Sea.

The other is a crimson, the color of blood. You will know what to do with them. And how to handle them with the greatest care. Do not remove the dark mold adhered to the back of the paper. That is where the most magic lies.

The final recipient will receive instructions on how the wallpaper is to be installed.

The wagoner is trustworthy.

I send these treasures with my love,
Carlotta

Giorgio sent a rider to the cardinale's palace with a brief letter that his audience with Ferdinando must be postponed until the following morning. That night, while the wagoner from Fiesole snored raucously in the hayloft, Giorgio set about forging iron hooks. The ring of metal against metal did not disturb the wagoner, who had heartily enjoyed the good red wine of the region.

Giorgio had to shake the man awake the next morning. He groaned, sitting up in the rustling hay.

"Good wagoner. You must set out on the road early. I have errands to carry out this morning but will bid you farewell first."

When Giorgio arrived at the cardinale's palace, he had to wait three hours for an audience with Ferdinando. In the meantime, he supervised the servants in unloading the cargo.

"I will unload the canvases myself," he told them. "Use the hooks attached to the sackcloth to carry the other packages. Use the utmost care, for they are easily damaged."

Cardinale Ferdinando de' Medici glowered when Giorgio was finally ushered into his study.

"How dare you cancel an appointment with me, Brunelli!" snapped the cardinale, once the door had been closed behind the attendants. "I am a busy man. I must inspect the paintings before they are delivered to Poggio a Cajano. Already the granduca is preparing his departure, and they have not been hung!"

Giorgio managed a shallow bow.

"And you!" continued the cardinale. "You must swear never to contact me through letter again. I have destroyed the missive."

"I swear I will never send written communication to you again, Cardinale."

"I will remind you of your oath, Brunelli."

"Your eminence," said Giorgio. "I was just about to depart from Vignano yesterday when a unexpected package was delivered from Fiesole."

The cardinale raised his brow. "Fiesole? From . . . ?"

Giorgio raised an eyebrow. "From the same source where I secured the pigments for my work. I did not want to arouse suspicion with the wagoner, so I awaited his departure before setting off for the palace."

The cardinale nodded. "Let me see what was delivered from the witch of Fiesole."

Anger caught Giorgio's breath. *How dare this de' Medici call my love a witch!*

"Pray, Signor Cardinale," he said at last. "Give me a blade so I may unsheathe the wrappings. Your guard has seized my own dagger."

The de' Medici cardinale looked at the Senese, a flicker of suspicion in his eyes.

"You either trust me, good cardinale," said Giorgio, meeting his eyes, "or we are both dead men."

Ferdinando de' Medici walked behind his desk and opened a drawer. A shining blade caught the morning sunshine from the open window. He handed it to the artist.

Giorgio's hand met the cardinale's on the hilt as he passed the weapon.

Giorgio slit the outer sackcloth with the sharp blade, then picked the point of the blade at the string that held together the gauzy serge.

He wrapped the discarded sackcloth over his hand, making a mitten to protect his skin. Carefully, he unfurled the wallpaper.

A shimmering green, the color of reflected water in a cavern, shone from the floor.

"My God," muttered the cardinale. "Never have I seen this color outside nature. It is a treasure of a pigment."

"It is meant by its maker to accompany my painting. The one of the start of the Palio at Santuccio."

The cardinale could not take his eyes off the washed emerald green.

"So brilliant, but so delicate. Regal yet ethereal," he mused, stroking his beard. "Let me see the other."

As Giorgio unrolled the bundle, Ferdinando noticed the crumbling mold adhered to the back of the paper.

"What is this?" he said in disgust. His extended his hand disdainfully toward the rot.

Giorgio pushed him away.

Cardinale Ferdinando sputtered, "How dare you touch me—"

"I am concerned for your life, Cardinale." Giorgio brought his mouth close to the duca's ear. "The wallpaper hangers must wear masks and gloves. They must be as careful with the paper as they are with the art."

Giorgio unrolled the second layer of wallpaper.

Both men stared at the vermillion, as intense as a pool of blood. The yellow-gold of the de' Medici palle was emblazoned against the brilliant red background.

"Again. Regal. The red of a monarch," pronounced the cardinale.

Giorgio nodded but didn't speak.

Or a cardinale red. Or the blood red of a killer.

CHAPTER 76

Tuscany, Poggio a Cajano
SEPTEMBER 1586

A coach pulled by a matched pair of black geldings approached the estate of Poggio a Cajano at midday. A masculine hand wearing a golden ring pushed back the curtains.

Cardinale Ferdinando de' Medici smiled wistfully at the sight of the villa, commissioned by his ancestor Lorenzo de' Medici. Poggio a Cajano, perched on a high point amid the undulating swells of the Tuscan landscape, had been his childhood summer home. A sculptor had conceived both the palazzo and its magnificent gardens, sited and executed with geometric precision.

A cool breeze swept through the long rows of trees, rustling their summer-dusted leaves. Ferdinando imagined the early morning dew on the foliage, ushering the first earthy scent of autumn into the shady portico. It would come soon, the welcome freshness.

It had been a mercilessly hot summer in Rome. Here in Tuscany, he finally breathed cool air and noted the first splashes of gold and russet coloring the leaves. Summer and autumn played tug-of-war with the season, the cicadas still frenetic as if they knew their days were numbered.

The cardinale sighed, recalling the pleasant childhood memories, chasing his brothers and sisters across the shaded terrace and into the vast gardens. Then he tightened his lips; he would never look at Poggio a Cajano with the same nostalgia again.

The granduca and granduchessa of Tuscany greeted him in the marble hall of the palazzo.

"Saluti," said the granduca, kissing the cardinale's ring.

"I bid you welcome to Poggio a Cajano," said the granduchessa, her voice a strained rasp.

Since the death of the two princesses, Cardinale Ferdinando had avoided Florence and his brother. Bianca had arranged the meeting, and Cardinale Ferdinando had reluctantly agreed. His fortune and ambitions were inextricably tied to those of his brother, the granduca. Pope Sixtus had employed the strife between the brothers as an excuse to ignore de' Medici petitions. The de' Medici power was splintered by their family feuds.

Ferdinando, who had not seen Bianca in several years, suppressed a wince at the sight of the frail woman who greeted him. Bianca looked bloodless, her once plump cheeks withered and pale. The fat she had accumulated over decades of de' Medici indulgence had diminished, leaving white parchment skin sagging where once there had been plump flesh.

Bianca noticed his stare. Her hand flew up to her face, for she was still vain, even in illness. She coughed hard, trying to speak. The reconciliation between her husband and his brother was important to her—and all Tuscany.

"You are not well," said the cardinale. He looked at his brother the granduca, who glared at him. A lady-in-waiting offered the granduchessa a linen handkerchief.

"Nonsense. I am as fit as a Tuscan peasant," she said, dismissing his words with a sweep of her hand and moving on. "I must thank you, Ferdinando, for your generous gifts. We have enjoyed them all summer.

"The paintings are masterpieces . . . like none I have ever seen."

"I am so pleased you like them. When I took the liberty of hanging the wallpaper and art, I hoped they would please you."

"Please me? Oh, they do indeed! And that divine wallpaper matches the girl's contrada colors! Exquisite. You selected the best of the two for me. The girl and stallion in the mossa, filled with energy, ready to explode into motion. She dominates my bedroom and cheers me when I am confined to my apartment. Ah, how I remember that day! The detail of the horse and rider are exquisite—"

Francesco interrupted his wife.

"It is romanticized too much by the artist for my taste," he sniffed. When he saw his wife's shoulders fold like an injured bird, he repented by adding his own compliment.

"The true masterpiece is the horse shying at the Via del Capitano turn." Francesco's lips pursed in satisfaction. "The white-ringed eye of the horse, the girl's determined face dissolving in shock at having victory snatched from her grasp. Two other riders galloping past her, leaving her defeated in the dust. Magnificent!"

Bianca managed a smile.

"The red wallpaper on the south-facing wall is brilliant," she said. "So masculine in comparison with my ethereal green. Who created such exquisite wallpaper? And wherever did you find the artist, Ferdinando? Such passion!"

"An anonymous illustrator at the Siena Palio charged with capturing the action at the last stretch of the race. He was employed by the Balia to produce sketches for the archives. He made the paintings from his sketches and peddled them in the market of Il Campo. A servant of mine purchased them, seeing great talent. I had him repaint them with the best pigments Florence could procure. I hope they cheer you."

The cardinale looked out toward the splashing fountain in the garden. "I meant them to remind you of our father's conquest of Siena."

"I have had my bed moved so the painting is the first thing I see when I open my eyes in the morning," said Bianca. "When I hear the cry of the morning hounds of the hunt, I rush to the window to see their departure. I am bidden by my handmaidens to return to my bed. I look at the Senese girl and pretend I still ride the hunt."

Francesco grunted at the reference to Virginia Tacci. And he had never liked Bianca's following along with her ladies on the hunt, their chatter disturbing the hounds and alerting the prey.

"And you, brother?" asked the cardinale.

"I have moved the painting closer to my writing desk," said Francesco. "I like to remember the great folly of having a girl ride a Palio. Especially a Senese girl."

"Over your writing desk, you say?"

The granduca felt his brother's eyes inspecting his face. He wiped a bead of sweat from his forehead.

"Is there something wrong?" he asked.

"Of course not," said the cardinale. "Why do you ask?""

"You are staring at me in a strange way, brother."

"It has been such a long time since we have met in person. I feel I have almost forgotten your face."

Bianca took her brother-in-law's hand and joined it with her husband's.

"No more estrangements, I pray," she said, smiling at both of them.

She began to cough. Her bony shoulders heaved with the effort. A lady-in-waiting rushed to her side, leading her away.

"With your permission, I will accompany the granduchessa to her apartments," the maid said, curtsying to the granduca. She glanced at Ferdinando. There was something about the younger brother that bode ominous, despite his holy red robes, the swinging crucifix around his neck, and the cardinale's ring on his finger.

——————

The evening meal was celebrated with a fine prosecco from a de' Medici vineyard only a few miles from Poggio a Cajano. A servant approached the table with a silver bowl of water scented with lemon.

"How did you pass the afternoon, brother?" asked the granduca, dipping his hands in the bowl and drying them with the offered towel.

"I walked the gardens, remembering our childhood," said the cardinale.

"How delicious a pastime!" said Bianca, smiling. "These gardens, this house, must be full of memories for the two of you."

Francesco shot an ugly glare at his wife. Her smile dissolved.

"And you, brother?" said the cardinale, pushing up the sleeves of his robe to wash his hands. "How did you pass the afternoon hours?"

"In my laboratory," the granduca answered.

Bianca tsked. "Stifling hot in that room. Dark and stuffy as a coffin. A miniature version of the studiolo in Palazzo Vecchio, without the grandeur."

Ferdinando looked at his brother.

"What are you working on, Francesco?"

He had heard rumors that the granduca had grown overly fond of his studiolo and the alchemical foundry in Florence. The cardinale was startled to hear of a similar room here in the family summer villa.

"I am testing some alchemy experiments, notes I have obtained from Emperor Rudolf's chemists," said Francesco.

"He thinks he will turn mercury into gold," retorted Bianca. "I thought with the death of Giovanna, we had rid ourselves of the chicanery of the Habsburg Court."

The granduca winced at the indelicacy of his wife's remark. He started to open his mouth, then shut it again, seeing Bianca's pale moon face.

"There is treacherous gossip that accuses the granduca of manufacturing poisons," continued Bianca. "That he carries killing powders in his ring. Arsenic, is it not, my sweet?"

The granduca looked pointedly at the servants who lined the walls.

"Malicious rumors," he said. "I am not Lucrezia Borgia, if that is what they mean to imply. Nor am I the Duca di Ferrara!"

A servant approached Ferdinando with a *pasticcio alla fiorentina*, a honey-crusted pie with pasta and shimmering meat sauce.

"I had the cooks prepare your favorite foods, Ferdinando," said Bianca quickly, smiling. "Wild hare stewed in wine with candied orange peel, pine nuts, and raisins. Then partridge with juniper berries—so delicious this year!—cooked in marsala. Delectable, I assure you—"

Cardinale Ferdinando gave a curt nod. "I thank you for your excellent memory and kindness."

As he met Bianca's eyes, he nearly regretted the purpose for his visit. Then he remembered how she intended to place her Antonio, a peasant's son, as the Granduca of Tuscany.

"How fares your health, my lady?" inquired Ferdinando, as a servant offered him partridge.

"She is the granduchessa. You shall address her as such!" snapped Francesco.

Startled, the servant almost dropped the platter of partridge. Three escaping juniper berries stained the ivory tablecloth with splotches of deep wine. The servant sucked in his breath in horror.

"Voi mi perdonate, mio serenissimo!"

Ferdinando stared down at the stains.

"I will not allow any disrespect of the granduchessa!" continued Francesco, fuming.

"The cardinale meant no disrespect, I am sure," said Bianca, coloring for the first time. "Martino, continue serving our guest."

"Of course, Serenissima," said the servant.

"Granduchessa," Ferdinando said, articulating the word with great difficulty. He raised his eyes from the stains to his brother, then to Bianca. "I beg your pardon."

"Thank you . . . for inquiring about my health. I am recovering slowly," she said. "The pregnancy and loss of child were difficult. It is only that."

She darted a look at her husband. "I do not suffer the marsh fever, as some would claim. It was the pregnancy. So debilitating. It reminds me of my difficult confinement with our first son."

With a wave of her hand, she changed the subject.

"After dinner, I should like to invite you to visit my apartments, along with my husband. You may see where I have placed your magnificent gift. Every time I look at it, I see another nuance in the horses. And the girl—ah, the girl. I remember that day so clearly."

"I should very much like to see it once more," said the cardinale.

"You shall see my painting as well," said the granduca. "The defeat in the girl's eyes is palpable." Francesco plunged a finger into his mouth, digging at a piece of partridge lodged in his back molars. He leaned back, smiling in satisfaction, remembering.

"It is said that the girl Virginia Tacci disappeared from Siena," the cardinale said. "Shortly after the Palio."

Francesco blotted his mouth with a napkin. "Perhaps she has married and moved away. A husband wouldn't want her seen astride a horse once he had taken her as his wife."

"It is doubtful she would simply vanish," said the cardinale, watching his brother across the table. "She is a Senese legend."

"Siena!" said the granduca, scowling. "Such a wretched thorn in my side. I wish we had starved them all to dust and bones in the siege."

Ferdinando studied the mask of hatred that contorted his brother's face.

"What did you think of the artist's execution of the horses?" The cardinale steered toward safer waters.

The granduca's eyes lit up, his ugly expression fading. A smile spread across his face.

"Truly remarkable. The artist is most certainly a horseman. You say he worked chronicling the Palio for the Balìa?"

"Sì," said Ferdinando, surveying the fruit tray the servant offered. He selected a ripe pear.

"He obviously knows his way around a horse," said the granduca, peeling an orange with a knife. "I do not know that I have ever seen such skill at expressing an equine."

———————

Cardinale Ferdinando found it hard to sleep at Poggio a Cajano. The crickets had not yet quieted into their winter slumber. And in his restless nights, memories plagued him, keeping sleep further away.

During one such night, the cardinale heard noises and hushed voices in the hallway.

He opened the door and saw a rush of servants and two doctors he recognized from Court.

He caught a manservant by the arm.

"What is it?"

"The granduca is suffering convulsions," said the servant. "As if the devil himself were shaking him."

After that, night after restless night, he would hear the servants hurrying through the villa—and if he listened very carefully, he could hear the violent sounds of a man vomiting.

In the mornings following such nights, nothing would be said. Each day, both Francesco and Bianca looked more pale and wan. The black circles under the granduca's eyes deepened into bruised shadows.

One morning, the cardinale ventured to ask about his brother's health.

"You are not looking well, brother," he said. "Did you sleep last night?"

The granduca straightened his posture. He looked disdainfully at his brother. "Like a baby."

"And yet," the cardinale persisted, "the dark circles beneath your eyes . . ."

"The doctors tell me I have a poor diet. Incompetent quacks! They say I eat too many sweets, too much rich meat. And some nonsense about drinking young wines."

"Certainly the fare we have dined on would fit that description, Francesco."

"Bah!" said the granduca. "I have no faith in doctors. They say my piss is too dark—you should see them gathered around my chamber pot, sniffing and prodding the contents. All charlatans!

"Besides, Ferdinando. I am developing my own cure in my laboratories at the studiolo. An essence of scorpion. Young Antonio is distilling the experimental oil at the Uffizi foundry. But until I return to Florence, I cannot finish the preparation. Antonio carries on in my stead."

The cardinale watched his brother struggle to swallow.

"This terrible dryness in my throat. Bring me cold water," said the granduca to a servant.

A silver pitcher flashed, catching the morning sunlight.

"And the granduchessa? Will she be joining us for breakfast?"

"No," said Francesco, gulping down the water and nodding for more. "No, but she begs you to accompany her at tea on the terrace this afternoon."

The cardinale watched the glass tremble in his brother's hand. "Francesco. You should not take such cool liquid on a hot day. It—"

"Mind your own business, Ferdinando! And you will call me granduca, especially in front of the servants."

CHAPTER 77

Tuscany, Poggio a Cajano
SEPTEMBER 1586

Cardinale Ferdinando de' Medici frowned at himself in the looking glass. He did not relish the idea of spending time with his shallow, conniving sister-in-law.

He descended the sweeping stairs to the loggia terrace.

"Ah! Brother Ferdinando, please join me." Granduchessa Bianca sat at a wrought-iron table tiled in azure. The wind lifted a strand of her blond hair from under her lace cap. "I am afraid my husband cannot join us. May I pour you some tea?"

"Yes, please. Is the granduca in poor health?" he asked.

Bianca shot a look at the cardinale.

"The doctors say he is rash with his diet. He drinks new wines, exercises in the heat, then insists on drinking cold water."

"Yes. I know he has been advised against it. And your health, my lady?"

Bianca looked out over the sun-scorched hills. "More delicate than I would like. I hoped this sojourn at Poggio a Cajano would restore my equilibrium, but I sleep fitfully. I have strange dreams."

"Dreams?"

"You are a man of the cloth. Perhaps you can counsel me, dear cardinale. You will think me strange, but I often wake and look at the painting of the Senese girl. The youthful determination, the excitement in her eyes—"

The cardinale swallowed his tea, waiting. "Yes?"

"It is as if she wanted to tell me something." The granduchessa frowned. "Something urgent, but I cannot decipher the words. You know, I saw her race, saw the horse stumble—"

A cuckoo called from a knot of trees.

"How divine! A cuckoo! I so rarely hear them now, confined as I am. Whatever is he doing away from the forest?" Bianca chattered.

Bianca poured a cup of tea without looking at the cardinale She put two teaspoons of sugar into the cup and stirred.

"Here, my good brother," she said, passing the cup to the cardinale. "You do not really know our darling Antonio, do you?"

Ferdinando looked over the brim of his cup at his sister-in-law. *What is she playing at?*

"Of course I have met Antonio over the years at Court."

"And you are fond of him, as a loving uncle?" Bianca stirred her tea with a tiny spoon. The spoon made a tinkling sound against the cup.

"I think we should not revisit that question," he said. "As cardinale, I bless his soul."

"And as a de' Medici?" said Bianca, clicking the spoon against the brim of the cup.

Ferdinando took a deep breath.

It has come to this. So be it.

"As a de' Medici, I find him lacking in every characteristic known to the family." He eyed his adversary. "You know, Serenissima, Antonio cannot and will not inherit the dukedom. Pietro and I will oppose him."

"No, Cardinale. I do not accept that," the granduchessa said, setting her jaw. "It is a treasonous pronouncement. My son is Francesco de' Medici's legitimate heir."

"Please!" the cardinale could not control his anger. "Why do you persist with this myth? All Florence knows the truth of Antonio's birth." He slammed the cup into its saucer, careless of the fragile porcelain. "You want to deceive your husband, deceive our entire family. Why bring up this this unpleasant subject again? Was I not invited to Poggio a Cajano to reconcile our differences?"

Bianca drew a deep breath and looked out once more over the browning hills. She forced the air out noisily through her nostrils, a gush of hostility.

"Yes, dear brother cardinale," she said, acid dripping in her words. "Reconciliation."

Bianca said little at dinner that evening, allowing the brothers to discuss the politics of Rome and how Cardinale Ferdinando might reach the pinnacle—Pope of the Holy Roman Church.

"You must cultivate alliances among the cardinals," said Francesco. "Align yourself with those who support Sixtus—he has written that he will honor us with a visit to Florence."

The granduca chuckled triumphantly. A papal visit was a rare honor—the other princes of Italian states were furious that the Pope had granted this favor. Especially Francesco's greatest foe, Alfonso d'Este, Duca di Ferrara.

Ferdinando watched his brother's spiteful glee. Then he turned, looking down at his ring. He rubbed his finger over the stamp of the Vatican.

"It is not so easy to align wholeheartedly with Sixtus. Politics within the Vatican are fraught with danger. An alliance could turn sour overnight, depending on a marriage, a land dispute, or politics within the church. A friend becomes a foe in the blink of an eye."

"You are not hearing me, brother," said the granduca, petulantly. "Do what is best for our family."

Cardinale Ferdinando took a sip of wine.

Yes, brother. I will do what is best for the de' Medici.

He noticed Bianca watching him. For all the fanfare about reconciling the brothers—an intention sanctioned by the Pope himself—the cardinale still did not trust her.

After a rich ragù of wild boar, the servants brought platters of fruit. A lady-in-waiting bowed to the granduca, excusing her presence. She whispered in the granduchessa's ear.

"Sì, Giulietta," she said, nodding. "Please bring in dessert." She turned to the cardinale. "I have prepared the most exquisite pear tart for us to enjoy. I made it with my own hands this afternoon. With you in mind, dear brother."

Ferdinando swallowed hard, smiling.

Giulietta brought in the pear tart, golden dough crisscrossed in thin strips across the fruit, which shone frosty green and white with crystalized sugar.

Ferdinando's eyes widened.

Green. The same shimmering green of the painting and wallpaper.

"Oh! What a delicious treat so perfectly executed, my sister," said Ferdinando without hesitation. "I had no idea you were so skilled in culinary rites. Look at the golden perfection of the crust! The green of the pears—such a rich, unworldly color."

Bianca dipped her head, acknowledging the compliment. She regarded her brother-in-law through lowered eyelashes.

"Here, my dear brother cardinale. The pears are from the orchard. Welcome back to your boyhood home of Poggio a Cajano."

The granduchessa accepted a silver knife from the table steward. The blade flashed under the flickering flames of the candle as she sliced a generous portion.

Cardinale Ferdinando licked his dry lips.

"Oh, but dear sister Bianca! After the repast you have served me, I cannot possibly eat more. I am well satisfied."

Bianca's hand stopped midway through the slice.

"But you must!" she said, a wounded look on her face. "You cannot refuse. I made this tart expressly for you—"

"I simply could not eat another bite—" her brother-in-law protested.

"Serve my brother the portion you intended," commanded the granduca sternly. "He has the good manners our mother taught us. He will savor the tart, surely."

The cardinale shot a look at his brother. "No, I beg you, granduchessa! I cannot. I—I have foresworn sugars and delicacies."

"That did not keep you from eating the crystalized orange peels you seized by the handful when you arrived," observed the granduca. "The greedy appetite you have always had for sweets. You will partake in dessert, dear brother. I insist."

"Please, dear brother. I cannot. I—"

Bianca's face crumpled. Both men realized she was about to cry.

"Here!" shouted the granduca. "Your precious tart will not go to waste. I will eat my brother's portion and mine!"

He stood up and seized the knife from his wife.

"No!" she cried, trying to pull away.

"Stop it!" he said. "What is wrong with you?" He cut a large portion and slid it onto his plate.

His wife stared at him, unblinking. "Oh, Francesco!" she said, her voice strangely hushed. "Remember the doctor warned you not to eat too many sweets. Come, my treasure, please? The doctors said—please! I beg of you. Per favore!"

The granduca glared across the table at his brother and unceremoniously stuffed a forkful of the tart in his mouth.

"No!" she cried, her hand flying to her face.

Francesco stopped chewing and looked at her. A river of fire passed between them, blazing from her eyes to his.

"Delicious," he said. His speech was muffled by the unswallowed tart in his mouth.

He threw down his napkin, pushing himself away from the table.

"Good night," he said, storming out of the room.

Once out in the hall, he turned and spat furiously, the half-chewed remains of a mouthful of pear tart staining the stone floor.

CHAPTER 78

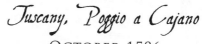

OCTOBER 1586

Weeks passed, the ivy on the walls of the villa turning red with the first cold touch of autumn. Cardinale Ferdinando was careful to avoid further altercations with his sister-in-law. He was as wary of the granduchessa as he was of his brother.

One mid-October morning, Granduca Francesco appeared at breakfast, white-skinned and sweating. His brother watched the small drops of perspiration bead his forehead as the granduca guzzled goblet after goblet of water.

"Are you well, brother?" asked the cardinale.

"I have never felt better in my life," muttered the granduca.

"You look pale—" said his brother.

"My darling. It is true!" said Bianca. The cardinale observed the equally dull color of his sister-in-law's complexion.

Like the underbelly of a toad.

Bianca Cappello grasped her husband's hand. "My darling! Let me—"

The granduca shook free of his wife's hand.

"Nonsense, my health has returned to its peak. Today we shall have a stag hunt! In the de' Medici tradition, Ferdinando. We will recall our youth."

"But my treasure!" said Bianca, knitting her fingers together. She launched into a fit of coughing.

"What do the doctors say?" she managed between hacking coughs. "You really do not look well."

"To the inferno with my doctors! It is a warm day, sunny and glorious. We shall hunt today, as we did in our childhood."

The cardinale's thoughts raced back to the hunts with the de' Medici family, in particular with Isabella.

"Come, Ferdinando. I have a brilliant gelding for you to ride. Proud cut—he still thinks he is a stallion," said the granduca, smiling. "See he doesn't mount a mare on the field. It would be quite a spectacle, a Vatican prince astride a rutting gelding."

A tinge of color returned to the granduca's countenance as he conjured up the image. He clapped his brother on his back.

"Perhaps a mare would be more fitting," said the cardinale. "One of my carriage horses—"

"Carriage horse! Nonsense—the gelding will be yours for the hunt. Bold of heart, he will take any obstacle—flying on air!"

Ferdinando smiled grimly. He hoped he could survive whatever mount his brother had chosen for him.

———

The day was indeed warm. The men sweated nearly as much as the horses. Before midday, the brothers had slain two stags. The beasts were tied to long poles and carried on the shoulders of the huntsmen out of the forest to Poggio a Cajano.

The sun blazed down on the vineyards. Cardinale Ferdinando saw that the grapes had already been harvested. The few that still clung to the vine had withered to raisins.

As the brothers approached a hillside villa, the granduca said, "I have a thirst that would kill a lesser man." He motioned to one of his servants. "Alfredo. Go and see if the proprietor there has wine, at the granduca's request."

Cardinale Ferdinando reined in his prancing horse as the gelding skipped sideways.

"A beautifully bred horse," said the granduca, grinning.

"High-spirited," Ferdinando called over his shoulder. "Isabella would have loved this one."

The granduca snapped his horse's head around to face his brother.

"Ferdinando! Never mention her name again in my presence!" he said. The gelding shied at the loud voice, leaping into the air in a series of sidesteps and rears.

"Tranquillo, tranquillo," the cardinale coaxed his horse. When the horse had settled, he turned to his brother in rage.

"She was our sister, Francesco! My sister. You may forbid the rest of Tuscany from mentioning her name, but not me! She is in my heart and in my prayers. And your dispute with her will be settled before God."

The estate owner hurried out to the granduca.

"Please, good duca! Come, taste my wine. I have some new vintage and grape juice to quench your thirst as well."

"Now that is the answer to my prayers," said the granduca, dismounting. He threw an angry look at his brother. He accepted an earthen jug of grape juice, warmed in the vat from the sun.

He tipped the jug up to the sky, emptying it.

"More!" he said, wiping his mouth with the back of his sleeve like a peasant. The proprietor hurried away to refill the jug.

The servant Alfredo murmured to his master, "Pardon me, my lord. The doctors begged me to remind you—"

The granduca waved his hand in disgust.

"Grape juice! Now I cannot be allowed to drink the purest Tuscan beverage, the fruit of the vine?"

"But my lord, the strong essence, the doctors say—"

"Silence!" roared the granduca. "Fie on the doctors! God, how will I ever slake this infernal thirst?"

"Here, Your Majesty!" said the proprietor, returning with a full jug.

Cardinale Ferdinando noticed his brother's arm shaking violently as he raised the jug to his lips. Crimson drops of juice bloodied his sweat-stained tunic.

A violent convulsion seized him, shaking his body from head to toe.

The granduca's steward Alfredo stepped closer to catch him if he fell.

"Come to the cool shade of my well, Your Highness," said the proprietor, casting a worried eye from the granduca to the cardinale. "There is a spring there—shady and damp. It will cool you."

"Fetch the doctor from Poggio a Cajano immediately," whispered the cardinale in Alfredo's ear. "Bring him in a coach. The granduca is not well."

───────────

That night, Francesco called for the servant who slept on a mat outside his door. He jangled a bell by his bedside.

"My lord granduca!" said the servant, his eyes heavy-lidded with sleep. "Are you ill?"

"Help me sit up. I cannot breathe."

The servant placed his hand under Francesco's arm, helping the granduca off his pillow. His master's back was drenched in sweat, soaking the bed linens. The smell of fever, acrid and pungent, filled the room.

"Water," mumbled Francesco.

The young man poured water into a cup. He tipped it to the granduca's blanched lips.

"I will fetch the doctor at once!" said the chamber servant. "Let me call for your other attendants to sit with you."

As the servant opened the door, he saw one of the granduchessa's favorite ladies-in-waiting come running down the hall, her skirts flying behind her.

"The granduchessa!" she gasped. "Where is the doctor? She is dying, I am quite sure of it."

The granduca heard the soft slap of leather soles running down the hall, the sound diminishing. His gaze followed listlessly to the closed door. His eyes focused and unfocused, looking around the room.

Granduca Francesco de' Medici found himself staring at the painting of Virginia Tacci and her black stallion. Something about her expression appeared to have changed. She seemed to be looking straight at him.

PART VII

The Reign of Granduca Ferdinando

ANNI 1586–1591

CHAPTER 79

Florence

OCTOBER 1586

After the death of his brother and sister-in-law, Cardinale Ferdinando wasted no time in renouncing his position as cardinale of the church and returning to claim the dukedom of Tuscany.

Ferndinando's first act of kindness as duca was to release his stepmother, Camilla, from the convent. Sadly, she had spent too many years in sorrow. She arrived at the Pitti Palace a stooped and demented old woman, barely able to make sense of her surroundings.

The new granduca quickly declared Antonio to be illegitimate, with no de' Medici blood in his veins. The rumor of his true birth spread like wildfire through the streets of Florence. Yet once that was done, Ferdinando kept Antonio as a member of the Court and as a royal envoy. As long as Antonio was not a threat to the dukedom, he would remain in the embrace of the de' Medici. Granduca Ferdinando also saw that Isabella's children, Virginio and Nora, were brought up in the de' Medici Court.

But despite these good deeds, the granduca forgot one promise he had made.

A visitor approached Florence's walls on a black stallion. He dismounted at the Porta Romana, asking permission to enter the city walls.

"I am here to see Granduca Ferdinando. He knows me."

"What business do you have with the granduca, Senese?" said the city guard.

"I cannot speak of it. But Granduca Ferdinando knows me."

The guard scoffed.

"A Senese with a country accent and no papers. If the granduca wishes to see you, his secretary will send you a letter of admittance to these gates."

The stranger and the big black stallion with the white star on his forehead set off a trot away from the Florentine walls.

"You ride a good-looking stallion," the guardsman called after him. "For a Senese!"

The man didn't look back. He was deep in thought. In the past, Cardinale Ferdinando de' Medici had summoned him to Florence. But now, because he had become granduca, the path to an audience was harder. But no matter. Cardinale or granduca, Ferdinando de' Medici owed him a great favor. He would find a way.

With the death of Francesco, Granduca Ferdinando inherited the dwarf Morgante. He was quite old now, and dwarves usually lived short lives. The little man tried his best to entertain the children of his new master, though he was too aged to juggle or caper.

But the granduca himself, struggling with the effects of his brother's ruinous reign, found Morgante's company comforting, for there were few who had hated his dead brother more.

"I have often wondered about the man from Siena. If he had anything to do with the death," said Morgante, watching the granduca's eyes scan the wall where his sister's portrait once hung.

"What's that?" Ferdinando was startled out of his reverie. His face grew pale.

Could Morgante know about the painter from Siena?

"Here in this room," said Morgante. "A man who wore a black silk scarf. There was a look in his eyes that chilled my heart. I remember thinking a man like that could murder a princess."

Ferdinando sat up, unfolding his hands. He breathed freely now. Of course. The death of Isabella.

So many de' Medici deaths.

And even though he now knew Morgante was speaking of the death of Isabella, Granduca Ferdinando thought about his brother. The dwarf was still prattling on. Something about a donkey and visitors. But the granduca wasn't paying attention. He was remembering his promise to a Senese artist.

He shook his head, ridding himself of the memory. It was far too soon to associate himself with the artist whose paintings hung in the death chambers of his brother and sister-in-law.

Giorgio Brunelli must wait.

CHAPTER 80

Fiesole

AUGUST 1587

The trip to Fiesole was harder than ever. Giorgio had developed headaches that seized his whole body, nauseating him. Under the heat of the sun, his vision was blurred.

But this was worse.

He knelt on the hard stones of the floor. "Why will you not marry me?" he pleaded. "Have I not shown you my love, my devotion? Come with me to Siena!"

Carlotta shook her head, making the veil of her hair wave. "I cannot. I must remain in this house all the days of my life. I love you, and I will always be your lover. But I cannot marry you, Giorgio."

"But why?"

"I belong to this house. I cannot leave."

Giorgio's face burned. "You could not be a Senese?"

"Fiesole is my home. I do not wish to leave here any more than you could leave Siena."

"But . . . you—"

"But I am a woman? You think I should follow a man and take his identity, like wearing a new cloak?"

Giorgio looked into her eyes. She was right.

He looked down at the foot-polished stones of the house as if he could find some consolation there. His hands were clasped as in prayer.

Carlotta took his hands in hers.

"Can you not survive on my love without marriage?"

She grasped his hand. He still did not look up. He felt her inspecting his fingers.

"Giorgio!" she said. "Look at your fingernails!"

Cazzo! I speak of my eternal love, and she chides me about my cuticles.

"You have the sign of the crescent moon in the nail beds. What should be pink is speckled with white stars. Oh, Giorgio!"

Giorgio looked down at his hand.

"How strange," he said. He did not spend time studying his hands.

"Giorgio! The paints! I warned you never to touch the pigments."

He thought of the day his left hand had shot out, the nail on his pointer finger etching Virginia's face on the canvas. Was the poison that had killed the de' Medici to take his life now?

"State your business," said the granduca, his eyes focused on the papers on his desk.

Carlotta let the silence draw out for a moment and then, when Ferdinando still didn't look up, said, "I request the favor that you look at my face when addressing me, Granduca."

Now he looked up. Astonished.

"How dare you!"

"Good, I have your attention. I come to you to discuss some unfinished business."

"Ah! Compensation for your—services—to my younger brother, Duca Pietro?"

Carlotta narrowed her eyes in disgust.

"I rendered no services to him. When I was finished with our relationship, we parted ways. And there is no compensation due from a lover who asked me for poi—"

"Enough!" He cut her off midword. There was a moment of silence. Ferdinando looked at the door, making sure it was shut tight. "You tread on dangerous ground. What business do you have with me, Carlotta Spessa?"

"You know very well the business we had together. Some special paints, do you recall? And an arrangement was made between you and a certain Senese artist."

Once more, the granduca's eyes flicked to the door.

"He delivered his services," Carlotta continued. "Now he finds you impossible to reach." She paused. Her look was opaque. "You may not have known—"

"Yes, yes," Ferdinando interrupted. "Do not play games with me."

"So. I come to collect the debt long overdue."

"You come on a very dangerous mission, Carlotta Spessa. I am sure you are aware of the long reach of a granduca. Fiesole is my back garden. I can pluck what I like—"

"I do know the reach of the de' Medici. But I also know you are a most honorable man, unlike your brothers."

He inclined his head, acknowledging the double-edged compliment.

"You are not a bad man, Granduca Ferdinando," said Carlotta, fingering a pearl seed in her hair. "Merely a forgetful one. It is time to pay your debt to Giorgio Brunelli."

The Granduca of Tuscany sent messengers to every convent within his land.

Nothing.

He made a trip to Siena, summoning Giorgio to the de' Medici palazzo. Looking down from the balcony, he saw the artist dismount from a black stallion with a constellation of white blazing its forehead.

Look at this wreck of a man, thought the granduca.

Giorgio's face had wrinkled like a pumpkin left in the snow. His cheeks and eyes had sunken, his freckled skin withered over his thin face.

There is a despair about this one, a weakness from much more than the sun and the years.

When Giorgio was shown into his presence, the granduca could see the frost obscuring the once fierce red hair. He could almost smell the dull husk of age that clung to his visitor, a premature decay that bespoke grave failure.

"How is your father?" he asked.

"He died last winter," answered Giorgio, unblinking.

"I am very sorry. He was a great horseman. Governor di Montauto was forever praising him."

"Dead, too, of course," said Giorgio, dismissing the memory with a wave of his hand. "A year after Virginia's ride in the Palio. He was more Senese than Florentine—Siena mourned his death."

As if agreed to, the two men bowed their heads in silence. They could hear the ticking of the gilded clock, a present from the Habsburg Court in Vienna.

"I want you to know that I have sent emissaries to every convent in Tuscany," the granduca said finally. "There is no record of Virginia Tacci."

Giorgio drew in a breath, letting the air rest in his lungs. He expelled it in a gush.

"I thank you for that—although that is ground we have already tilled. Perhaps you should have questioned Giacomo di Torreforte."

The granduca wrinkled his forehead. "Di Torreforte?"

"He was a visitor to your brother's court. A frequent visitor, he would have everyone believe. He always bragged of his presence there."

"I know the di Torreforte family. The old *conte* is a distant cousin. This is the son, I presume?"

"The eldest son. His coach was seen near the Tacci pastures the day Virginia disappeared."

The granduca's eyes narrowed. "But you have no proof he kidnapped her?"

"None whatsoever," said Giorgio. "Just the word of a shepherd, a cousin of Virginia, who saw the di Torreforte coach in the vicinity."

The granduca folded his hands together, reminiscent of his long days of prayer.

A long moment of silence passed. Giorgio leaned forward, his voice hot with torment.

"I have killed two souls, and the one I seek is lost forever."

"I am sorry," said the granduca, fingering a ruby ring that had replaced his cardinale's signet. "But if it is any consequence to you, I can tell you it is doubtful your paintings were the cause of my brother's and his wife's deaths."

Giorgio stared at him.

"The paints were potent. I am certain. I am proof of that."

"Perhaps," whispered the granduca, bringing his face close to the artist's. "But the cause of my brother's death was arsenic, baked in a pear tart Bianca prepared. Meant to poison me."

"I have heard that report," said Giorgio. "There is no end to the wild fantasies and Florentine gossip! But we know better, you and I. You and I, Granduca Ferdinando. You and I."

The granduca's eyes lit up in anger. Giorgio held his gaze.

"We both know it was my work—our work, *ours!*—that killed them both," said the artist. "Vengeance has been just. And now it kills me."

"God will forgive us both more easily if we were not murderers," said the former cardinale, clasping his hands in prayer. "As will history, in my case."

"God," said Giorgio, "knows the truth. No matter what we say. And for my part, I do not care how history colors me or whether I am included or not. I only care about Virginia. I regret that I did not poison di Torreforte. Would that I had pulled the ends of his black scarf tight around his neck until he strangled."

Ferdinando unfolded his clasped hands and stared at Giorgio. "Black scarf?"

"He always wore a black scarf tied loosely around his neck. Summer or winter. An affectation. Pretending to be an artist—"

"Wait!" said the granduca holding up his palm. "The dwarf Morgante spoke of a man in just such a scarf."

Giorgio leaned forward. "Serenissimo! What did he say?"

Morgante arrived from Florence two days later in a de' Medici coach.

Standing before the granduca, the aging dwarf craned his neck like a turtle.

"Forgive me, my hearing is gone," said the dwarf. "Would your grace please be so kind as to repeat the question?"

The granduca spoke directly in the little man's ear.

"The man from Siena, the one with the black scarf who met with my brother Granduca Francesco? Did he speak with a Senese accent?"

Morgante's tongue poked around in his mouth, trying to remember.

"No. A bit queer, but no. He spoke like a Florentine, perhaps from the provinces. A nobile, all the same."

"And you mentioned . . . something about a donkey, was it?"

Morgante swung his head back and forth.

"I beg your forgiveness. I have grown old and forgetful. I cannot remember."

"Yes. Yes, you did. There was a donkey. I am certain." Granduca Ferdinando's eyes slid upward, unfocused in thought. "Yes. And a mention of visitors. No visitors. That's what you said. No visitors."

"A convent!" blurted Giorgio. "So it is true. She was sent to a convent!"

"Not any convent in Tuscany. And my contacts have found nothing in Rome. Morgante, you are dismissed."

The dwarf suddenly raised a finger in the air. "I remember now. The granduca said she was 'in the heart of the enemy.'"

"Bravo, Morgante," said Granduca Ferdinando. "Rest here tonight—tomorrow the coach will deliver you back to Florence."

The old dwarf bobbed his head in gratitude. He shuffled toward the door.

"Take care, good servant," said the granduca.

"You are a kind master," said Morgante. His gnarled hand reached up to the handle of the door.

Giorgio watched the little man list left, then right, like a rocking boat, as he tottered out into the hall.

When the door clicked shut, the granduca's eyes lit up. "'Heart of the enemy.' Yes, that is what I remember now, too."

"It is hard to think of what states are not enemies of the de' Medici," said Giorgio.

The granduca flashed an acid look at his visitor. "You would do well not to forget your place, Senese."

"My place is finding Virginia Tacci. Nothing else."

The granduca rubbed a finger back and forth over his mustache, thinking.

"So," said Giorgio. "What quarrels and enemies come first to mind?"

"Siena, of course," said the granduca, fingering his cropped beard. He gave a curt chuckle. "But no Senese convent would keep such a secret."

Giorgio glared at him, saying nothing. His dark look sent the granduca back to thinking. He chewed his lip.

"Again, Milan. The Sforzas are envious of the status of granducato that the Pope gave our Tuscany. France is our sworn enemy. Napoli detests the de' Medici for the murder of Leonora. The Habsburgs bear a grudge for my brother's treatment of Giovanna—"

"In short, most of Europe," said Giorgio, throwing up his hands. "I cannot search every convent!"

"Let me think upon it. I will use every contact I have in Rome. I will search for Virginia Tacci."

"Unless the bastardo di Torreforte gave her a false name," said Giorgio.

The granduca looked at his visitor and sighed. He said nothing, but looked around the room at the portraits of his family in the Senese palazzo.

I will restore the Bronzino of Isabella to the Pitti Palace. I need her comfort. And the one of her in the green velvet dress. The little dog in my sister's lap, a garland in her hair. How that portrait gave my father joy.

"My brother was very good at erasing women when they did not suit his purposes," the granduca said, closing his hand. "Give me time to think. In the meantime, I must concentrate on my wedding celebrations."

Giorgio cocked his head.

"Ah," said the granduca. "I suppose the news does not travel as quickly as I thought from Florence to Siena. I am marrying the princess Christina of Lorraine."

"A Frenchwoman?"

"She is the granddaughter of Catherine de' Medici—so she has our blood in her veins. Her grandmother was our sworn enemy, but no matter. I am weary of unrest. It is time to make peace."

Giorgio said nothing more. He could not understand why anyone—especially a de' Medici—would settle for peace over revenge.

CHAPTER 81

Siena, Brunelli Stables, Vignano

AUGUST 1587

Giorgio rarely saw Riccardo anymore. Shared memories of Virginia made it too painful for the two men to meet. But upon Giorgio's return from Florence, he wrote for his old friend to meet him in the country stables.

"Have you found her?" Riccardo said even as he dismounted, swinging off the horse so quickly, his mount shied away.

"Not yet. But I am certain di Torreforte kidnapped her. Now beyond a doubt—"

"I will kill the bastard!" said Riccardo, his entire body stiffening in rage.

"No, no!" said Giorgio, putting a hand on his friend's arm. "Let us find Virginia first!"

A tremor shook Riccardo's body.

"How can you stand there so coolly, Giorgio? We must have revenge!"

Oh, my friend, I have had revenge. If you only knew.

"I am trying to find her, Riccardo. We can settle di Torreforte's fate later."

"Where is she?"

Giorgio shook his head.

"No one knows for sure. A convent. Outside of Tuscany."

"So only di Torreforte knows for sure—" said Riccardo.

"Perhaps. Only—"

Riccardo gritted his teeth together, baring them like a wolf. "I shall find out!"

Shaking Giorgio's hand from his arm, he gathered the reins in his left hand and swung back into the saddle.

"Where are you going?" said Giorgio

"To confront the bastardo!"

He wheeled his horse around and took off at a gallop for Siena.

———————

Riccardo found di Torreforte on the perimeter of Il Campo, drinking outside a tavern. He was sampling a Montepulciano wine from a keg the proprietor had just tapped.

The sun was bright, making the Florentine squint as he brought the cup to his lips. A group of Florentine bankers and nobili sat on plank benches around an overturned cask, serving as a table.

"*Delizioso!*" di Torreforte pronounced. His entourage murmured similar sentiments, draining their cups.

A rider trotted across the bricks of the piazza. His eyes searched the crowd. When he spied di Torreforte, his face contorted.

"You, signore!" said Riccardo, pointing his gloved hand. "You!"

"Are you addressing me, Signor De' Luca?" said di Torreforte.

Riccardo gave the reins to the tavern boy.

"You scoundrel! You kidnapped Virginia Tacci."

"What?" said di Torreforte, looking about the crowd that gathered instantly.

The name Virginia Tacci spread across the piazza. The pigeons shot up from the brick pavement, their wings beating madly.

"You are quite mad, sir!" said di Torreforte.

"You know where she is!"

Di Torreforte set down his glass. He wiped his lips against the back of his hand.

"Everyone knows that you were madly in love with the villanella. You made a fool of yourself spouting poetry, besotted by a poor shepherdess. Now you have some insane notion that I am to blame for—"

Riccardo seized di Torreforte by his shirt. "You know where she is! You liar!"

Di Torreforte leaned into his attacker, his breath sour with wine. "If I did, I would never tell you, you piece of shit!"

He tore away from De' Luca, giving him a shove. He straightened his cloak and scarf.

"You would do best to forget about that little whore of a shepherdess. She is probably in a field somewhere rutting with someone from her own despicable class."

Riccardo's face paled with rage. He took a step forward and slapped di Torreforte hard.

"I challenge you to a duel, Signor di Torreforte," he said. "To defend the honor of Virginia Tacci!"

The crowd gasped. Duels were outlawed in the province of Siena on penalty of death. As one the crowd turned, looking for the de' Medici guards. Surely they would have heard the commotion, seen the crowd gather.

One of di Torreforte's Florentine companions shouted, "Your challenge is illegal, Signor De' Luca. Retract it at once!"

"My proposition is between two gentlemen," said Riccardo. "Let Signor di Torreforte decline to meet my challenge, not one of his henchmen."

Giacomo di Torreforte licked his lips. The skin of his face looked puckered like an old man's.

"What do you say, di Torreforte?" Riccardo insisted.

"Make way! Disperse!" shouted a voice of authority.

A guard broke through the crowd.

"What is this disturbance? Who are the perpetrators?"

Riccardo looked past the guard, pointing his finger. "Do you accept my challenge, you coward?"

Di Torreforte slid his eyes toward the guard. Two more appeared.

"He challenged me to a duel. Arrest him!" said di Torreforte. "What are you waiting for?"

CHAPTER 82

Siena

SEPTEMBER 1587

Signora De' Luca held her beloved Riccardo in her arms next to her bosom, crying the burning tears of a mother who has lost her son.

His trial had been simple. He had broken the laws of Siena by challenging Signor di Torreforte to a duel. The Florentine witnesses testified on di Torreforte's behalf. The Senese would say nothing.

Granduca Ferdinando intervened to spare his life, but Riccardo was banished forever from the city and province of Siena.

And now soldiers had come to enforce that order.

Riccardo De' Luca chose Ferrara as his home of exile. His father had contacts in the d'Este Court through trade and marriage, as well as friendships forged before and during the siege of Siena.

"I would give you Caramella as a gift," his father said, barely able to look into his son's eyes. "But I fear she could not make the journey. I have picked out three good mares for you. I will send more when you are established."

"Thank you, Babbo."

"Our alliance with Duca Alfonso will serve you well. He has always supported Siena. They love their horses, their Palio."

At the last word, Riccardo wiped a tear from his eye. Then another.

———

Three soldiers escorted Riccardo De' Luca to the border of Emilia-Romagna.

The lieutenant took out the decree signed by Granduca Ferdinando. He read aloud, the wind snatching his words.

"Thou, Signor Riccardo De' Luca, shall not enter the Duchy of Tuscany for the rest of your living days. Your crime: challenging Giacomo di Torreforte to a duel and disrupting the peace of Siena. The death sentence has been converted to banishment by the mercy of Serenissimo Granduca Ferdinando de' Medici. Your banishment is inconvertible—you will enter Tuscany only under penalty of death. Do you understand?"

"Sì," said Riccardo, looking over the hills in the direction of his beloved Siena.

Then he turned his back on Tuscany and took a firm grip on the lead ropes of three shiny-coated chestnut mares, who bobbed and pranced behind the gelding as Riccardo headed down the dusty road toward Ferrara, never looking back.

CHAPTER 83

Ferrara, Castello d' Este

Ercole Cortile, Ferrara's ambassador to the de' Medici Court, rested at home for three days before he made an official visit to the Palazzo d'Este. Ferrara had not the same grandeur as Florence, but the green waters surrounding the crenellated palace walls, the wisps of morning fog, and the refined Court cultivated by Alfonso were a balm to his soul.

He had spent too many years listening to—and paying for—the many ears pressed to the doors of de' Medici intrigue. The murders and scandals sickened him as he grew older. It was no longer the celebrated Court of Granduca Cosimo, and Cortile was no longer the dashing ambassador who enjoyed the sordid bits of gossip he procured for the Duca di Ferrara.

Both Ercole Cortile and Duca Alfonso had grown old.

Cortile had missed his homeland. Under Alfonso, Ferrara was a haven for artists, musicians, and scientists, free from the rancor and reprisal that haunted the de' Medici Court. Alfonso welcomed visitors from other lands whose diverse experiences and opinions would enrich the culture of Ferrara.

Most of all, Duca Alfonso enjoyed thumbing his nose at Rome and at the de' Medici, his mortal enemies.

The De' Luca family had appealed to Alfonso to grant Riccardo asylum in Ferrara, and he was inclined to grant their request.

"They say Riccardo is a superb horseman," Cortile said, reading the letter from the elder De' Luca. "I do know that his father breeds magnificent Palio horses."

"A breeder of Palio horses, a foe of Florence—what better qualities to recommend him to the House of Este!" said Alfonso, taking a sip of wine. "But what is this about a duel?"

"Apparently Signor De' Luca believes a de' Medici henchman kidnapped Siena's shining star—Virginia Tacci."

"And she is?"

"The girl who almost won the Palio some years ago."

"Ah, sì! The Senese shepherdess! Such a tale!"

"Indeed. Her horse shied in the last stretch. Some *bastardi* threw boards out into the road. Still, she finished third. But after the Palio, she disappeared. There has been no record of her existence."

"Kidnapped?" asked Alfonso, raising an eyebrow.

"Riccardo De' Luca is convinced of it. And so he challenged a Florentine—the man whom he thought responsible—to a duel."

"You think Granduca Francesco had a hand in this?"

Ercole Cortile shrugged and laid the De' Luca letter on the desk. His stomach roiled at the name Francesco de' Medici.

"All that is certain is that she is gone—and that Siena worshipped the girl. Virginia Tacci represented the independence and passion of their old republic," he said. "The rest is speculation."

Alfonso nodded. He suddenly felt a cold shadow floating over him. He thought of the murder of the beautiful Leonora de' Medici, cousin of his first wife.

"Perhaps they feared this Virginia Tacci could have sparked a rebellion. Siena's soul is restless. A de' Medici who is capable of murdering his own sister and his sweet cousin—yes, I could see how such a girl might disappear mysteriously."

Ercole Cortile nodded. He knew well of what Francesco had been capable.

"Did this scoundrel accept the challenge of"—Alfonso glanced at the letter lying on his desk—"Riccardo De' Luca?"

"No. He waited like a coward for the guards to arrest the man. And now Signor De' Luca is within our borders. He brought three gorgeous chestnut brood mares, already in foal."

Alfonso savored his wine, his tongue swishing it around his palate. He swallowed, taking a deep, contented breath.

"I must pay our guest a visit. And we will learn even more when those mares give foal. I am always looking for good prospects for our Palio."

CHAPTER 84

Siena, Brunelli Stables, Vignano
OCTOBER 1587

In accord with Cesare's last wishes, Orione became a standing stud in the Brunelli stables. Senese horsemen coveted the Maremma bloodline mixed with Stella's thoroughbred breeding, especially after Orione's performance in the first contrada Palio of the Assumption. Few outside Siena understood the nobility and spirit of the stallion, grumbling that the stud was too heavy-boned for Palio stock. They feared the offspring would not be fleet-footed as a thoroughbred. But the Senese knew the true value of heart and agility. They looked for the strength and courage bred in their own land.

Caramella's first Orione foal had her sire's black coat and white star. The filly came straight from the mare's womb into life, pulled to her hooves like a puppet on a string.

Giorgio remembered the night of Orione's birth, how Virginia had crawled across the blood-stained straw to breathe life into the stillborn colt. His freckled face streaked with tears at the sight of Caramella's newborn filly.

He alone attended the birth, the memories flooding back to him. Never had he felt so lonely. How he wished his father, Cesare, had lived to see this filly born. And . . . Virginia. She should be here to see Orione's first foal.

The filly belonged to the De' Lucas. When the time came for her to be weaned, Giorgio would take her to Ferrara, where Riccardo had established his stables. Giorgio shook his head, thinking of Riccardo forever beyond Siena's city walls.

But at least Ferrara was horse country . . . and they hated the de' Medici. The filly, christened Celeste, could thrive there.

She will outlive me. Orione's offspring will outlive all of us. If only I could paint her.

Giorgio clenched his trembling hand, no longer capable of grasping a paintbrush.

———

A man in d'Elci's livery rode into Vignano, leading an aging chestnut mare. The children in the streets stopped playing in the puddles on the cobblestone road in front of the church.

"She must be a Palio mare," whispered one, whose older brother worked shoveling manure at the Brunelli stables. "Look at her beautiful head."

"She looks old and moth-eaten to me," said another. "Her coat does not shine like the great stallion Orione. No horse is as great as Vignano's!"

He made sure his voice was loud enough for the rider to hear.

"Get out of the way, you ragamuffins! This is the great Stella, the dam of your Orione. Show respect."

Giorgio Brunelli was already out in the cobblestone yard when the rider approached the stable. He winced seeing the once beautiful Stella, now swaybacked, her luminous reddish coat mottled with faded tufts.

"Giorgio Brunelli," said the rider, dismounting.

Giorgio stroked the big mare's neck. She lowered her head.

"Why is Stella brought here? She is—"

The rider produced a letter from his pouch. "La Duchessa d'Elci sends this in explanation. She is on her deathbed, may God and Santa Caterina bless her noble soul."

Giorgio opened the folded parchment.

Esteemed Giorgio Brunelli,

After a good long time here on Earth, I am told by my doctors I am approaching my end. I have asked my secretary to take down my last words.

I think I have lived this long only in hopes of seeing Virginia Tacci return to Siena. Now I see that I shall have that joy only by looking down from heaven, if our merciful Lord sees fit to accept my soul.

I entrust you with my beloved mare Stella, who has served Siena well, not only in winning two Palios but in giving birth to our Virginia's Orione.

I fear that she has little life left to her. No one can tell me a remedy for her present sad condition. I know that your father has taught you much about the cure of strange illnesses, so I commend her to your care.

See that she is treated with the good care she merits, and that, when the time comes, her end is noble. I trust you know what I mean, being a true horseman.

I am in your debt.

Lucretia, Duchessa d'Elci

CHAPTER 85

Ferrara, Convento di Sant'Antonio

OCTOBER 1589

Conversa Margherita had watched the postulant Silvia grow from a child to a young woman, twenty-two years of age.

Again and again, Silvia told Margherita she dedicated her prayers to Santa Caterina, for only that saint knew her true self and sorrow.

"One day my saint will turn her countenance upon me," she said fiercely. "And my name—Virginia! My name will be known once more."

Margherita said nothing, but she opened her arms and pressed the young woman to her bosom.

The postulant squirmed free of the embrace.

"You still do not believe I am Virginia Tacci."

Margherita thought of the bits of hair and salt she had found on the young postulate's clothes and the one boot she had preserved in a small trunk in her hovel outside the convent walls.

"I am forbidden to have an opinion beyond what the mother superior tells me," said the conversa. "But I know that I love you, and so does Jesus. Santa Caterina would be proud of your devotion."

The young woman sighed, making the sign of the cross.

"You are a good woman, Margherita, devoted to the church and to God. One day I will prove to you that I tell the truth. I am the girl who rode the Palio."

Margherita blinked back tears. She had long ago given away the right to think for herself. The church, this abbey, were all that existed for her. Anything that ran counter to what the mother superior told her was evil.

Sometimes she woke up at night, wrestling with what she knew—the boot, the salt, the horsehair—and what could not possibly be real: a girl riding the Palio. The collision between the two caused her real pain as she blinked in the darkness, listening to the rustle of straw in her family's cots. They needed the money the convent paid. It was little, but the coins were enough to put a bit of meat and bones in the soup pot.

Margherita envied Silvia's spirit but understood why she could not take the veil graciously. No . . . take it eagerly. Had Margherita been born to a family who could afford a dowry to the convent, she would have joyously dedicated her life to Jesus and to God.

Instead she emptied the chamber pots of the privileged nuns, who were Jesus's own brides.

It was as close to heaven as she could hope for.

———

Riccardo began a small breeding farm along the Po River. His three fine mares were already in foal, and he acquired four more from nearby farms. His father sent a stallion, the sire of Caramella. With the good breeding of the mares, Riccardo had a new beginning in Ferrara.

He had heard that Caramella's filly, Celeste, was a prize foal, strong-willed and strong-boned. She sounded just like her sire, Orione. He could not wait to see her when she was old enough to make the journey to Ferrara. In the meantime, one of his own mares was in foal by Orione.

Now the Duca di Ferrara, Alfonso II d'Este, was to pay him a visit. If the duca looked upon his mares with favor, his future in this new land was blessed.

Despite all the work that had to be done around the new farm, Riccardo set aside a few hours each day to paint. Only painting and long rides eased his mind. Ferrara's haunting mists, shrouding the countryside and city buildings, caught his artist's eye. He dressed warmly and rose early from his bed, starting to paint even before the horses nickered for their breakfast. His brushes and paints captured the moody tones of blue and gray, the mystical light as the muted sun burned away the clouds most mornings.

And when the sun was vanquished by an approaching storm, the land and its people enveloped in the gray mantle—Riccardo De' Luca liked this best.

It spoke to his soul, gray and despondent.

The day Duca Alfonso and his ambassador Ercole Cortile came to visit was one such gray, misty day. Riccardo could barely pull himself away from his painting—the urge to capture Ferrara's moodiness was almost an affliction. He cleaned the paint from his brushes hastily.

Still carrying the faint odor of linseed oil, he received his visitors and thanked Duca Alfonso profusely for giving him refuge.

"I should have nowhere to go if it were not for the kindness of Siena's ally."

"Bah! The de' Medici are a pack of murderous imbeciles," said Duca Alfonso. "Renegade bankers, not true nobili. I invite you, Signor De' Luca, to attend my Court."

Riccardo bowed deeply. "It shall be my honor, my duca."

"You will see how favorably our Court compares to Florence's," said Ercole Cortile.

"I have never been to the de' Medici Court."

Ercole Cortile inclined his head slightly in apology.

"Forgive me." He motioned to the palette and paints sitting on a wooden table in the garden. "May I assume you are a painter, Signor De' Luca?"

"I am a horseman first. But yes, art is a serious occupation for me."

"Perhaps one day, you will show me your work," said Duca Alfonso.

"I am honored, but I think you will find my horses more appealing."

"Ah, yes, the purpose of our visit," said Duca Alfonso. "I want to see the brood mares. Will they foal soon?"

"The beginning of the year," said Riccardo. "Come, I will show you."

In the stables, the chestnut mares nosed at their hay, fat and contented. The immaculate stalls smelled of fresh hay without a trace of rancid urine.

Duca Alfonso drew a deep breath, smiling. The good smells of healthy horses washed away Court concerns.

"May I see them more closely?" asked Duca Alfonso.

"Please. Would you like me to bring them out?"

"That won't be necessary," said Duca Alfonso. He slipped under the rope into the stall with the flexibility of a young man.

The mare jerked her head and snorted. Duca Alfonso reached out his hand and stroked her neck slowly, comforting her.

"Tranquilla, bella. Tranquilla," he soothed.

His hands traveled down her legs, feeling their conformation and soundness. His fingertips sketched the length of her spine, from withers to rump.

"Look at the brightness in her eyes," he said at last, patting her neck. "She is a beauty."

She bobbed her head at his touch. He slid his hand down her blaze, cupping her velvety nose in the palm of his hand.

"Brava, ciccia! You say she has run a Palio?" asked Duca Alfonso.

"Two. She won once and was second another time," said Riccardo. "She would have won but had a stone bruise. We retired her."

Duca Alfonso nodded his head. "The sire of her foal to come? What is his lineage?"

"A Maremma stallion. A great black horse, stout and mighty. He was a gift from Governor di Montauto to Virginia Tacci."

"Ah! The girl who rode the Palio," said Duca Alfonso, watching Riccardo's reaction.

"Ferrara has heard of her?" Riccardo's eyes blazed bright in the misty air.

"La villanella! Well, sì, all horsemen throughout Italy have heard of her, I would imagine," said Duca Alfonso. "What brave girls you breed in Siena."

Riccardo's eyes dropped for a moment to stare at the straw on the ground.

"Yes, she was indeed brave," he said, raising his chin and meeting the duca's eyes. "With an uncanny sense with horses. She feared nothing."

"What has become of her?" asked Duca Alfonso

"My duca, she has disappeared. If I may speak frankly, sir, I believe that it involved Granduca Francesco and a Florentine who resides in Siena—but I have no proof, no recourse. This is why I was banished from Tuscany. For challenging the Florentine coward to a duel."

"I am sorry for your predicament," said Duca Alfonso, "but you have brought good horses to Ferrara. We shall rejoice! The de' Medici loss is Ferrara's gain."

He reached out and clapped Riccardo on the back. Ercole Cortile smiled. Such a gesture was rare and a great tribute.

"I want to see the foals when they are born," said Duca Alfonso. "Maremma stallion, eh? I need another Palio prospect. Ercole, have the groom bring my horse. We should let Signor De' Luca get back to his painting."

"You see, I take artists seriously," said Duca Alfonso, resting his hand on Riccardo's shoulder. Then he added in a low voice, "I hope Siena finds her beloved Virginia Tacci."

As the duca prepared to mount his horse, he took another look at the mares, then at Riccardo.

"You will not be challenging anyone to a duel in Ferrara, will you, young De' Luca?"

"No, of course not," said Riccardo, bowing. "I honor the House of d'Este for giving me refuge. I will not disturb the peace of your city."

Duca Alfonso slipped his boot into the stirrup and swung up into the saddle while the groom held his horse.

"Have you tried the convents?" he asked.

"The convents?" said Riccardo, stunned.

Could Duca Alfonso know of our search?

"Granduca Francesco has a history of locking up bothersome women in convents, including his own stepmother. If he could have done the same with his sister Isabella, she would still be alive."

The duca paused for a moment.

"And little Leonora, the lark," he sighed. "But neither woman would have stood for it. They would sooner have hanged themselves than be confined."

Again Riccardo's eyes dropped to the ground. The duca watched, his face tense with emotion.

"Well, Signor De' Luca, I will look forward to seeing the foals. Remember—one has my name on it. I think . . . the one sired by the Maremma stallion. Virginia Tacci's horse."

"Of course, good duca. It will be my pleasure. And a good choice."

As Duca Alfonso d'Este and Ercole Cortile turned their horses, Riccardo quickly wiped his eyes with the back of his hand.

"He must have been in love with the girl," said Alfonso as the two men rode away. "Ercole, send Signor De' Luca an invitation to next Saturday's ball. I would like to introduce him to Court. He will find there are Ferrara women who rival Siena's beauties."

The duca smiled. "Perhaps my beautiful cousin, Lucia d'Este, could turn the Senese's head."

CHAPTER 86

Tuscany, Poggio a Cajano
MAY 1589

Thousands of burning candles lit up the Poggio a Cajano, illuminating the sumptuous wedding festivities of Granduca Ferdinando and Christina of Lorraine.

"After the mock sea battle in the Pitti Palace, Poggio a Cajano seems quite rustic," Ercole Cortile said to the ambassador from Venice. He sighed, quite content to have come out of diplomatic retirement for the de' Medici marriage festivities. The House of d'Este was closely aligned with the French by marriage.

"I find it strange that the granduca chose Poggio a Cajano as the location for such festivities," grumbled the Venetian. "Is this not where the late granduca and Granduchessa Bianca…um…breathed their last?"

Ercole Cortile lowered his voice. "It is, ambassador. But I think you would be wise not to bring the subject up at this celebration."

The Spanish ambassador leaned over to join the quiet conversation. "Granduca Francesco is surely cursing in his grave. His brother marrying Catherine de' Medici's granddaughter, aligning

Tuscany with France—and after Spain gave Siena to Florence following the siege? Loyalty? Ha!"

Both Cortile and the Venetian ambassador cast a worried look at the Spaniard. He was getting far too drunk for diplomacy's sake.

The Spanish ambassador drained his glass. "At least the wine is favorable."

"Compared to the swill they drink in Madrid," Ercole Cortile murmured to the Venetian ambassador, "I should think so!"

The Venetian ambassador laughed. Before the Spaniard could react, Cortile rose to toast the marriage of the Tuscany and France, leaving the enraged Madrileño sputtering.

Ferdinando shot up in bed, gasping. His shoulders and back were soaked in perspiration.

The damp smell of lovemaking mixed with rosemary strewn—and now crushed—in the bed linens gave off a heady scent. He breathed deeply, trying to ground himself in the real world beyond his nightmare's reach.

"It was a nightmare, my darling, you are safe," said Christina, stroking her new husband's shoulder.

"Did you dream of your brother?" she asked.

"Yes," he said. The granduca grasped his wife's hand. "But . . . but there was also a Jewess. From Naples. A friend of my mother."

"A Jewess? Friend of a de' Medici?"

"Benvegnita Abravanel. She came to visit us in Florence when I was a child."

The duca's breathing regained its calm. "Benvegnita fled Naples shortly after my parents married. She was welcomed by my father, Cosimo. I remember the delight on my mother's face whenever she entered the Palazzo Vecchio."

Christina continued to stroke her husband's back. She could feel his muscles relax under her touch.

"What happened in your dream?"

"I was in the Pitti Palace gardens. Francesco had caught a fish. A beautiful fish, gold with fanned fins. He set it on a rock, watching it gasp for breath."

"And that frightened you?"

Ferdinando closed his eyes.

"It was dying. Its mouth opening and closing. Francesco watched it so carefully, doing nothing. Nothing at all. I said, 'Throw it back into the water, so that it might breathe!'"

"Did he?"

"He turned to me and said, 'Do you really care? Here you are. You watch it die and do nothing. That is your way, little brother.'"

"But darling, it was just a fish!"

"No, it was something more. With every gasp, I felt a pain in my heart. I felt . . . sin. Incredible guilt. I began to cry . . . I was just a child. Francesco was laughing."

He started breathing more rapidly again.

"And then Benvegnita came. She struck Francesco's fingers hard with a cane. 'Jew!' he cried. 'My father will have your head.'

"She turned to me. 'Toss the fish back into the water, Ferdinando. You have much work to do. Start with the fish.'

"And, though the fish was half-dead, I threw it back into the pond. It floated to the top, stunned. Then it swam away. And it swam up into the air and it turned into a black horse. It reared, its hooves slashing high above my head."

"No wonder you screamed out," said Christina. Her fingers toyed with a ribbon at the neck of her nightdress.

Ferdinando pulled his wife close to him.

"I have many sins to atone for, dear wife," he whispered.

CHAPTER 87

Siena, Palazzo Dei
DECEMBER 1590

Giacomo di Torreforte had lived a careless life gambling, drinking, and painting. But now his father had developed a racking cough that shook his old body, rattling the wattles on his throat. With the specter of death in his near future, Signor di Torreforte turned a stern eye to his eldest son, demanding he start paying attention to the matters of the banking business of Monte dei Paschi.

"Your brothers have learned the banking business. Now it is your turn."

"But father, I am an artist! I have no head for figures, you know as much. And as eldest son, I am heir to your fortune—"

The older man winced. "Yes, you are heir to my fortune, but you will also become head of our family. Our fortunes are in Monte dei Paschi. I have neglected my duty as a father. You are spoiled and unfit to take the reins after my death. You will now make up for the time you have lost."

And so di Torreforte began rising early in the mornings alongside his brothers. Grudgingly, he learned the rules of investments and loans, to assess risks, to capitalize on good ventures. His brothers complained bitterly behind his back at his ineptitude with mathematics, his mistakes with the ledger, the inkblots and corrections requiring a scribe to rework his figures on new parchment.

They mocked his mistakes, and they feared his fondness for making loans to his friends and social contacts.

It became evident that Giacomo's father would not survive much longer. His ragged cough worsened with the winter rains, and when snow blanketed the red terra-cotta rooftops of Siena and whitened Il Campo, old Signor di Torreforte was confined to bed by his doctor.

One bitterly cold afternoon, he summoned his eldest son to his bedside.

"We have a serious issue to discuss," said the sick man. "One that pertains to your character. Rumors I have heard."

Di Torreforte looked at the glassy eyes of his father.

"Father, you are not well. The fever has seized you. We should speak of serious issues when you—"

"No!" shouted Signor di Torreforte, triggering another spasm of coughing. "We should have spoken of these matters years ago. I have spoiled you as my heir and firstborn. Now I am on my death-bed. We will speak!"

Di Torreforte bowed his head, fingering his silk scarf.

"You were challenged to a duel by Riccardo De' Luca. But you did not respond. You refused to accept."

"The scoundrel was arrested, you know that," sputtered Giacomo. "Banished from the city! It is against the law of Siena to—"

"You acted the coward!" said his father. "In front of all Siena."

He broke off, racked by coughing again. His son wondered if the old man was going to die right then, right before him. But the coughing subsided, and the elder di Torreforte gathered his strength to speak again.

"The cowardice is shameful. But there is still worse that we must confront. I hear ugly rumors that you know the whereabouts of the villanella. That somehow you arranged for her to be spirited away from Vignano."

Signor di Torreforte locked eyes with his son.

And the son did not answer. He dropped his eyes to the carpet.

"That girl belongs to Siena, to no one else," said the old man, beginning to cough again. His thrashing wound the bed linens tight around his arms. He slumped against the pillows, gasping.

Giacomo took his father's arm, supporting him.

"Father, you should rest. Do not trouble yourself with—"

"Let me speak, damn you! I want that girl returned to her birthplace. I can see now that the rumors are true. Yes, I will die. Soon. But if you do not remove this blasphemous stain from our family name, I will haunt you from my grave."

Giacomo's eyes widened.

"And that grave shall be here in Siena. I will be buried as a Senese," said Signor di Torreforte. "My coffin shall be taken to Il Campo and nod its respect to the Torre del Mangia in the city I love. Not Florence, do you hear me! Here! My bones will rest under the floors of San Domenico until our Lord shall come to raise them."

He focused a cold eye on his heir.

"But wherever I may be buried, you will not avoid my specter if you do not bring the villanella back to Siena."

Giacomo di Torreforte shuddered.

CHAPTER 88

Ferrara, Convento di Sant'Antonio
DECEMBER 1590

I raked the dirty straw from the donkey's stall into a heap. Because my arm had never healed properly, I was slow and clumsy at my task. Even then, my arm ached. The mother superior would say it was God's just punishment for my disobedience.

I wiped the sweat from my face, knowing my white scarf would be stained with dirt and perspiration by the end of the day. The conversa Margherita would have to pound the cloth hard against the rocks of the Po to clean it to the strict standards of the abbess.

"God bless you," said Suor Loretta, entering the little shed. "You keep Fedele's shed clean and smelling sweet with fresh straw."

"It is good straw, Sorella Loretta. It smells of heavenly fields and summer sunshine."

The suora laughed. "You notice even the little things. Yes, we procure the best from the duca's stables—"

She clamped her mouth shut like a turtle, but not before I noticed her consternation.

"The d'Estes give us this straw?" I asked. I pitched a forkful onto the ground, spreading it around. "That is an unusual contribution to a convent, is it not?"

"Duca Alfonso is generous to the convent," she said. "A donkey is a religious symbol. For the Holy Bible says both Christ and the Madonna were carried on an ass."

She was fumbling for an answer, though I could not imagine why.

"I will leave you to your labor, Silvia. I have been summoned to speak with the abbess."

"Oh?" I said, stopping. "Is everything all right?"

"It is a small matter," answered the suora, waving her hand. "I will see you before Vespers, I am sure. Make sure you scrub out Fedele's bucket. There is green scum forming on the sides of the wood."

"Sì, Sorella Loretta. I shall do so."

She turned and left the shed. I watched her black robes retreating toward the abbess's office.

"I am sorry, but there is no alternative," said the abbess. "The family promised a dowry of a hundred ducats a year. They have not sent payment in nearly two years now."

"But, Madonna, the postulant Silvia is a godsend!" said Suor Loretta. "She works the skin off her hands caring for Fedele—"

"A financial arrangement was settled upon. The family has not kept their bargain. And she refuses to take the veil. She can be transferred to another convent—"

"*No!*" said Suor Loretta.

The abbess stiffened her back but said nothing.

"You cannot send the girl away," said the old suora. "She has suffered enough! And I think you are well aware of the depth of that suffering, Madre."

The abbess worked her mouth.

"The hundred ducats—"

"You know, of course, that I will procure them," said Suor Loretta. "Send parchment and fresh ink to my cell. My supplies have dwindled. I will write to my family immediately."

Suor Loretta pressed down hard on both carved armrests to raise herself from the chair.

"And do not dare breathe a word of this to our . . . Silvia," she said. Without asking permission, the suora walked to the door, turning her back on the abbess.

CHAPTER 89

Siena

JANUARY 1591

Giacomo di Torreforte winced in the cold wind that blew through the little passage leading to Il Campo. The black hearse descended the narrow vicolo into the great piazza, the black satin coverings fluttering in the wind.

How could my father insist on being buried in Siena? Florence is our ancestral home, the root of our fortunes. The grandeur, the legacy of Florence—

He accompanied his father's horse-drawn hearse to the center of the piazza. His youngest sister, walking behind, began to sob as the coffin was removed.

He moved to comfort her, but his brother Giovanni had already thrown an arm around her, pressing her face to his breast. He whispered words of comfort. They turned their backs to him.

Di Torreforte felt inexorably alone. The raw wind bit his skin, playing capriciously with his silk scarf.

He felt all the eyes of Siena were on the coffin . . . and on him. His hand seized his scarf, tucking the foolish ends under his woolen cloak. He cringed, thinking about the Florentines' opinion. His father's funeral was a tribute to Siena's traditions.

He watched the pallbearers as they removed the coffin from the hearse and stood it on end. His father's last wish was sacred: He would show respect to the city in the Senese fashion. As the bells at the top of the Torre del Mangia rang, the pallbearers tipped the head of the coffin in respect, a last nod to Siena.

Both the Florentines and the Senese bowed their heads to the man who had been the head of the most powerful bank in Tuscany. Many charities had profited from Monte dei Paschi's generosity and the open hand of Signor di Torreforte. The nuns escorted the children of the orphanages to Il Campo dressed in warm clothes the dead signore had provided, their little bellies full of bread and warm soup paid for by Monte dei Paschi.

The bell tolled.

The coffin was carefully returned to the hearse. Slowly the horses walked back toward the northwest of the city, where Signor di Torreforte's body would be laid to rest in sacred ground, under the floors of San Domenico in the Contrada del Drago.

His father's bones would rest deep below the mummified head of Santa Caterina of Siena.

———

Giacomo di Torreforte worked alongside his brothers, still struggling to learn the banking profession. As he battled with the ciphers, he raked his fingers through his hair, leaving it standing on end—and leaving him looking like a madman.

As heir, he commanded respect from his younger siblings. The family house on Via di Giglio in Contrada della Giraffa belonged to Giacomo now, and most of the family lived under the same palazzo roof.

But it was clear to everyone that di Torreforte was dismal at figures, poor at calculating risks, tight-fisted with charities, and wretched at cultivating alliances both in the banking community and within the cities of Siena and Florence.

The next oldest brother, Simone, had gracefully taken over most of the tasks that should have fallen to di Torreforte. Simone's head digested figures in the ledger book easily and instantly. His hand was open to charities, especially to Maria della Scala's orphanage, just as his father's had been.

One day, bent over figures in a ledger, Giacomo di Torreforte realized he had made a great error—thousands of scudi—on the parchment. He flung his pen, dripping with ink, across the room. The deep indigo splattered against the white plaster, the impact leaving a radiant star.

He stared moodily at the thin spokes emanating from the heart of dark color.

A perfect starburst of passion.

Di Torreforte had not picked up his paintbrush since weeks before the death of his father. He felt unmoored. His family treated him with the respect owed to him, but nothing more. They did not seek his companionship. His sisters avoided him altogether, rarely speaking at the dinner table unless a question was directed to them. They did not love him. They were afraid of him.

Only a small boy named Gregorio, a scabby-headed kitchen urchin who slept on a heap of rags on the stones at the corner of the kitchen, always smiled when he saw the master.

———

One early spring day just before dawn, di Torreforte walked the halls of the palazzo, unable to sleep. He spied a figure struggling with a burden in the dim light of a single lantern. Gregorio was toting two buckets of vegetable peelings to be boiled into a broth for the workers. Crossing paths with his master, Gregorio beamed.

"What do you have to smile about?" snapped di Torreforte.

"Why, it is the day of the birth of Santa Caterina!" answered the boy, putting down a bucket to scratch his head with his dirty fingernails. "March 25th. All Siena is light of heart on this day. Only the devil himself would not find joy in his soul."

The devil himself be damned!

"Might I be excused, signore? Otherwise the cook will box my ears," asked the boy, wiping his nose on his sleeve.

"Go, get out my sight, you little beggar!" snapped di Torreforte. "Santa Caterina's birthday indeed!"

It does not change the fact that you were born in rags and will die in rags. You still exist only because of my father's misguided hand on his purse strings, adopting ragamuffins as kitchen workers.

Di Torreforte's anger fed an urge to get out of the palazzo.

My father let too many scudi fall from his hand to these orphans. That money could have been used for paints, art, brocades, velvets. A new carriage, horses. What was he thinking? And now my brother Simone argues to do the same!

He let the metal-covered door slam behind him. He walked the streets of Siena, his father's silver-tipped walking stick in his hand. He was not sure why he had adopted this habit of carrying the stick. But in the days after his father's death, when he saw the familiar *bastone da passeggio* leaning forlornly in the corner of the front hall of the palazzo, his hand had reached for it. Now it was always with him.

It had rained hard the night before, and the gray stones of pietra serena gleamed in the sunlight. A pigeon dipped its beak in a puddle and threw back its head, letting the water dribble down its throat. The winding streets filled with voices as the Senese opened their shutters into the early morning sunlight.

"Buongiorgno!" cried one servant to one another, sweeping the entrance to a palazzo with the stiff branches of her *granata*. The shopkeeper at the end of the street whistled a tune. The wine merchant joined in, rolling kegs off a wagon.

The lively chatter in Via di Giglio, the bright ring of horses' hooves on the stones, only made di Torreforte wind his scarf tighter and turn his collar up. He hunched his shoulders and walked on.

He found himself winding his way up through the Contrada della Giraffa into Piazza Matteotti and the Contrada del Drago. He hurried from the open piazza into the descending streets, narrow and confining.

The street broadened. He looked up to the rose-colored bricks of San Domenico. He entered, blinking. He was not sure why he was there. He had avoided the great church since his boyhood, returning only for his father's burial.

A bright shaft of sunlight pierced the stained glass windows, illuminating a Dominican priest looking at di Torreforte through the bright color in a haze of spinning dust.

The old man spoke to him from the sunbeam.

"Have you come to see her?"

"Who?"

"Saint Caterina, of course. Have you come so early this morning to have her grant you peace and blessing?"

Di Torreforte's mouth twisted into a sneer. The priest's expression did not change, the milky blue eyes staring back.

The sneer melted. The holy man was blind. Di Torreforte stared back at the priest, bathed in light.

"Well, my son?"

"Yes," mumbled di Torreforte. "I wish to see her."

"Come," said the old priest. "This early, you will have a chance to be alone with our saint."

He beckoned blindly, listening for the approach of the visitor. "She is sheltered in the crystalline case just there, of course."

Di Torreforte knelt at a pew in the darkened chapel. Two candles glowed, their flames dancing in the cold draught of the church.

Santa Caterina's head, uncannily preserved, stared out at him. He looked at her sunken eyes, her sharp cheekbones, her gray-white skin. Words of prayer would not come.

The head of a nun! What is so holy about an empty skull and broken teeth? Charlatans pawn off splinters from the true cross of Jesus, the hem of the Virgin Mary, the hair of St. Paul, a peg from Noah's Ark—

"You are a good son to come and pray to our Saint," said the priest. "You are Signor di Torreforte, sì?"

Giacomo looked at the priest, startled.

"You recognize me? But—"

"But I am blind? I recognize much more now than I did when I could see. I remember you as a little boy, signore. Your voice gives you away. You come to pray for your father's soul, no doubt, and for the benediction of our patron saint. A good son. I will leave you here to receive her blessings in solitary peace."

Di Torreforte looked down at his feet.

The crypt is just below this floor, I tread above my father's body.

He kneeled on the stone floor, clasping his gloved hands in prayer.

Father, I—

The candlelight leapt—a door must have opened somewhere in the church. The illumination shone bright on the eyes of Santa Caterina.

Father, I am not the son you wanted me to be.

She stared at him from her sunken eye sockets. Her eyes were blue. Unmistakably blue.

Di Torreforte did not cry out, he did not move.

He stared back. He waited for her to speak. She said nothing, but looked at him unblinking. Accusing.

And in the fierce gaze of those impossible blue eyes, Giacomo di Torreforte felt something within him shift—perhaps slightly, perhaps forever.

But his mind could not accommodate what his heart felt.

———

As he left, he saw the blind priest mumbling a prayer. The old man made the sign of the cross and kissed his fingertips.

The priest turned. "Is someone there?"

"It is I, Father."

"Ah, yes, Signor di Torreforte. Did you find peace, my son?"

The light streaming through the rosette window blinded him. He put up a hand to shade his eyes.

Peace?

"You know, she never took the holy orders," said the priest. "She was a laywoman, a tertiary, and worked amongst the poor, the lepers, the afflicted. Her letters convinced the Pope in Avignon to return to Rome, the gaping schism of our great church healed."

"Letters? She was literate?"

"Some people say it was Caterina's scribe who wrote the letters, but others insist she did learn to read and write. She was the poor daughter of a Senese dyer, one of twenty children her poor mother bore. Humble beginnings. But she became educated in order to help others."

The priest smiled, his unseeing eyes staring into the distance.

"Such a simple Senese woman. And yet she healed us all."

Di Torreforte's hand reached for his scarf. He savagely untied the precious silk from his neck and placed it in the priest's hands.

"This is for the poor," he said, watching the blind priest's blue eyes widen at the touch of smooth silk.

"My son!" said the priest, his fingers running across the fabric. "It—is costly. It feels like the lining of a drappellone for the Palio!"

"For the Palio? Yes, perhaps it will be someday. A good destiny for it—it should fetch a good price and feed many orphans.
Arrivederci, Father."

———————

Giacomo di Torreforte converted his apartments into a studio. He
told his brothers that they would manage Monte dei Paschi, and
that he would hear their report each month. At his instruction, the
usual stipends from Monte dei Paschi to the poor, the hospitals,
and the orphanages were resumed. The di Torreforte family could
raise their heads once more in the streets of Siena.

Giacomo locked himself into his studio and began to paint. To
paint her.

The colors were bright, the lines muted. He adopted the Senese
style of the old masters. The black mantle and white veil of a tertiary matched the colors of the Senese republic. In her hand was a
lily, the sign of innocence and purity . . . and of rebirth.

For weeks, di Torreforte refused to leave his apartments. He
did not bathe, only splashing cold water on his face. Ants crawled
over crusts of bread on platters, flies rubbed their greedy forelegs
over rinds of fruit.

He refused entry to anyone. He worked alone.

The saint held the lily in her left hand, her right hand extended
toward the lips of a young girl. The maiden looked up into the
great saint's face, her hands crossed over her heart, accepting the
blessings bestowed upon her.

———————

One day, a visitor arrived at the door of the palazzo on Via di
Giglio in a carriage that was rickety with age and neglect. He lowered himself painfully from the carriage with help from a peasant.

The man was stooped and balding. His hands, spotted with purple blotches, were twisted into claws. He struggled to grasp the great iron ring of the knocker, letting it fall on the metal door.

"May I help you?" said a manservant opening the door.

"I have come to visit Master di Torreforte," rasped the visitor. He craned his neck, trying to see the servant.

"Is he expecting you?" said the servant, knowing well that di Torreforte received no one, not even his family members.

"Tell him . . . tell him Giorgio Brunelli has come to call. Tell him! I have not much time left on this Earth, and we should bid farewell face to face."

Di Torreforte's brother Simone heard Giorgio's reply. He stepped into the entry hall to greet the visitor.

"Come, signore. Sit here. Massimo, send for some wine and panforte for our guest."

"I will not trouble you long," said Giorgio. He turned his eyes up to Simone di Torreforte, unable to move his neck. "I only wish a few words with your brother."

"Of course, I understand," said Simone. "But my brother. I—he is not receiving, I fear. He does not speak with us. He has locked himself in the garret upstairs, where he paints all day and throughout the night."

"Painting?" said Giorgio. "He still paints?"

"He stopped for a year after my father's death. But then one day, he came home and renounced his duties as the head of the bank. Since that day, he has become a hermit, seeing no one."

A tremor coursed through the left side of Giorgio's face. "I must talk to him."

"Signore, I swear to you. He receives no guests—"

"Except for this one," said a voice.

Di Torreforte, bearded and gaunt, appeared at the top of the stairs. His bony fingers grasped the wrought-iron railing for support.

"Bring my guest to the studio," said di Torreforte, his voice thick from disuse. "I will await him there."

CHAPTER 90

Siena

MARCH 1591

Two days after the visit of Giorgio Brunelli, Giacomo di Torreforte returned to the Basilica San Domenico.

"*Buona sera*," said di Torreforte, grasping the old priest's hand. He watched the blind man's mouth curve up in a wide smile.

"Have you found peace, son?" asked the priest, staring in his direction. "Has your father's soul comforted you, Giacomo? The dead can soothe the living."

Di Torreforte's face fell as he heard the priest's words. He felt his heart tighten in anguish.

"Peace?" said di Torreforte, examining the word as one would inspect a strange insect. "What is peace? My sins are too great for there ever to be peace in my lifetime."

"You must confess your sins, my son."

"Oh, Father!" said Giacomo, looking up at the basilica's ceiling. His words echoed in the vast space. "There is no way to tell you the wrongs I have committed. If I could, I would surely do it."

"You speak under the roof of the Lord," said the priest. "Take care you do not tell a falsehood. Confession will give you a portion of peace and God's absolution. And it is your religious duty."

Giacomo closed his eyes, rubbing his forehead.

"If I tell my sins, you will surely hate me, Father."

"I have heard many sins and always given God's absolution. It is my obligation to offer forgiveness, not blame. Come with me."

Giacomo di Torreforte followed the priest into the small wooden confessional.

"Forgive me, Lord, for I have sinned. Against you . . . and Siena."

Giacomo saw a slight movement through the grille as the priest's back stiffened.

When Giacomo began his confession, he watched for a sign that the priest would absolve and even console him. But as the confession continued and the priest heard the name Virginia Tacci, he sunk into himself like a mollusk into its shell.

"You must give me absolution," prompted Giacomo as finished his long tale. "I have unburdened myself with this confession to you and God."

"Bless you, my son," muttered the priest, his voice barely audible. "I absolve you . . . in God's name."

Giacomo placed his fingers on the grille, looking at the priest. "But you . . . *you* do not forgive me!"

"It is God who must forgive you," said the priest. "Not I." A silence stretched out in the dark of the confessional. "How can I forgive?" the old man said finally, his joints creaking as he rose.

"I am Senese."

———

Giacomo wandered the streets of Siena for the rest of the day, his collar turned up against a cold March wind. Eventually, he stood in the shadow of the Torre del Mangia, where he watched families mingle, eating hot chestnuts and drinking mulled wine, though already talking of the approaching spring. Children chased the pigeons across the shell-shaped piazza, laughing joyously. Everywhere Giacomo walked, he heard talk of the next Palio, contradas boasting of their strategies to win.

They might be talking of Virginia now. They would be talking of her chance to win. I have robbed Virginia and Siena of that.

As an arc of pigeons flew over Il Campo, Giacomo walked toward the southeast section of the piazza entering the Via del Porrione, the entrance to Contrada della Torre and the small Jewish ghetto within its territory.

The narrow streets were filled with the aroma of a foreign cookery: garlic, oil, and anchovies, scented with herbs he could not name.

He walked past the synagogue, where an old man with a thick white beard sat on his heels, talking to an adolescent boy.

"You must give back the coin," said the man. "God will forgive you, but you must make right the wrong you have done."

The pair looked up at the Christian, who was listening intently to their conversation.

"Go now!" said the man, touching the boy's arm. "Do what is right."

The boy scrambled to his feet and set off running. The old man rose, rubbing his back.

"If only all sins were so easily remedied," said Giacomo.

The man shrugged.

"And why should they not be?"

Giacomo exhaled sharply, a sound of despair. "Some are simply too ugly to confront."

"Those are the best to remedy," said the man. He narrowed his eyes and jutted out his chin, challenging Giacomo. His white beard bristled.

"It is just—" said Giacomo. "I have just come from praying at my father's tomb at San Domenico."

"Ah," said the man, bowing his head in respect.

"He died months ago," said Giacomo. "And now . . ."

Giacomo was not about to confess to this Jew that his father's spirit hovered over him.

"It is a powerful bond, a man and his father," said the man. "I lost my father many years ago in the fight against Florence. He died of starvation during the siege."

Giacomo stared at the Jew.

"You look surprised," said the man. "My family has been here in Siena for three centuries. We fought alongside our fellow Senese, starved with our brothers. There is no difference between Jew and Christian in a siege. We all suffered and fought in her defense."

He took a little dig at the air with his chin, glaring at Giacomo. "I may be more Senese than you, my friend."

Under any other circumstances, Giacomo would have struck the impertinent Jew. He remembered how proud he was of his Florentine roots, how bewildering his father had become, claiming Siena as home. Siena the conquered.

Why should I care about being identified as a Senese? I am Florentine!

But something felt wrong within.

"Am I right?" asked the man.

Giacomo's mouth collapsed, his two eyebrows colliding in sorrow. Tears flooded his eyes.

"Come with me," the man said, grasping Giacomo by the elbow, his hostility changing to concern. "I can offer you a moment of privacy."

Giacomo followed him into the darkness of the synagogue. Few candles were lit, despite the approaching twilight.

"Can I enter here?" Giacomo suddenly felt like an intruder.

The man shrugged. "I have invited you. This is God's house."

"Are you . . . the rabbi?" The word felt strange in Giacomo's mouth.

Again, the man shrugged.

"Here. Sit on the bench, I will leave you in peace," he said, turning to leave.

"There shall never be peace for me," said Giacomo, plunging his head into his hands. The man hesitated.

"Yes," he said. "I am the rabbi of this congregation. Tell me why you will never know peace."

Giacomo's words rushed out, unconsidered, unchecked. "Because I can never wash clean the sins I have committed. When you said you were more Senese than I, you were right! I have betrayed Siena, my God, my conscience."

The rabbi sat down beside him, making the joints of the bench groan.

"Siena?"

"I cannot explain. It is too much of a burden even for a priest to hear. At least a Senese priest, as I have just discovered. I confessed my sin, and he turned away in hatred. I shall burn in hell for all eternity."

The rabbi smiled. "Hell? Is that all?" he said.

Giacomo uncovered his face, still wet with tears.

"What?" he said, glaring at the rabbi. "What worse fate is there, Rabbi?"

The rabbi made a swift huffing sound, dismissing his remark. Giacomo felt his rage growing in the darkness of the synagogue.

"We Jews do not believe in your heaven or hell. We do not live only to be rewarded after our deaths. We are called to do good because it is our obligation to do right in the world, as God commanded. We look for no further reward."

"You—you do not believe in hell?"

"Hell is what we create on Earth. There is nothing in the Torah—what you call the Old Testament—that describes this 'hell' you Christians fear."

Giacomo's brow creased.

"And heaven? Do you not believe in the angels on high?"

The rabbi shook his head. "No, not the angels you believe in. Human souls with fluttering wings and halos. Very pretty indeed. No, death is permanent. We have a deep respect for it. And also for life."

Giacomo blinked in the dim light. The candles had a queer scent he could not recognize.

"How can you not believe in heaven, where Jesus sits at the right hand of God?"

"Jesus was a good Jew, he believed in doing good on Earth: charity, healing, honoring the commandments. But heaven with clouds and cherubs? A fairy tale gone too far."

Giacomo was too bewildered to speak.

"Jews do not invest in dreams of heaven."

"What is the point in living, then?" asked Giacomo, exasperated.

The rabbi smiled. "You do God an injustice, signore. There is much to do here on Earth. To live *right*. To do right, despite all odds. To appreciate the great gift of life that God has given us. That is the point of living. Not because there is a sweet at the end of the journey to entice little children to behave properly."

"Rabbi!" said Giacomo, raking his fingers through his hair. "There are wrongs far too twisted to make right. Ever. A priest has just told me as much."

"Pfff!" said the rabbi. "You forget the history of the Jewish people. We have forgiven—but not forgotten!—many sins. A Senese priest, on the other hand . . ." He opened his hands in supplication. "Well. We Senese are a proud people."

Giacomo felt an urge to laugh, though he was speaking of his eternal damnation. This rabbi was strangely disarming.

"You confuse me, Rabbi. Our own priest cannot forgive me. You tell me there is no hell, but no heaven either. What is the use of confession, then?"

The rabbi took a deep breath, expelling it noisily through his tufted nostrils.

"Good question, signore. Have you considered rectifying your wrongs, rather than simply confessing them? Perhaps that would assuage the guilt. We Jews believe in *tikkun olam*. It means 'repairing the world.' We have an obligation, all of us, to heal wrongs."

"There is no way I can ever right this wrong. And if I were to tell you my transgressions, you would howl for my arrest."

"*Allora!* Fine . . . do not tell me," said the rabbi, opening his hands with a shrug. "Confession is a cheap substitute for retribution. Charter your own way out of your darkness. Then settle your accounts with God."

Giacomo raised his head, looking at the rabbi.

"Who . . . are you?"

"I am called Rabbi Mortimer Borghi. I do not know your name."

"Giacomo. Giacomo di Torreforte."

"*Ah!*" chuckled the rabbi. "Signor Monte dei Paschi!"

"I am a very poor businessman," said Giacomo. "I have left the family business in the hands of my more capable brothers."

The rabbi considered this.

"Then who are you, Giacomo di Torreforte?"

Such impertinence! Di Torreforte swung his face toward the man.

"I am an artist," he said defiantly.

"An artist," said the rabbi, nodding his head. "A good one?"

Giacomo considered the question.

"Once I thought there was nothing in the world more important than my painting." He knew it wasn't really an answer to the question, but it was all he had to offer. "Now I paint with an obsession, trying to find—something! I do not know what I chase. But I am haunted."

"Yes. Then you understand passion, my friend! You know human nature," said the rabbi. "You must recognize the grip that passion—for good or for evil—can have on the human soul. You must understand the darkness that is part of us. Understanding is the light to give you passage out of this black hole."

Giacomo did not say anything. He had a fleeting memory of a painting. The lines of a reclining beauty in ecstasy, ravaged by a swan.

"Our eternal mistake is to deny the darkness in each of us. All of us. When we confront darkness without recognizing its universal nature, we are catapulted into chaos. We abandon our compass, which shows all directions, not just one.

"The Old Testament is brimming with cruelty as well as mercy. Darkness and light live in each of us, awakened by passion. Such strong emotion can persuade us to do the very worst . . . or the very best. Passion can hurl us into the blinding light."

Giacomo said nothing. He looked around the house of worship. It was a simple room. Plain.

How different this synagogue was from the cathedral! Where were the gold altarpieces, the precious jeweled chalice, the masterpieces of art?

Even the smell was different. Beeswax from the candles and an ancient scent, musty and dense.

"My friend. My advice to you is to right your wrong, no matter how ugly it may be. You have taken an eye—replace it. A tooth, a life—make retribution. Not because you will be a hero, not because you will go to heaven. Because . . . *voi dovete.*"

Voi dovete . . . you should. You must.

CHAPTER 91

Florence, Palazzo Vecchio

APRIL 1591

"I should have you imprisoned," said Granduca Ferdinando. "If your noble family weren't allied so closely with Florence—"

And if your family did not manage Monte dei Paschi so profitably.

"Forgive me, Granduca," said di Torreforte. "But hear me, I pray. I come to make amends for past deeds."

The granduca took a moment to control his anger. Then he nodded. "Proceed."

"Serenissimo, I carried out the express wishes of our late Granduca Francesco. And the villanella's aunt gave written permission. Granduca Francesco had all the proper legal authority. I obeyed his orders."

Granduca Ferdinando glared. This matter would further stain the de' Medici name. As if Francesco had not done enough damage already.

"So." He took another moment to calm himself. "You took her to a convent?"

"Sì. I suggested it to spare her life. Granduca Francesco wanted to—"

"What convent? Where?" Ferdinando did not want to hear what his brother had wanted.

"In Ferrara. In the city of Ferrara."

The granduca nodded fiercely. His mind worked quickly. "Does Duca Alfonso know about this?"

"Absolutely not, Serenissimo."

The granduca scowled, pulling at his beard. "What about Ercole Cortile? Surely you must have had papers to move across the borders and within the walls of Ferrara."

"I was a messenger of Granduca Francesco. As an emissary of the granduca, I had official papers. But I never went as far as the d'Este Castle. My business was at the Convento di Sant'Antonio in Polesine."

"And so, Virginia Tacci is—a nun?"

"I am not sure. She was a most unwilling postulant. The granduca paid a dowry of one hundred ducats a year to keep her within the convent walls. I do not know what happened after your brother's death."

"Dio mio!" muttered the granduca. "I ordered those payments stopped when I audited the treasury. I could not see why the de' Medici coffers should be opened to a Ferrarese convent."

"Then . . . I do not know. Perhaps she is no longer there. Perhaps they cast her out, if there was no more dowry. They would have sent her to a much poorer enclave. We may not be able to find her."

"Why are you here now, di Torreforte?"

Giacomo looked straight into the granduca's eyes.

"I want to right a grievous wrong. And I am answering a request from a dying man. One you know. Giorgio Brunelli."

The granduca lifted his chin. He looked away from his visitor, out the open window.

"You did not suspect as much, Serenissimo?" Giacomo asked.

"Why should I suspect anything?" he snapped. "What do you mean, signore?"

Di Torreforte held the gaze of the granduca.

"Certain paints are deadly, as you well know. To those on whose walls the paintings are hung, perhaps. To the painter, most certainly, Serenissimo. Giorgio Brunelli turned a deaf ear to warnings. His love of his art and his devotion to the villanella were his only guides. That has led him to a dark end, I fear."

The granduca said nothing but turned away, looking out the window of the Palazzo Vecchio down to the red bricks of the piazza.

"You must find the girl," he said, without turning. "Find her and free her. But you must not drag the de' Medici name into this matter. And she cannot return to Siena. She could be indeed a spark that lights the fires of rebellion."

Giacomo di Torreforte glanced at the profile of the great granduca.

"I will find her," he said.

As the door shut quietly behind di Torreforte, the granduca drew a heavy breath. He sat down at his desk, dipping a sharpened quill into the inkpot.

Giorgio Brunelli, whom I hold in high esteem,

It has been brought to my attention that we have unfinished business to discuss . . .

CHAPTER 92

Ferrara, Convento di Sant'Antonio, Polesine
AUGUST 1591

The conversa Margherita opened the door of the dispensary. She had come to pay her last respects to Suor Loretta.

"Who is there?" The old woman's voice was scarcely intelligible.

"It is I, the conversa Margherita, sorella. I—I ask permission to speak."

"Please, speak now," whispered the suora. "I fear I have little time left on this earth."

"I ask your counsel," said Margherita. "And then your forgiveness."

"What, my child? I am no priest. I cannot grant absolution."

Margherita inhaled, drawing in the medicinal smells of the dispensary and the dying woman.

"Your personal forgiveness is what I seek. I have kept secret for ten years some evidence. I believe that the young postulant Silvia was brought to our convent shrouded in a lie. The story she tells—that she is a rider of horses—I believe is truth."

The old suora pulled her blue-veined hand over her face. For a long time, she did not speak.

"What evidence do you possess?" said the suora finally.

"I kept these things—little things—from the fire when her clothes were burnt. I believe they are horsehair. Chestnut hairs, black, even white. And salt. Her clothes were stained with a brown mix of salt and dirt. Horse's sweat, I believe."

Margherita unfolded her linen cloth, displaying the hair, the flakes of salty dirt.

"Silvia says her real name is Virginia Tacci. One of my cousins works in the stables at the d'Este Castle. He says there was indeed a girl who rode the Palio of Siena in 1581. A girl of fourteen. He says her name was Virginia. He doesn't remember her family name."

"Dio mio," gasped the old suora. "Have you told the mother superior?"

"Sì," said Margherita. "I showed her my evidence over a year ago. She told me to hold my tongue, that this was the devil's work. I would lose my position and she would put Silvia under stricter watch, take her away from you and from her work with the old donkey."

The conversa's face twisted in a spasm of pain.

"Then she seized the hair and dirt and cast them into the fire."

Suor Loretta drew her bony hand over her face. Margherita noticed the meandering blue veins coursing through her translucent skin.

"How is it that you still have the evidence, as you call it?" the suora said finally, pointing to the cloth.

"I took half to the mother superior and kept half . . . in case I needed it. I also have a soiled riding boot with traces of horse dung."

The old suora's face slowly transformed. She smiled.

"You are far too wise to be only a conversa, Margherita. Now we must decide what to do with your pieces of dust, hair . . . and footwear." Suor Loretta chuckled, setting off a long spell of coughing.

"There must be some contact outside the abbey," said the suora at last, her fingers clutching the coverlet. "My nephew Duca Alfonso must see this evidence. Only he could wrest a confirmed novice from the grasp of the convent."

The conversa bowed, hearing the name of the Duca di Ferrara.

"Bring me a pot of ink and parchment," said Suor Loretta. "I shall write my nephew while I can still hold the quill. You have done the right thing, conversa. May God bless you."

Margherita kissed the suora's hand. It was cold as ice.

CHAPTER 93

Ferrara, Convento di Sant'Antonio, Polesine
AUGUST 1591

The toll of the chapel bell resonated in my heart. I knelt, praying as hard as I could.

God receive Suor Loretta's beautiful soul.

I shook my head as I prayed.

So much time lost! What has become of all whom I love in Siena? What of Orione? Did he mend, or was my godfather forced to take his life to end his suffering?

This last thought tormented me. I began to sob, slumped over my clasped hands. I heard the rustling of linen near me. A gentle hand grazed my sleeve.

Anna Rosa took my hand in mine.

"Virginia," she whispered. "I know how much you loved her."

She paused, looking into my eyes. "Suor Loretta called me to her bedside last night." She had been whispering; now she dropped her voice so low that I could scarcely hear her. "She and I were related. She never wanted anyone to speak of her origins. Only the old nuns know—"

"Know what?"

I strained to hear—and to understand. Anna Rosa's hand reached out from under her black habit, beckoning me to follow her outside.

"Know what?" I repeated once the fresh air touched my face. "What do only the old nuns know?"

"Suor Loretta was the aunt of Duca Alfonso."

I stared at my friend.

"I am her second cousin. I grew up calling her Zia Loretta. Both of us are of the House of d'Este."

"The House of d'Este? Related to Duca Alfonso?" I had heard what she said, but I could scarcely believe it.

"The duca is my cousin. Suor Loretta was his favorite aunt. He gave her Fedele the donkey."

It explained why the abbess and the old suoras looked the other way when Anna Rosa was sharp-tongued. Never had she been made to lie prostrate on the floor in penitence.

"Before she died, Suor Loretta told me to see the conversa Margherita, that she had something that could remedy a terrible sin. The conversa gave me something to show my brother," said Anna Rosa. "The one who has a stable of Palio horses."

"What did she give you?"

"Some flakes of sweat-caked dirt and horse hair. And a boot. A girl's riding boot, tanned light brown."

"It must be mine! I had such boots when I entered the convent."

"I have written my brother that he must visit me immediately," she said. The sun passed from behind a cloud, warming us. A smile blossomed on her pale face as she squinted in delight.

Anna Rosa kept glancing toward the wrought-iron grille, knowing that the nuns were always eager to eavesdrop. She beckoned her brother, Sandro d'Este, to lean close.

The moment Anna Rosa finished whispering and placed the little bundle in her brother's hands, he gave a curt nod. Anger darkened his face.

"Do not worry, little sister. I know a Senese who will be interested in what you have given me. The duca must be made aware of this as well."

"Will he dare fight with the church?" Anna Rosa whispered.

Sandro sucked in his breath, considering. He expelled it, shaking his head. "I doubt it. Duca Alfonso knows to let Rome conduct its affairs without interference. He has yet to produce an heir, and Rome sits like a fat crow on the walls of Castello d'Este, waiting for the chance to swoop in and carry away Ferrara." He looked at his sister and raised his hand to her forehead, smoothing away the furrows.

"But Riccardo De' Luca, the Senese—what he will dare to risk for Virginia is another story."

CHAPTER 94

Ferrara, Convento di Sant'Antonio, Polesine
AUGUST 1591

The old donkey hung his head low, his soft muzzle touching the straw.

"He is dying," I told the abbess.

The abbess, who knew nothing of livestock or even cats and dogs, bowed her head.

"The earth is freshly mounded over his mistress's grave," she said. "And so leaves the faithful donkey. She told me once the beast had a soul. The most blasphemous utterance."

I wondered if the abbess had made her do penance. I never saw any punishment of Suor Loretta. Nor Anna Rosa, despite her rebellious nature. And now I knew why.

"I was told that Fedele would be buried here," I said.

The abbess flashed a look in my direction.

"Who told you that?"

"Suor Loretta herself. It was decided years ago, I was told. You gave your permission, she said."

The abbess's fingers sought her rosary beads tied to her belt.

"We discussed it," she said finally. Her fingertips rubbed hard against the beads. "I assuaged her concerns about the donkey, saying that we would care for it generously during its lifetime. I have kept my word."

"She told me you promised he would be buried here, close to her."

The abbess was silent for a minute. I knew she was measuring her words carefully.

"Postulant Silvia," she said, her eyes narrowing. "Do you really think that the hallowed ground of a convent is the suitable graveyard for a common ass?"

"Suor Loretta said you had come to an arrangement. She told me—"

"If the bishop should learn that an animal is buried alongside the great Beatrice d'Este, I shall lose my position! The cemetery is consecrated to the brides of Christ."

"But—"

The abbess dropped her hand from her rosary. Her face tightened, the skin pinched at the edges of her wimple.

"Do not dare to argue with me! Suor Loretta is beyond such matters. She is with God. And I shall keep my promise of caring for the donkey. You may stay here in the shed and forgo prayers in the chapel. I will expect you to pray here, of course. On fresh straw."

"Sì, Madre."

"When the time comes, we will send for the knacker." With that, she turned swiftly toward the door, her robes fluttering behind her.

I closed my eyes, stroking the old donkey's back, his ragged breath the only sound.

"Come with me, faithful donkey," I said. I took Fedele out of the shed to stand in the sunshine near Suor Loretta's fresh grave.

He lowered his gray muzzle to the mound and let out a stillborn bray, a choking sound that wrenched my heart.

I stared at the freshly turned earth, thinking of its weight on the fragile bones beneath.

Anna Rosa found me standing by the grave with the donkey's lead rope in my hand.

Her fingers sought mine, taking my free hand in hers. "At least she is finally free," I said.

She looked around, making sure no nun was within earshot.

"We shall be, too, Virginia," she said. "One day."

I squeezed her hand. "Of course. Until that day."

My heart would stop beating if I ever thought I would not see Siena again.

———————

I was stationed at the dying creature's side when I heard rocks being thrown over the wall. It was during Vespers, when the watch nun was at prayer in chapel. The pelting of stones hitting the slate roof of the shed made Fedele lift his head once more, swiveling his ears at the sound.

The stones were wrapped in parchment. I collected them one by one.

I unwrapped the missive from one:

Virginia Tacci! Are you truly within these walls? Riccardo

"Riccardo?" I whispered.

I called in a voice as loud as I dared.

"Riccardo? Is that you?"

"Virginia? Virginia!" he called back.

"How did you find me?

How did he know I could read now? That I would be there at the donkey shed alone?

"*Senti!*" he called. "Listen! I will come tonight at Matins prayers. I will scale the wall—"

"The top layers are not mortared. The bricks will fall. You cannot—"

"I shall have help. I will have rope. You need to be ready to climb."

"I—oh, God, yes! Riccardo get me out of here!"

"At Matins, then. I will return."

———————

Fedele's condition worsened. His head hung so low, his puffs of breath scattered the bits of straw at his feet.

"God, please end his suffering," I prayed. I called on the abbess to report on his health.

"I think he will die very soon," I said. "There is no luster in his eye, and he cannot lift his head. He refused hay, even grain."

"Stay by his side, Postulant Silvia. Report to me in the morning," she said, barely looking up from her papers. "You are dismissed."

As I left, I saw her eyes slide toward me under her glasses.

I fell into a restless sleep, right after Compline. I dreamt again of the donkey flying across the convent wall. I woke to the sound of Fedele's breath rattling hoarsely in his throat.

I moved next to the poor creature, stroking his neck. "Forgive me for not being by your side when you pass," I whispered. "But Suor Loretta would have wanted this for me—my escape, Fedele."

Would she indeed want this for me? Yes, she would. She showed me the fresco of Christ on the wall of the chapel. "He is making a choice by climbing the ladder on the cross. It is his own volition. That is the way we should all approach God. Willingly."

And I had not made that choice willingly. I was kidnapped, sealed within the convent. Still, as I listened to the bell toll Matins prayers, I thought about what Suor Loretta had said about the convent providing a home, a sanctuary of peace and protection for women who might otherwise be abused by unloving husbands, shut away as spinsters, or forced to make their livelihood as puttanas in the back alleys.

It was a refuge for many. But not for me. Never for me.

Fedele made a strangled sound in his throat, trying to bray. Warning me of his death.

I crept out of the tiny donkey stable when the bell finished tolling, leaving Fedele to die alone. My heart was sickened, but I couldn't miss my chance to escape with Riccardo. The stars were bright overhead, the sliver of a moon low in the horizon.

I heard a brick fall. Then another.

"Riccardo?"

"Merda!" I heard him curse, along with more tumbling bricks. *"A le guagnele!"*

"Be careful! The bricks—"

I heard the crashing of something heavy fall to the ground.

"Oh! Santa Maria!" I cried. I ran through darkness, guided by soft moans.

It had been nine long years since I had seen him, but I recognized him in the dim light. The high cheekbones, the strong nose.

"Riccardo! Have you hurt yourself?"

"I think—I think I am all right. It is my hand, my forearm."

He held his left hand against his chest like a child would hold a baby bird.

"Let me see—here, come into the shed where there is a lantern."

"All right," he said. "But first, Virginia . . . "

He pulled me tight against him with his good arm, making me lose my balance. He kissed my lips. His mouth opened against mine, spicy and warm. The taste of his kisses made me hungry for more. I opened my mouth, breathing in his masculine scent.

"I love you, Virginia. I have always loved you."

I did not answer. I had never loved him—or any man. I had never spent any time thinking about men. But nearly a decade had passed since the Palio, and I had not so much as seen a man, except for the old priest and an occasional bishop.

The sweet taste of his mouth, his breath! A pull that brought me into his body, surrendering me to his embrace. My spine tingled as he held me; a warm rush climbed to my cheeks. I felt suddenly alive again after a long sleep.

He let out a hushed scream, but his lips still sought mine. In our passion, he had tried to press me closer using his injured arm.

I pushed him away.

"Basta! Let me look at your hand and arm!" I took his good hand and led him to the stable.

"We must work quickly. The suoras will be returning from Matins soon."

In the light I saw his wrist, already swollen to two times its normal size. His arm was turning blue-black with blood.

"I think you have broken your wrist, at the very least," I said.

He closed his eyes tight.

"We must get you over the wall," he said. "Come! I will tie you to the rope and we will hoist you up."

It was then he noticed my crooked arm.

"Virginia! What happened to you?"

"I fell, just as you did, years ago, trying to escape. The nurse did a bad job of setting the bone. I cannot straighten it."

His eyes widened. "Do . . . do you think you can scale the wall with my companions pulling the rope?"

"I do not know. What I do know is that you must go first. If the nuns catch you, they will turn you over to the duca for justice. You will be flogged and thrown in prison, Riccardo. The church will destroy you. The abbess will see that you are punished without mercy."

Riccardo turned pale.

"I cannot anger the duca," he said. "I am here under his protection. I would lose my farm, my horses, my—"

"Come then," I said pulling him behind me. "We must get you over the wall at once."

The rope dangled against the bricks. Riccardo tugged it down, looping it around his waist. I had to tie the knot because his left arm was useless.

"This will be difficult," he said, wincing. "But watch me. I will place the sole of my foot against the wall and pull myself up with the aid of the rope."

"With one arm? Do you think you can?"

"I must," he said.

"Then I will have to do the same."

His eyes flickered with panic. "You must, Virginia!"

"Show me," I said. "I will try with all my heart. Show me first."

He pulled me close, kissing me passionately.

"Basta!" I said pushing him away. "The Pope will demand your life if the nuns catch you here."

Riccardo nodded. He tugged three times on the rope.

The slack in the rope immediately went taut. He pulled hard with his right hand and slowly began scaling the wall. I heard him cursing in pain.

As he neared the top of the wall, I could hear him gasping for air as he struggled to hang on to the rope.

There was a small gap at the top of the wall where several of the bricks had fallen. He tried to swing his foot up to the top, flinging it like a puppet jerked on a string.

But he couldn't kick high enough, and he just knocked more bricks down on the far side. He swung from the rope tied to his waist, groaning,

Again he tried. And again. Without the use of one arm, he could not hoist his weight up.

The great door to the chapel creaked open, and I heard the rustle of habits. The suoras were returning to their cells. While it was quite dark in the corner of the courtyard where Riccardo struggled, he would be spotted soon enough by the sharp-eyed nightwatch.

If the abbess learned of this escape attempt, she would confine me to my cell for weeks—months. Stale bread and water to starve me. With Suor Loretta dead, there was no one to intervene on my behalf.

I spotted the nightwatch lighting her lantern at the portal of the chapel. The flame grew bright as the oil fed the fire.

I whispered, "Riccardo! The nightwatch approaches!"

He spun a half-turn on his rope, looking over his shoulder. He called to his friends.

"Ranieri! Giuglio! *Venite su, aiutatemi!* Subito!"

The nun picked up her lantern, walking her rounds. She checked the cells first. She was coming our way.

A head appeared at the top of the wall. The young man hung down headfirst, his legs apparently anchored by invisible hands on the other side of the stonework. He looped his arms under Riccardo's armpits, hoisting him high enough to swing a leg over the wall.

As the path of light from the nightwatch's lantern touched my face, I saw both men disappear.

I heard a thud on the other side of the wall, muffled cries.

"Riccardo! Riccardo!" cried men's voices. "Dio mio!"

Then silence.

"Silvia," said the nightwatch, spotting me. "What are you doing out here?"

I bent over, pretending to vomit.

"The heavy smells of death from the donkey sickened me," I said. "He is purging his last. I had to breathe fresh air."

The suora's face puckered in concern. She brought the lantern to my face.

"You look pale indeed. Shall I escort you to the dispensary?"

"No, no. Only a few minutes of fresh air. Then I shall return to my charge. Suor Loretta's donkey will not live much longer, I fear."

———————

That night, a few hours before dawn, as Fedele's legs buckled under him, I knelt beside him, stroking his neck.

I walked to the door of the little shed and stared out into the starry predawn sky.

Had I really been so close to freedom?

Nothing had changed. I was accompanying a dying donkey to the edge of his life. He would surely die before dawn.

I had tasted kisses for the first time, finding them irresistible. I ached for the touch of Riccardo.

But I would remain alone, a prisoner. Suor Loretta had left me, and with her death, I lost my protection from the abbess. The abbess hated me for my knowledge of her lie. I knew she had forsaken her promise to grant the earnest wish of the old nun.

I touched my lips, my tongue remembering the spicy warmth of Riccardo's mouth closing over mine. I had felt a weakness in my legs as he pressed me against him. I recognized for the first time an urgency, a passion for something other than horses.

Would I ever feel that sensation, that desire again?

Fedele's eyes lost their focus, clouding under his long lashes. He struggled to breathe, a hoarse gasp expanding his rib cage, then the guttural grunt of air expelled. My fingers stroked the cross on his back, tracing down his spine, gently finishing the black horizontal line across the top of his shoulders.

Fedele drew his last breath just before dawn. His body shuddered, a massive spasm, and lost control of all his muscles at once.

Urine soaked the hem of my skirt as I pressed close to stroke his long ears.

Then he lay very still.

But I could still sense his spirit lingering there in the dim light of the shed. I cried quietly so as not to chase it away too quickly.

CHAPTER 95

Ferrara, Castello d' Este

AUGUST 1591

In the early evening, Alfonso, Duca di Ferrara, greeted a guest: the scion of the Monte dei Paschi banking family, Giacomo di Torreforte.

"I am glad to make your acquaintance finally, Signor di Torreforte." The duca beckoned the visitor forward into the Lion's Tower. With a gesture, he dismissed the manservant who accompanied the visitor.

Giacomo raised his eyes to the frescoes high above him.

"This is the Sala dell'Aurora," said Duca Alfonso. "The winged goddess driving the chariot of three white horses carries the sun, the light of day. She follows Aurora, who runs ahead with two candles."

"Magnificent," murmured Giacomo. "The power of the horses, the strength and beauty of the goddess."

When the doors of the apartment were closed, the duca stepped closer to his visitor. "I awaited your visit a decade ago . . . but you never appeared, Signor di Torreforte."

Di Torreforte bowed his head. "Forgive me, Duca, for that great error in decorum. But many events have transpired since that first folly."

"Indeed?" said the duke. "Pray tell me. In detail."

"I obtained permission to visit the d'Este Court and Your Serenissimo under false pretense, at the specific request of Granduca Francesco de' Medici."

Duca Alfonso arched an eyebrow.

"I appreciate your candor. I am aware of many transgressions of the de' Medici. One more does not surprise me. Continue, Signor di Torreforte."

"I shall confess all if you are willing to hear, Duca," said Giacomo. "But I also require your favor to rectify my errors."

Alfonso settled back in his chair.

"You surprise me, Signor di Torreforte. You admit to a lie—you entered Ferrara as an envoy from Florence, yet never appeared for an audience. And now you have the gall to ask me—no, to require—a favor?"

"If you would grant me the good grace to listen to my story, I will tell you how I have erred, committed unforgivable trespasses against man, woman, and God. Then I will beg you to help me right a grievous wrong committed here in your dukedom."

Duca Alfonso nodded.

Who is this Tuscan who now betrays the de' Medici?

"Begin. I am curious to hear your tale."

The oil burned low in the lamps. The duca listened in silence, his eyes occasionally blinking in astonishment.

When Giacomo di Torreforte finally concluded his story, there was silence in the room for many minutes. At last the duca nodded. "I must consider what you have told me," he said, "and decide what course of action to take."

As di Torreforte rose to take his leave, a messenger arrived from the convent with a letter from the abbess. With it was a folded parchment sealed with red wax bearing the imprint of a crowned eagle . . . the emblem of the d'Este family.

"Wait!" commanded the duca, lifting his hand. "This news may concern you, Signor di Torreforte."

Alfonso scanned both letters, then walked to the fireplace, tossed the parchments into the flames, and watched them burn.

Stirring the ashes, he turned his head and said, "You may have a chance to atone for your sins more quickly than one might have thought, Signor di Torreforte."

CHAPTER 96

Ferrara, Convento di Sant'Antonio, Polesine

AUGUST 1591

When the royal horsemaster arrived at the convent, the mother superior's hand reached for her rosary beads.

Why would the horsemaster come here? This is only an old ass that finally died.

The abbess met the horsemaster at the door of the convent. Besides Ercole Cortile, ambassador to the court of Francesco de' Medici, there was no man more trusted and esteemed by the duca in all Ferrara.

His face showed no love for the abbess, his eyes glinting cold blue. He stood in the doorway, reluctant to cross the threshold.

"Please, come sit close to the fire," said the abbess. "We keep it burning in my apartment for visitors, thanks be to God and the generosity of Duca—"

"Spare me, Madre Superiore," said the horsemaster, refusing the offered chair. "I happen to know how much the duca gives annually to this convent. You could have a bonfire every day of the week."

"And we pray fervently, several times a day, for the souls of all the d'Este family, as the convent has for centuries—"

"Do you pray as fervently for all the good women housed within these walls?"

The abbess rubbed her rosary beads hard between finger and thumb. Her skin began to burn with the friction. "What do you mean, signore?"

"Never mind," said the horsemaster. "I will get to the heart of the business at hand. The duca wishes to have me interview the suora who took care of the donkey."

"What?" said the abbess.

"Duca Alfonso d'Este wishes to know the nature and trajectory of the animal's disease. He died only days after the death of the duke's well-loved aunt."

"I—no, that is impossible. The suoras here—as you well know—are entirely cloistered. You may not speak with her. It is forbidden."

The horsemaster rose, his lips set in a grim line.

"Then I shall return with the duca himself. And I promise you he will not arrive in a generous mood."

"The duca?" said the abbess, her hand flying to her throat. "Here, at the convent?"

"When he hears that you have refused his request, I can only imagine what might become of your fine wines, steady fire, and comfortable fare."

The abbess's hand slid off her rosary beads, fluttering to her face.

"Good signore! I follow the rules of Rome and our holy order. This is the only reason I would dare decline to fulfill the duca's wish. We are a cloistered order. I could be excommunicated!"

"So be it."

"I do not understand the nature of the request," she said. "The donkey died of natural causes. He was quite old. "

"So you say, Madre Superiore. The duca wonders at the astonishing coincidence of the ass's death following so closely after that of the great suora Loretta d'Este."

The abbess pressed her lips together, bleaching them of color.

"It is the duca's express wish to interview Postulant Silvia?"

"No, Madre," said the horsemaster. "It is his command."

He nodded stiffly, preparing to leave.

"I would be present, of course," said the abbess.

"No. You shall not be present. The duca requests the honest word of the suora in charge of the donkey's care. There can be no other witnesses who might interfere with the truth."

"How dare you!" said the abbess. "You imply that my honesty is not beyond reproach? I, the mother superior of this convent?"

"You waste your holy breath with me, Madre. The duca will be here tomorrow an hour before Vespers to speak with the young woman in question. And he will come with a wagon to transport the donkey carcass. If you have any complaints, reserve them for Duca Alfonso himself."

The horsemaster turned at the door. He saw the abbess's fingers clinging to her rosary beads.

"And do not think those church trinkets will save your soul when you finally meet your maker, Madre."

He left the door open as he strode down the convent hall, scattering the suoras like frightened crows.

CHAPTER 97

Siena, Brunelli Stables, Vignano
AUGUST 1591

Giorgio's three brothers had never shown any interest in horses or the farm in Vignano, despite their father's urging. Each had sought his fortunes elsewhere. Alvise, the eldest, was a prosperous cloth merchant selling bolts of fine fabric dyed in L'Oca at Fonte Branda. Michele was a clerk at Monte dei Paschi, swiftly climbing through the ranks under the watchful and encouraging eye of the di Torreforte brothers. Dario was a partner in a vineyard in Chianti, just north of Siena's walls.

The three sent money to subsidize the horse farm after their father's death. Their one sister, Delia, a spinster of thirty-two, cared for Giorgio, whose condition worsened steadily. And one by one, the great stock of brood mares dwindled as Giorgio's health failed. He could no longer train horses. Only the stud fees for Orione kept the stables in hay and barley.

Stella, who had shown initial improvement under Giorgio's dedicated care, relapsed into a pathetic state of health.

Giorgio, carried now in a litter to the stables, saw the change in the mare. Her coat had grown wavy and thick. She was losing muscle tone, though Giorgio blamed himself for not being fit enough to ride her.

But the mare's thirst was the telltale sign. The grooms were ordered to stable her for observation, counting the number of buckets the horse drained in a day.

"Twenty buckets, Master Brunelli," said the head groom. "My back aches from carrying water. Her thirst is unquenchable."

That same evening, as Stella yanked hay greedily from the manger, Giorgio noticed a bulge filling the natural depression above the mare's eyes. He ran his thumb across the horse's skull. He felt the fat beneath the skin.

He knew the fate of the mare. He knew his own.

"You and I are looking at the end of our lives, old girl," he said. "And quite a life it has been."

Giorgio knew the progression of the disease. Within weeks, the mare would lose all remaining muscle tone; the slight sway-back she had developed would become more pronounced until her body resembled a fleshy washtub. She would become lame, and finally her legs would buckle underneath her. As had Giorgio's own.

The summer solstice was long past. Autumn approached, and now, as the days shortened, so would the remaining fragment of Stella's life.

She would not survive the winter.

Giorgio listened to the grinding of the mare's teeth working over the hay. He heard the nicker of a horse stabled farther down the line. It was Orione, calling to him. He sighed, shaking his head as he left the ailing mare to her feed.

Orione pressed hard against the door of his stall, his big head emerging over the door, shaking his mane at Giorgio.

How docile Orione has become—was it the time we have spent together forging a friendship? Waiting for Virginia. Like two old men in love with the same girl. We have a mutual understanding.

He watched the spinning motes of hay dust linger in the twilight. Giorgio reached through the golden air, his hand resting on Orione's blaze.

"I will not let all Siena see what has become of your good mother," he promised the stallion, running his fingers through the horse's forelock.

"We must preserve her legend. And you, my friend. I will send you back to the Maremma hills to run wild with the mares."

CHAPTER 98

Ferrara, Convento di Sant'Antonio

AUGUST 1591

The abbess pulled the heavy velvet drape away from her apartment window. She watched as the gatekeepers bowed deeply to the duca's entourage. In the windows below, she could see her nuns' wimpled faces peeking through the gaps in the curtains.

The wagon approached first. It was no ordinary knacker's cart, but a lacquered flatbed in gold and red, the d'Este colors, with two liveried grooms driving a matched set of gray mares. They pulled up to the interior gate of the courtyard. Riding behind was the horsemaster. He flicked his eyes up at the abbess's windows, scowling.

"Madre," said Suor Adriana, rushing in with only a perfunctory knock. "The gatemen say Duca Alfonso is coming!"

The abbess swallowed hard. She had hoped that the horsemaster's threat was only a bluff. Would the duca really concern himself with the carcass of a very old donkey?

"I will descend with you at once," said the abbess. She made a hasty sign of the cross, lowering her eyes to the stone floor. By the time she had reached the ground floor, the horsemaster was questioning the timid Suor Petra, assigned to deal with visitors to the abbey.

"What can you tell me about the donkey's death?" he demanded.

Suor Petra squirmed, her eyes beseeching the mother superior.

"Horsemaster, please! The suora does not know anything about the matter. Only one postulant knows the answers to your questions."

"Then the duca and I will question her at once. Open the doors to the chapel as well. The duca wishes to visit the frescoes while he interviews the postulant. He has given his permission for you to watch through the grille."

What little color the abbess had in her lips faded to white.

The horsemaster smiled, savoring his words. What a delicious reversal. Every Sunday and all holy days, the public of Ferrara stood behind the grille to watch the nuns singing the mass, accompanied by the organ and harpsichord. Now it would be the abbess herself who would watch from behind the grille as the duca questioned the girl.

Before the abbess had time to answer, the clatter of hooves rang across the first courtyard. Duca Alfonso rode up to the chapel doors. A groom accompanied him, dismounting at once to hold the reins of Alfonso's mount.

The abbess curtsied deeply before her most generous benefactor.

"Good day, Madre," said the duke. "And the postulant?"

"I shall send for her at once," said the abbess. "May I welcome you to our humble convent, and may God's blessings be bestowed—"

"I will wait inside the chapel for the girl. Instruct the gatekeepers to unlock the inner courtyard."

"My duca, I must first accompany them to the donkey's shed. The girl waits there, guarding the carcass as you requested—"

"Open the gates at once, Madre."

The abbess did not hesitate. "Yes, my duca."

She gathered her robes high enough on her ankles to hurry across the gatekeeper's station. In her rush, she glanced at the two men on the bench of the wagon. One quickly turned his head away from her.

Is there indeed holy shame among the duca's men, as there should be, for this foul invasion?

But just as the bright fire of self-righteous anger rose in her heart, a strange flicker of uneasiness grew beside it.

Who is that man? Have I seen his face before?

Despite her hurry, she paused, her fingers fumbling in her pocket for her bone-rimmed glasses. When she brought the spectacles up to her eyes, the man had disappeared.

The interior gates of the convent creaked on their hinges. The gatekeepers were obliged to keep a guarding hand on the wood so it would not disintegrate. The wagon entered the inner courtyard, the abbess walking behind in its wake. All the nuns and postulants had been secured with the walls of the convent hours before. Except one.

"I will notify her that you have arrived. Be aware, she may be overcome with emotion. The two deaths—Suor Loretta and now the donkey—have affected her most profoundly. She is an odd girl. I think that it would be best if I were by her side to give her spiritual support."

"I think I have made it abundantly clear that I wish to interview the postulant in private," said the duca, his voice betraying impatience. "I want to know of the last hours of my dear aunt's life. I want to know that the donkey was not poisoned."

The abbess's mouth dropped open. She raised her hand at once to cover it. "My duca! Poisoned? Who would poison Suor Loretta's donkey?"

"Questions are mine to ask, not yours. Introduce me to this postulant at once, Madre. Stand beyond the door while my horse-master inspects the donkey's body. We have brought along a respected horse surgeon."

The man who had turned his head away from her only minutes before descended from the flatbed wagon. As the abbess turned to take a closer look at him, he again turned his face from hers.

"Madre, bring the postulant to us at once!" repeated the duca, furious.

The abbess lowered her head in respect, pushing open the shed doors.

An overpowering smell of decay greeted the visitors. A thin girl knelt beside the dead donkey, her simple verge dress soiled. The cloak on her back was matted with straw, her hair tied back in a dirty white kerchief.

She made the sign of the cross and rose to her feet.

"My lord Duca Alfonso, this is postulant Silvia. Postulant Silvia, show your proper respects to Duca di Ferrara, Serenissimo Alfonso II," said the abbess.

Virginia curtsied deeply, bowing her head. When she rose, she looked at the duca.

"Duca Alfonso," she said. Her eyes caught a glance of the man standing just behind the duke's shoulder.

It was him! The face she had seen in her nightmares—

The postulant's face froze, her mouth partially opened to scream.

The duca made an almost imperceptible shake of his head, his eyes holding steady on her face. She dipped her head, saying nothing.

"Postulant Silvia," he said. "I know this is a shock to you—first the death of my beloved aunt Suor Loretta, then the donkey whom you cared for with such devotion. My aunt wrote of you often. Especially in her last days."

The abbess's eyes flashed open in astonishment.

"And I thank you for your loving care. I would like you to answer a few questions the horse surgeon has for you."

With a wave of his hand, the duke indicated the man at his shoulder. Giacomo di Torreforte. Di Torreforte took a step forward, bowing.

Virginia took a step back, her heel wedged against the dead donkey.

"This examination of the donkey's remains will be most indelicate. We will certainly excuse the abbess from the few minutes these procedures are carried out," said the duca.

The abbess looked at him, preparing to speak. He held up his hand for her to keep her silence. "Then the rest of our interview will be conducted in the sanctity of the convent's chapel, in full view of the abbess. Though I will insist you sit behind the grille."

"But . . . my duty—" sputtered the abbess.

"Abbess," said the duca. "You will excuse us."

"My good duca, hear my plea!" the abbess protested. "I cannot let the girl be unchaperoned for an instant. I have a duty to God, to our Holy Order—"

"I understand, Madre," said the duca. "Send at once for Suor Anna Rosa, my cousin. I am, of course, permitted to visit with members of my family. Suor Anna Rosa shall be present throughout our questioning, thus assuaging your concerns for . . . God's protocol."

The abbess bowed.

"Yes, Serenissimo. I will send for her at once." As she turned to leave, she tried in vain to take a better look at the horse surgeon. But he had already moved next to the donkey, throwing back the blanket.

A swarm of flies buzzed up angrily from the decaying carcass.

"Go! Subito!" ordered the duca, his hand flapping away the flies and stench.

The abbess hurried out of the shed toward the convent.

CHAPTER 99

Ferrara, Convento di Sant'Antonio
AUGUST 1591

I stabbed my finger at di Torreforte, who brushed the flies from his velvet sleeves.

"I will not trust my life to this villain!" I said. "He is source of all the misfortune that has ever befallen me."

Giacomo looked at me, having the gall to lower his face as if he felt shame.

As if he could.

"I am well aware of his treachery," said Duca Alfonso. He wrinkled his nose in disgust at the smell of the decaying donkey. He took a lace-edged handkerchief from his pocket and applied it to his nose.

"Che puzza!" he said. "Virginia Tacci, we do not have time to sort out grudges and mortal enemies at this point. Your countryman, Signor di Torreforte, has a plan."

"He is not my countryman," I said. "He is a de' Medici spy!"

"Basta!" snapped the duca. "You can either follow his instructions faithfully or spend the rest of your days in this convent.

Though I would suggest you take the orders if you do—a postulant of your advanced age does not speak well for the convent."

————————

Several nuns, including Suor Adriana, were stationed just outside the chapel doors, making sure none of the young postulants or younger suoras grew too curious to see the great duca.

"Fetch Suor Anna Rosa at once!" called the abbess, her black habit flapping as she strode across the lawn.

"She is in chapel," answered Suor Adriana. "I will call her at once."

Suor Anna Rosa appeared immediately and followed the abbess across the courtyard. She adjusted her brass-framed glasses, focusing on the agitated face of the mother superior.

"You must report every question posed to the postulant Silvia," said the abbess. "If anything is untoward, you must evoke God's name and force a halt to the impropriety."

"But Madre," said Suor Anna Rosa. "This is Duca Alfonso d'Este. You know I cannot contradict him."

"See that you intervene in some way," said the abbess, ushering the suora toward the tiny stable. "It seems the duca suspects foul play in the death of the beast. What unholy interest could he possibly have in a lowly donkey?"

Suor Anna Rosa said nothing, but she saw the abbess's lips pinched so tight they turned the white of marble.

The abbess pulled at the stable door. "What treachery! They have slid the bolt!" The abbess rapped hard on the splintered wood.

The horsemaster opened the door only enough to admit the young suora.

"We will question the postulant only a few minutes as the surgeon inspects the donkey's body. Then the duca will keep his word and move to the chapel, where you can observe the interview personally."

The abbess thrust the suora forward, pushing her finger into the small of her back.

The horsemaster bowed deeply to the duca's young cousin.

"Suor Anna Rosa, it is indeed an honor to see you again," he said. "It has been many years since I have had the pleasure."

Anna Rosa blushed. She had always adored the d'Este horsemaster. One glance at him brought back a rush of childhood memories.

What is he doing here in Convento Sant'Antonio?

———

Once the shed door was closed, the horsemaster took Suor Anna Rosa aside. I watched how he held her elbow, making her face him.

"You must listen closely," he said. "We brought you here not to witness Virginia Tacci's questioning but to aid us in her escape."

"Escape?" said Anna Rosa, barely breathing. She looked up at her cousin, the duca. "You will help her?"

The duca did not answer right away. When he spoke, he spoke to all of us.

"The word 'escape' has not been mentioned in my presence, Cousin. I leave these matters entirely in the hands of the Senese visitor. I will have nothing to do with any arrangements whatsoever. I do not understand the matter to which you refer. I hope this is clear."

"Sì, Serenissimo," she answered.

I could barely look at Giacomo di Torreforte. His hazel eyes bore into me. I turned away, unable to stand the sight of his face. But I listened.

"I beg your forgiveness, Virginia Tacci," di Torreforte said. "But you must look at me. I want to know you understand the risks involved."

"I cannot look at you, you villain!" I hissed. "You snatched my life, my horses, away from me—how can I ever forgive you? What a pointless word is forgiveness, when I have lost so much."

"But if you will hear my plan, you may find freedom again," pleaded Giacomo di Torreforte. "And peace between us!"

I shook my head. I wanted to spit in his face.

"How can hatred ever find peace?" I hissed. "How could I possibly trust you?"

"Because you have no choice. And neither do I," di Torreforte said quietly.

Anna Rosa sought my hand.

"Raise your eyes, Virginia," she said. "Look at him. Hear what he has to say. My cousin the duca would never risk so much if the cause were not just."

My eyes slowly climbed up to meet di Torreforte's. I saw the face I had hated for years. In my memory. In my nightmares. Even in my prayers. But now there was a light in his eyes that had never been there before. It was that light I focused on as he told me what to do.

"How can I help?" asked Anna Rosa when he was finished. "How is there a part for me?"

Di Torreforte nodded, his eyes shifting from mine at last.

"The abbess will be watching closely. When we have completed our interview in the chapel, she will expect to see Virginia emerge from the shed after we load the donkey on the cart. That is where you will play your part."

———————

We sat under the great fresco in the convent chapel: Suor Loretta's favorite, *Gesù Sale alle Croce*. Duca Alfonso's eyes gazed up at the gilded halo of Jesus as he mounted the cross.

"Our savior looks so certain, so assured," he said, nodding up at the fresco. "What a gift to know that what you do is absolutely the right thing. No matter how you will suffer."

"It is the gift of faith," said the abbess from her position behind the ornate grill. Her voice resonated in the small chapel, reminding me that she could hear every word uttered.

As her words faded away into silence, I waited for di Torreforte to speak. His eyes were riveted on the painting. I turned in my pew, the ancient wood creaking. I feared he had forgotten all about me, the plan.

Di Torreforte said nothing for far too long. His mouth moved soundlessly. I doubted he was praying.

What does he see in that painting?

I began to sweat, cold rivulets meandering down the small of my back.

Finally I spoke, trying to shake di Torreforte from his trance.

"Suor Loretta always said that our fresco is the only depiction of Christ showing his volition, Duca. He climbs the cross voluntarily, knowing his destiny."

The duca nodded. "She was a wise woman and my favorite aunt." Then he shook his head as if dismissing an idea. He turned to see the abbess watching intently through the grille.

"I want to question you, Postulant Silvia, on your knowledge of this donkey," the duca said. "I shall ask the horse surgeon to pose a few questions."

Di Torreforte snapped out of his reverie. He looked my way.

I avoided his eyes. "Sì, Serenissimo."

Di Torreforte cleared his throat. "You have told us that the beast became seriously ill the day of the suora's death?"

"Sì," I answered. "He was old but not unhealthy. A day or so before she died, his head drooped and he would not take his feed. When the bell tolled for her death, he dropped to his knees."

"And he sickened precipitously after that?"

"Yes. Quite suddenly."

I heard the bench scrape the floor as the abbess moved closer to the grille.

"Do you think there was any coincidence in Suor Loretta's death and that of her beloved pet?" asked di Torreforte.

I did not answer. I glanced at the abbess.

The duca said, "Please answer the question, Postulant Silvia."

"I think it is uncanny how quickly Fedele died. The earth still freshly mounded on his mistress's grave. But I have heard tell that donkeys are faithful. I do not know donkeys," I said, looking again toward the abbess. "Only horses."

"Ah yes! I have heard your fantasy. You think you rode the Palio in Siena. Yes, all Ferrara will have a good laugh at that!" said di Torreforte.

I could not help but clench my jaw, sticking it out at him in defiance.

"I did—"

"Answer my question, Postulant!" di Torreforte snapped. "Do you think it a strange coincidence for a donkey—or a horse—to die at the same time as his master or mistress?"

"Not so faithful that they roll over dead on the spot," I answered quickly. I glanced at the duca, trying to gauge my response. "That seems too much of a coincidence."

"Serenissimo. I have inspected the tongue," said di Torreforte. "And noticed some telling characteristics. First, Postulant Silvia. Was his tongue swollen before death?"

"Yes, sir. Fedele could not manage to eat for several days, as I have mentioned."

"My duca. In the donkey's stool, I found remnants of oak leaves and acorns."

"That is very strange," I said. "We do not have any oak trees on the grounds. I fed him only sweet grass and dried hay. Occasionally, he had a ration of good oats."

"But never oak or acorns?" asked di Torreforte.

"Never."

Di Torreforte turned toward the duca. He paused, stroking his beard.

"Serenissimo, it is my opinion that this donkey was poisoned intentionally by someone within these convent walls."

"*No!*" cried the abbess from the grille. "That is impossible!"

"Silence!" shouted the duca. His voice resonated against the vaulted walls of the chapel ceiling. "Outrageous! What villainy is this?"

"I request a full inspection of the donkey's remains in my dear aunt Loretta's name," said the duca, anger edging his words. He turned to look at the grille. "Madre Superiore, I will require a private audience with you at once."

The abbess could barely speak. She took a few seconds to compose herself.

"Madre Superiore? Do you hear me?"

"Sì, Serenissimo. Please join me in my apartments. We can speak privately there."

"Go," whispered di Torreforte to me. "Remember what I told you."

As I turned to leave the chapel, I took one glance back. I saw di Torreforte's gaze riveted on the painting, his finger reaching up to trace the rungs of the ladder.

———————

I wiped the fat black flies out of my eyes, my nostrils. They clung to my temples and tickled my legs. I felt the slick maggots working the donkey flesh resting against the back of my calf.

My flesh still lives. Surely they will not feed on me!

In that suffocating heat, each breath was more of a coffin then of life.

Breathe, Virginia. All you have to do is keep still and keep breathing, he said.

This man who had caused such sorrow and suffering. This same man I was forced to trust now.

What did he see in that painting, damn his soul! For a moment I thought all was lost.

I could never forgive him. But what other chance did I have?

I thought of the sweet kisses, warm from Riccardo's lips. The world outside the convent. Giorgio! Cesare, my padrino!

And most of all, Orione. Padrino will have cured him, nursed him back to health! My padrino could cure any horse, surely.

They all awaited me in Siena. My fate was in di Torreforte's hands.

Will he kill me as a last oath to Granduca Francesco? Was his task to wash clean any remaining stain of his treachery?

My blood suddenly ran cold.

Jump! Jump before he slits my throat!

The ropes were tight on the thick canvas tarp, weighing heavily on my shoulders, and the reek of putrid donkey made me swallow the acid in my throat.

I sought an airhole to breathe, my fingers working desperately against the oiled cloth and rope.

"God protect you, Virginia Tacci," whispered Anna Rosa. Her fingers wiggled through the tarp, finding mine.

"Thank you. Good-bye, my friend."

I could hear a choking sob. Her fingers squeezed mine, and she whisked her hand away.

"You were my only friend," she said, her voice low. "I will never forget you. I shall pray for you every day—"

Every day.

I no longer wanted to jump out. I thought of the long days of convent life, endless prayers eight times a day. Where do those prayers go? Do they drift up to God and heaven, like the incense the priest swings from his brass pan? Or do they vanish like the mists that shroud the town, disappearing as the sun burns them into oblivion?

There was indeed suffering beyond the walls of this convent. The hovels of the city, infested with plague and marsh fever. The louse-infested orphans of Maria della Scala, begging for bread. The poor farmers whose families chewed roots and bone-broth soup when their crops failed. But along with that suffering, there was life. And I needed to live.

I hoped that for her sake, Anna Rosa could finally find peace in God's service within these convent walls, as Suor Loretta had.

But I could not.

"I will never forget you," Anna Rosa said again.

Nor will I ever forget you.

Under the foul decay of the donkey, I smelled Anna Maria's familiar odor in her nun's habit, which I now wore. I wondered how long it would take the near-sighted abbess to realize that under my dirty white kerchief was the head of Suor Anna Rosa, cousin to the duca.

I thought of the conversa Margherita, puckering her lips in dismay as she pummeled the dirty kerchief against a rock in the river Po. Once the stains were washed away, it would cover some other postulant's head. Over and over again, until it was relegated as a rag to rub beeswax into the choir seats, and finally to wipe clean the chamber pots.

Would the conversa ever think of me again? Did she ever believe me when I told her my true identity?

"May God guide you back home, Virginia. To Siena," said my friend.

I closed my eyes tight, trying to remember the smoky smell of winter fires, the aroma of fresh hay–cut fields, and the warm scent of horses. I thought of the rippling fields of red poppies in the Senese spring, the tolling of the clock of the Torre del Mangia. The songs of the contradas, starting with the one lone male voice, singing in the darkness.

Nella Piazza del Campo . . .
I moved my lips, singing silently.
. . . ci nasce la verbena.
Viva la nostra Siena,
viva la nostra Siena!

I heard the driver cluck to his horses and felt the shudder of the wagon. My head thumped against the donkey's stiff leg as we rumbled forward across the cobblestones of Ferrara.

———

The horsemaster accompanied the flatbed wagon to the duca's stables. There the driver and his lackeys unloaded Fedele's carcass. They pulled the donkey by its tail toward an open grave, where the diggers still sweated, finishing their work. The creases of their brows were lined black with dirt.

They must have been warned not to look at me, for not once did I see a servant cast a glance in my direction as I slipped off the side of the wagon.

I turned away. The tugging caused the poor creature's body to pour forth excrement and deep yellow piss.

No, I would not watch. This donkey had saved my life. I would preserve his memory with dignity. He was not a horse, he could not help it.

But he was my savior.

"The duca instructed me to speak with you," said the horsemaster. "I speak with his voice. What has transpired here can never be spoken of. You are free, but not to return to the same life."

"What do you mean?" I said. I could smell my own sweat obliterating the smell of the gentle Anna Rosa.

"You can return to Siena's regions, but not to Siena itself. If anyone should learn that you were confined to a convent, then released, with both de' Medici and d'Este assistance, we would have the Pope's armies at our gates. Neither Granduca Ferdinando nor Duca Alfonso want to bring Rome north to battle us."

"But I—"

"Should you share your secrets, you ensure the trial and death of this man who sacrificed so much to save you," said the horsemaster, gesturing at di Torreforte, who stood just behind him.

"But he was the cause of all my suffering!" I hissed. "Why should he not suffer, too?"

"You are not one to forgive, are you, Virginia Tacci?" said the horsemaster. "The convent did not cultivate a willingness to pardon sins?"

"To the fiery inferno with forgiveness! I will never, *ever* forgive him. My youth, my life—my horse! Every dream I ever had—snatched from me!"

Giacomo di Torreforte winced. He came nearer, wary of my fists.

"Do you think for a moment that Siena has forgotten you?" he said. "Forgotten your Palio? How you stayed up on that stallion, despite his spectacular fall, racing him to the finish?"

"I *lost*," I said. "I came in third. I wanted to race again—and win! You robbed me of that chance!"

"I did what I had to do to save your life. And Siena will always remember your spirit. You *won*, Virginia Tacci."

But I remembered what he had done.

"And the boards? Thrown on the street in front of Orione? You were there at Via del Capitano—I saw you right before Orione fell!"

"They were thrown from the rooftop. I shouted at the villains! There was nothing I could do."

The horsemaster held up his hand, demanding our attention.

"Virginia. Understand well. The condition of your release is this: while you may return to Siena's countryside, you may never enter its gates. By the decree of Duca Alfonso II."

"But—not enter Siena again in my life?"

"There is a delicate arrangement here between two dukes, sworn enemies. Both stand to lose much. The pope would like nothing more than to seize Ferrara as a papal state.

"You must swear to remain outside of Siena for the rest of your life. And to never again be known as Virginia Tacci." His voice was deadly serious. "Or I will personally return you to the convent myself this minute. Do you swear to the duca's conditions?"

I stared at the man, dressed in his fine livery. "Never enter the gates of Siena?"

"You may never approach any closer than Corsano," said the horsemaster. "You can see the city from a distance from the Crete hills."

"But! Never to—what if someone recognizes me in the Crete?"

"Forgive me, Virginia," said di Torreforte. "The many years in the convent have—changed your looks. And you are a woman now, not a fourteen-year-old villanella. Only your closest friends would recognize you now. Perhaps."

My hand reached to touch my face. I had not looked at my face for over a decade. There was no looking glass in the convent.

"I cannot—I cannot contact my friends? What of Giorgio, of Cesare—my godfather? My uncle!"

The horsemaster slid his eyes toward Giacomo. "Signor di Torreforte, this is for you to tell," he said.

The words were dry parchment on di Torreforte's lips. I watched him try to speak.

"Tell me!" I said.

"Virginia," he said. "Siena has changed, too."

I held his eyes. They had shifted color to a dark, moody green, as when a cloud passes over the water in stream.

"What do you mean, changed?"

His face contracted as if he had a severe headache. I saw the muscles move in his throat as he swallowed.

"There is a place for you, Virginia. I will take you back to Corsano, where our family raises Palio horses in the Crete. On the road toward Monteroni d'Arbia."

"No! I want to go back to Vignano. I want to see my zio, my padrino, Giorgio, Contessa d'Elci—"

Di Torreforte put his hand on my shoulder. I let it rest there, testing its weight.

"Virginia," he said. "They are all . . . gone."

I tried to focus on his face, but it suddenly blurred into jagged fragments.

All the people I loved, blown away like the dry leaves in winter.

I had never had a chance to thank them.

"No!"

The horsemaster closed his eyes. His horse fidgeted under him. The rider stroked his fingers through his mane.

"My presence here was Giorgio's last wish," said di Torreforte, his words suddenly spilling from his lips. "If he is not dead already, he will be soon."

My tears, hot on my cheeks, astounded me. I touched my fingers to the wetness in wonder.

"You cannot return to Vignano. You might be recognized there. Your aunt, the village priest. Your cousins."

"It will be better for you," the horsemaster said softly. "A new start, a new identity. Signor di Torreforte can care for you in Corsano, where so many Palio winners are born. I have bought horses from Signor di Torreforte for the Duca d'Este's stable—they are indeed magnificent. You will recover your spirit through the horses. All true horsemen do."

"Women," I said. "I am a horse*woman*."

"Sì, fantina," said the horsemaster. "You have indeed earned that."

Giacomo dared to pull me closer. "Virginia. You could dress as a young man and ride. No one will know the difference. There is no reason—"

I pushed him away. I looked up at them both, these two men who talked nonsense. I wiped the burning tears from my eyes, only to have more appear.

"I am not a boy," I said. "I am Virginia Tacci."

CHAPTER 100

Siena, Brunelli Stables, Vignano

AUGUST 1591

No one noticed the horse and rider slip out into the darkness. A light rain muffled the hoofbeats on the muddy road as they cut south and west across the hills.

By the time they reached the edge of the Crete hills, the sky had cleared and the moon blazed on the eastern horizon, throwing long shadows in front of the crippled rider and his stumbling mare.

For a Senese, there was no more sacred country than the Crete. Its expanses and rolling hills were the unobstructed view of the unfettered, indomitable spirit that was Siena.

Stella wanted to run. Weak though she was, her spirit was strong. Giorgio felt her prancing step, though every so often she lost her footing, almost buckling to the ground. Still, the night air fed the mare's spirit; the wide, never-ending fields of the Crete invigorated her.

"Not just yet," said Giorgio, wincing. He pulled the mare down from a canter to an extended trot. Stella had lost muscle along her backbone, making a painful ride for the sick man as her sharp bones cut into his buttocks.

Giorgio turned the horse on the crest of a hill, just outside the village of Corsano, and looked back to Siena. There was no finer view of the city, set on three hills, rinsed in the bleached light of the rising moon. He rode to a single cypress tree where a swelling breast of disturbed earth mounded a grave.

"Babbo—" he whispered. But he could not say any more as tears gushed from his eyes.

Giorgio turned away from the cypress and removed his cap. He looked across the rolling hills to the city of Siena. "They will never forget you, Virginia," he said. "Nor will we."

He spurred Stella into a breakneck gallop, descending the hill recklessly through the dark. A reckless gallop toward a steep ravine. Deep enough to kill a horse—and a rider, too, especially one who was half-dead already.

CHAPTER 101

En route from Ferrara to Siena

AUGUST 1591

The unmarked coach whisked us away from Ferrara. Giacomo rode beside the coachman, whether to avoid me or the stench emanating from my close encounter with the dead donkey, I did not know or care.

I bathed that night in scalding hot water in a shallow wooden tub in the village of Malabergo. The innkeeper's wife was paid extra to bring oil soap and a reed brush to scour my skin. Giacomo had purchased a few simple linen blouses and skirts for me, and a pair of leather slippers. They had been delivered to my room in an oak chest.

The woman who bathed me must have been paid a pretty coin, for she said nothing about my stench, the nun's habit, or the Tuscan signore who paid for my lodging. She bundled the clothes together and delivered them to Giacomo's room—along with me, in light blue linen. My hair was still wet from the bath; my skin stung red and raw from the scrubbing.

"Grazie," said Giacomo, nodding curtly to her. "That is all."

After she had closed the door, Giacomo threw Anna Rosa's habit into the fire.

"You look a damned sight better than you did a few hours ago," he said, stabbing savagely at the burning cloth with an iron poker. A whiff of the pestilent fabric, smoking and acrid, assailed my nostrils. I covered my nose.

"I suspect I smell better, too." I said, watching the garment turn to ash. I walked over to the window, opening the shutters. It rained quietly outside, mist rising slowly from the earth, shrouding the town.

I looked at the table, laid with a cloth, a roasted chicken, and savory dishes still steaming. A jug of wine was filled to the brim. The smell of herb-roasted fowl and crisp pancetta made my knees weak. I closed my eyes, breathing in the aroma.

"I thought we should eat. You must be famished."

"I am used to it. Hunger is a virtue in the convent, gluttony a sin."

He said nothing but pulled the chair out for me.

"We will fatten you up again, Virginia Tacci," he said. "Regain your strength so you can ride colts again!"

I did not know how to respond. I sat across from the man who had brought such bitter sadness into my life. Giacomo di Torreforte had stolen a decade from my life, a decade during which all the people I had ever loved had perished.

Now he had intervened to free me from my prison.

"I do not owe you anything, Signor di Torreforte," I said, twisting my napkin in my hands. "I do not know why you have saved me, why you risk so much to take me back to Siena. How you convinced a de' Medici to align with a d'Este. What advantage do you seek?"

Giacomo drew a deep breath, settling into his chair. He looked at me and then back at the fire.

"I have caused you irreparable pain and sorrow. I know this."

"I will not tell you sweet tales, Signor di Torreforte," I said. "I will never forget your treachery. I am your worst enemy—"

He put up his hand, stopping my speech. For second, I thought he was going to strike me.

"I think you have painted a very clear picture for me, Virginia. No further elaboration is needed. And I indeed have a great deal to atone for," he said, carving the fowl. He filled my plate with succulent slices, glistening in pan drippings and studded with roasted juniper berries.

"Come. Eat."

"You do not expect me to ever forgive you, do you?" I said, accepting the plate from him. "Because I cannot."

He paused, his hands still on my plate as if we were playing tug-of-war.

"No," he said, releasing it. "I suppose you cannot. Yet. But perhaps someday."

I thought of Giorgio and my padrino, distraught over my disappearance. My uncle dying without me at his side. Most of all, I thought of never seeing Orione again.

"Never," I said. I stabbed at the meat with my knife and began to devour my food in silence.

Di Torreforte did not attempt to engage me in conversation. He refilled my wineglass, but he did not press me to speak. But I saw a dark shadow pass over his face.

"I am sorry we did not have an opportunity for you to pay your respects to Riccardo De' Luca's family before we left Ferrara," he said finally.

My respects?

In my mind, I heard again—from a dark night that seemed so long ago—muffled cries. "Riccardo! Riccardo! Dio mio!"

I swallowed, clutching my knife, a chunk of meat still speared on the tip.

"He died in a fall, broke his neck. A failed attempt to rescue you." Di Torreforte took a sip of wine. He watched me over the rim of the glass. "Or so went the rumor amongst the d'Este family."

I thought of Riccardo's deep kiss, despite his suffering. I remembered how he had pressed me close against him, wincing. His breath intoxicated me.

"He was very brave," I said finally.

"Really? His wife did not think so," he said, dabbing his lips with a napkin.

I stopped breathing.

"I—had not realized he was married," I stammered.

"Indeed," said Giacomo, watching me with a ferocity I remembered from the day he kidnapped me. "Did he not tell you that?"

He took another sip of wine. He seemed to be wrestling with his dark emotions.

"Lucia d'Este thinks her husband was a fool to have risked so much. Better to have left these matters in the hands of her uncle, Duca Alfonso. Had Riccardo been caught, he would have been banished from Ferrara as a matter of course. *Persona non grata* in two dukedoms—"

"Two dukedoms?"

Di Torreforte looked down into the red depths of his wine glass, brooding.

"He was in Ferrara because he had been banished from Siena," he said at last.

I could feel the thud of each pulse of blood reach my head.

"Riccardo De' Luca was always a reckless fool." I heard the bitter disdain in his voice. "Did you know him well? Or was his botched attempt simply to honor Siena?"

I gathered my skirts, preparing to rise from the table.

"Forgive me, Signor di Torreforte. I think it is best if I return to my room to rest. The long ride has tired me."

Di Torreforte poured himself more wine. "Everyone in Siena knew the fool loved you, but a married man risking—"

"Shut up!" I shouted, pounding my fist on the table. My wine spilled, staining the white linen. "Why—why did you hate Riccardo so?"

Di Torreforte's face contorted, muscles twitching under his skin. I suppose the long day, the risks he had taken, the conflicts he suffered, provoked him to confess what he said next.

"I hated him, just as I hated all the other Senese, for detesting my Florentine blood. But then! Then he accused me of sneaking into the Drago stall to cut that mare's fetlocks—I would never have done such a thing! I would sooner murder my own mother than harm a horse."

I thought of the gentle care di Torreforte had given his horses—the insistence of a rubdown and rest, despite his haste to reach Ferrara.

"Then who?" I said. "Who cut Caramella's fetlocks?"

His voice was harsh. "The Granduca Francesco was behind it. I am certain of it. Just as he was behind the boards thrown into Via del Capitano."

Giacomo di Torreforte stood, quickly striding to my side to ease out the chair.

"Virginia. You have had a most exhausting day," he said, casting his eyes down at the floor. "Forgive me. I have much to atone for. My temper and rancor are just two of my sins."

I looked at his face.

Did he have any idea how many dreams had been crushed in the past few hours?

I thought I was returning to my old life, my memories.

But that life was no more than the smoking ashes in the hearth.

CHAPTER 102

Siena, Crete Hills

The sight of Siena rising above the hilly country of the Crete was magical. Somehow the distance enhanced the walled city and its towers, a magical vision rising over the sun-bleached hills.

I hung out the window of the carriage, staring. The wind made my eyes sting, so I finally had to withdraw into the cabin.

"Even our view from Vignano—so close and perfect!—does not compare with this," I said.

"There is something special about the perspective," said di Torreforte, smiling for the first time since I had met him. "The perfect distance from the city, the surrounding hills for contrast. Wait until you see Siena in the winter mists. It is magical."

His words echoed my own thoughts. How strange that we should think alike about anything.

"You should paint it," I said, turning away from him to look again.

It was the first time we had shared a moment of peace together, where I had addressed him as a friend. I wondered if my heart was softening toward him.

"I could never do it justice," he said with a curt wave of his hand. "I do not have the technique for landscapes." He gazed down at the muddy floor of our coach. "I have too many failures. My betters have proved that."

I shrugged. "Perhaps portraits would suit your talent better?"

He opened his hands, a gesture of surrender.

"The maestro once told me I had a talent for drawing anatomy and facial features. But he also told me I had not learned to love my subjects enough to find their spirit. He said my portraits were cold and stiff as the canvas on which they were painted."

He stole a look at me, like a young boy. "The maestro accused me of being misanthropic. At the time, I considered it a compliment."

I nodded. I knew too well the man he had been. But part of me was alert to the man he was becoming. "What else did your maestro tell you?"

Giacomo looked out the window toward Siena. He laughed sadly, shaking his head.

"He told me to find a muse. That was his answer to any artist's dilemma. Find a muse and a passion. Like Giorgio had for painting horses."

The stone buildings of the di Torreforte family's Villa Corsano were imposing, standing solid and grand on the brow of a hill overlooking the vast vineyards and pastureland.

We passed a chapel across the road from the di Torreforte villa. In the slanting sunlight of late afternoon, the stone took on the tawny color of the grass field beside it.

"That is Pieve di San Giovanni Battista a Corsano," said di Torreforte, nodding. The Parish of St. John the Baptist. "The young priest dreams of running a little school to teach the poor and orphans how to read. Perhaps, Virginia—"

"Do not say more. I need time to adjust to these changes."

"Of course. Forgive me," he said, bowing his head. "Changes take time."

"It looks quite old," I said, looking at the weather-worn stone.

"They say the baptistry was built more than five hundred years ago," he said.

"San Giovanni Battista. Aren't you Giacomo Giovanni? Were you named for the saint?" I asked.

Di Torreforte looked at me, then turned away.

"Yes," he said, his voice muffled. "My father was very fond of San Giovanni. I think I disappointed him. It is a fine church. But . . . I haven't set foot in the parish since my boyhood days."

He looked away again. "We visited here often. I spent long stretches of my boyhood here. Many of our Palio horses were bred right here."

"Not in Florence?"

"No. Florence was my father's family home."

"You are a Florentine by birth—"

"No," he said, shaking his head. "I was sent to school in Florence, living in our family house on the Arno. But my mother was from Oca, and I was born and baptized there in the contrada."

An Oca? A Senese?

I did not have time to consider further as we entered the gates of the estate.

A great crowd of servants had gathered in the cobbled court-yard to welcome us. Di Torreforte helped me from the carriage. I studied the maids, grooms, cooks, scullery maids. I saw no one I recognized amongst their eager faces.

"This is my cousin, Silvia Notari di Giovanni," said di Torreforte. He looked at me intently. "Signorina Notari di Giovanni will be here at Villa Corsano for an extended stay. Please welcome her and give her any service she may require. The signorina should be considered the mistress of Corsano for the duration of her stay, which I hope will be a very long time."

It took me a moment to realize he was referring to me as a signorina, now of the nobility.

The women stared hard at me, then spread their skirts wide in their outstretched hands, curtsying. The men ducked their heads, eyes lowered to the paving stones.

I felt Giacomo di Torreforte take my arm, escorting me through the foyer into the searing heat of the kitchen. Over a crackling fire in a wide hearth was an array of pots simmering with rich dishes seasoned with wild Tuscan herbs: rosemary, sage, and oregano. Haunches of meat hung from the ceiling on a long bar running from wall to wall. A calico cat looked up expectantly at the red hams, waiting for any drop of fat to fall on the stone floor.

"Let me show you to your room," said the housekeeper, dressed in gray with a white kerchief tied over her hair. I nodded, following her to the stairs.

At the first step, her waist jingled with scores of keys. The sound made me start. I jumped away from her, stumbling. I clutched the bannister, gasping.

"Signorina! What is wrong?" she asked.

The keys. Mother Superior and her power to keep me locked forever behind the convent walls.

I collected myself. "Nothing. The coach ride has left me reeling still."

"It is a long trip from Ferrara," said the housekeeper. "You may not have your legs steady for some time."

I said nothing. My legs would be steady once I was back on a horse.

———

We argued, though only briefly, the first day I was ready to ride.

I refused to dress as a boy.

"The servants know full well who I am. I am Signorina Silvia Notari di Giovanni." My new name still felt strange in my mouth. Hard enough to get used to the name of the woman I had suddenly become without the extra confusion of dressing as the boy I never could have been. "Why should I try to disguise myself?"

Before Giacomo could object, I stamped my foot. "I am proud I am a woman, a ragazza-fantino." Then I shook my head. "Ah, but look at me. I am not the villanella who rode the Palio. After so many years without riding, I have lost my hands, my seat, my legs. Give me a gentle horse until I recover my riding skills."

Giacomo found a mare that the housekeeper's grandchildren rode. He had a groom bring the saddled horse to the courtyard.

"Here, she will do," he said. I saw the sadness in his eyes. The villanella riding a children's mount.

"Good," I said. I put my hands on my hips. "Now take off the saddle, Signor di Torrforte."

His face brightened like a child's. The groom unfastened the girth and withdrew the saddle.

"Give me a boost up," I said, bending my leg. "I can no longer swing up the way I did as a girl."

Giacomo cupped my foot in his hand. *"Uno, due, tre!"*

I settled on the horse's back. To feel the warmth and the symmetry of the horse under me gave me a rush of memories.

"Open the gates!"

I fell off many times. With age, I learned, each fall is harder to endure. I limped for months.

The mare, who was gentle enough and well used to such foolishness as a rider who could not stay on her back, looked at me almost in remorse every time I tumbled off. Slowly—too slowly for my impatience—I recovered my muscles and balance.

One day, I rode to the ancient church, its walls covered in moss. A young priest was sweeping the paving stones.

"Buongiorno!" I greeted him. "I am . . . "

"Excuse me, signorina, but I know who you are!" said the priest, smiling. He set his broom against a column. "I am Prete Mariano. Welcome to Corsano, Signorina Notari di Giovanni."

The name still didn't fit me, as if I were wearing someone else's clothes. Still, it served its purpose to conceal my identity, as I had sworn to do. I owed that much to those who had risked so much to save me.

"I come with a proposal, Prete. I wish to teach the village children how to read and write."

"Signorina, how generous!" said the priest. But the smile slid from his face. "I regret we have not the money for such instruction,"

"Signor di Torreforte will pay for the books, parchment, quills, and ink," I told the priest.

"Have you consulted him, Signorina Silvia?" the priest asked. "Such a generous gift—"

"No, not yet," I answered. "But he will provide all we need for the school. I am quite certain of it."

I knew Giacomo would deny me nothing.

———

I taught the boys and girls—for I insisted girls be included—the rudimentary skills of reading and writing. The poor children of Corsano could spare only a few hours away from their chores each week, but slowly I taught them their letters and the magic of the written word.

I called our little school L'Accademia di Santa Caterina.

Then, one morning, I awoke to a shrill neigh in the courtyard and the strike of iron horseshoes on the cobblestones.

I opened my shutters to see a chestnut mare, her neck as defined as a Roman sculpture. Those strong curves and bulges, the fine solid head and body, made my heart skip a beat.

"Buongiorno, signorina!" called Giacomo, smiling up at me, though he could barely tear his eyes away from the mare.

"Come down and meet your new mare, Celeste."

"She is—she's bred from—" I could not finish my sentence.

"Sì! Caramella and Orione. It took a pretty penny to pry her away from the d'Este stables in Ferrara. She is in foal, and he was not the least inclined to sell her. But it seems someone whispered in the granduca's ear who would be her new owner."

I raced down the stairs so fast, I did not realize I was still in my bedclothes. My linen shift fluttered as I raced across the cobblestones, making the mare shy. Then she swung her big head around toward me.

Caramella's eyes. Orione's neck. His body.

I pressed my nose into her warm neck and sobbed.

———————

One day the following spring, I was riding home from the hills when I saw a coach approach Corsano. A woman with a young boy with red hair, perhaps ten years old, descended. The driver unloaded a leather bag from the top of the coach, and the woman and boy each took a handle and walked toward the villa.

I cantered up to them. The woman was a striking brunette, her hair shot through with streaks of silver. Her green eyes sparkled as she gazed up at me and smiled.

"Virginia Tacci," she said in a Florentine accent. "I see you are riding again."

I hesitated, astonished. "I am afraid you are mistaken. My name is Silvia."

"Oh, I am not mistaken, Virginia. I want you to meet my son, Giorgio."

My heart stopped. I could not breathe. I slid down from the mare.

"Go on, Giorgio. Give your Zia Virginia a kiss," said the woman. Her eyes held mine. "I am Carlotta Spessa. We have a special bond between us, villanella."

I swung down from the saddle, held my reins in one hand, and opened my arms wide to the boy in front me.

In a heartbeat, I recognized him.

"Mamma says you will teach me to ride," he said. I studied his brown eyes, soft as his father's. His white, freckled hands were sensitive, his artist's fingers as tapered as altar candles.

I wrapped my arms around him, squeezing him hard. The gelding's head swung toward us, his reins pulled tight. Then the boy looked at me impishly, taking a stubborn stance the way his father used to do, with his palms turned out at his side.

"I want to ride the Palio," he said. "Like you did."

I was forced to wipe the tears from my eyes with one hand. I could not let go of the little boy's hand. I felt each throb of his heartbeat, my fingers enlaced tight with his.

"How did you find me?" I asked Carlotta, watching her strap her bag onto my mare's saddle.

"Granduca Ferdinando told me. He is a very different from his brother, Virginia. It gives me hope for Tuscany. For us."

"Who—how did—" I asked.

"It is best you ask no more questions," she said quietly. "I have promises to keep."

I shook my head in wonderment.

"Come, Giorgio," I said, releasing his hand. "Lead the mare. Yes, there on the left side. Do not let her lead you! She knows the way back to the stables."

We walked together, our boots mashing down the dry winter grass, exposing the new green of the coming spring.

"I have a surprise for you, Giorgio," I said when we reached the stables. I handed the mare to a groom, directing him to carry the bag into the villa after that.

I took them to the stall to see Orione's newborn grandson.

"You will ride the Palio, Giorgio. On this horse, one day. I have never been more sure of anything in my life."

Giorgio's eyes grew large, his freckled face breaking into a lop-sided smile.

"May I pet him?"

"Pet him! Oh, Giorgio, he is *yours* . . . you must spend every hour with him, feed him, groom him, sleep in the stables by his side. I shall talk to Signor di Torreforte, but I am sure he will agree most wholeheartedly."

"Mine!" cried the boy. "Mamma, did you hear! My own horse!"

The foal nickered, sensing the emotion in the air. The high-pitched whinny of a foal never failed to make me smile.

He approached little Giorgio and began exploring the boy's smell, his tiny horse nostrils flaring wide.

Carlotta took my hand and squeezed it.

"We have waited many long years for you to return, Virginia. Your secret is safe with us. I have instructed Giorgio to call you Silvia in public. I have told him Virginia Tacci is a magic name, a secret never to share with anyone."

I turned toward her. She was a beautiful woman with high coloring, despite the streaks of silver in her black hair. Her looks were dramatic, lightning and thunder. I could see why Giorgio had fallen in love with her.

"A magic name," I murmured. I stared off into the distance, toward Siena.

"Sì. Perhaps it is."

A fortnight later, a carriage arrived at night. I heard the ear-splitting whinny of a horse and the efforts of the driver trying to calm him.

"Tranquillo, tranquillo," he called. Then he muttered, just loud enough to hear, "You devil!"

In the moonlight, I could see that the horse causing the trouble was not the one that pulled the carriage but one tied to a lead, following behind. He balked, rearing at the torches in the courtyard.

I pulled on my tunic and skirt, hurrying down the stairs. Giacomo was already in the courtyard, paying the coachman.

"He has been the devil to lead," said the man. "I thought he would break his rope more than a dozen times on our way from the Maremma. He almost overturned the coach itself. Look how he rears!"

I stopped dead, staring at the horse. A white star on his forehead gleamed in the moonlight. I turned to Giacomo, my face frozen in shock.

"Go on, Virginia," he whispered. "He is yours. Take him."

In an instant, without thinking, I hugged Giacomo fiercely. Did I? Did I really hug the man I had declared my enemy forever? Yes. Yes, I did.

And then I spun again and rushed toward the black stallion with the white star, wanting to fling my arms around his neck. He would not let me. He shied away.

I was not the skinny shepherdess he had known since birth.

I approached him again, and he shook his head and reared, his front hoofs slashing the air.

"Easy, boy," I said. And then I began to whistle.

Nella piazza di citta . . .

Orione hesitated, not quite remembering. His ears pricked up, focusing on me. Then he lowered his head, snorting in my scent. I approached him, my hand out to his muzzle. Giacomo untied the rope silently, fastening the end in a knot under the halter.

He held his arm out for me silently to give me a leg up.

I heard the barefoot clap of feet on the stones. A boy's voice said, "Where is she taking him, Giacomo?"

"Wherever she wants," he said.

Then I rode out the gates into the Crete moonlight.

———————

We galloped through the fields, our silhouettes stretched long under the rising moon. I swung off Orione's back at the foot of a lone cypress. I let him graze as I watched the torches on Siena's walls. The city's towers had diminished even more during my long absence, taken down stone by stone by the de' Medici. Still, the great walls of Siena shone mystical and mighty on the hilltop. There is no better view of Siena than from Corsano. My padrino Cesare was right about that.

"Grazie, Padrino," I whispered, kneeling in the grass. Giacomo had told me Cesare Brunelli had been buried here according to his wishes: in the Crete hills, overlooking Siena.

Grazie, Giorgio.

Orione mouthed at my hair the way he used to do as a colt, when I was a lonely shepherdess who dreamed of riding the Palio.

"Andiamo," I said, standing up. I stroked his neck.

I led him to a rock wall and climbed up onto his back, gathering up the lead rope as reins. We headed across the rolling hills of the Crete in the bright moonlight that bleached the summer grass white, casting unworldly shadows. Under me, I felt the powerful muscles of the stallion contract and release as we galloped over the fields. On my left in the distance glittered the torchlights of Siena as the bell of the Torre del Mangia tolled the midnight hour.

In front of us was a fallen olive tree. Orione did not hesitate as I reined him toward it.

I laughed with abandon, just as she had so many years ago, as we soared through the air. Weightless.

ACKNOWLEDGMENTS

In my search for historical documents on Virginia Tacci, I am indebted to many people and sources. Thank you all for the essential information that was the backbone of my novel.

IN SIENA:

So many people have helped me! This book is dedicated to them.

Contrada del Drago (and della Giraffa!): Deep gratitude to former Drago capitano Antonio De Luca and Dr. Silvia Giovani De Luca, a loyal *giraffina,* who have sat beside me for hours, explaining the *prova*, the *tratta*, and the intricacies of the Palio. We have attended the *cena generale* of Drago, witnessed blessings for the horse and jockey in the De Lucas' Drago and Giraffa contradas, watched sons Francesco and Giovanni's *alfieri* (flag-throwing) talents in the Palio parades, and been included in many moments of Senese life through them.

Historical archivist of Contrada del Drago, Walter Benocci. Thank you for giving us the historical tour of your museum that snowy February day, and for making us feel like a part of your celebrations. *Vai Drago!*

Dragaiolo Fabrizio Gabrielli's article on Virginia Tacci was one of the first I encountered that succinctly traced the history of this legendary hero of Siena. Thank you, Fabrizio, for your excellent introduction to Virginia Tacci.

To the Mignone family: Anna Rosa (Goga), Alvise, and Margherita. Goga, you introduced me to *so* many who have helped my historical research. Your beautiful Villa Corsano is featured in the last scenes of the novel. Your hospitality and friendship helped illuminate the wonders of Siena.

Thanks to Luigi Bruschelli, il Trecciolino, horseman extraordinaire. Gigi, my gratitude for spending time with me and introducing me to your magnificent horses. Your insight into the Palio as a *fantino* inspired many moments in this book.

Enormous admiration and gratitude to Rosanna Bonelli, "Rompicollo." Meeting you was a highlight of my research. I thought of your words of experience as I wrote the character of Virginia Tacci. I will forever admire your courage. (And I hope you don't mind my borrowing "Rompicollo" for Virginia. I hoped to have her spirit in my novel match yours.)

To the d'Elci and Pannocchieschi family: Writing this book in the d'Elci palazzo above Il Campo inspired me every moment. Thank you for our months there with you in the heart of Siena.

Accademia dei Rossi: Their journals (*riviste*) were a major source of information. Thank you, Ettore Pellegrini, for your assistance and gracious nature. And for your help in navigating sixteenth-century Italian poetry . . . and expletives!

Petra Pertici, scholar of medieval Siena. Thank you for your help and friendship.

Carla Galardi—your knowledge and love for Siena shines through in your historical tours.

Grazie a Cinci, La Contesessa Angiola Piccolomini. Thank you for your hospitality and the exquisite joy of spending evenings at your lovely palazzo. While sipping champagne and conversing, I was secretly writing scenes for this book in my mind!

Viola Carignani, *Stelle di Palio* editor in chief. Thank you for all your help. I enjoyed our interview on Toscana Canale 3 during Palio week 2012 and now follow your Palio coverage via live streaming in Colorado.

To Gina Stipo and your knowledge of Senese cookery in the renaissance. Experiencing the Palio with you was a blast! Kelly and Linda Hayes, thanks for our introduction years ago.

My stay at Castello di Quattro Torra with hosts Nicola and Laura Guerrini inspired several chapters of the book. What a setting! Thanks to Caterina for introducing me to Antonio De Luca!

Thank you to Patrizia Turrini and staff at the Historical Archive of Siena. Ms. Turrini was one of the editors of *The Palio and Its Image*, a magnificent tome for anyone interested in the Siena Palio.

Former captain of Aquila Vittoria Nepi, *grazie* for sharing your knowledge of both the Palio and Siena.

Silvia Notari, thank you for your friendship and our afternoon Italian lessons.

Simone Bocci, the proud *chiocciolino.* Thank you for including me in the festival dinner in the streets of your contrada.

Maria Serena Fantechi of Scuola Leonardo da Vinci. Your knowledge of and enthusiasm for the Palio sparked my imagination. How I loved your lectures and guided tours of Tuscany!

In Florence:

Alessandra Marchetti, Florentine guide extraordinaire. Thank you for your help walking through the Medici corridors of history.

Sheila Barker of the Medici Foundation. I could spend weeks just listening to your knowledge of the Medicis. Thank you for helping me find my way around the Bia research browser and the visit to the Medici archives. I would love to find another novel featuring the Medicis . . .

IN FERRARA:

I am grateful to the kind sisters of Monastero di Sant'Antonio for my guided visits.

IN GENERAL:

Caroline Murphy's book *Murder of a Medici Princess* was instrumental in researching the deaths of Isabella de' Medici and Leonora de' Medici. Her book is highly recommended for further reading about the family of Cosimo I.

The Palio in Italian Renaissance Art, Thought, and Culture (2005): This dissertation was a treasure trove of information for me. Thank you, Dr. Elizabeth MacKenzie Tobey. What incredible research! You are a true sleuth for historical tales.

In researching Bianca Cappello, I relied heavily on Mary Steegmann's book published in 1913, *Bianca Cappello*.

The poetry of Virginia Tacci is translated loosely from the Renaissance original of 1581. Riccardo De' Luca's words of ardor were actually the poetry of Domenico Tregiani: *In lode de virgin a tacei corsiera il Palio ed Giove per il Dragoî* (In praise of Virginia Tacci, rider of the Palio of Jupiter for the Drago).

Lucia Caretto helped me to translate and understand sixteenth-century documents written in Italian. In addition to teaching me Italian, she has long been a supporter of my fiction and a good friend.

Nancy Elisha, my beloved sister, has always encouraged my writing. She accompanied me to Siena in February 2012 while I researched this book.

Bridget Strang and the breathtaking Strang Ranch of Carbondale, Colorado, gave me inspiration every day. Bridget and Marie McAteer's understanding of horses helped me, particularly in writing about Virginia's training sessions. The venue for two National Sheepdog Finals, Strang Ranch gave me the opportunity to observe sheep 365 days a year, in addition to providing stellar horse training for my young mare, Shiner.

Thanks to the Aspen Writers Foundation, especially Jamie Kravitz and Maurice LaMee. Also *grazie* to Aspen's Pitkin County Library: Susan Cottle and Margaret Durgy.

Isabella Kirkland, our friend and extraordinary artist. I appreciated your loan of books on renaissance painting and Max Doerner's *The Materials of the Artists and Their Use in Painting*. Your careful demonstration preparing egg tempera paint (in your houseboat studio in Sausalito) inspired me.

Sarah Kennedy Flug and Marty Flug, thank you for your friendship and support. *Angel Glow* recharged me to continue writing during trying times.

Thank you to my great Amazon team: Jessica Poore, Gabriella Van den Heuvel, Susan Stockman, and Dennelle Catlett, among many others. Special appreciation to Danielle Marshall, my new editor at Amazon.

To Lindsay Guzzardo, former Amazon editor, now screenwriter. I will never forget you.

To my copyeditor, Mia Lipman. Your careful work made this novel better. I am grateful to you.

To Phyllis DeBlanche, my proofreader: Thank you. I know it was extra hard work proofing with all the Italian words!

Thanks to all the production and design team at Amazon, especially Sean Baker.

Mumtaz Mustafa: You created the perfect cover.

Melody Guy, my developmental editor, is an incredibly sensitive editor who draws my best work from me. I love working with her. I have been blessed having her guide all four of my published books.

Terry Goodman has championed my work for several years now—book #4! Thank you, Terry, for your support and good nature. It has been a pleasure. Happy retirement!

Special thanks to Jeff Belle. I'm a happy—and grateful—Amazon novelist.

To my foreign rights team at Curtis Brown, especially Sophie Baker and Betsy Robbins. Thank you for spreading Virginia's story to other lands and in other languages.

The team at Gelfman Schneider/ICM Partners has guided my contracts and all matters of business, looking out for me all along the way. Thank you especially to Cathy Gleason and Victoria Marini.

To my friend and agent, Deborah Schneider . . . you have been behind this book from the first second of inspiration. What a fun ride!

To my beloved parents, Betty and Fred Lafferty. You raised all your girls to love books, storytelling, and horses. We love you more than you can possibly know.

Finally, my profound gratitude to Andy Stone, my husband, research assistant, and first editor. You are the love of my life. I don't know if I ever could have written all these books without your love, encouragement, and hard work. And that's the truth.

Author Notes

In writing *The Shepherdess of Siena*, I primarily used documents that were part of the de' Medici archives, but also everything I could track down about Virginia Tacci. Of great help was the Accademia dei Rossi and specifically Ettore Pellegrini, who shared all the information he had found in his own research. Also the dissertation of Dr. Elizabeth M. Tobey, *The Palio in Italian Renaissance Art, Thought, and Culture*, was of enormous help to me. (Even the Senese were astonished by her depth of research.)

Sarah Dunant's marvelous novel *Sacred Hearts* was of tremendous research value. For those who want to learn more about convent life in Ferrara, I highly recommend Dunant's book.

Among the many books on the Palio I used for reference, the following were brightly fanned with sticky notes: *La Terra in Piazza: An Interpretation of the Palio of Siena* by Alan Dundes and Alessandro Falassi; *Palio and Its Image*: *History, Culture, and Representation of Siena's Festival* by Maria A. Ceppari Ridolfi; *Tutta Siena, Contrada per Contrada* by Piero Torriti; *Palio: The Race of the Soul* by Mauro Civai and Enrico Toti; *Io, Rompicollo* by Rosanna Bonelli.

The de' Medici family's story is so well documented that I basically followed the storyline. Caroline Murphy's book *Murder of a Medici Princess* was indispensable. I really didn't have to create drama—the de' Medici family provided it. There are some plot points I have modified slightly.

Mary Steegmann's book *Bianca Cappello* (1913) gave me insights into Francesco de' Medici's mistress and wife.

Thanks to the Medici Archive Project, and especially Sheila Barker for her assistance. I found a document that showed the Granduca Francesco's gratitude to Pietro for the gift of a hunting eagle. The letter shows a very cordial—even lighthearted—correspondence between the two brothers. If Francesco de' Medici were not complicit in the murders of the two women, I doubt he would have maintained such a good relationship with his brother, the murderer.

As mentioned, the de' Medici family is well documented. Virginia Tacci's story, on the other hand, was much harder to investigate. I could not find any record of her life after 1581. The second half of her story is my invention.

Orione, too, was poetic license. However, it is part of the historical record that Federigo Barbolani di Montauto, governor of Siena, gave Virginia Tacci a horse as a present. The governor was a great admirer of hers, as evidenced in this letter to Granduca Francesco de' Medici in 1581:

This young woman has begun to practice this art of race riding . . . not without manifest danger of breaking her neck . . . but she doesn't make any sign of falling, but rides with much artfulness and dexterity . . . . She not only knows how to master and hold the mature and unbridled race horses, but also the hot-tempered and speedy colts, and she is able to assert herself with many of them, such that, tamed of their ferocity, they become gentle with her.

ABOUT THE AUTHOR

Linda Lafferty taught in public education for nearly three decades, in schools from the American School of Madrid to the Boulder Valley schools to the Aspen school district. She completed her PhD in bilingual special education and went on to work in that field, as well as teaching English as a second language and bilingual American history. Horses are Linda's first love, and she rode on the University of Lancaster's riding team for a year in England. As a teenager, she was introduced by her uncle to the sport of polo, and she played in her first polo tournament when she was seventeen. Linda also loves Siena, Italy, and the people of the region and has returned to the city half a dozen times in the past three years to research her novel. Linda is the author of three previous novels: *The Bloodletter's Daughter*, *The Drowning Guard*, and *House of Bathory*. She lives in Colorado with her husband.